LEE HUNT

HERALD
THE DYNAMICIST TRILOGY
BOOK TWO

FIRST EDITION
Herald © 2019 Lee Hunt
Cover art by Jeff Brown
Interior design & typesetting © 2019 Jared Shapiro

All Rights Reserved

This book is a work of fiction. Names, characters, places, and incidents are either a product of the author's imagination or are used fictitiously. Any resemblance to actual events, locales, or persons, living or dead, is entirely coincidental.

Distributed by
Ingram Spark, and IslandBlue Book Printing
P.O.D.

Library and Archives Canada Cataloguing in Publication

Title: Herald / Lee Hunt.
Names: Hunt, Lee, 1968- author.
Description: First Edition. 2019
ISBN 978-1-9990935-2-5 (soft cover); 978-1-9990935-3-2 (Ebook/PDF)

Edited by: John McAllister

HERALD

Novels by Lee Hunt

Dynamicist Series

Dynamicist
Herald
Knight in Retrograde

For my wife, Lori. She says she doesn't need to be singled out ... but she should be.

Prologue.
Price of Memory

I fear nothing in Elysium or Earth. No man, woman, god, or monster. They are all of them, external; they are orthogonal to me, to my ethos, to my incumbency. Only memories of the future concern me, for am I not responsible for the future that I herald?

▽

ROBERT ENDICOTT HASTILY PUT *THE LONELY WIZARD* ASIDE. MEMORIES OF HIS HERALDIC dream hurtled forward, dominating his mind. They were more real to him than any book, more painful, more to be feared. And like the Lonely Wizard, he felt compelled to review them again and again.

He stood by the slough, his dog beside him. It was quiet and peaceful. A duck squawked somewhere in the reeds.

My mother has just died. Thanks to Sir Hemdale, I know what the memory means now.

Then the dream scene shifted.

Koria and Eloise were walking the dark paths of the campus. The streets were empty but for the two glorious girls. Endicott's heart soared as he looked upon them. In the whole of the heraldic dream, this was the only buoyant moment, the only time he felt love or happiness. He loved both girls, though differently. Eloise was everything he could hope for: a man's strength and ferocity, the pinnacle of female beauty, and an enormous, hidden heart. But Koria was his soul mate, darkly elegant, melancholy from her own hidden knowledge of the future, smarter, and much more mature. Wiser. He had finally earned Koria's trust, but was he wise enough to act on what he had foreseen? Could he prevent what was coming?

The two girls passed the agricultural greenhouses, and an enormous, cloaked figure stepped out of the shadows. It followed them.

No.

Even in review, he could not maintain his dispassion.

Koria looked over her shoulder and cried out in fear. Endicott could not hear her, but seeing her muted expression of terror evoked an answering terror in him.

No!

His reaction at this point was always the same, no matter how many times he relived the awful, vivid memory.

The girls ran, but the hulking figure closed on them. At last they turned to face it. A wall of blue flame sprang into being and rolled soundlessly from the hooded stalker towards the two girls. Koria raised a hand, and when the flame passed over them, they were not burned, but Koria shivered, frost-covered, and fell to one knee.

No!

Eloise drew her sword and lunged forward, striking the cloaked figure. It fell back but drew a long, black spear from its cloak. They dueled, the hulking figure fighting with a peculiar, otherworldly style. Eloise struck again, fast and hard, but her opponent caught her sword with the blade of its spear, and Eloise's weapon shattered. Even holding only the jagged hilt, she did not back down but stepped boldly in front of Koria, challenging the colossus facing them. The spear went through her chest and drove her into Koria.

Nooo!

It was real. Endicott knew it was real and could watch no more. He never could watch it all. With a powerful wrenching, his consciousness snapped elsewhere into some other dark night.

Bethyn was coming out of the Lords' Commons. The figures of Endicott and Gregory ran up to her. They spoke silently for a moment and then began walking back to the orchid together. No.

Syriol was curled up in the back of a carriage. Two men made her drink from their bottle and brutally violated her. No!

Endicott and Gregory were back at the Orchid. Eight Knights, no!

Tiring of their sport, the men dumped Syriol's body on the side of the road. Three individuals separately walked by but ignored the battered, bleeding body. It lay on the curb until morning, by then breathing no more.

Nooo!

His memory of the dream had not drifted, softened, or faded, but its impact was as searing as ever, even if Endicott could now control, barely, the destructive mania it induced. A heraldic dream was indistinguishable from memory, indistinguishable from fact, but it was not a memory. It was a vision of the future. And terrifyingly, *this* vision never changed.

When the day finally comes, will I be able to change it then?

Chapter One.
The Lonely Wizard

When most people are alone for any length of time, they feel lonely. I do not.

I do not like people.

Any time I am with people, they feel compelled to talk about feelings. They deny this, of course, as if their denial could hide what their actions inevitably prove.

Every conversation about feelings with someone devolves into an inward-outward turning multiplication of those feelings. The other wants to operate some mathematics of emotion upon my mind so that what was once a small thing becomes much larger. The price of sharing is a journey towards the endpoints of emotion, whether that is fear or happiness, desolation, or outrage. Why must every feeling be made into an extremity of passion? Why outrage, for example? Cannot a thing simply be what it is and be discussed for itself? Why must everyone be cast as either protagonist or antagonist? Why must the other squeeze sentiment into their selfish story, ruining the rational enjoyment of the world through the application of bias and selective narration?

I can only conclude that most people are deeply unhappy. Why else this compulsion to share their thoughts, inflict their feelings, project their aspirations? The curious disease of the free is that they are never truly happy. They never have enough, never earn enough, never become enough. Because their future is unwritten by some ultimate authority, they are never happy with what they write for themselves; it could always have been a better story. In their freedom they freely inflict the spiteful residue of their failed dreams upon everyone else. They do not understand what true freedom is and hate the freedom and success of others.

I prefer it when my thoughts are autonomous, untangled from the need that others have for explanation or ornament. I do not desire the indulgence of explanation or the gratification of extraneous validation from anyone other than myself. I am the only authority with whom I must evaluate my feelings. My authenticity is through me, with me, and in me, not through, with, or in someone else.

I love to be alone.

This part of the Ardgour Wilderness was empty, pitiless, and still. I wondered if any human narrative at all remained in this abraded, worn-out landscape. If it did, it could only have been brought by me. I stood and listened but heard no human sound, felt no thoughts, saw no sign of new construction, progress, or invention. All was in ruins. There was no mind to sully the beautiful objectivity of nature with dreams and imaginings of fanciful things.

Had I come home?

Strangely, after being alone for so long in the Wilderness, I noted a curious lack of color in the world. Was it the uniform yellow stalks of wheat, the single hues of the barley beards, or the greens of the trees that were missing? No, there was color there, but its pallet was a muted, uniform pastel. Heterogeneity was missing.

The mountains lay behind me now, along with the lone, long-dead guardian I had left standing vigil on the rocky path. I had passed well beyond the marches of the Ardgour Wilderness into the dead core of the abandoned county. There was some spoor of skolves but not nearly as much as there had been nearer the borders. I doubted this was because the skolves now feared and avoided me. Skolves guard their territory with a profound jealousy. They always attack an invader and never retreat.

Unless they face their gods. Or now, me.

There simply was too much vegetative homogeneity—and animal heterogeneity—here in the center. The grains were uneaten, untrampled. The skolves were not eating this wheat. Their tracks were few here—they themselves were few—but there were other beasts. I had glimpsed a forest lion and a host of deer. I guessed that the skolves could not eat our deer. Rather than the Wilderness being empty of all life due to the skolves' greed, as one might have expected, it was filled with life of a different sort.

But not people. They were long gone, their homes eroded, their works degrading.

I passed over a scrubby hill and was surprised to encounter what was perhaps the oldest monument to those lost people. An ancient ring of menhirs stood grasping from the tangle, its tall stones partially hidden by time and the entropic growth of bushes, grass, and even a few stunted trees. I rubbed my hand along one of the monoliths, removing a layer of dark fungal growth that had covered it. The stone was revealed to be a pale granitoid. Not local rock at all. Some call the menhirs calendar hills due to their assumed connection to time and season. The connection to planting is probably correct; menhirs are scattered about in every land where seed crops grew. They predate written language and, like mathematics, are symbologies of their own. Wherever I have found them, I have always marveled at these archaic, timeworn monoliths. The great circles of old stone are all so ancient that no one knows precisely what they mean or even who first came up with the idea of building them. The size of the stones here, and their non-local provenance, indicated that building such a calendar circle must have been a monumental undertaking that would have required an enormous number of people acting in cooperation. Yet the idea would have had but one author, one inventor.

I could only suppose that this inventor had been murdered by Nimrheal. Was the original inventor's monument even built, or was the idea rediscovered later, reinvented later, incurring no punishment at all? The price can only be paid once. All the same it is difficult to convince anyone to innovate now even without Nimrheal. How did an ancient inventor convince people to undertake such a large and costly operation? What narrative was spun on that day? Or was it possible that the objective, quantitative merits of planting on time were enough? Perhaps. In desperate times basic facts must triumph or the people perish.

Shaking my head, I *did* marvel at the obelisks. They must have been awe inspiring in their time. I stepped on a wild rose that had sprung out from under one of the massive, dark blocks. Its thorns could not touch me physically, but it pricked a thought. The circle was now little more than a memorial to its long-vanished builders, its former precision lost in the jumble of untended growth. No shadow could tell a dead farmer when to plant now. The time and season for humanity had passed here.

I counted the crumbling homesteads, unused and unmaintained, as I moved on. The ones made of stone had resisted time best, and the Wilderness was dotted with old crumbling towers, the broken castles of the most successful. It seemed as if there were a lot of them only because the towers were almost all that was left. Of the homes made of wood, all that remained were the rough tents of rotting roofs, sitting half covered by wheat like rude, square mushrooms. Or like an old, abandoned hat. The stone fences had fared better: those heaped walls did not disappear so quickly. Passing deer, bears, and lions had rubbed themselves against the corners of these walls, leaving coarse fur and musky smells in place of the odor of bread that must once have been baked in the houses beyond.

A semicircular, wheat-filled draw stood off to my left. It may once have been used as a silage pit. No one would fill it now to keep their cattle fed in the winter. No heat would build in its core as it fermented and created life of its own. No smell would waft from it, no earthy odor. No sounds of insects or call of birds' overhead, drawn to the grain. No farmhand would pile or rake it, thinking private thoughts and dreaming of what might be.

Now I saw none of those things. There was no silage, for there were no more farmers and there were no more dreams. I realized that, before encountering this ruined land, I had forgotten one thing that comes of the calculus of passion. From the taking of facts, the drawing together of ideas, and from the multiplicative transformations of feeling into narrative comes sometimes something else: creation.

I had forgotten that true creation requires a step beyond the quantitative reality of the known. It requires a subjective leap across an immeasurable distance, a landing in a new world. The unknown inventor of the menhir likely had an objective, measurable motivation to build that monument to time and season. She may have convinced the local peers or lords to authorize the circle on such a basis, but she could never have come up with the original idea without something beyond objectivity. Her inspiration had arisen from something more. It must have. It had a magic that could only arise from something greater and more beautiful than objective calculus. And the incomparable, euphonic wave of that creative act had been beautiful enough and powerful enough to wake the ire of a transcendent being.

Perhaps I had never appreciated this reality before because it is so exasperating. I do not like people. I do not like narrative. And yet creation requires more than just facts. It is galling to me that any such innovation—even pure mathematical creation—needs a surplus of feeling, an excess of ego, and a distasteful indulgence of both.

Well, there was none of that here now.

I passed over a stone fence style from one ancient, abandoned field to another. No one sat there, wheat stalk in mouth, writing poetry or creating fables. I supposed that here, where no people gathered, where all who came now must necessarily come alone, that a curious thing was true. Here there could be no non-linear alteration of fact and feeling to create an original story or idea. Here all would be fact, not fiction, all fact and no invention. In this place I had found the true test of objectivity: is there meaning in the quantitative when there is no mind to appreciate it? This was the test of the pure thing-in-itself.

If objective fact needs a mind to give it value, then this truly was a wilderness. All that could endure here would be the endless null space of an empty thoughtlessness. All would be unchanging, except through the slow timeless march of entropy.

Even though he was gone and could come no more, Nimrheal had won after all.

Chapter Two

The Secret School

"**M**AY I BORROW THAT ORIGINAL EDITION OF *THE LONELY WIZARD*, THE ONE YOU GOT from Keith Euyn?" The request came from Jennyfer Gray, the diminutive, blond poet that Davyn and Heylor had met on the terrible night. Lord Jon Indulf was standing proudly with her in a formal jacket, a hand resting on her lower back. "And why are you so bruised?" she added, staring at Endicott's face. "You look like you got rolled over by one of those ice carriages."

Robert Endicott looked up from his porridge. He had been thinking about his heraldic dream and the impending murder of his friends that it foreshadowed. As he dropped his spoon into the bowl, it made a ringing sound. He needed a moment to clear his head and remember where he was and who he was with.

His friends. Koria. Eloise. *Not dead. Yet.*

Endicott touched his temple. *Still sore.* "I was planted by something bigger than the average ice wagon."

And much, much crueler.

"I think you owe us an explanation now," Lord Jon Indulf said, trying out the unaccustomed act of smiling at Endicott. The two had not exactly stood on the same side of the field since arriving at the New School, and smiles or jokes were something new between them.

The smallest change.

Many things had changed since that terrible night. For most of those involved, the changes had been enormous. And for the worse. Syriol had been horribly assaulted by two men, traumatized perhaps forever. Endicott had nearly brought on his own thermodynamic death in rescuing her. Eloise had beaten one of the rapists to death. The other had been hanged. No one close to the event was the same. The survivors were forced to remember what had happened. They were not allowed to forget.

Endicott returned Indulf's smile, unsurprised at how much better this simple exchange of goodwill felt than any of their previous interactions in the Lords' Commons. "Eloise's uncle, Sir Hemdale, beat the porridge out of me." He *was* beaten up. The big knight had backed him all around the sand ring and turned him into a wreck. The twenty-four-hour-test had had far more corporal punishment built into it than he had studied for.

Indulf's thin, blond eyebrows climbed towards his hairline. "You fought Sir Hemdale?"

"And lived!" boomed Davyn.

"Sort of," added Heylor waggling his left hand but smiling widely and with unmistakable pride.

"The stupe should have brought me with him," Eloise said, scowling. She was still angry that she had not been invited to do battle at his side. Endicott could not help but smile at the thought. Eloise was tall, strong, and beautiful. More of all three than just about any woman he had ever met except for Koria, who was much shorter than Eloise but even more beautiful to him. Some thought that Eloise's crooked nose detracted from her goddess-like appearance, but Endicott knew her too well. Her nose was perfect.

"But why?" Jennyfer asked, jumping in before Indulf could ask another question.

Good skolving question. To make me remember standing at a pond while my mother died. But to what end?

Endicott had no idea. He still could not remember his mother's face. Perhaps he never would. The beating had uncovered all it could short of covering him permanently in the dirt. He turned back to Jennyfer Grey in relief. "The original edition of *The Lonely Wizard*, did you say? What do you need it for?"

Jennyfer looked startled by this redirect but recovered with an enigmatic smile. "I did say," she pronounced, her blue eyes catching the light. "I think there is a secret message in the book."

"But that the altered versions might be obscuring it!" shouted Davyn in Endicott's ear.

Endicott thought for a moment while he waited for his ear to stop ringing. "It's not my book to loan, but if you came by and read it in the Orchid, it would avoid us having to ask the great man for permission."

"Surely you're not afraid to ask." Jon Indulf spoke with something like his former sneering tone. Or was it skepticism?

"Surely he's too smart to ask," said Deleske laconically.

"Keith's a grump," explained Heylor.

"He's certainly moody," murmured Bethyn.

"He's just old," finished Koria, her bright, green eyes flashing keenly from her dark face.

"He might remember to ask for it back too," Gregory mused, staring at Eloise surreptitiously.

"I get to visit the Orchid?" Jennyfer said. "That's a very easy deal. I will even let you read the poem I write about it when I am done."

As they chuckled at the prospect, Jeyn Lindseth approached the table. "Ready?" asked the tall, subtly graceful soldier. As usual he wore a sword on each hip but walked as if nothing was there at all. He waited for Jon Indulf and Jennyfer Gray to move out of earshot before continuing. "We are going to leave in a moment—" he began, waving at Heylor to remain seated—the skinny young man had sprung out of his seat at the word "we"— "but we don't want to attract attention."

Endicott remembered Bat Merrett calling him an attention whore during the twenty-four-hour test. It had been one of the more moderate things that had been said to him at the great Keith Euyn's request, all to test the young man's temper. Personal insults had never bothered him and now, looking around the enormous main dining room of the Lord's Commons, Endicott saw that quite a few of the other students were looking in his direction. Like the insults, the attention had little effect on him. Still, it would not do to ruin the secret location of the dynamics lab they were about to visit for the first time.

I need to be there. I need to be ready.

He turned back to Lindseth. "We will leave separately," Lindseth was explaining, "in small groups, then gather by the statue of Sir Heydron. She will provide our cover." Lindseth smiled his gentle smile. "Don't forget to tuck in your medallions."

Jeyn led the reassembled group to the edge of campus, across the ring road, and down the slope that marked the border of the Academic Plateau. Endicott walked with Koria, holding her hand.

"You are still being very mysterious," he whispered to her. After it was announced that they had all passed the examination, Koria had only smiled when Endicott asked her what was next. It was far from the first time she had kept secrets from him, but he suspected this secret was less important than her former stalking of him. The standing wave of dimples on her face had spoken of excitement and happiness, not the fear and anxiety of her heraldic dreams about him.

Of course Koria had always known more than he did. She was not only older and wiser, but together with Gerveault and Eleanor, she had planned much of the redesigned program after the disaster that had left her the sole survivor of her own class. She had known nothing of Sir Hemdale's plans for the twenty-four-hour test, but she supported the distraction test that Bat Merrett and Keith Euyn had administered.

"I know it was unkind, but they had to take everyone to their limits, Robert," she had said before they went to bed that night. "That includes emotional limits."

Being told his father had died because he was careless was probably not meant as an indictment of the long-dead man. It likely had more to do with the perceived recklessness of Robert Endicott than his father. The violent, dangerous conduct of Sir Hemdale had not been as easy to account for.

What does the fact that I cannot remember my mother's face have to do with anything? Sir Hemdale had only replied, "You can't change if you don't know who you are."

The young man finally acknowledged, reluctantly, that his emotional background merited examination, even if this was painful, yet he wondered if his family history had really needed to be aired so painfully during what was supposed to be a test of mathematics and physics.

In the end Endicott decided that Koria was probably right—as usual—and that he should bury his doubts. He had more important things to worry about than the buried memories of his mother's death. The manic anxiety of his heraldic dream was under control now, but its bitter residue still seized him viscerally at unexpected moments. His ruthless preparation for the test had been effective as an emotional management tool, but management could no more remove his memories of the dream than it could remove the blood from his heart. Endicott was still the volatile but optimistic young man who had arrived at the New School. He carried powerful new fears now, but he also enjoyed the positive feelings of success, and more profoundly than that, the sublime buoyancy of love. Regardless of the jumble of his thoughts and feelings, he was who he was, and right now he was excited to see what new changes and opportunities were about to be disclosed to him and his classmates.

As the walk continued, Koria seemed to enjoy the mystery of where they were going more and more. She almost skipped, and though Endicott's unsatisfied curiosity was frustrating, seeing Koria in such a light and happy mood buoyed him up. He hoped he would one day see her jump on fences and flit about as Eoyan March had described.

Perhaps I can help bring that about.

Far from the Academic Plateau now, they were approaching the river at a point near the edge of the city. Before them rose an intimidating, tall stone fence topped with razor wire. Its heavy iron gate was closed, but Endicott could see the enormous compound it guarded through the thick bars. Two heavily armed guards in full armor opened the gates. A horse-drawn covered carriage rolled out of the gate and passed them, Vercors Ice Company was emblazoned on its side.

This is where the ice carriages come from.

"Show us your medallions please, lords and ladies," one of the mailed guards said. The other held a loaded crossbow. It was pointed up, but the archer was watching them carefully.

The gate closed behind them, and having satisfied the guards, they approached the main building of the compound. Endicott could make out an enormous loading zone, which reminded him of the Bron grain elevator. A paved pathway led around one side towards the river, where he presumed there must be an inlet to some part of the building. Smoke rose from a stack at the rear, and on the far side the sun glinted off a wide array of glass. They approached a large, heavy iron door.

Lindseth knocked with the palm of one hand. Bat Merrett opened the door from the inside and stepped back to let everyone through.

"Care to test who really can beat who, Bat?" Eloise challenged as she passed him. Endicott smiled, guessing that claims of physical prowess or vulnerability had been part of Eloise's distraction test.

To everyone's surprise, Merrett apologized. Sort of. "I didn't mean it. Well, I *can* take you, wench, but it wasn't personal." Merrett took in the whole group of with a wide glance. "For anyone." He stared intently at Endicott. "Except you, blouse."

Endicott found this hilarious and could not stop laughing.

The heavily muscled soldier led them down a wide hallway into a large classroom. Gerveault and Eleanor Brice, Duchess of Vercors, waited there for them. Today she acted simply as Professor Eleanor, unburdened by wig, powder, gloves, or formality, and seemed happy in her role as professor while with her students. Endicott had yet to reveal to her his knowledge of her royal identity. Looking at her paper-thin, blue-veined white skin, he was loath to go against Eleanor's wishes. Whenever he took conscious note of her age and human fragility, he felt a visceral discomfort.

Gerveault was another matter. Like Koria he was a member of the old Engevelen aristocracy. He had very dark skin and light eyes. Again like Koria he was wise, but he behaved with a rigid sense of old-fashioned propriety. Most of the time at least. He could also seem unsympathetic, opaque and emotionless—he was the man, after all, who had written *The Lonely Wizard*—but now he glanced deferentially at Eleanor. She took a half step forward to address the students.

"I am so glad that you have all made it through the testing process successfully." Her gravelly voice was even-handed but kind. "We weren't sure we would have such a good result. Was it worth the time and planning, Koria?"

"Well worth," Koria answered, her happiness plainly written on her face.

Eleanor pointed to a series of paintings on the rear wall. "Those are the previous classes over the years. The painting on the right is Koria's old class. As Professor Gerveault informed you some months ago, apart from our fair daughter Koria, the class was unsuccessful … in the extreme. You have been held to a higher standard. Much higher, but it has all been for good reasons. Congratulations. Professor Gerveault will explain what happens next."

Endicott frowned at the paintings. He could see a younger, grinning Koria staring back at him. Her name was written under her likeness: Koria Valcourt. It was strangely disconcerting seeing her image on the wall so unexpectedly. Beside her in the picture stood two very tall young men who were virtually indistinguishable, and another, both taller and larger, vacant-eyed boy who bore the twins a strong resemblance. Their names were also written out under their likenesses: Arron Derryg, Allyn Derryg, Eldred Derryg.

All dead but her.

Gerveault took the floor while Eleanor stepped back, resting her lean body against a chair. "Today we take the first steps in connecting mathematics to empyreal manipulation. Keith Euyn is … indisposed again, but he is as proud of you as Eleanor, Annabelle, Meredeth, and I are. Try not to be too sad, but I will be your primary guide for the remainder of the year. Let us begin with a tour of your new home."

They passed by several other classrooms some large, some small, all empty, and a small kitchen and dining room. A dark-haired woman in her mid-to-late twenties was making a cup of tea as they passed through. It was Elyze Astarte, whom Endicott and Gregory had not seen since the greenhouse encounter on the terrible night. She smiled a sharp and knowing—some might say predatory—smile at them and called out.

"Come and help me when you have time, Robert! You come too, Gregory."

Eloise scowled at them all.

"At least I was an afterthought," muttered Gregory at Elyze's back, but she was already on her way elsewhere and past hearing.

They emerged from the hallways, classrooms, and offices and descended several steps into a large warehouse-like space divided in the center by a stone channel. The channel carried a steady stream of water.

"From the river, as you must have already realized," supplied Gerveault. "We use water throughout the facility as a heat sink."

And sell the ice afterwards!

Gerveault showed them three forges with large pools of water, stacks of fuel, and cabinet upon cabinet of metal feedstock. He led them to smaller stone rooms, some with chairs and benches where other, smaller work was done. These rooms also had pools of water, though the stone containers were smaller than the ones in the forges. One of the chambers had a cabinet full of solder and other rolled metals along with clamps and assorted tools. Another room had a water-powered metal lathe. Gerveault eventually guided them to an enormous greenhouse, much larger than the one on campus, with stone walls but a glass ceiling. It also had a series of long troughs full of water set in parallel to earth-filled planter boxes.

"It seems a little deserted in here," Davyn observed.

"Except for the guards," added Gregory.

Most of the people they had seen who were not dressed in the armor of guards worked in the greenhouse. Endicott saw that Vern was hard at work not far from Elyze Astarte, who must have come from the kitchen by another route. There were a few others here and there whom Endicott did not recognize. He resolved to have a closer look at the other paintings.

"Yes, there are projects and room enough for eight classes, so do not fear that you shall have too little to do." Gerveault said cryptically. "You are needed. The guards are needed."

Gerveault paused before the wide entrance to yet another room. "This building is a closely held secret that you must never reveal. To anyone. When you come here in future, come in small groups with your amulets hidden. Refer to the building as the Vercors Ice Company warehouse if you must."

"Why the big secret?" asked Heylor.

"Few people know what a dynamicist is, Heylor Style, and fewer still are comfortable with wizards. There is plenty of unrest out there without us adding to it." Gerveault gave the skinny man a long look.

We don't need protestors here too.

"The unsteady sweep of change is seldom comfortable," Gerveault added wryly. "And there is competition to think about as well."

"I can keep a secret," Heylor said.

"Hmm," said Gerveault. "This next area is important."

He led them into an antechamber that opened into two small changing rooms. "Ladies, take the left-hand room, please. Find a free locker for each of you and put the shorts and shirts you were given into it. Then pass through the door at the back and meet me."

Gerveault ushered the boys into the right-hand room, which was filled with benches, cubbies, and metal lockers. "Leave your shorts in a cubby, gentlemen, and come with me."

They emerged into a cozy, humid chamber, well-lit by hanging lanterns. A large, steaming bath dominated the space.

It must be twenty feet or more across.

"This may save your lives," Gerveault pronounced. "We added this room only very recently, but it has already seen considerable use. Using this, we can train you a little harder with less risk. It was Koria's idea actually."

Endicott remembered the terrible night and the use they had made of the Orchid baths. He reached his hand over the stone wall into the pig pool. The water was extremely hot.

Aren't you smart? He smiled at Koria.

Gerveault walked to a cubby set against the back wall and produced a wooden box. He held it out. "Take one."

Endicott reached into the box and pulled out a long, thin tube with a small reservoir on one end filled with dark fluid. Regular lines crossed the tube's short axis at regular intervals. His grandpa had a large thermometer, but Endicott had never seen one so small. A thick black line ran across it two thirds of the way up.

"Dynamicists do not use wands," Gerveault said with a thin smile. "They use thermometers. You will log your temperature every day when you arrive and check it periodically throughout the day. If you feel cold at any time, change into the shorts, come here, and sit in the bath until you are warmed up. If you measure more than four degrees below normal, it is mandatory that you come here immediately, no exceptions, no delays. If you think one of your colleagues is cold, take their temperature and bring them here. If they are more than four degrees below normal but refuse to come, you may call any of the guards to compel them. No one may leave the building until or unless they are at normal body temperature."

Davyn's hand shot up. "When it's just among ourselves, what do we call this place?"

"Call it the Bifrost, Davyn Daly."

THE FIRST EXERCISE GERVEAULT GAVE THEM INVOLVED SIMPLE HERALDRY. THIS WAS SOMEthing that all the students had done before being chosen for the New School, but their professor now issued a warning. "From this point on, do not herald any further or in any other way than as I direct," he instructed.

Eleanor had rejoined him by this time. The students sat facing them on the far side of one long table. They had each been provided with a feather pen, a pad of paper, and two ten-sided dice.

"This is to prepare you for dynamics," Gerveault continued calmly. "First you must become proficient at the lesser breakdown, then we will see what you can really manipulate. The instructions are as follows: achieve the lesser breakdown and focus on your next roll of the dice. You will roll every two minutes at the top of the minute. I will call the roll. You will sit far enough from each other that you cannot see anyone else's dice. Whether you achieve the breakdown or not, you will roll the dice at the top of every two minutes. This will control the experiment and minimize the heraldic uncertainty. Your challenge is simply to herald your numbers. Note down what you herald on the paper in the left column and what you actually roll in the next column. Take your temperature at every interval and write that in the last column."

Davyn's hand shot up, "How do we win? What dice game are we playing? Is it Knights and Demons?"

Eleanor laughed and placed a restraining hand on Gerveault's arm. "You aren't playing any sort of game today, Davyn, so it does not matter what you roll. Any roll is as good as any other. You win, if you want to put it that way, when you accurately predict the roll."

"Thank you, Professor Eleanor, I had not thought of mentioning that," Gerveault said. "Please divorce yourself from *caring* about the numbers. Prejudice may affect the heraldry. Even thinking about statistics should be avoided."

"Roll," came Gerveault's voice, and Endicott rolled. The dice came up a three and an eight, for a total of eleven. That was just as Endicott had heralded. He sat with the thermometer in his mouth and wrote "11" in both columns.

His temperature had not changed, but he was not surprised. Heraldry had become almost second nature to him as he grew up. His grandpa had taught him that it was like an old man peeing in the middle of the night. It required a certain relaxation that was not exactly relaxation. He had to open a window into the empyreal sky and then hold that window open with what his grandpa called an effort-not-effort. The technique could be elusive. It could be frustrating. And apparently it was what urinating in the night would be like for him in a few decades, if he lived that long. Endicott had performed enough clandestine heraldry recently to make that peculiar sweet spot of concentration come easily. Too easily, some might say. Only the most gifted experienced heraldic dreams, and usually only after decades of heralding. But Endicott had already suffered a heraldic dream of epic proportions, a vivid foretelling of a future in which Eloise and Koria were murdered by an enormous cloaked figure. It was a memory Endicott could not get out of his head. It frustrated him, drove him, angered him. If he let it, it would make him desperate and manic again.

After writing down the numbers, Endicott opened himself to the empyreal sky again. He thought about peeing, did not actually pee, and achieved stable heraldry. The room did not flicker or vibrate. The table did not change shape. If the future was an inverted cone, then the further Endicott looked, the greater the possible changes he could observe. Most of his previous attempts at heraldry had looked further ahead in time, much further than he needed to do in order to predict the dice rolls. At the grain exchange, he had seen the variations of events as a deck of cards, unfolding, spraying out across perception, fanning like the splash of a peacock's feathers.

This effort was very different, vastly simplified and orders of magnitude more controlled. He *knew* the moment he was looking for. It was prescribed. He saw, just a moment ahead, the dice roll. Or rather he saw a multitude of rolls, their numbers changing, the exact position of each die shifting, blurring. The longer he watched, the smaller the blur became and the tinier the shifts in position. He came to understand that the most likely rolls had a hotter, more opaque appearance, while the less likely appeared more transparent. As the moment approached, only the most certain results remained, vibrating marginally, blurring imperceptibly.

I must see through the less likely possibilities.

And he did. Most of the time. Endicott rolled the dice twenty times and was correct eighteen of them.

"To the baths, Heylor Style," he heard Gerveault ordering off to the side followed by the muttering, unsmooth departure of the skinny man.

"Roll."

This went on for what began to feel an interminable time. Heylor came back and left and came and left again. "I'm turning into a prune," he complained the last time. Gregory, Deleske, and Bethyn left for the bath, and finally even Eloise had to leave. Endicott, Koria, and Davyn kept on rolling. The heraldry continued to come easily to Endicott, and it did not take long before he found he could achieve the breakdown and an accurate prediction in a very few seconds. Soon he had extra time to think. A notion occurred to him.

Maybe I can win.

He decided to try more than prediction. He would try to influence the dice to come up one-one, the legendary Nimrheal roll. His grandpa had taught him to manipulate the arrangement of metals in his dagger to a very unlikely kind of randomness, a perfect entropy that would form the strongest alloy. He considered that manipulating the dice rolls should be much easier than rearranging the molecular structure of a dagger blade. The odds were only one in a hundred, and the dice could be perturbed quite easily.

How much energy can it take?

"Roll." He did not achieve snake eyes. He had missed the greater breakdown.

Davyn was the next to leave. Only Endicott and Koria now remained.

Endicott bore down on the problem. Suddenly he broke through and achieved the sensation he thought he needed. It felt akin to simple heraldry, only instead of being a passive observer, he fixed the result he wanted in its place in the empyreal sky, pouring energy out of the air and into its possibility. The opacity of the desired event increased until every other possibility became more and more transparent and eventually disappeared. The cone of future possibilities narrowed to a single event—a certainty. It was heraldry with a selective bias and a certain application of force. It was both similar and profoundly different from the heraldry he had performed on the futures of the protestors near the Apprentices' Library. That act had focused on single lines of probability but had remained passive and unselective, observing them one at a time as options. This new act obliterated all options but one, crossing an ineffable line in the sky to *make* an event happen—and borrowing energy to do so.

"Roll." He rolled and, as he did so, knew he had a one-one even before he looked. He wrote it down, adding an asterisk, but he did not notice his breath cloud the suddenly cooler air around him or that Gerveault was frowning at him from across the room.

Is this what I did to Sir Hemdale? He had made Hemdale stumble and miss in the sand ring, though he had done it instinctively. It had cost him more to make the big man fail, if only for an instant. He had nearly frosted over, perhaps only escaping unharmed because he was already overheated from fighting. The temptation to continue, to understand analytically what he had done instinctively was overwhelming. And he had the opportunity to do so.

Let's do it again.

"Roll." He knew it would be a one-one again without looking.

Nimrheal again.

Endicott felt the effect of the operation this time. He shivered slightly but felt more interested than alarmed. He knew the probability of a Nimrheal roll was one in a hundred. Rolling one-one twice in a row should have been a hundred times more improbable, yet it had happened. He had *made* it happen. And the cost felt about the same as the first time rather than a hundred times higher.

"Roll."

Nimrheal again. No harder than before. Yet the odds are now a million to one!

Endicott wondered if the difficulty would have been greater if he had chosen to force three successive Nimrheal rolls right from the start rather than make three individual decisions.

I wonder if I should talk to Meredeth Callum about this?

"Robert Endicott, you are suddenly down two degrees." Gerveault's voice was right in his ear.

Does he know?

"Maybe it's time for everyone to have a little soak. Off you go. You too, Koria."

When Endicott came out of the changing room in his shorts, he saw something that made him stumble. Eloise was standing in the tub with her hands on her hips but no top. Bethyn and newly arriving Koria both wore the shirts they had been given. Endicott hurried into the tub, standing beside Koria and trying not to look at Eloise.

"No shirt, Eloise?" Eleanor's voice asked the question that everyone had been thinking of asking, some with a different intent. The older lady had just walked in and was shaking her head.

"Why waste the washing, Professor?" Eloise answered in a falsely sweet voice. "The boys don't have to wear them."

"Well," said Gregory in an odd tone of voice, "fair's fair."

Davyn's hand shot up. "Tit for tat?"

"Shut up, stupe," snapped Eloise, her perfect breasts riding along the top of the water. "This is simply more comfortable.

"For *you*," Bethyn hissed, red-faced.

"How did everyone do?" Koria asked, a welcome change of subject for Endicott at least. Her hip nudged his under the water.

Endicott was glad the dark water hid his instant and enthusiastic erection.

The answers varied. "Not so great" from Heylor. "Spotty" or "mixed" or "so-so" from everyone else. Except Davyn, who could herald on demand about two thirds of the time and was happy to say so. Koria of course had heralded effortlessly. Endicott's participation in the discussion was constrained by the enjoyable distraction of Koria, who kept brushing him with her hip or thigh. She did it so surreptitiously that anyone else might have thought it was an accident unless they noticed the tiny smile playing on her lips. It annoyed him that she could do this and still engage in the ongoing discussion of their results as if nothing were going on under the water.

"It will come more easily with practice," Eleanor said. "By the end of the week, you will see a significant improvement in your predictive acumen."

"We get to do this every week?" asked Heylor, staring gormlessly at Eloise's breasts.

Gregory tapped him sharply on the back of the head.

Merrett walked in and whispered in Eleanor's ear. "It is time to go, everyone. Join us in the kitchen when you have dried off and changed."

Eloise, Bethyn, and Koria walked out of the hot pool immediately. Koria glanced back at Endicott. "Are you coming, Robert?"

He shook his head. "In a minute. Uh, I'm still cold." He could not risk leaving the concealing water until he had calmed down.

"I'll keep him company," said Gregory, looking at Eloise.

"Me too," boomed Davyn, his voice echoing off the stone walls. "Because I am such a good friend."

Deleske said nothing but stayed where he was. The girls laughed and strolled off, looking behind them and grinning at their stranded classmates.

Heylor shrugged. "Well, I'm ready to go." The skinny boy walked out of the hot pool with no hint of shame or self-awareness, his erection preceding him.

Chapter Three
Small Ways

CLACK, CLACK, CLACK-CLACK-CLACK. Endicott's wooden sword met Lindseth's as they maneuvered across the fenced-in sandpit. Up, down, or sideways, they moved at three-quarter speed. It was a walk-before-you-run lesson from the taller man, and winning it meant winning smoothly. The effort was deeply concentrative, yet Endicott's mind bifurcated, one part in the urgent now, parrying Lindseth's fluid and seemingly spontaneous movements, and the other leaping through the breakdown to herald. That part of him focused solely on the coordinated acts of mock combat, finding the one movement he wanted of the many possible. Some responses gave an advantage to future moves, while other possible responses left him out of balance. Some of the available options required only a small amount of energy from Endicott. Others would draw from his strength unsustainably.

A third part of his mind was altogether elsewhere, remembered words from months past.

You are going to become a person who can change the world in small ways.

Professor Gerveault had said that.

When you change the world, you will change it in a way you expect at the cost you have calculated.

Endicott *did* want to change the world. He had thought about changing the world in vague terms before coming to the New School, but those terms had become much clearer. He now wanted to create a world where his heraldic dream was unlikely to the limits of probability, unlikely enough to become effectively impossible. He wanted to utterly remove the cloaked figure's murder of Eloise and Koria from the cone of the possible. He wanted to manipulate the dice so that Nimrheal's one-one never came up.

"Shout, shout

Redoubt, redoubt
Redoubt Empyrean!
It's echoed, echoed
In the halls of Elysium!"

The chanting was coming as a sing-song back-and-forth from a group of ten students the incorrigible Eoyan March was leading through a series of exercises in the next room. It was the most common of the many training chants he had learned since he started training. Endicott recognized the song's provenance. It was from a poem in *The Lonely Wizard*.

I kind of prefer the song.

"Sir Robert and Sir Gregory are in there, lads and ladies, let's see you put up some effort in case they're watching!" Eoyan March enjoyed teasing Endicott and Gregory when he could. He was a little more cautious with Eloise, perhaps due to her habit of hitting people who irritated her. She was the best fighter of the three who had been knighted after the terrible night, and the most likely to land a blow.

Clack, clack, clack-clack-clack, clack-clack.

Lindseth was quieter than Eoyan, less easy to read. The tall man was not so much tight lipped, like Merrett, as economical in his words. He fought with the same easy parsimony as he spoke: centered and with no more movement or force than was necessary.

For a fleeting second Endicott had an image of what would be, the image preceding what *was* by less than a second. It was a micro-heraldry, but for one sequence of moves it enabled Endicott to react milliseconds before the event. His previous attempts to use heraldry in combat had failed for a variety of reasons, and one of them had been timing. If the heraldry reached too far ahead of the act, cause and effect could become decoupled and prediction tactically useless. This time Endicott hit, almost by accident, on the right lead time. Perhaps his success now was because of the work at the Bifrost predicting dice rolls. Perhaps. His heraldry was ahead of Lindseth but by such a small margin that it did not spoil the causal relationship between him and his opponent. The lead might have been one hundred or two hundred milliseconds, and Endicott managed to flow with it intuitively instead of fighting it so that the heraldry felt instinctive. The tiny lead time also eliminated the multiple probabilities problem that had confused him in the past.

Clack-clack, whup, whup, whup.

Endicott had trapped and disarmed Lindseth. The tall man looked incredulous, but he bowed fractionally and retrieved his wooden sword.

"What was that, Robert?" Gregory was contending against Merrett on the other side of the ring.

"I think it was a moment of millisecond certainty!" Endicott was too fully in the moment with his pleasure to worry about sounding conceited.

"Let's see you do it again, blouse," Merrett growled.

Can I? Endicott was not sure.

Lindseth, sword recovered, returned to guard and only smiled at his opponent. Then he lunged.

Clack, clack, clack-clack-Ouch.

There was only the certainty that Endicott had taken a blow to the ribs. He bowed to Lindseth, and they continued. The smooth flow of cause and effect absorbed his attention and his perception again split. He remembered the lessons of the last several weeks at the Bifrost.

"Heraldry is not completely understood, Davyn," Gerveault had explained. "Some say that when we herald we are dreaming the future, that we see a random-seeming selection of what might be, but multiplied by the filter of our own desires like the impulses of a dream. That school of thought suggests that our own interests affect the accuracy of what is seen, and that in extreme cases of subjective bias, the informational value of heraldry is little more than a reflection of our own daydreams and desires, an echo chamber of our prejudices."

Endicott wondered if that would explain the poor outcomes that seemed to afflict the Justice family whenever Gregory's father heralded.

"Others say heraldry is the observation, both forward and back, of other worlds, alternate realities where the chance contained in every endeavor plays out differently. Of course, if that is true, there must be an infinite number of worlds, infinitely growing as each new chance is taken up."

"Knights and skolves," swore Heylor, shifting uncomfortably. The skinny man had hoped that passing the twenty-four-hour test meant lectures were over. He had been sorely disappointed. Gerveault never tired of exposition and theory.

"That view allows for the possibility of bias in what is seen. The assumption is that the mind can preferentially select certain of the infinite possibilities." Gerveault paused, pointing his index finger up to the cold stone of the ceiling. "My preferred theory, at least for the time being, is that heraldry is the observation of a kind of energy emanating from the future that somehow travels backward to be interpreted by our minds. Reverse—sometimes called retrograde—heraldry, or seeing the past, is understood by this theory as being enabled by a very slow-moving wave of energy. Like sound, but even slower, the past is revealed by the turtle-wave to the careful observer."

Davyn's hand shot up. "Why do we see a range of possibilities even in the most controlled experiment, then, Professor?"

Gerveault smiled like a wolf. "Some of the possibilities come from the other worlds, Davyn Daly." He paused. "And what does this tell us?"

"That you can't make up your mind," shouted Eloise to general laughter.

Gerveault shook his head patronizingly. "No, Mrs. Kyre. It means you must clear your mind of emotions and biases. You must leave your desires, narratives, and delusions at the door. Only the objective mind will draw full value from heraldry."

$\triangledown$

"Well done, Robert." Lindseth extended his hand, and they shook, sparring session over. They cleaned up quickly.

"Are you ready, Gregory?" Endicott whispered.

Gregory smiled, and the two of them slipped out the back door. For weeks they had wanted to take another look at the estate the two obnoxious, bald, sign-carrying protestors had visited. That the campus was ringed, even stalked, by protestors was strange enough. Endicott had seen protestors before at the Battle of Nyhmes and at court. That these two seemed to associate with someone in an opulent, well-guarded estate across town was perplexing. Endicott wanted to know if the protests were being directed and, if so, why. His awful heraldic dream had interrupted that idea, and the twenty-four-hour test had delayed the return to it. The first weeks at the Bifrost, with their intense introduction to dynamics, had put off matters further. But now a break in the schedule had come up. Eleanor,

Gerveault, and Koria had been called away on some mysterious errand at the Citadel, and Eloise was spending the day with her uncle, Sir Hemdale. An opportunity presented itself.

"There. They. Are." Endicott spied the two protestors on the edge of campus by the ring road. They were walking back and forth at their usual spot near the Apprentices' Library. Heavily built but of average height, they bore a striking resemblance even in their facial features. Same large noses, same smooth bald heads, same fixed looks of contempt and discontent. They could have been brothers. As usual they carried large signs raised over their shoulders, spelling out–or misspelling–their daily message in large, bold print. The first sign was typically positive and uplifting:

"You will reep what you sew.

Duke's wizzards grow poison

And spit on the past.

Return to the old ways!!"

The second man's sign was no more encouraging:

"Evil grayn grows, people die!

Wizzards have secret plans for you.

If you don't pay the price, we will collekt!

Skoll and Hati will take you to Hell!"

"But we're not here for *them* this time." Gregory said in a low voice, trying not to be obvious as he watched the protestors.

"Not this time," Endicott whispered. *This time we will see who is behind them.*

They backed away, staying at the perimeter of campus, waiting for the protestors to pack up and leave.

"How are you feeling, Lord Justice?" Endicott had been taking note of his tall friend's pensive look. It was an expression Gregory had been wearing more and more often in their weeks at the Bifrost. The protestors were packing away their signs now. Gregory adjusted his sword, and the two would-be detectives started across the ring road. "Fine. Good. Excellent, thanks." Endicott said nothing, merely staring at Gregory until his friend looked at him and put his hands up. "Okay, perhaps not excellent. It doesn't bother me, really, that I am only about a tenth as good as you and Koria. And I'm happy that you are the hero of the terrible night, and I am very pleased that you just disarmed Lindseth, who is a wizard with his swords. I—"

Endicott interrupted him. "That was a lucky moment, Gregory. You know I'm usually the worst of us. And let's face it, Lindseth was only using one sword." Jeyn Lindseth was a thing of beauty with one sword in each hand.

"Right," Gregory said, sounding unconvinced. "But none of that bothers me anyway. You are my brother." He pounded the top of Endicott's shoulder. "I just don't know what to do about Eloise. Or Rhiain."

"Perhaps pick one and focus on *her*?" Endicott tried to avoid sounding sardonic but realized too late that Deleske would probably have spoken in just that way.

Gregory spun and faced him, bringing him up short. "This coming from the man who professes love to every woman he meets! It wouldn't be a problem if they did not, in their way, reciprocate."

You're flirting with Rhiain because I'm *close to everyone? No. Because I'm close to Eloise.* Endicott took hold of his friend's shoulders. He thought he understood. "So this is about Eloise, then? You've decided to commit yourself fully to courting her? You love her?" He lowered his arms, and they turned by some mutual, unspoken consent and continued walking.

Gregory's eyes were wet. "For the longest time I thought she was in love with *you*. She was so provocative … She never acted that way with me, even after the terrible night, when we all slept together. But over time it's become clear that she has no jealousy of you and Koria, so I have started to think that maybe I don't understand her at all. Perhaps she is not in love with you. Perhaps she even likes me."

"So you do love her," Endicott mused. "But you have been suppressing your feelings because of … things. Okay. That's okay. You should tell her."

"I'm not you, Robert," Gregory spoke slowly now and with much less heat. "I can't say the words so easily."

Endicott thought about that. "You know the words are important. They shouldn't be misused. But don't hoard them like gold. Love should be shared. It's the only coin that multiplies with the spending."

Gregory laughed quietly, nodding.

Endicott continued. "Eloise is from Armadale. Her uncle, Sir Hemdale, is a Deladieyr Knight. Do you know what blood runs in her veins? It is a beautiful, over-the-top kind of romantic blood, Gregory. You need to tell her how you feel. Or show her with some chivalric gesture."

"Like what?" Gregory said quickly, seizing on the idea. "Fight for her? No. Mostly I fight *with* her. You gave her that wonderful cold-forged sword, Robert. I couldn't make her one if I tried. I don't think flowers are going to do it for her."

"You could scale the Orchid and climb into her room."

"And get thrown off, possibly after being beaten *and* beheaded." Gregory looked up dramatically. "Humiliated, dead, *and* alone."

"How about writing a poem? That seems to have worked for Jennyfer Gray on no less a romantic than Lord Jon Indulf."

"Eloise laughs at poetry unless it's about battles."

"Carry her books?"

"And get a punch in the face. It would be an insult to her."

"She is … difficult. Let me think." The two young men walked in companionable silence for a few moments. They had just started working with the thermal equation at the Bifrost, which meant they might have access to the forges soon. An idea began to form in Endicott's mind. It would serve several purposes if it worked.

"What if," Endicott said with growing excitement, "you did something clandestine?"

"Sneaky? Maybe," Gregory responded with a mix of skepticism and hope.

"And personally dangerous."

"It sounds like this could be the right stroke. What else?"

"Totally against the rules and all good sense."

"A little redundant, but that sounds like the kind of thing Eloise might like."

"Something no one else can do."

"Even better. What else?"

"Martial in nature."

"She is going to marry me!" crowed Gregory with uncharacteristic abandon.

"Yes." Endicott raised one eyebrow. "You will have her children, Gregory."

"What is it? What sneaky, dangerous, unlawful, unique, and martial thing am I doing?"

Endicott jumped over a curb. They were almost at their destination. "You, sir, are going to make Eloise a cold-forged shield."

"Excellent skolving idea, Robert," Gregory said, exasperated, his fire doused. "How am I supposed to make a cold-forged shield? I don't understand the metallurgy, and I can barely transfer enough heat to make a cup of tea."

"Don't worry, my friend. Tea today, shields tomorrow. I will help you."

Gregory grasped Endicott's shoulders. "Thank you, brother."

"I love you too."

"You always go too far."

Yes, I do.

They were now within one block of the estate. A slow drizzle materialized as if out of nowhere, almost as if the tiny droplets had suddenly manifested from the ether. A tall blond woman hurried past them, covering the basket she carried with a dark blanket or cloak. Endicott did not get a good look at her—she passed them too quickly—but he caught an anxious sound in her breathing. It set him momentarily on edge. The small sound, whatever it was—a sigh, a whimper—shot through him and he found his heart beating faster, his eyes more sharply focused, and his hands clenching into fists.

Why?

Endicott had always responded to a woman's distress this way, autonomically, instantly, sometimes uncontrollably. It was akin to the way most people react to the sound of a baby crying, and it had grown worse since the terrible night and the heraldic dream. He knew that women were not helpless babies, but even so, anyone could need help at some point. In any case being aware of his propensity did not make it stop. Wherever the response came from, it was somewhere deep inside him, and it was immune to reason or negotiation. He did not wish to think about his dead mother and the inability to remember her that Sir Hemdale had made an exclamation point of. With his sword. He doubted that remembering would make a difference. He doubted it could change him at all. *This is just the way I am.* He blew out a breath and slowed his pace.

"Let's stop here," he said quietly, "and see who comes and goes and what they do. The drizzle should cloak us some."

They stood on the corner of the block and watched the gate of the big private residence from the corners of their eyes, pretending to be in conversation. Endicott relaxed and allowed his perception to split again, part of him watching, the other part remembering what they had learned in the Bifrost and how some of that reminded him eerily of the precocious acts they were perpetrating now.

"It is time to apply the mathematics you spent so much time learning. In front of you are two stone vessels of water. They each hold one standard cup. The heat capacity, shape, and mass of each cup is noted on the charts in front of you. You are going to transfer some of the thermal energy from one cup to the other." Gerveault's pedantic tones were a familiar patter in Endicott's ears. Eleanor still attended many of their lessons at the Bifrost, but Gerveault was their only real instructor.

"This seems too complicated," declared Heylor, pushing one of the small vessels away. "Why don't we just start with one cup?"

Gerveault stopped dead, his face blank. "How would you increase the heat energy in your single cup, Mr. Style? Where would that additional energy come from? Or if you chose to lower the temperature in your single cup, where would you put the extracted energy?" He narrowed his eyes. "Remember what I told you on your first day: we cannot create or destroy energy, we move it. We borrow it. Carefully."

"Oh."

Davyn's hand shot up. "How much heat do we move, Professor?"

Gerveault relaxed his squint and smiled. "The first half of the exercise is to calculate how hot one cup will become and how cool the other one will be as a result. The second half will be to enact the empyreal manipulation. For that you will use a mathematical framework, the thermal equation, and your understanding of heat capacity."

Gregory shook his head. "It is easy to hear the words, but what do they mean? I don't know what *you* mean, sir."

"It is always easier to speak a thing than make it true, Gregory Justice." Gerveault's voice droned on, describing the creation of a sampled field in three dimensions and how that field would be populated by properties observable in the Empyreal Sky.

Endicott did not miss the reference to The Lonely Wizard. It made him uncomfortable coming from the author, but he set aside his strange reaction to Gerveault's phrasing and thought about what the man had said. He knew how thermodynamic manipulation could be performed. He had done it several times with his grandpa, sometimes even with a cup of tea. Those efforts had been performed instinctively, in the style of the old wizards, or so he assumed. Endicott had imagined what the mathematical, or dynamic, method might look like a month previously, right before the twenty-four-hour test. The fact that the imagined method of his own invention was in fact the correct method was intoxicating to him. It fed an irresistible curiosity.

Why not just try it?

Without waiting for Gerveault to finish describing how it should be done, Endicott began. He built a three-dimensional grid in Empyreal space and populated it with the thermal properties he saw there. He tightened the grid and compared the two vessels, imagining two inversely related dipoles positioned in the center of each cup. Then he broke through.

The first cup began to steam slightly. He placed a thermometer in each vessel. The first vessel was nine degrees hotter, the second was eleven degrees cooler. The table around the cups was marked by a series of condensation rings. He adjusted his dipoles and broke through again. One cup was now twenty degrees hotter, but the other was partially frozen. The rings changed too. The closest was frosty now, while the outer ones remained simply the products of condensation.

"Where are your calculations, Mr. Endicott?" Gerveault's voice boomed in his ear. Endicott looked up. Everyone else was staring at him. They had still been working on the calculations that Endicott had skipped. Koria's eyebrows were raised, whether in alarm or admiration was hard to say. She glared at the steaming mug and then at the frost-covered work area. Not alarm or admiration—alarm or anger.

I am in so much trouble. And I'm shivering…

Endicott was jolted out of the uncomfortable memory by two armored men walking noisily by. One brushed Gregory's shoulder as they passed, almost nudging him into the gutter. Their arms were the archetypal plate and mail of Armadale. Gregory smiled ingratiatingly at them and said something about the weather to Endicott. They watched the men clank their way through the gate and up the cobbled driveway of the same stone mansion they were watching.

"That was almost worth getting bumped by those skolves," Gregory scowled.

"Let's see who else comes," Endicott replied.

Endicott made the calculations that Gerveault demanded using two fresh cups of water. He decided to bring one vessel to a uniform boil hovering just at or minutely above the boiling point. The other would be reduced to a temperature significantly below freezing. He also created a rough heuristic based on the observed heat loss from his dipole experiment to ensure he would precisely achieve the result he wanted.

Endicott glanced around before he acted. Heylor had broken his pen, Bethyn was frowning, and Deleske was staring hard at his vessels but to no apparent effect. Gregory's cups also remained inert. Eloise's were broken, and water had spilled on her pages of paper, but Endicott did not think the cups had been broken by empyreal manipulation.

Davyn seemed pleased as he scratched away with his pen. Koria's left cup was steaming mildly and a ring of condensation surrounded both vessels, but it had a smaller diameter than Endicott's. He wondered if that had to do with the lesser amount of energy he estimated she had managed to transfer, given that her cup was not steaming very much, or if it was a function of support. He decided to make his support smaller.

Endicott made his grid tighter by a factor of two, increasing the number of points in his observational field eight-fold. *Ah, the price of support.* He broke through and executed his manipulation.

Both cups exploded.

One of them cracked down both sides from the solid block of ice it suddenly contained, while the other sprayed a shower of superheated water and steam over Endicott, his papers, and immediate environs. A few errant drops hit Davyn, Koria, and Gregory. Endicott's face, hands and arms were scalded, but before he could yelp, a curtain of freezing water hit his face. Koria had emptied her cold vessel over him. The rest of the class quickly followed suit, ostensibly to help him, though their grins told a different story. Eloise used one of Heylor's.

Gasping, Endicott tried to explain what he had done. He faced Gerveault as he spoke, but he was really talking to Koria, whose foot tapped with irritation. Gerveault interrupted his explanation. "What did we learn from this, class?" Gerveault asked.

"That Robert is an idiot," said Eloise fiercely.

"Yes, though we hardly need reminding that Sir Robert tends to go too far and too fast," replied the old man, giving Endicott a withering look. "But we learned something else. He changed the support in his calculation, but his heuristic for losses was based upon a coarser level of support. Finer sampling yields more accurate results and smaller losses, class. That is what you learned. I wonder if Robert will ever learn the lesson about jumping in with both feet? We will see."

Koria did not play delicious games with him in the hot pool that day.

"Look at that, Robert!" Gregory just managed to avoid pointing at the covered chariot that had stopped at the gate. A man of average proportions emerged, resplendent in a purple cloak and an enormous decorative chain. He was quickly flanked by two plate-armored attendants.

"Who do you suppose that is?" Endicott wondered aloud.

"That, Sir Robert, is the ambassador for Armadale." Gregory's forehead crinkled as he saw the question on Endicott's face. "I *am* of noble blood, I will have you know, and not a total idiot. That is obviously an ambassador's chain, and he is being guarded by Knights of Armadale. Ergo," he added archly, "he is almost certainly the ambassador for Armadale."

Endicott had never seen an ambassador's chain, but he trusted Gregory's background and confidence. "Perhaps we should go," he suggested, fearing that they may have pressed their luck by loitering for as long as they had.

"Yes," Gregory agreed with some satisfaction. "It's starting to rain harder anyway."

They decided by mutual paranoid consent to take a circuitous route back to the Orchid. The drizzle had turned to a light rain, which was now starting to turn heavy. It shrouded the city like a semitransparent curtain, reminding Endicott of the forced view of a single reality through heraldry.

I wonder if we ever see the world as it truly is, or is what we perceive always some best guess of what might be?

One's view in the dark or in rain is colored by mood. If lonely, the rain and dark set one inalterably apart from the world; if frightened, the world becomes an unknowable, threatening, haunted place. What we perceive is a function of how we feel.

They passed near a seedy-looking tavern. Endicott read its name.

The Black Spear. Conor's tavern!

A crude image was carved beside the name. It was of Nimrheal holding his spear aloft. Endicott had always meant to find the place, had always meant to look for Conor again, but had never had the time. He was about to suggest they go in when he noticed an abrupt hitch in Gregory's step.

"We are being followed," Gregory whispered.

Again?

"Is he wearing a cloak?"

Endicott let Gregory search for a reflection in the tavern windows as they passed while he took the opportunity to covertly loosen his sword in its sheath.

"Yes!" Gregory's whisper was almost a croak.

A familiar anger surged in Endicott, but an excitement too. The idea of confronting the long-standing threat of the cloaked figure was exhilarating and almost overwhelming.

Be calm.

"We are going to get him this time, Gregory," Endicott whispered while his heart pounded, and his blood screamed. "At the next corner." They rounded the next block and darted ahead and to the side, hiding in the shadow of the building, listening for the footfalls of their stalker.

Clop, clop, clop, clop. Then nothing. Whoever it was had stopped at the corner.

Endicott could not miss his chance. He practically vibrated with impatience. He drew his sword and leaped out and around the corner, holding the blade level at the tall, cloaked figure. Gregory followed a step behind, cursing to himself. His entropic sword sung its familiar hum as he swung it around to the level, ready to destroy.

"Who are you! Why are you following us!" Endicott roared it into the rain.

The tall cloaked figure stumbled and threw up her arms, exclaiming in a female voice, "I-I'm no one."

Both Endicott and Gregory kept their swords level in the pregnant moment.

"Please don't hurt me!" the voice cried.

Her terrified cry pierced Endicott's soul. He sheathed his sword, feeling sick and foolish. The adrenaline coursing through his body, finding no outlet, intensified the sensation of illness that seized him.

"Would you mind lowering your cowl?" demanded Gregory, less affected than Endicott and apparently less surprised to discover they had been followed by an exceedingly tall woman rather than a man. His sword was still levelled at her.

The figure lowered her cowl with visibly shaking hands. She was the tall blond woman who had passed them on the street corner earlier, the one carrying a basket. Her eyes were a piercing blue, cool and incongruous on her panicked face.

"We won't hurt you," soothed Endicott absently pushing at the flat of Gregory's sword so that it swung away from her. "We thought you were following us."

"I *was* following you," she replied, lowering her arms and crossing them in front of her. "I saw you by Armadale House. I need your help."

Armadale House.

Gregory had barely sheathed his sword before Endicott was leaping to her assistance. "Did the knights at that estate … do something to you?" Endicott's heart pounded again.

"No," she said. "But I am behind on my sewing for the Ambassador's valet."

Endicott's mental charge stumbled, his heart rate slowed, and confusion superseded gallantry in his collapsing emotional tableau. Gregory stepped forward. "Perhaps if you could tell us who you are and exactly what you need, we could help you." His voice was calming.

"My name is Freyla Loche," she said, looking reassured. "I'm an arts student at the New School." She uncrossed and then quickly recrossed her arms as if uncertain how to proceed. "I've seen both of you in the Commons. Everyone knows who you are. So when I saw you on the street, and with the way everything has gone for us the last few days, I had to see if you would help."

"Help you with sewing?" Endicott asked, still nonplussed.

Freyla nodded her head eagerly. "My mother owns the Eight Stitches Sewing Company. It's how she has been able to put me through school. I work with her when I have time and help as much as I can between classes. This winter we finally bought three stitching engines."

Ahh.

A trickle of cold rainwater ran down Freyla's face from her forehead to her angular cheek and then to her firm jawline. "Someone broke into our shop four days ago and damaged the engines. Now we're behind on our orders!" Freyla sobbed. "We still owe money on the engines, and if we don't meet our orders, I don't know what will happen."

Gregory shook his head skeptically and asked, "What do you expect us to do, Freyla?"

She stifled another sob. "You all have stitching machined clothes. Word is that Sir Robert built his own stitching engine. I thought you would be able to fix ours." She turned her big, blue, watery eyes on Endicott.

I didn't make it. That was my uncle.

"Everyone says you'll do anything for a woman who needs help," Freyla explained, keeping her pleading eyes fixed on him. Gregory began to laugh and did not stop for rather a long time.

For the first time Endicott regretted not paying more attention when his uncle had reverse-engineered the stitching engine. He was far from confident that he knew enough to help Freyla, but there was no doubt in his mind that he had to try. And so, fifteen minutes later, he found himself at the Eight Stitches Sewing Company trying to understand what had gone wrong with the engines.

Freyla's mother, Veygdis, was roused and split her attention between watching Endicott examine the engines with Freyla's assistance and listening to Gregory's stories about the New School.

"Freyla, can you just slowly work the treadle while I try to look under here." Endicott struggled to get his head in position to examine the underside of the feed mechanism of the first machine without putting his head in Freyla's lap. With her cloak off, her strong, young feminine figure was unmistakable. She wore a yellow skirt and had long smooth legs that reminded the young man of Eloise. He wondered how they had possibly mistaken her for the menacing cloaked figure of his heraldic dream.

Endicott tried to look away from her legs, but despite his maneuvering, his head *was* practically in her lap. "Maybe crouching would be better than sitting, Freyla." He felt awkward, rudely masculine—and suddenly, unexpectedly —embarrassingly tight in his pants. He did not want to give the tall, beautiful young lady the wrong idea as he tried to squeeze himself under the table. All he wanted to do, he repeated to himself, was to see what was awry with the mechanism while she simultaneously worked the treadle. After much straining and readjusting, he found a position that worked without being distracting. "Thanks. That is perfect now."

Endicott took his time examining the engines, losing himself in the analysis. The work reminded him of his days back at the Bron elevator. At the elevator he had opened himself to the empyreal sky in order to detect metal fatigue and other deep-structural problems, but here the problem was mechanical. The mechanism required that the needle, rotating hook, treadle, belt, flywheel, and feed mechanisms all work in precise concert, and although he had happily pushed the boundaries of recklessness at the Bifrost repeatedly over the past weeks, he felt cautious about what he could do with Freyla's stitching engines. She had explained how expensive, uncertain, and slow a commercial repair would be, and he had come to appreciate that this seemingly minor problem held vast significance for the women. Their livelihood, and Freyla's future at the New School, depended on solving it. To make matters worse, he saw at once that the machines had been sabotaged. They had numerous dents, abrasions, and gouges. Someone had deliberately damaged them while the women slept in their apartment above.

Endicott took a deep breath and announced his conclusions. "You have three major problems. First this broken pushrod needs replacing. A machinist should be able to make a new one in a few days depending on how busy they are. The second issue is with the damaged feed on this other machine." He pointed to the second engine. "Someone has mashed the presser foot and the feed dogs. I'm not sure how it was done, but I suppose enough indiscriminate whacking could have managed it. That shouldn't be hard to replace either, but it's fine work. Lastly we have a broken rotating hook on your third engine. It is a delicate piece, but it could be recast at a forge or machined fresh. Without it you cannot make your lockstitches, which means you cannot sew."

"But you can fix it, Sir Robert?" Freyla asked, hands wringing.

"If I had a day or two and a forge, yes." Endicott shook his head. He had never even seen the Bifrost's forges fired up yet. It was something he could do if he had a few days to prepare. "But I have neither right now."

"We're ruined." Veygdis declared in a peculiar, flat voice.

Endicott looked at Gregory. The tall young man shook his head subtly. He looked at Freyla, whose eyes moved from her mother and back to him, and then at Veygdis, whose eyes looked dead. When he had found Syriol in the carriage on the terrible night, Endicott hadn't been sure exactly what to do, but he had instantly known he would do anything to help her. While this situation was very different objectively, his reaction was the same. It did not matter why someone had damaged the machines, why Veygdis had overstretched her financial resources on the engines, or why she could not find a smith or machinist to help her. All that mattered to him was her undeniable need for help.

"How much water can you boil for me?"

"Are you skolving out of your mind, Robert?" Gregory hissed. "You might have the affinity, but you also blow up more cups of water than you boil. I've never met anyone who could burn water, let alone make it explode until I met you. What are you going to do?"

That's actually a very good point.

"I'm better with probability, Gregory." Endicott winked, projecting a confidence he did not have.

Gregory was unimpressed. "What in Hati's Hell does that mean?"

"Look," Endicott said, "the pushrod is solid iron. I know its heat capacity, I know how much of it there is, and I can work on it in isolation, so the error field won't ruin anything else. I can fix that thermally. I've worked on things just like it with my grandpa. I just need a clamp and a hammer. The other two pieces I can fix with probability manipulation."

"This escalation is insane, Robert! You're going to die like the stupe Eloise says you are. And if you don't die of hypothermia, both Koria and Eloise are going to kill you again. Me too, probably." Gregory's voice had risen as he spoke, and Freyla was staring at them both, open mouthed.

Endicott waved away his friend's objections, hoping to calm the situation. It didn't work.

"Don't kill yourself!" gasped Freyla. "Who said anything about killing anyone?"

Gregory turned to her. "There's always a price."

"I don't understand any of this," she said.

Endicott stood up and faced her directly. "He's exaggerating. But don't tell anyone else about this." Endicott turned to his friend. "Gregory, you're right. Can you run and get a horse and carriage and bring it here? There isn't a bath in the house. If things go wrong, we'll hop in the carriage, drive to the Bifrost, and you'll dump me in the pool."

Gregory left, scowling.

A few moments later Veygdis arrived with a cauldron of steaming water.

I need to tilt the field.

"How much more hot water can you boil?"

Suddenly Gregory was back, breathing hard and dripping water. Endicott paused in his arrangement of water and materials. He looked inquiringly at his friend. Gregory could never have found a carriage-for-hire this quickly.

"A real friend would not let you do this, Robert."

"What?"

"This is not you, Robert. Use that mind of yours." Gregory tapped his forehead. "That has to be the best thing about you. There must be seven other things we could do that are less dangerous."

"You heard these ladies. The don't have time for anything else!" Endicott felt hot.

"They don't know what they are asking!" Gregory stepped closer, his hand on the hilt of his sword.

Endicott eyed Gregory's hand, and the tall young man shook his head. "I'm not going to draw on you, Robert. Not with the sword your grandpa made for my dad. Not ever. You are my brother." He stepped closer. "But you haven't been … right ever since the heraldic dream. It's ruined your judgement. You've been reckless in class, but this is *so* much worse. This is no emergency that justifies putting yourself in mortal danger. What would Koria say? What would your grandpa say?"

Freyla put a hand on Endicott's arm. "Is he right? Is this really that dangerous?"

Endicott closed his eyes and listened to his heartbeat. He had not been aware it was pounding so hard. He felt the heat in his body, smelled the sweat, and sensed the tautness of his nerves. He imagined what might happen if he proceeded with his plan.

The carriage charged down the wet streets, careening around corners, and nearly plowed into the gates at the Bifrost. Moments after that Gregory and one of the guards flung the shivering, frost-covered body of Robert Endicott into the steaming pool. It shook violently and then shook no more.

Endicott opened his eyes. He remembered everything Koria had said about consequences and care. He remembered what Lord Brice had said about being desperate. Even remembering all that, it was difficult for him to stay above the rising tide of anxiety that threatened to drown his analytic abilities at every reminder of the dream.

How am I supposed to protect Koria and Eloise when I cannot even manage a problem as small as a broken stitching engine?

I have been reckless and desperate. I'm not right in my mind.

Admitting to the problem was some relief, though the underlying tension remained.

"You're right, Gregory. I have been out of control. At every opportunity, I have pushed ahead at the Bifrost. You know *why*, but the reason doesn't matter." He nodded. "Thank you."

With this, the tension finally seemed to leave Gregory's body. "So what are we going to do?"

Think carefully!

Endicott turned to Freyla, who was still grasping his arm. "If I could repair two of the engines tonight, would you be able to meet your obligations?"

She nodded, tears running down her face. "With help from hand sewing, yes. But don't hurt your—"

"There will be no risk, just work." Endicott took her hand and squeezed, then let it go. "Now I need a few tools. Gregory, you can help me."

Freyla's mother brought her small toolbox, and Endicott explained what needed to be done.

"We are going to remove the rotating hook, presser foot, and feed dogs from the engine with the broken pushrod. That machine is out of commission for at least the next day or two. We will take those pieces and use them to replace the broken elements of the other two machines. Once that is done, we should have two working engines. Sir Gregory and I should be able to make repairs to the broken pieces over the next couple of days and get the third engine up and running."

The work took longer than expected. The Eight Stitches Sewing Company's tool set was missing a few pieces. The young men had to return to the Orchid and locate Endicott's needle- nose pliers as well as a knockout pin. Luckily Heylor had stolen neither of these, so they did not have to turn over his room to find them. Deleske was the only one still up when they retrieved the tools. He barely glanced at them as they came and went.

Once they had everything they needed, the replacing, readjusting, and testing took less time than they expected. Nevertheless it was very late on that still-rainy night when the two young men walked back to the New School, side by side and proud.

"Just tell me if that happens again," Endicott said quietly.

Gregory laughed, completely at ease now. "At least you didn't profess your undying love this time."

Endicott thought about what had happened, smiling. After the two machines had been restored to life, Freyla and her mother had tried to insist that their saviors should sleep there until morning. *That* had seemed a very bad idea to Endicott, though he realized it was prompted only by relief and a desire to return at least some hospitality after being helped so crucially. Endicott guessed that they had never fully believed the machines would be fixed until the job was done. The engines were not complicated, but they were new, and Endicott supposed that people were still intimidated by them and felt helpless when they were damaged or needed repair.

He thought about how easy it was to picture people's hopes and dreams as tides that could shift the world as they rose and fell, but saw that mostly they are nothing of the kind. The worries and concerns of almost everyone are small and mundane. Most people want to have food, a home, and love. A small mix of objective needs complemented by a more complex subjective satisfaction is the driver of most human life. On the terrible night Endicott had for a moment been part of a dramatic, unequivocal struggle for life, and while it had in some way irrevocably changed everyone involved, he suspected it might not prove to be the most important thing he would ever be involved in. It was possible that a life concerned only with mending the small things could have just as much value.

Chapter Four.
A Criterion for Entropy

"I NEED YOUR ADVICE." ENDICOTT RESTED HIS HEAD ON KORIA'S LAP. THE FEEL OF HER smooth, curved skin under his face, of her hair tickling the back of his head and her hands gently stroking his shoulders, helped soothe the tempestuousness that had affected his behavior since the heraldic dream. Koria's lap was the endless half-space of love that made him feel whole.

And fortunate. Very fortunate.

She said nothing, but he knew she liked it when he asked. She thought it showed good sense. It was unclear who had the greater intellectual capacity, but Koria was a year older and more experienced. Endicott was more dynamic and therefore less stable. They both knew who was by far the wiser of the two. Endicott was well aware of his emotional turbulence. He felt his passions and ideas as powerful tides and knew they were difficult to turn aside even when he knew them to be unwise or dangerous. Gregory's recent comments had not been lost on the young man. Endicott knew his friend had spoken correctly. The possibility that his emotional maturity seemed to have turned retrograde due to the trauma of the heraldic dream shocked and scared him. He clung to Koria's smooth ebony legs, to that half-space of love and stability. He knew he needed this. He needed her.

And so Endicott spoke.

He told her everything that he and Gregory had seen and done, the promises he had made, and the stitching engine pieces that still needed repair. Then he tried to describe the rising tide of anxiety that had nearly led to a new and unnecessary act of recklessness.

"How often have you and your grandpa repaired metal like this?" Koria's first question was strangely matter of fact.

Endicott sat up so he could see her luminous green eyes. "You aren't going to give me hell for working myself up so badly over some other woman's problems?"

"Why?" Koria's eyebrows barely went up. "It's all of a piece. Your heraldic dream, this girl Freyla, you not remembering your mother. Maybe somewhere deep inside, all women are your missing mother to you, but accepting that theory from Hemdale is not going to suddenly unravel all this other trauma." She kissed Endicott on the cheek. "You are *damaged*, Robert. I don't think you are going to magically undamage until we start to solve some of these problems. Perhaps you cannot save *everyone*, as Eloise would say, but saving *someone* might be a step in the right direction."

"Is that what you are doing with me?"

She punched him on the shoulder. "Don't be an idiot. Now back to the question at hand, please."

Endicott covered her clenched fist gently with one hand. "Did Grandpa and I fix metal like this? Pretty much all the time, though we did the work discreetly."

"Did you manipulate the materials thermally or probabilistically?"

It did not occur to Endicott, nor apparently to Koria, that discussing such technical details in the bedroom was unusual, though he did weigh his choice of words before responding. He and Grandpa did not use the same jargon that Gerveault taught. "In most cases, let's say it was … thermally *aided* probabilistic manipulation. Sometimes we did both but in a specific order."

Koria clapped her hands together in a girlish display of delight that surprised Endicott and recalled Eoyan March's description of that earlier, carefree Koria. "That could be *perfect*! And well beyond what we were ever taught before my class ended. Let's talk to Gerveault before breakfast."

Endicott locked away the little memory of Koria clapping her hands. He kissed her and stood up to leave. Before he reached the door, he remembered Gregory's secret shield project and told her of that plan. She suggested they tell Gerveault about this too. It could be another test of the method.

Gerveault lived in a two-story stone house just inside the ring road. Endicott had never visited him at home and without Koria's prompting would never have dared disturb him so early. The old man received them placidly and made no comment about the hour. Endicott could not read Gerveault's mood or reaction as he spoke of his plan with the stitching engine repairs and requested materials for the shield project with Gregory.

"I believe we can do something about the repair work, Robert Endicott, if you think you can reign in your enthusiasm during the actual operation." As he spoke, the old man gazed at Endicott with an intensity that would have made most people uncomfortable. Endicott knew this gaze for what it was: Gerveault was evaluating him. He was trying to decide whether they really could work together to execute the lesson Koria had laid out. "I will work with you, Professor. Just signal me when you need me to wait or slow down."

"Hmm." Gerveault's face betrayed what might have been the hint of a smile. "Can you hold your manipulation if I suggest you should?"

Endicott relaxed, knowing they had entered the negotiation stage. "Yes, though we should talk throughout given the need for continual thermal control."

Gerveault's feet turned slightly away. "I'll have the forge lit, then. Bring the pieces with you."

Endicott dared one last question. "And the shield?"

The old man shook his head. "The materials alone could be prohibitively expensive. Manganese, cobalt, and tungsten are rare and difficult to obtain. There is also the safety factor to be considered. It would be significantly more dangerous than fixing a few stitching machine pieces. I will have to speak with Professor Eleanor."

Endicott struggled to remain diplomatic. "Respectfully, my grandpa and I have done this work on dozens of alloys dozens of times. We've managed it safely every time."

"Just because you have not *managed* to kill yourself yet does not make you safe this time!"

A little uncharitable, even if the reasoning is sound.

Endicott considered Gerveault's hard face and thought about his own recent history. He realized it would have been better not to have used an argument based simply on previous successes. Koria noticed him looking at her. She stepped into the gap. "Perhaps we can assess how Robert does with the repairs and go from there."

"You shouldn't be worrying about every woman you stumble over, stupe." Eloise glared at Endicott over a spoonful of porridge.

He winked at her, refusing to rise to the bait. Her tactic of berating him over everything he did that was not firmly directed towards Koria was too familiar. Bethyn, however, surprised him.

"Don't you think she might be using you?" Bethyn rarely agreed with Eloise, but both women were nodding now.

"It all sounded a little contrived." Deleske did not even look up as he spoke, creating the effect of a disembodied, if still sardonic, presence.

"She was certainly aware of your reputation already," Gregory added.

Endicott put his spoon down. "And what if she is using me? I am not sure that matters. They *do* need help, and I—we—can help them." He shook his head, certain of himself. "If I built a wall between myself and other people's problems, assuming I even could, wouldn't I lose as much as I gained?"

"I wish *I* could help people." Heylor's wistful sincerity argued against the possibility of sarcasm. "Nobody ever asks me."

"Well, you *are* good at helping yourself," interjected Davyn loudly. "You stole my boiled egg." The big man's fork speared an egg off Heylor's plate. "There. I just saved you from going to hell."

The trip to the Bifrost was quieter. The rule against descending directly on the secret location remained in full effect. A circuitous route was always taken, and they even mixed who walked with whom. This time Endicott went with Heylor. As usual the skinny young man could hardly keep still. He was in constant motion: skipping, hopping, or just flailing about randomly with his arms while moving his head in restless, rapid fidgets. He was a walking distraction.

"How come I never get to go with you on any of your knightly exploits?" Heylor whispered this for no apparent reason. Perhaps, Endicott wondered, he thought whispering would add an extra layer of interest to the tedious question.

He thought fast.

Whether any of his actions qualified as "exploits" was one thing, how to answer Heylor without hurting his feelings was another. *There are many true answers, but which one to use?*

"It could be dangerous. Gregory has his sword." Endicott did not know when the cloaked figure would come, but he would come eventually, so his words were therefore not a lie. The truth was that Endicott did not trust

Heylor not to make any situation worse. In fact it would be truer to say he *expected* Heylor to make most situations worse.

"Justice?" The skinny young man's eyes lit up. "Make me one, then," he pleaded.

"What?"

"I know. It's pretentious, but that's what Gregory calls it. His sword, I mean. Justice."

Endicott's forehead crinkled. "You have yet to even practice with a sword, Heylor."

"Well, I will from now on."

There was a stubborn tone in the man's flighty, vibrating voice. Endicott had no idea what might come of this.

"My sword will be light and fast. I will name it Style." Heylor abruptly leaped forward in some parody, caricature, or perhaps sincere attempt at reproducing a duelist's lunge. Sincere or not Endicott thought the gesture tended towards one of the former. He said nothing, for there seemed nothing to say that would be constructive. The skinny boy-man seemed to take silence as agreement and continued his herky-jerky way down the street in apparent satisfaction.

They passed through the gates after showing the guards the medallions they otherwise kept tucked away and with the other students followed Gerveault and Eleanor towards the first forge. Koria slipped in beside Eleanor, and the two of them quickly fell into some deep conversation that continued as they passed through the open door and then through a heavy wall of warm air leading to the forge. Endicott remembered that he had missed every opportunity so far to find out what special project Koria had assisted Eleanor with at the Citadel on the previous day.

A guard and a very muscular, thirty-something woman awaited them at the forge. Her heavily veined arms and shoulders were perhaps not as big as Eloise's, but she was also only of average height, making them seem enormous for a woman. The large hot pools and the glowing forge made the room hot, and the sweat ran down her face and stuck her thick brown hair to her scalp. The guard looked even worse off dressed in full mail with a heavy tunic belted over this. He was drenched in sweat and seemed to struggle to move at all.

"You can all thank Lil Hilliard of our second dynamics class and Jeyk Johns of our guard for bringing the forge up this morning," Gerveault said, inclining his head slightly in the general direction of them both.

Jeyk Johns nodded and made an awkward, unceremonious—and definitely relieved— exit. He paused only to retrieve his longsword and loaded crossbow, both of which had been propped near the door. Lil was a different story. Her lively brown eyes scanned the room with a confident, unhurried gaze. "It was a nice break from working with grain."

She nodded to Koria and Eleanor and raised an eyebrow as her eyes passed slowly over Endicott. "This is your first probability dynamics lesson?" Her lips made a little "wow" gesture. "Mind if I stay and watch?"

"Not at all, Lil." Gerveault said. "This lesson is being tailored on the fly to fulfill the latest quest that our young knights have taken up."

Lil's eyebrows scrunched in confusion.

"It's the quest of the over-leveraged maiden and the broken stitching engine!" said Davyn in a loud singsong.

"Thank you, Davyn. Unnecessarily facetious but more or less correct," said Gerveault. "Robert, why don't you begin the heating process while I start the lecture?"

Endicott nodded and retrieved the stitching machine parts from his bag. Next he selected a heavy tray, tongs, and two sets of heavy leather gloves from a shelf. Before placing the items from the stitching engines on the tray, he took several hammers and a wire brush and set them down beside the large anvil. Endicott checked his tools twice more before donning a pair of the leather gloves and using the tongs to place the loaded tray into the forge. He glanced over at Gregory, who was standing next to Davyn. "Stay handy. I may need you."

Gerveault watched what was happening and nodded to himself. "Probability manipulation is a powerful and flexible subset of our study of dynamics. There is little that cannot be done with it provided the dynamicist satisfies what we call the entropic hypercriteria. These criteria are as follows: a complete understanding of what needs to be done and its mathematical probability, the ability to envision the targeted outcome in detail, a high affinity for probability manipulation, a reliable source of energy, and finally what we call specific preparation. In a few moments Robert will explain how his specific preparation is going to make the manipulation at hand feasible."

"Five things!" blurted Heylor, incorrectly. "Wouldn't it be easier to just do it the old-fashioned way?"

Gerveault nodded. "Most of the time yes, Heylor Style. Though you miscounted; the hypercriteria has six elements. More importantly, there are times when one wishes to create a work of art. To wit, the swords that Sir Gregory and Sir Eloise carry. As you know, they are the envy of the city. Why? Because they are impossible to create without specific and careful entropic manipulation. Sir Gregory's sword, together with Sir Hemdale's, are in fact the greatest pieces of metallurgy I have ever seen. Both created by Sir Robert's grandpa, the great Finlay Endicott. We will talk at length about *those* works of dynamic art as well as the minor differences they have with Eloise's sword in another lesson."

"So are we going to make an indestructible stitching engine?" Heylor asked, grinning.

Lil Hilliard covered her mouth with one hand.

"No. May I carry on with the lesson?" Gerveault mock frowned at Heylor. "Of all the subfields of dynamics, probability manipulation is the most difficult. Would any of you care to suggest why?"

Heylor held one hand out, all five fingers splayed. "Six things!"

Gerveault's eyes narrowed. "Any other guesses?"

Endicott was busy assessing the temperature of his trayed items, but Davyn's hand shot up. "It has to be the difficulty of quantifying the probability."

Gerveault nodded. "That is correct, Davyn. We normally start this lesson with dice, just as we do in the lessons on heraldry, so that we can calculate and calibrate the required energy and effort to the probability of the manipulation, but once we leave the simplicity of dice behind, it becomes very challenging to understand the probability of any manipulation. If we do not know the cost, we cannot pay the price." He paused to scan the group. "And when the price is not paid, someone tends to die. That is why most dynamicists with a high probability affinity end up working on only one kind of problem. They work it and work it in the lab until they know the cost very precisely. One must specialize in *one* thing to understand its probability. This quandary is also why probability manipulation has the most ... *feel* to it, and why probability dynamicists are sometimes called wizards despite all the training we do here. Is that not correct, Lil?"

Lil Hilliard smirked. "So *that's* why I have been working on the same problem for fifteen years? Good to know." She surveyed the class again. "I've made an awful lot of uniform, identical blocks of ice. Maybe one of you can give me a break."

Endicott turned the metal over in the tray with his tongs.

"Me too." The new voice was Elyze Astarte's. She walked through the open stone doorway, Vyrnus Hedt in tow. "I wouldn't mind seeing this."

Gerveault shook his head but gestured to the back of the room. "And as you can see, our probability manipulators are always interested in seeing new tricks. Just stay silent once he begins. We are taking some chances here."

Endicott did not like the sound of that last remark, but he understood the reasons for Gerveault's caution and felt proud that the old man trusted him to try something new, especially before an audience that included other expert practitioners.

I just hope this turns out to be a proof of concept rather than a cautionary tale.

Endicott went back to watching the metal's coloring. He adjusted the position of the objects on the tray and nodded to Gerveault. "Almost ready."

Two other individuals had entered the room while he was examining the metals. Both were older than the average student, at least in their thirties, maybe older. Endicott was too absorbed in the task at hand to give them much attention, but he assumed they must be two of the other dynamicists working in the agricultural area of the Bifrost. The forge was now a little crowded, and the onlookers had to take care to stand well away from the hot end of the matter.

"Sir Robert Endicott has made a promise!" Gerveault's voice boomed as he gestured grandly, almost theatrically. "You may laugh if you consider that he is only repairing a stitching engine, but if your livelihood depended upon finely machined parts and your options were few, you might not find this so funny. We all live and prosper because of the smallest things, the smallest changes, no matter how smart or special we think we are. Perhaps repairing a stitching engine is a small quest, but here at the New School we meet all our promises, large or small, with as much perfection we can." He turned his eyes upon Endicott. "Kindly walk us through your intentions and your plan, step by step please, and in conformity with the entropic hypercriteria."

Endicott adjusted his heavy gloves and threw the other pair to Gregory. He used the tongs to grip the pushrod. "The pushrod is an essential element of the stitching engine, and this one is cracked so badly that it is almost in two pieces. Now we are going to put it back together again. See the color? It's glowing. That tells us it is almost molten. But if you make the lesser breakdown for a moment, you will see that directly." Endicott broke through and observed the tight crystal lattice of the iron start to fray probabilistically.

"We need to weld the crack such that the breaks and void spaces are gone. Our sources of energy are that pool of water," Endicott pointed to one of the pools, "and of course the energy of the forge itself." He looked at Heylor. "This work could be done traditionally, through normal welding techniques, and so we are going to use traditional techniques as our method for specific preparation. This should make the work as easy and efficient as possible. We will time our manipulation up to the point at which we would, in a conventional welding operation, manually weld the object."

Endicott put the pushrod back into the tray and released the tongs. He nodded to Gregory. "Please take the tongs and hold the rod tight where I can get at it."

After a moment of hesitation, perhaps of doubt, Gregory looked over at Eloise, who was watching intently. Eyes still on Eloise, he nodded to himself. Endicott could guess what his friend was thinking about. Gregory took up the tongs and held the pushrod in place for Endicott while he rubbed at the crack with the wire brush.

Elyze Astarte laughed, and Eloise called out, "I think it's getting bigger."

"It's not the size, ladies," Endicott replied as he cleaned the surface. "It's the purity. We must make sure no foreign particles are present before we make the weld. Okay, Gregory, thanks. You can put it back on the tray now."

Endicott took up the tongs from a relieved Gregory and looked over at Gerveault. "This is going to happen fairly quickly now, professor. Any comments?"

Gerveault pursed his lips. "Just as in heraldry, there are several theories of the physics of probability dynamics. One interpretation of what is being done is that we are reaching into all the many futures and locking in the one that *we* choose. This ties directly into the probabilistic cost equation and is fairly easy to imagine as a kind of proactive heraldry. In this interpretation it is simply heraldry using a greater breakdown. Another theory is that probabilistic dynamics is the actual creation of the reality you desire. That is, an object is broken or it is healed; it is up or down. Molecules and objects move according to a choice that is made. The choice also has a cost, of course, one that is commensurate with the difficulty of the action or the extent of the change. Experiments have been done to test both hypotheses, but no experiment has managed to do more than show that when you set out to support one theory, you end up supporting it."

Davyn's hand shot up. "So both theories could be correct, just as in heraldry?"

Gerveault smiled tightly. "Perhaps both theories simply mean the same thing from some distinct perspective that we do not yet understand."

"I am going to lose the temperature if I don't act now, okay?" Endicott looked urgently at Gerveault, who nodded calmly.

Endicott held the pushrod on the anvil with the tongs and took up the hammer with his other gloved hand. "Please achieve the lesser breakdown. You will see the cleavage plane. In a weld I would tap the pushrod with the hammer and slowly work the cleavage until it closed. If it was at the wrong temperature, this would not work, but it *is* at the correct temperature and is quite ready to flow to my tap. If foreign particles or dirt were on the weld, the strength of the weld would be poor. Depending on how well I control the rod, the temperature, and the hammer, I can make a weld of sufficient strength. Right now all it takes is a tap of this hammer to start the process. This is my final specific preparation. The situational physics is *specifically* in my favor. Watch closely."

Endicott raised his hammer. Achieving the lesser breakdown, he imagined the crystalline structure of a repaired pushrod. He started to swing his hammer at the rod and simultaneously achieved the greater breakdown, closing the crack, eliminating all voids, and forcing the molecules into the order of his imagination, all the time drawing energy from one of the pools of water.

Tap. Tap. Tap.

The pushrod was in one piece.

Endicott achieved the greater breakdown a second time, held the molecules in the order he wanted, which was highly entropic, and then removed the heat from the rod, rapidly cooling it. He moved a portion of the excess heat back into the pool of water, melting the skiff of ice that had formed on its surface. The pushrod was repaired. A highly reflective, glass-like band now occupied the area where the old fracture had been. The forge was silent except for the hissing of the flames as they rolled over the coals.

Eleanor rushed in front of Endicott and pushed a thermometer into his mouth. "Hold still a moment, Robert."

"I stand amazed," said Lil Hilliard, perhaps grudgingly. Striations stood out on her taut, veiny neck as she smiled with a strained incredulousness. "He actually performed four separate and almost simultaneous manipulations."

"Well, I am not surprised," said Elyze Astarte. She looked at Gerveault. "Remember what I asked you."

Endicott barely heard this last remark. He was trading significant looks with Koria for helping him arrange the use of the forge, and then with Gregory, who was surely thinking about what they might now accomplish on the shield project.

"Your temperature is good, Robert." Eleanor put a hand on his forehead as if to double-check. "Well done."

"I guess it helps if you're already a blacksmith," added Deleske sarcastically.

"Correct, Deleske." Gerveault pointed his index finger up. "The more you know about a thing, the better the specific preparation will be. That was done with surpassing efficiency."

Endicott performed similar repairs on the other objects as Gerveault amplified and augmented the younger man's description of what he was doing. The presser foot and dogs were the most difficult pieces to repair due to the complexity of their shapes. Gregory seemed to take pride in his role as assistant blacksmith, and the class as a whole clearly enjoyed the attention of the older dynamicists, who stayed until the last piece had been repaired.

Arrangements were made for Koria to take over the class when it adjourned to the dice room so that Gerveault and Eleanor could confer about some other project. As he watched his girlfriend patiently and coolly arranging everyone around the table and providing them with their ten-sided dice, Endicott couldn't help wondering about her double role as both student and mentor. It was not just that she was so obviously intelligent and mature, he reflected. Koria clearly also had a massive natural talent in dynamics, yet her patience with him and the whole class seemed endless. A thought occurred to him.

I responded to my heraldic dream with a mad frenzy that could have destroyed me and others. She responded to hers with patience and a plan.

It was not lost on Endicott that he and the others were now the beneficiaries of this patient planning. He could only hope his own scheme would turn out to be as helpful. The deadly cloaked figure of his heraldic dream was still out there.

We need Eloise to have that shield. Soon.

The night before, Endicott had solemnly vowed to himself that from now on he would patiently follow instructions and dutifully learn everything he could in class. Above all, he had promised himself he would not be reckless, but at odds with all his good resolutions was the fact that he was also massively and naturally talented and so far ahead of the others that the classroom work often seemed pointless.

Endicott forced his attention back to the classroom. Once again everyone had several cups of hot water, a pad of paper and quill, and two thermometers. There were only two slight differences in the experimental design, the first being the use of only a single ten-sided die. The paper was quickly divided into three columns as before but with the second small difference. This time they were to write the number they had *decided* to roll in the first column.

Without consulting Koria, Endicott took a second and a third die. He had effectively mastered how to control two dice back when he was supposed to be practicing heraldry. He wrote "1–2–3" in the first column, and when Koria called "roll" he achieved the greater breakdown and without difficulty rolled a one, a two, and a three. Then he began playing with controlling the order of the dice and how the cost—as measured by temperature changes in the cup of water—changed if the one, two, or three were allowed to come up on any die or only on a specific die. To his surprise he found it easier to produce the more specific outcomes. This seemed to contradict Gerveault's lesson on probability.

"That's an effect of how you envision your outcome and your affinity, Robert," Koria said, passing him a fresh cup of water to replace the one he had frozen. She did not frown too much over his unauthorized use of three dice. "The tightness of your vision is crucial."

"Roll."

Endicott decided that he would try one more experiment.

Can I force everyone else's roll to be a one?

"Roll."

Endicott quickly calculated the odds and realized he would need to counter the energy being poured in by his classmates as well as providing enough of his own for each die to come up one. He achieved the greater breakdown and gritted down on the idea of a roll of one all around the table.

One, one, one, one, one, spinning dice, exploding cup.

Eloise, Bethyn, Gregory, Heylor, and Deleske each rolled a one, but Davyn's die spun crazily. Endicott's cup had flash-frozen and failed under tension from the expansion of the water. He shivered violently and looked over at Davyn, who was grinning back at him.

"That was you, Robert!" Davyn boomed, laughing. "You interfered with our manipulations."

"A dangerous and unpredictable practice," Koria admonished. She followed this with a long lecture about not ruining the calibration and efforts of the rest of the class. Endicott lowered his head in contrition, trying to hide his minor hypothermia, and went back to the long, repetitive exercise he had been assigned. After the intense effort of interfering with his classmates' dynamics, it took him some time to warm up again, but as soon as his shivering subsided, he quietly added two more dice to his rolls.

By the time Endicott got up to eight dice and could make them come up with any combination and sequence of numbers he wanted, Heylor could no longer contain himself.

"You won't be able to gamble anywhere, Robert!" he exclaimed.

"Because he won't be *gambling*," added Davyn, who was now working with two dice and eying a third.

"Keep taking your temperature, please," Koria said. "Roll."

Even with all his effort Gregory was still able to control his single die only about half the time. He was still shivering after the lesson as he made his way to the hot pool with Endicott and Koria. "Kn-knights, th-that was h-hard," he stammered.

"And yet you wish to try things much more difficult." They whirled to find Gerveault standing only a few paces behind them. He had appeared as if from nowhere. The old man smiled opaquely before beckoning the trio to come with him.

Eleanor was waiting for them in the empty classroom. It was the one with all the paintings. Endicott always thrilled when he saw the one of Koria's class. His heart performed little summersaults to see her looking so much younger and more carefree. Now he also recognized Elyze Astarte and Vyrnus from the third-year painting and the muscular Lil Hilliard from an even older picture.

"Professor Gerveault and I have been discussing your request for certain rather specialized materials along with the use of the forge to create an entropic, amorphous alloy shield." Eleanor looked tired. She retained her kindly, sympathetic demeanor, but her skin looked more papery-thin than ever. He felt remorseful for not noticing this when she had so solicitously checked his temperature earlier in the forge.

She smiled, but her eyes were red. "Why do you want to create this shield?"

Gregory took a step forward. "I want to gift it in courtship to Eloise."

Both Gerveault and Eleanor laughed. "A fitting present, Sir Justice," Eleanor declared. "Is that the only reason?"

Who acts with only one reason in their heart?

"No," Endicott said. "I too want Eloise to have the shield."

"Why?" asked Eleanor.

Endicott's heart raced. He took a breath. "I never thanked you for looking after me when I was sick, Eleanor. Or you either, Professor Gerveault. I know you both have many pressing duties." He smiled at the old lady. "I know who you are, Eleanor. I have wondered why we have been so well looked after, so considerately cared for, especially by someone with so many other priorities."

Eleanor was clearly listening intently, but her expression gave nothing away, even though he had just made it clear he knew her secret.

"Why do you think that is, Robert?" Eleanor asked him in an even tone.

He smiled wryly. "For more reasons than I may ever know probably, but one of them must be that it is in your nature, Eleanor. So thank you for being who you are."

"Still a romantic," she said quietly.

Endicott saw Gregory frowning at him.

Don't worry, brother, I am not about to profess my love.

Gerveault was frowning as well. "What does this have to do with the shield, Robert?"

"It has to do with my heraldic dream." Endicott struggled to maintain an even tone. He turned his head and looked at Koria as he continued. "I don't believe the threat has suddenly gone away. How could I? I do not know if I will ever get it out of my head, but I am certain I won't be at peace until we find the person in the cloak. We have not found him yet despite efforts from many quarters, but *he* may yet find *us*. Eloise has the best sword I could give her. I would like her to have a shield of similar quality with which to protect herself and Koria if I am not there."

Endicott was not sure whether this admission would seem patronizing to Koria or Gregory, but he felt it was important to fully disclose his motivations. Koria gave him a tight smile but said nothing. Gregory did not appear to be surprised, which was interesting.

"Oh." Gerveault, however, did sound surprised. "That actually makes sense."

"What a nice set of motivations it is," added Eleanor in her gravelly voice. "Love and protection. Very Heydron-like." She nodded to Gerveault.

"We will grant you the materials, time, and resources you need, but there are conditions." Gerveault waited a moment before continuing. "The first condition is this: Robert and Gregory will accompany Elyze Astarte as special guard on her agricultural mission to the Castlereagh Line during the late summer break."

"I don't want to leave Koria here without me!" Endicott protested.

Gerveault made a calming gesture. "It will be during the break, Robert. Lady Koria will go home for the week. With Eloise."

"That's fine," said Koria with a certain sharpness that Endicott recognized from all the times he had behaved in ways she deemed reckless, "but why is Elyze Astarte so interested in Robert and Gregory?"

Is that jealousy?

Endicott thought it might be, which in a strange way felt nice, but he also thought Koria was too intelligent to have reacted only for emotional reasons.

Gerveault hesitated. "I am really not sure, but Elyze has had this idea since the night Endicott and Gregory met her, the night you rescued Syriol Lindseth and became so prominently spoken of in the school. She thinks that Endicott and Gregory are important. She says she has a... feeling that our two gentlemen knights may make a crucial difference in her experiment, and she has been lobbying for their involvement ever since."

Koria crossed her arms. "I don't think I care for that explanation."

"The experiment at the Line is important," Gerveault said evenly.

"What is it?" asked Gregory, clearly perplexed.

"The answer to that is very long and involved," said Eleanor. "We will be happy to go over it with you before the event but not before then." She gave Koria a meaningful look. "It is connected to our meeting yesterday."

Something passed between the two women, but Endicott did not know nearly enough to guess at its significance.

"Which means the experiment is pressing as well as important," added Gerveault dryly. "Will you agree to this stipulation, gentlemen?"

Endicott thought for a moment, looked at Koria, who was still frowning, and finally nodded his head. His curiosity, he decided, could yield to his ambition to make the shield.

Gregory saw Endicott's affirmation, smiled, and said, "I would do a lot more if it helped us make the shield. We should keep this project a secret, though, should we not?"

"From whom?" asked Gerveault.

"Eloise, for one," Gregory replied. "It would be Hati's Hell if she learned before the deed was done that we had joined a conspiracy concerning her."

"*After* the deed may not be so pleasant either, Sir Gregory," said a chuckling Eleanor.

"Eloise doesn't like surprises," warned Koria.

"Well, what does she like? With Eloise it's always a rough ride on a fast charger." Gregory threw his hands up in exasperation. "It will not do for her to know about this gift before I can give it to her."

"Fine. Secret it shall be. We will all try to forget the charger comments." The old lady smiled. "There is another proviso," Eleanor said. "I will also ask you to make a second, similar shield for Lord Kennyth Brice."

Endicott had no hesitation over this condition. It only made sense, considering that Eleanor was Brice's mother. "Certainly," he said. "Once we make one shield, the second will be easy." He reflected that it might even be silly not to make more than one shield once they had gone to all the trouble of sorting out the challenges involved.

"There is one final condition." Gerveault smiled mischievously. "You both must pass an upcoming test to be delivered by Lady Koria before you make any attempt at the shields."

"Which test?" Endicott asked, looking at Koria.

"You will have to bake a cake."

▽

"A cake?" Endicott asked. The day was over, and his head rested in Koria's lap once again.

"Are you afraid of more delicate work?" she asked, lying back in the bed and closing her eyes. "You seem to have some talent for it."

Endicott kissed her upper thigh, breathing lightly on the spot where his lips had been, and sat up, remembering something else that Eleanor had said. "What was that about a connection to your meeting yesterday? What happened?"

Her eyes opened, but she did not sit back up. "The Ambassador for Novgoreyl is visiting. He has been here for two weeks already and will probably be here at least that much longer. We are being offered the opportunity to take over the Ardgour Wilderness with their blessing, provided only that we can recolonize it within a prescribed time period."

Eight Knights!

Endicott grudgingly took his eyes off her as he thought about the monumental nature of the opportunity. Thousands of skolves and a couple of demons stood in the way of any pacification of the territory. "What if we fail to, as you say, recolonize it in time?"

"Then Armadale gets it."

A loaded proposal. Or perhaps a poisoned chalice ...

It was daring even to consider going into a territory that eight Methueyn Knights and an army had not been able to hold at the height of their power, but it would be a disaster if Armadale ended up controlling the county.

"What do our duke and duchess say?"

Koria sighed. "They don't know what to say. Gerveault heralded the proposal inconclusively. Keith Euyn heralded it and apparently went almost as mad as you after your heraldic dream. He was so distraught that he was removed from the project."

So that's why he hasn't been seen.

"Dear Knights," Endicott said. "Is he okay?"

"Who knows? Keith is not very well most of the time. And he really flipped his position on Novgoreyl."

Endicott frowned. "They didn't ask you to herald, did they?"

"No, silly," Koria said, smiling. "I was there to evaluate the ambassador. Surreptitiously, of course."

"And?"

"He was ... complex."

Endicott did not know what that meant, but he let it pass. "Is there a connection between this potential deal, treaty, or whatever it might end up being called and Elyze Astarte's agricultural experiment at the Castlereagh Line?" The Castlereagh Line bordered the Ardgour Wilderness, and despite Koria's past admonitions about the meaningfulness of coincidences, Endicott thought the timing must be connected somehow.

Koria shook her head. "I don't know, Robert, but Elyze had better keep her grubby hands off you."

Endicott enjoyed the growl in her normally sweet voice and couldn't help chuckling.

Koria reached for a pillow, perhaps for hitting him, but it was too far out of reach. She gave up the uncharacteristic attempt at boudoir violence and continued. "I was there long enough to hear something that I *can* tell you. In his response to the ambassador's point about recolonization Lord Kenneth Brice referred to a long-term resettlement plan called Lighthouse, but he did not explain what the plan was or connect it explicitly to Elyze Astarte or to wheat."

Endicott made a frustrated sound in his throat. "Lighthouse? Strange name. I suppose this is not something we should talk about with anyone."

"Clearly," she said flatly. "But I'm not keeping any secrets from you, especially given the likelihood that you will become involved anyway in a few weeks."

"Sometimes I feel more confused and ignorant that I was before I arrived at the school," Endicott confessed.

Koria reached up and caressed the side of his face. "Nonsense. You've learned some very important things, my darling. And as you know, one thing leads to another. In point of fact, weren't you just working on a new and delicate experiment?"

She closed her eyes and reclined, arching her back and luxuriating in the sensation.

One thing does lead to another, and sometimes the unpredictability makes it better.

Endicott kissed her upper thigh again, finding the most unpredictable path that still followed the overall arc and composition of the story he was reciting upon her skin. There was always an appropriate criterion of entropy.

Chapter Five
Cake and Ice

"How is the poem coming along, Jennyfer?" Endicott was surprised to find Jennyfer Gray curled up on the couch of the boys' quarters well before breakfast. She had not struck him as a morning person. Aside from that one morning at the Lords' Commons, he had always seen her in the evening, usually well after dinner.

Who let her in?

Someone had let Jennyfer in during the night. The doors of even the boys' floor had been strongly reinforced since his heraldic dream. Endicott had been surprised, even a little alarmed, to see them open when he descended from the girls' floor. He looked around. There was no one else in the common room. And no one in the baths.

Hmm. Bethyn?

Jennyfer put down the original edition of *The Lonely Wizard*, blinking rapidly as if to clear her eyes. "It's coming along very well, thank you." She blinked her eyes again. "But I needed to check again that my research was correct. The writer hid his message in the tiniest details. I didn't want to get it wrong."

"Why don't you just ask Professor Gerveault?" Endicott said flippantly.

Jennyfer laughed darkly. "Oh, I did."

"And?"

She twirled one blond lock in her finger. "Let's just say the interview did not go well."

"He can be moody." Endicott sat down in a chair opposite her.

Jennyfer's blue eyes were clear now, and she seemed to look straight into Endicott. "I have, however, completed one interesting poem. It's about the night you rescued Syriol. I have decided to give it the name everyone seems to be using, *The Terrible Night*."

Endicott shot to his feet but couldn't step backwards because of the chair. His heart raced. "Please don't publish it."

Jennyfer stood up and reached out a hand for his arm. "I'm sorry! I didn't think you would mind."

Endicott took a breath and tried a smile. "I just don't like to think about it, Jennyfer. It still ... hurts to imagine it."

"*Imagine* it?" Jennyfer's nose scrunched up, her hand still extended towards Endicott. "It *happened*, Robert."

"You're a poet, Jennyfer, and a very good one." Endicott stepped forward, leaned down fractionally, and very gently rested his forehead against hers. She did not move, but he could sense her stiffen. "You know that everything that occurs physically also goes on up here in our minds," he pointed to their foreheads with one hand, "and is held in memory as a thing imagined."

He raised his head, stepped sideways, and started towards his room.

"True enough! A good writer makes the imagined real and gives imaginary voice to the real things we need to share." Her voice floated up behind him, certain of herself now. "The terrible night, of all nights, should never be forgotten."

Yes.

He remembered opening the door of the coach to find not Bethyn but Syriol inside. Broken. Dying. He remembered the two drunken men who had done the breaking and how they had assumed he and Gregory would gladly take part in their fun. He remembered breaking through into Elysium and reaching for the infinite fire that waited there, remembered that he had fully intended to burn the two men from the world. He remembered being saved from that mistake by Koria and Eloise.

Endicott felt a trace of wetness in his eyes. "I suppose I know how Gerveault feels about your questions then, especially if he actually is the Lonely Wizard."

He took the door in his hand but turned back to Jennyfer who, he saw, had taken several steps in his direction. "Do one thing for me, though, please."

"What?"

"Ask Syriol before you release that memory."

"Is everyone up early today?" Endicott said, pointing at the two stocky, bald men.

Gregory chuckled. "Why, I think you're right. We *have* never seen them before at least midday, have we?"

"They've brought some friends this time." Endicott scanned the dozen or so others who stood on the corner opposite the Apprentices' Library, apparently in support of the bald sign carriers. None of these others were carrying signs, but as a group they created quite an impression. The signs themselves had undergone some alterations. The first one read:

"You will reap what you sew.

Nimrheal will git you for

Grayn is toxik

Why duke feed poison?"

The second sign seemed to complete the admonition this time:

"Evil grayn grows, people die!

The end is coming soon.

If you don't pay the price, we will collekt!

Skoll and Hati will take you to Hell!"

"Do you want to talk to them this time?" Gregory asked.

Endicott considered his earlier heraldry and thought it might be a better idea to summon the constabulary. "Maybe we should—" He cut himself off. He recognized one of the protestors. It was Conor.

"What?"

Endicott grabbed Gregory's arm and pulled him aside until they were out of sight of the protestors. "I *know* one of them. It's the man I told you about, the one from the registered seed riot, the fellow who looks like my father."

Gregory's forehead curled. "What an odd coincidence."

Let me count them.

"Despite what Koria might say, it does strain credulity, doesn't it?" Endicott pursed his lips, considering what they should do.

"It's not illegal just to stand there." Gregory mused. "At least not yet. I would bet they could be cited at some point for harassment."

"It might be what they want," Endicott suggested, still thinking.

Conor thinks I am one of them.

He could not help but smile. "We could bypass the confrontation being offered and simply go and speak with Conor at the Black Spear later."

"When?" Gregory sounded eager.

Endicott thought about the affinity test that Gerveault had mentioned was coming soon as well as his continued references to baking a cake. The summer break was still a little over two weeks away, and they needed time to make the shield before then.

No wonder I can't seem to finish half my projects; there are too many of them.

"I'd like to go tonight, but perhaps we should see what other surprises are coming our way first. In any case let's not allow the week to get away from us."

"Patience," Gregory nodded thoughtfully. "I like it."

Endicott smirked. "Well, thank you, Lord Justice, though I wonder if the constabulary should be notified about some of these possibilities."

Gregory reached into his jacket and with a flourish pulled out a cream-colored letter. "It so happens that Vice Constable Edwyn Perry sent us a letter last night." He paused. "Don't even think of scowling at me, Robert. I very thoughtfully did not interrupt you and Koria last night, even though *you* have your love and *I* as yet do not."

Gregory tapped the letter against his lips twice. "I *am* very thoughtful, aren't I?"

Endicott muted his reaction to offer his friend less satisfaction. "Very good. What does it say?"

Gregory handed him the letter. "Nothing material unfortunately. They have not yet found the person or persons responsible for the damage to the Eight Stitches engines, but they are continuing the investigation and enrolling the additional patrolmen we requested."

"A small relief is better than no relief," Endicott said softly. "Well, why don't you or I write back to him during one of our breaks today and point out some of the ongoing coincidences."

"How about whoever gets the least wet today writes the letter?"

"The twenty-four-hour test will not be your last examination," Gerveault was not smiling. "By the end of today you are going to be presented with your next big challenge. You will need to use everything you have learned to pass. Including mathematics."

Heylor kicked the table.

Endicott sympathized with his nervous classmate's truculence. Every day of the past fourteen had in fact been a near perfect reproduction of the one before with only a few exceptions. Waking up with Koria was a beautiful thing that only Endicott experienced, but for him that represented the glorious start of each day. This was followed by breakfast at the Commons, a walk down to the Bifrost with one of his classmates, followed by lessons in thermal manipulation, heraldry, and probabilistic manipulation. This took most of the day. Lunch and mandatory trips to the hot pools were all that broke up their work with dice, paper, quills, thermometers, and water.

The return trip from the Bifrost now saw everyone except Deleske, Bethyn, and Koria go to the military school for training. True to his promise Heylor had started working with a sword usually under the gruff and heavy-handed tutelage of Bat Merrett. Davyn had lost a little more weight but mostly through a process of firming up rather than shrinking. Eloise continued to get the better of both Gregory and Endicott most of the time, though Endicott usually maneuvered the situation so Gregory would spar with her rather than himself.

Gerveault would not admit it out loud, but Koria had confided that something in the program seemed to be working. Everyone in the class could now herald to some degree most of the time, and everyone except for Gregory could perform thermal manipulation without having to be shipped off to the hot pools almost at once. A direct drawback of a weaker affinity, which appeared to be Gregory's issue, was that the time spent in thermal recovery was time lost in training. Despite this one hitch the class apparently was far exceeding the old professor's expectations and according to Koria was an order of magnitude better than previous classes.

Probability manipulation was not so easily compared.

On this particular morning Gregory had turned up with a rather beat-upon demeanor after walking with Eloise to the Bifrost. His hair was messed up as if he had developed a new and aggressive cowlick, and he walked with a limp. They had been late, but a smiling Eloise denied any malfeasance on her part. Gregory had said nothing about his disheveled appearance as he tucked his shirt into his belt and tried to stand straight, but now he could not seem to make his dice do anything.

"Did you use up all your luck on the way here?" asked Davyn in the loudest stage whisper Endicott had ever heard.

Gregory said nothing and rolled a three instead of the eight he had targeted.

"Someone did," said Bethyn under her breath, looking sideways at Eloise.

Endicott had decided to try a new trick with eleven dice. On the call, he threw them and manipulated entropy with a twist. All eleven dice danced, spinning on their corners for an improbably long fifteen seconds.

"What do you call that?" Heylor's eyes were wide.

Endicott thought for a moment. "The Methueyn War: three demons and eight knights dancing."

"And all eventually falling," finished Davyn.

"What you call it matters less than what it costs, Robert Endicott." Gerveault had managed to materialize beside him again. "Take the measurements and repeat the experiment until you know exactly what the price is and can pay it with efficiency."

The old man held a third thermometer and a fresh cup for Endicott, which he placed beside the nearly frozen one. He checked Endicott's body temperature before moving on.

Koria threw seven threes and smiled at Endicott before recording her data. She could herald considerably better than Endicott, sometimes managing to predict as many as thirty-two simultaneously thrown dice, which happened to be the limit of how many she could hold in her cupped hands. He seemed to have an edge with probability manipulation, though, all things being equal.

But what two things, situations, or people are ever truly equal?

So far Endicott had mostly succeeded in keeping his vow of patience and caution, but he was still a young man, full of curiosity and high spirits. A certain recklessness flowed in his blood, and he enjoyed pushing his own boundaries. He could not help feeling that the safe, controlled environment that had been created for them at the Bifrost was exactly where such boundaries should be pushed. At the same time he continued to labor under the dark memory of his heraldic dream, which hung like a black shadow over his future. He could no longer feel that he had all the time in the world to make himself ready for that future.

But what about Koria?

He could not be sure how she defined risk. She had lost all her classmates to their own recklessness, and she was by nature a cerebral, careful actor. Her affinity might be masked by her personality or by her own plans. It was possible that she had a better gift for everything but did not show all of it. Endicott was sure she could still jump onto any fence pole, even if she did not choose to do so.

Someday she will jump again.

"Roll."

He glanced over at Heylor and saw something strange. Heylor's two dice disappeared. The skinny young man did not see Endicott looking. Without hesitating, he reached into his pocket and pulled out two dice.

The same two?

Endicott watched Heylor while the sand clock went around, passing up the opportunity to perform his own manipulation.

"Roll."

It happened again. Heylor's dice vanished, and he immediately fished two dice out of his pocket.

"Professor Gerveault!" Endicott called. "Is it possible to move two objects through space with probability manipulation?" He gave Heylor the briefest look.

Gerveault frowned. "Yes, though with very great difficulty."

Heylor was looking down at the table, but Endicott thought the question was worth pursuing. "It fits the duality observation, doesn't it?"

"Yes," the old man said. "Why don't you explain how?"

Endicott flipped his dice in the air. "There is always a chance when I throw a die in the air that it will end up somewhere other than the table. Maybe somewhere far away, certainly somewhere unexpected. Such an occurrence would have a probability that we would struggle to define, but it would have a probability."

"Very good. Call it probability teleportation." Gerveault raised his voice. "But don't try it with anything big or across any great distance. It would be exceedingly ill-posed and therefore exceedingly costly. Now what is the alternative interpretation?"

"That the dice have simply … tunneled elsewhere," said Davyn breathlessly.

"I wish *I* could be elsewhere," whispered Bethyn, possibly in an attempt at humor.

"Indeed," Gerveault said, though to whom he spoke was unclear. "Shall we continue?" And they did.

"Keep working on it," Endicott whispered to Heylor.

▽

"Let us discuss geometry for a few moments, class," Gerveault said much later in the day. The class, minus Eleanor, had been led to a long, open stone room near the Bifrost loading docks. Five rows of stone, each about five feet wide and four feet tall, ran lengthwise down the room. Cuboid spaces were cut into the stone at precise intervals, creating basins. Each basin was filled with water and its volume etched on the outside walls. The volume of the basins varied from four cups to five barrels.

"No," whispered Heylor, fidgeting.

"Yes," whispered Bethyn in parody.

"Imagine two triangles," Gerveault continued. "The first triangle describes the limitations of accuracy you might get from a dynamic innovation. Each point of the triangle is significant, and we name them estimation accuracy, transformational accuracy, and support. Did it need to be a triangle? No, but we like triangles. Other issues with the … lack of perfection in our innovations are simply heaped in with one of our three categories. Konrad Folke, who you may or may not have met—he was a late arrival at Robert's demonstration of probability and metallurgy last week—has suggested that the triangle should include considerations of the medium itself as well as certain issues to do with the irreducible noise floor. But Konrad has a way of equivocating, and we have not abandoned our triangle just yet. For now let us stick to thinking about these three things. If you work with the same medium, the triangle will tell you what you need to know to create consistent innovations and to make corrections as needed."

Davyn's hand shot up. "Is this another reason that dynamicists tend to specialize? For consistency."

"Yes, Davyn. Dynamics are ill-posed, and we need control wherever we can find it. The second triangle," Gerveault raised a finger, "is more generally about outcome. Its points are time, efficiency, and accuracy. You can at best have only two of these things. It is not normally possible to have both an accurate and an efficient innovation in a short amount of time. We would rather you gave up time here, class."

Gerveault gestured to the stone rows and their basins. "Today's first exercise is about scale. The stone basins contain water. The stone is a granitoid. I want you to calculate precisely how much heat needs to be transferred from a particular basin in order to freeze it to twenty-five degrees below zero. Use another neighboring basin as your heat sink. Start small and work your way up to larger basins. Beware of steam coming off your heat sink. You need to work both sides of the equation." Gerveault turned around. "What am I forgetting, Koria?"

She smiled at the old man. "The ice extraction."

"Oh yes." Gerveault nodded. "Some of our people will be along in a few moments to begin collecting the ice you make. To facilitate that, you need to lower these hooks into the center of your basins. *Before* you perform the innovations, please, or we will never get the ice out."

Gerveault gestured to a long stack of tall metal devices of varying size but similar shape. The devices terminated in four metal legs that pointed out orthogonally from a central shaft. The tops of the shaft were formed into a metal handle.

"What are the hooks made from?" Endicott asked.

Davyn's hand shot up, his quick mind immediately grasping Endicott's concern. "And can we measure their weight?"

Gerveault gave a tight smile. "They are made from iron, and both mass and volume graduations are marked on each of them. Very good."

A few moments later Endicott was preparing to make calculations for his first innovation on a single gallon-sized basin of water. He decided to use the same transformational approach and level of support he had used with the cups of water in the experiments of the previous weeks. That consistency would act as a control for losses. In addition to this he examined the height, length, and depth of the stone boundary and measured the temperature of both object and sink. As a last step Endicott estimated the losses expected from the hook, which he had already inserted into the water, and took care to double-check his measurements in the empyreal sky.

"Don't be too aggressive, Robert." Koria said, gripping his arm as she walked by, which made him smile briefly.

Endicott turned and saw a woman standing not far off, watching him. She was wearing a workman's outfit with gloves hung through her belt. He nodded to her and re-examined the empyreal sky, double-checking temperatures and ensuring the area around both his basins was clear.

"Innovating," he said in warning, just before he made the greater breakdown and froze the water.

Creeeek. Pop. He heard the ice expand, but the heavy stone of the basin held. A circular pattern of frost banding covered the surrounding stonework, and small waves of air rolled over him in cycles: hot, cold, hot, cold.

"Excuse me, sir." The woman stepped forward and pulled on the hook with one gloved hand. The ice came loose with a pop, and she hauled it away to the loading dock. Endicott took his temperature and the temperature of his steaming heat sink. His calculations were off slightly, probably, he thought, due to the way in which he had handled the effects of the stone basin itself. The error effects on the stonework around him were immediately observable as alternating, circular, frosted bands. The symmetric bands of heated rock were not visible. He measured the nearest cold band at minus ten degrees, and the nearest hot band at sixty degrees. He noted the width and number of the bands as well as their radius from the vessel, none of which were very large or concerning.

He moved to a ten-gallon basin, procured a much bigger hook, and prepared to make his next set of calculations, adjusting the thermal equation to better account for the boundary effect of the stone. Endicott was tempted to change his support since the huge change in volume increased the time and difficulty of the calculation commensurately. Despite the increased computational cost he decided he needed to maintain the tight support to control the experiment. After calculating the mass of the water, he added another hook and spaced the two hooks evenly. His calculations now needed to be adjusted to account for the second hook and the adjusted placements. The final computations had to be done on paper and required nearly a half hour to complete. When he was ready, he took two steps back from the basins and looked around to make sure nobody was standing close.

"Innovating."

The error wave this time was considerably more uncomfortable. It hit him hard like a series of body-sized slaps of alternately stinging cold and scalding hot air.

"For the love of Knights!" cursed the ice woman.

Endicott turned to look at her. A line of condensation ran down the lower half of her face. The upper half glowed red.

"Sorry," he said. "That was worse than I expected."

"It's fine," she replied. "I should have known better when I saw the size of vessel you were going after."

Not her first time at all.

Endicott started recording his observations. His temperature was down a degree. The innovation had taken more out of him than he expected. More worryingly the heat sink was not as hot as he had calculated.

Where is that error coming from?

"Can I pull it now?" asked the ice woman.

"No," he said, distractedly. "There is something I don't understand."

He returned to the ice block and saw a pattern around the edges at the top of the ice. There was more error there. He needed to think about it. While he worked on the mystery of the boundary pattern, part of his attention returned to the ice lady. She was of average height but had a stocky figure. "I'm Robert. What is your name, miss?"

"Myfan." Her brows scrunched up. "You aren't Sir Robert Endicott, are you?"

"The same."

He returned his attention to the ice. The edges had a corrugated appearance. The answer came to him.

It's the Lessingham transform! It can't handle the discontinuity of the boundary.

He shook his head, thinking about what Gerveault had said about the transformational accuracy point on the triangle and the nature of continuous mathematical transforms. He made a note of the wavelengths he could observe at the edges and realized that the problem had always been there. He simply had not noticed it in the smaller-scale experiments. "Okay, Myfan. You can take this block now."

"Great." She pulled on the near hook. The ice did not budge.

"Can I help you?" Endicott moved to grasp the second hook, but Myfan slapped his hand away, hard.

"That handle is frozen, Sir Robert. It'll stick to your hand." She handed him her other glove. "Here. Use this."

They both pulled on the hooks.

Pop. The ice came loose, but the block was heavy, a little over eighty pounds with the hooks. Endicott helped Myfan pull it out of the basin, and despite her protests that she did not need his assistance, he helped her carry it to the ice carriage.

"No need to hurt your back," he said after they put the oversized ice block down. It was the biggest one in the truck.

And I need to warm up.

"How did we enjoy that lesson, class?" Gerveault seemed amused. He had led them to one of the smaller workrooms just off the kitchen.

Everyone had managed to make some ice, but the sizes and quality varied. Gregory's efforts seemed to yield the poorest results. His two-quart ice block was only partially frozen, dripped sadly, and appeared banded. Endicott intuited instantly that this was the result of transformational inaccuracy and an overly coarse sample size. But he did not consider his friend's efforts as a failure. Gregory—and everyone else in the class—had achieved the greater breakdown.

"Can we burn something next?" asked Eloise with a gleam in her eye. She did not seem to have the level of talent that Davyn, Koria, or Endicott displayed, but she clearly took a fierce joy in changing things. Especially destructively.

"Like the Lonely Wizard!" exclaimed Heylor. He had attempted a five-gallon vessel and had to be carried off to the hot pool with hypothermia. Nothing seemed to keep him down long, though, and he appeared unconcerned about trying again.

Gerveault frowned. "Most definitely not, Miss Kyre. And there will be no lonely wizards here, Mr. Style, only dynamicists. We are moving on to the other half of today's objective, which is all about accuracy. The scale experiment you just participated in should have taught you a couple of things. First that scale is not as important as you might have thought. Thermodynamic losses are not linear with size. There is a large component of loss simply in the breakdowns themselves. Second, by playing at the larger end of the scale of things, a few of you also demonstrated to yourselves that the nature of the error field and the nature of your transformational mathematics are inextricably bound together. In an exercise where accuracy is critical, this must be given the highest consideration." He paused and gestured towards Koria. "Lady Koria Valcourt will now take you through an exercise that you *must* pass before progressing further in dynamics: baking a cake."

Davyn's hand shot up. "I like cake!"

"What a surprise," whispered Bethyn to laughter from Deleske.

I like making shields.

Endicott's vision focused and he leaned forward, ready to take in everything Koria had to say about cake. She smiled at him and took over from Gerveault, who promptly left the room. She held up a small piece of paper. "This is a recipe for cake. A simple white cake to be precise."

Davyn's beefy hand shot up. "What about the icing? Is icing included?"

Koria scowled. "We are not concerned with the icing."

"I like a whipped-cream icing," Eloise hollered.

"I bet you do," said Bethyn sarcastically.

Eloise turned towards Bethyn and looked ready to turn their cold animosity hot, but Davyn interrupted, shouting, "Everyone likes whipped cream!"

Koria shook her head in exasperation. "You can make whipped cream *after* you bake the cake. We have enough ice to cool it off. Now focus. There are alloyed cake molds in the kitchen with well-known thermal properties. What you are going to do is this: mix up the cake batter in the normal way but use dynamics to bake the cake. If you can bake the cake so that it is cooked consistently and throughout, but not burned, then you will have passed the test and can make your whipped cream."

"And eat it?" boomed Davyn.

Koria nodded. "Being good enough to eat is mandatory."

Endicott stared at the cake pan, or mold, or whatever it was called and considered the problem of baking the thing. He grasped a few of the relevant facts but not all of them. The cake recipe called for baking at one hundred and seventy-seven degrees for thirty minutes but specified a final internal temperature of ninety-nine degrees. He saw at once that there were five key issues.

First baking a cake by dynamics was an internal rather than an external operation, so he had to focus on the internal temperature. This was no problem, but the time at that internal temperature was undefined. Certainly it could not be instantaneous. Second all the dynamics he had executed so far, except for probability dynamics, had been virtually instantaneous. Third he did not know the thermal capacity of the cake batter. Fourth the cake was small, so he had to consider the error field carefully. Fifth he did not know what transformational mathematics he should use.

But perhaps he could get started on the task without defining the entire solution. The thermal capacity question was the simplest starting point. He made a very large amount of batter and poured it into three different but familiar vessels, then produced three cups of water of the same size and temperature. He knew the thermal capacity of the water and the losses he could expect with water and objects such as thermometers or hooks that might be placed within the vessels he had chosen. He readied six thermometers and used the three different amounts of batter as heat sinks while attempting to lower the water temperature by five degrees in each cup. By measuring the temperature of the three batter samples after each innovation, he could make an estimate of the batter's thermal capacity, and by performing the experiment three times, he could check the work against a variety of errors.

Interestingly the cake batter's thermal capacity was barely half that of water.

Endicott tapped his feather pen against his nose a few times, considering the problem.

It's just cake.

I will learn a lot if I just try something.

He decided to try an instantaneous manipulation to take the batter temperature up just a few degrees past ninety-nine and then let it cook while it cooled. He chose the tight level of support he had been using and the Lessingham transform. Calculations made, he announced, "Innovating."

Poof!

His cake exploded, spraying the classroom with bits of half cooked, scalding batter. Cries of surprise and pain filled the workroom.

Again?

Eloise was no mind reader, but she knew Endicott well enough to anticipate his intentions. "Again? Do you even know what you did wrong the first time, stupe!" she shouted, scooping a clod of batter out of her hair. Bethyn, Deleske, Gregory, Davyn, and Heylor were similarly soiled with variably cooked cake mix. Only Koria, safe at the front of the room, was unscathed.

He thought he *might* know what he had done wrong, but explaining it to an enraged Eloise did little good. Later, as he cleaned the bowls of raw batter out of his own hair—deposited there by Eloise, assisted by the rest of his classmates— he thought about his error. Eloise had shouted, "Are you learning anything? Are you learning?" as she poured the batter on his head while the others held him down. Koria had not intervened. She had only shaken her head and said gravely, but through a smile, "Lessons must be learned. That is what we are here for, after all."

Cake batter is really quite difficult to get out of one's hair, Endicott learned. Koria, caught between laughing and being angry with him for acting so rashly, confirmed the error. The cake could not be heated so quickly to that temperature without a method for outgassing.

Chapter Six
The End Is Nigh

"The end is nigh! The end is nigh!"

The sounds of Davyn's shouting from a floor below reached them in the girls' common room and even Koria's bedroom, where Endicott and Koria were enjoying some private time with the door firmly closed. That door abruptly swung open, and Davyn burst through, still shouting at his full, outrageous volume. Syriol, Bethyn, and Eloise followed close behind him. "The end is nigh! The end is—,"

Seeing what Koria and Endicott were doing, Davyn cut himself off mid-nigh. "What the—?"

"I am very disappointed in both of you," said Eloise, aghast.

"What are they doing?" cried Syriol, hands reflexively covering her mouth.

"You don't want to know," said Bethyn flatly.

Koria's bare legs were draped over Endicott's. She was dressed only in a long white silk shirt. Endicott was only wearing his hot-bath shorts. They were sitting up, each with a closed hardcover book in their laps. On each book sat two dice and a glass of water. Several other glasses of water dotted the nearby bureau and shelves. A thermometer protruded from each of their mouths. A small sand clock sat on the bureau.

"What?" exclaimed Endicott with as much of a smile as he could manage around the thermometer. "We're just practicing for the affinity test." The thermometer fell out of his mouth, and he fished it out of the blankets.

"Is *this* what you've been doing in here all this time?" Eloise asked, scowling and knotting her hands.

Koria gracefully removed the thermometer from her mouth and replied airily, "A lady doesn't tell." She grabbed her cup and Endicott's and carefully shimmied off the bed to put the cups on the bureau.

"I don't understand," said Syriol, staring at Endicott's shoulders.

Davyn put an arm around her waist and said, "Allow me to explain what happened in our lecture today." As Syriol stared at him with a mixture of amazement and confusion, Davyn proceeded with his tale.

Today we spent a little more time on the best project of the year. I mean, four months at the New School, and we were finally learning to bake cakes! It's about Knights' damn time, don't you think? Koria took up the lectern again and very calmly laid out some of the principals that Robert's exploding cake maneuver of the previous day illustrated.

Robert was good enough to share his thermal capacity data on the cake batter. That is a kind of measure that tells us how much energy is required to raise the temperature of a given amount of batter by a degree. If we know the thermal capacities of a variety of media, we can use the energy in one substance, usually water, to change the thermal conditions in another. Heylor interrupted him to ask what we were all perhaps wondering: "By Hati's hackles, Robert, are you going to kill us all, today?"

Death by cake. Well, Robert's eyes rolled up into his head, and Heylor covered his face as if expecting another explosion of incendiary batter, but Robert was only making a vain attempt to look up at his hair in case it might still contain some of the batter that Eloise had gracefully administered the previous day as lesson for his recklessness. Eloise has a very soft voice and lady-like demeanor, you know.

Hey, no hitting!

Well, anyway, my dear, we proceeded to make new attempts at baking cakes. I spent some time experimenting with the effects of adding chopped strawberries to the batter. It turns out that they do not change the thermal capacity very much, so a strawberry-white cake is definitely in the offing. Meanwhile our reckless adventurer continued with his destructive tests, only this time, the cake was kept under a lid.

As for myself I finally cleaned up the leftover strawberries and started on an idea based on the radial transform, which I thought might make sense given the well-known shape of cake. The transforming mathematics must fit the transformed object, you see. I explained the radial transform concept to Heylor, who had made little progress other than eating raw batter.

"By the fields of Elysium, Davyn, that's brilliant!" exclaimed Heylor, who was awestruck at my genius. His goggling and hero worshipping of me was interrupted by Gerveault, who stormed into to the room. The old man was on a mission. He was excited.

He was in a hurry for us to get better, which, you know, flies in the face of his stated goal of having us learn in an orderly and careful fashion. I think his new eagerness had something to do with the secret project that Sir Gregory and Sir Reckless—I mean Sir Robert—have been working on with him. The three of them have been meeting secretly, I've noticed, speaking about rare metals and conspiring about timing and the summer break as well. I don't know what it's all about, but I know they are up to something, and I concluded the old man's disequilibrium had something to do with this.

Nevertheless Gerveault raised a finger in his usual pedantic fashion and spoke in his normal crisp tones. "Enough of the pies, class, at least for now."

I knew then he had gone mad. We weren't even making pie.

"We need to go back and work on your thermal manipulation skills at once. I would like you to consider the error field and energy losses today, so please work through tests at as many orders of magnitude as you can. We are going to characterize the losses by the three terms in your accuracy triangle and by bulk losses to do with your affinity."

"My dear Professor," *said Sir Gregory in his best and noblest tones.* "However should we do that?"

Gerveault, author of The Lonely Wizard, *retired warrior, and current Professor of Dynamics, did not seem as patient as usual, especially when faced with such a well-phrased enquiry elocuted in such a superior fashion to that of Heylor and his usual exclamations.*

"Treat it as simply as you reasonably can, Mr. Justice," *he said closing his eyes as if pleading to his inmost self for patience.* "Start by tackling a multilinear equation."

"I don't want to, old coot," *complained Bethyn under her breath.*

"Is it something we can use in battle?" *asked Eloise, eyes narrowed.*

Heylor put his hand into his cake batter and seemed to be considering doing the same with his face. Gregory saw Heylor's angst and rushed in knightly fashion to his rescue. "Could you please elaborate, Professor Gerveault. We rarely performed multilinear regressions on my family's vast estates, and when we did them in class here at the New School, I was too busy ogling Eloise to remember how."

Ouch! That is *what he said! More or less.*

Gerveault nodded. He had noticed how Sir Gregory was always staring at Eloise. Deleske does it as well. Only I truly do not, for I have eyes only for Syriol. "That is the worst excuse I have ever heard, Mr. Justice," *Gerveault pronounced.* "The mathematics do not make allowances for your shortcomings and oglings. You can work out the details of the equation as an assignment, which I expect to be solved before you leave today."

Bethyn muttered and Heylor whimpered, which no doubt made Gregory realize he had only made things worse. But the mighty professor was not quite finished.

"The problem is not difficult enough to justify such groaning. Use the accuracy triangle terms as well as the amount of energy in each manipulation as your independent variables, though you are going to have to decide how to handle the losses through affinity. Usually they are treated as an additive term."

Gerveault noted that Koria was shaking her head at him in subtle disapproval. "What is it, Lady Koria?"

Koria had no problem taking the grumpy old man to task for his sloppy formula. "The affinity is really two terms, one for the lesser breakdown during analysis and another for the greater breakdown during manipulation. The greater breakdown is usually the dominant one for losses, but we have seen that this is not always the case. Remember Eldred Derryg? He had no affinity for the lesser breakdown. He could not herald at all, but his affinity for thermal manipulation was exceptional."

The old man's face took on a crestfallen expression at the reference to Eldred. "He was an exception, probably the oddest one I have ever seen. We should never have taken in his brothers, let alone him. But the exception often proves the rule. Lady Koria is strictly correct, class, though for this exercise we will stick to the simple view of matters. In an ideal world affinity should be broken into three terms: one for the lesser breakdown, another for the greater breakdown, and a last term, which I will mention for completeness, for the extradimensional breakdown. Each of these terms corresponds to the dynamicist's ability to break through the Heygan's modulus. None of you will attempt to borrow power from Elysium, so you likely need never worry about the last term."

"Why not?" asked the ever-intrepid Sir Robert.

"Because, as I have told you before, you would most likely die!" the old man nearly shouted. Sir Swashbuckler Robert often drives Gerveault to the limit of patience, and today did not appear to be the old coot's best day. "The greater breakdown into Elysium is an order of magnitude harder for most practitioners than simply borrowing energy from our own world. The Heygan's modulus is just that much higher. But the point here," Gerveault's tone came under better control, "is to remember that we only borrow energy. The dynamicist does not create energy, and he is not the source of energy for anything, except what he loses through his own inefficiency. This is an inverse way of thinking of affinity."

"By the hairy paws of Hati, why?" blurted Heylor. There had already been far too much talking for the jittery and impatient young man.

"Why do we estimate these things, Heylor Style?" asked Gerveault, unruly eyebrows quivering. "We need to test your affinity. It helps us determine where you should specialize and what kind of work will be safe for you to pursue. We will have a formal affinity test in a few days."

"And that's what these two have been working on, Syriol," finished Davyn. "Robert and Koria were practicing trivial heraldry and probabilistic manipulation to tune their affinities. It's like exercise; the more you do it, the easier it gets. Up to a point. Actually up to an asymptote."

Syriol punched Davyn's beefy arm. "Too much detail, Davyn!" She was smiling, though, and ran a finger over one of the thermometers. "You really use these?"

"I never called Gerveault an old coot," said Bethyn darkly.

"That Gregory better not be ogling me," vowed Eloise. She turned on her heel to leave but spun back in an aggressive pose, eyes intent. "What was that about a secret project?"

Davyn stumbled away, hands up. "I don't know anything more than I have said! Ask Robert!"

Endicott shook his head at her. He was not a comfortable liar, but he knew how to throw someone under the grain cart, and that seemed appropriate now. "I also am not saying anything about it. Ask Gregory."

Eloise looked like she was thinking about jumping on him and beating the information out of him. Her fists pumped a few times and her eyes widened. Endicott decided he was probably safe on Koria's bed, but with Eloise nothing was ever certain. Finally the tall woman turned and left Koria's room. Endicott could hear her pass noisily through the big stairwell door and clomp down the stairs. A collective sigh of relief went up from everyone once Eloise's heavy footfalls could no longer be heard.

Gregory is about to get mussed up again.

"Sir Robert," Syriol said.

Sir? Coming from Syriol the honorific made Endicott uncomfortable, but he gave her his attention. Out of the corner of his eye he saw that Davyn and the others were watching him.

"*The Terrible Night* has been published. Jon Indulf has paid to have it posted in every square in the city." Syriol left the statement there, but her moist eyes remained on him.

That Jon Indulf must really love Jennyfer Gray was the least of the thoughts that crossed Endicott's mind. He was more concerned about Syriol and her motivations. He thought it wrong that he should be the focus of attention, but he understood the complex sensitivities and feelings that night provoked in the few that had shared the experience. Now it was a night that would be shared by many more people. "If you think it will be of help, Syriol, I am glad for the song."

Syriol nodded, apparently satisfied. For a moment Koria watched her with obvious sympathy and then turned to Davyn. "What did you mean about the end being ... nigh, Davyn?"

Davyn held his hands up, palms out. "I *may* have stretched the truth a little in my story, but that part was true. I passed a big crowd of protestors by the Apprentices' Library making a fuss. They had signs saying that the end is coming. Those obnoxious bald fellows are there too."

Endicott sprang up from Koria's bed and grabbed his shirt. "They're still there?"

Davyn shrugged. "Possibly."

Endicott turned to say something to Koria, but she cut him off. "Yes," she said archly, "I gather you and Gregory are going to go take a look at the crowd. Just *try* to walk softly for once."

"And take Eloise with you!" she called to his back.

Chapter Seven
Peas, Poems, and Parsley

ENDICOTT, ELOISE, AND GREGORY EMERGED QUIETLY FROM THE ALLEY BEHIND THE Apprentices' Library. They had crossed the ring road well away from the public house so that they could creep up on the protestors from outside the New School. They had changed out of their school uniforms, of course, and taken care to conceal their medallions. Gregory wore a rather expensive tunic, but Endicott was in one of his plainer shirts without any special buttons or stitching. Over this he wore an old gray cloak. Eloise dressed in a simple black skirt and cloak. She had only agreed to set aside her questions on the secret project when the boys agreed that she could come with them and, as she put it, "help beat the stuffing out of the protestors."

Luckily for them the protestors were gone. The site of their protest was marked by piles of rubbish, including an old mitten and a beat-up sock, something that might have been offal, bundled haphazardly in a rag, and one small abandoned sign reading, "Grayn Is Poizon!"

"Well, since we're already out," said Endicott quietly, "we could try the Black Spear and see if any of them might have gone there."

"What, after a long day's hard work?" scoffed Eloise.

"That is probably how some of them view it," Gregory conceded.

"They are saving the world, you know," Endicott added, though he had not forgotten what his uncle had said about changing the world many months ago.

They took the long way to the Black Spear, which gave Eloise a chance to interrogate them. When she could not get anything out them concerning the secret project, she decided to challenge them about the protestors. "What is it you think these protestors have done wrong anyway? Other than wasting time and annoying hard-working people?" It was difficult to tell whether her truculent tone was aimed at her two friends or at the protestors.

"I don't think they have done it yet," Endicott said, looking up and down the street.

"It?" demanded Eloise.

"We don't know, but *it* has to be some kind of conspiracy," Gregory proposed, his eyes on Eloise.

"Hmm," she said, frowning. "Because the two of you stupes know something about conspiracies. How about evidence?"

"Mostly circumstantial, which is why the constabulary has done nothing about them." Endicott rested a hand on the hilt of his sword as they passed an alleyway. "But let me list what we know about them for you: first there was the riot at the Nyhmes registered seed compound. We know for a fact that was—"

"We've heard that story!" Eloise barked. "And to tell you the truth, it sounded to me like you and your uncle started that fight." Eloise gave him her wickedest, most knowing smile.

"We certainly did *not*, Eloise. They threw seeds at us."

Eloise howled. Gregory looked away.

"Stop laughing. In any case you can't deny that what happened there was a fact." Endicott extended one finger. "So that's the first thing. Then there was an attempt to burn down the Bron elevator. That was thwarted, but it is our second fact." He held up a second finger. "The investigation into who was behind the fire did not go anywhere beyond suspicions, but it is still important." Endicott saw that Eloise was readying another comment, so he continued quickly. "Moving on, one of the persons from the Nyhmes incident is here in town. His name is Conor. He told me that someone had hired him, *and* he cast aspersions at the grain industry."

"Aspersions!" Eloise held both hands in front of her and dramatically clenched her vascular fists. "Let's lock him up. After we beat the skolve right out of him."

Endicott slowly extended a third finger. "Okay, that is circumstantial, but Conor did join the bald protestors here, which is an odd coincidence, don't you think?"

Eloise raised one eyebrow archly. "Coincidences now? Didn't Koria teach you about those?"

Endicott gave Gregory a pointed look and jumped back into the fray. "There is something else, Eloise. The fourth thing." He brandished four fingers at her. "The bald protestors were seen by Gregory and me going into the Armadale ambassador's home."

"That is kind of interesting." Eloise frowned, opting not to pounce on this point. "How sure are you of that?"

"We saw him ourselves and checked the address and ownership with Constable Perry. So there's a good chance that Armadale is behind this *whole* thing," he concluded with some enthusiasm.

"Not a very strong case, stupes," Eloise said shaking her head. "It's a good thing you have me here to help you gather some real evidence on this *conspiracy*."

They were only a few blocks from the Black Spear when Endicott realized they had to take stock of their situation a little more seriously. He was anxious to unravel the suspected conspiracy, but he had learned how irrevocable outcomes can arise from undue haste or uninformed commitment. It was one thing to accelerate his understanding of dynamic bakery by detonating a cake, quite another to ruin his only connection to information, destroy what few advantages they had, or worse get someone hurt.

Be slow. Be patient.

Endicott motioned for them to stop. "We should talk about how we are going to do this." He looked at his two companions. Gregory appeared to be as determined as ever, even grim. Eloise's eyes were bright and wide, her breathing more rapid than usual. She was excited. They both looked back at him, waiting.

"We have to go in separately. We have to gather information separately, and we have to leave separately."

"Why?" Eloise looked skeptical.

Endicott spread his hands out. "If Gregory and I go in there together, we might be recognized as students from the New School. Someone may have seen us before, and if they see us together, the association might give us away. But *you*, Eloise, are another matter. There aren't many young—"

"—beautiful," interrupted Gregory.

"Beautiful," Endicott chimed in, "six and a half feet tall, bl—"

"I'm not six and half feet tall."

"Close enough," Gregory chirped.

Endicott closed his eyes, then continued. "Beautiful," he raised one finger. "*Almost* six and a half feet tall," he raised a second finger, "blond women," he raised his third finger, "from Armadale. How many of those are there around here?" He raised his fourth finger. "You might be recognized, Eloise, and if the three of us walk in there together, the grain will be in the grinder for sure. Alone is another matter. My appearance is unremarkable, and if Conor is there, I'll know someone who thinks I am on their side. We cannot ruin that. Gregory should be nondescript enough if he keeps his sword in his scabbard and avoids talking like a lord. You, Eloise, are going to have to keep your sword sheathed as well and, I don't know… slouch a little or something?"

"I'm going to be Freyla Loche," declared Eloise. She reached out and grabbed Endicott's arm and then Gregory's, pulling them both easily to her. "*Help*, me Robert, *help* me Gregory." She fluttered her eyelashes at them. "My engine's broken. Maybe you could stay overnight and fix it. *Both* of you."

Gregory's face and neck were red. "Freyla *is* tall, and she lives pretty close by." He gently blew strands of her hair out of his mouth. Endicott was not sure, but he thought Gregory might be blowing in her ear.

At least he's fighting back. Sort of.

Endicott tried to step away, but Eloise held him fast and hard. Gregory had been pulled in right beside him, but the two men were only peripherally concerned with each other. Eloise had Endicott's immediate, visceral attention. He could feel her hard, smooth leg against his and her breast against his shoulder and neck.

Why does she do this to me? Grain, grain, grain, grain. "Freyla doesn't carry a sword, Eloise."

Eloise pushed him away abruptly. "She does since her stitching engines got busted up."

Endicott was first into the Black Spear. Crowded and dark, with a motley assortment of patrons sitting on benches and at tables, leaning against the bar, or standing in groups, it looked no different from other public houses he had been in. There were no overt signs that it was a meeting place for dissidents. The various mottos, plaques, and pennants that adorned its walls seemed resolutely apolitical. It certainly smelled like a typical tavern. Its odor of beer mixed with greasy snacks, tobacco, and the sour-milk fetor of poorly washed men and women was the familiar bouquet of drinking establishments everywhere. Smoke from pipes and fags hung in a thick layer throughout the room, obscuring its already poor lantern light. A cacophony of clinking glasses and loud voices rounded out the unappealing ambiance. It was a place, Endicott mused, best visited at night with limited light and less expectation.

He made his way slowly through the tavern, assuming an air of casual curiosity while keeping an eye peeled for his man. A minstrel sat in one corner. He was aged and worn-looking, but he smiled and absently strummed his lute. Then he announced, "I have a new song from Jennyfer Gray tonight, gentle folks. It is called *The Terrible Night.*"

The song had an appealing melody and a catchy rhyme scheme and meter, but Endicott tried not to listen.

> "We all go out into the darkest night,
> We work, we drink, we eat; some like to fight.
>
> When in the dark, some do the darkness crave,
> They must then choose to be the knight or knave
>
> When we go out into the darkest night,
> Will we perceive, or ignore neighbor's plight?
>
> One eve two men brought rape and foul murder,
> Upon a child, someone's sister, daughter.
>
> When you hear evil in the darkest night,
> Will you protect or hurt or bring the light?
>
> They raped the girl in a dark covered coach,
> Hidden from justice, and safe from reproach.
>
> When you find evil in the darkest night,
> Will you stand down, stand up, and bring the light?
>
> There was one thing to which they gave no thought:
> The might and friends of Robert Endicott …"

He winced at the sound of his own name. The ensuing description of each of the players who had taken part in the drama of the terrible night was so poorly timed for his clandestine mission that Endicott might have laughed. But it was no laughing matter. Even if the song had not made him feel exposed, it would still have bothered him. He did not want to relive those memories. They were too terrible. The song faded behind the noises of the crowd, but its slowly altering chorus stayed with him, the last stanza resonating especially keenly.

> **"You will be out when there is naught of light.**
> **Where will you stand in the terrible night?"**

He pushed through a cluster of rough-clothed men and women, away from the song into another part of the room. In a corner at the back three black-armored Knights of Armadale sat at one table, talking in thick accents to a barman. There was a noticeable halo of space around the knights brought about by their well-deserved reputation for aggression. Endicott was tempted to linger nearby but remembered his goal.

That plate armor looks uncomfortable.

He wondered if they would do better to make Eloise a suit of armor, a comfortable, flexible one, rather than a shield.

Comfort won't stop a spear.

Thinking about the complex problem of Eloise almost made him miss Conor. The old hobo leaned against the main counter. His beard had been trimmed, but his clothes were starting to fall into disrepair again. He was wearing the same outfit as on their previous meeting, which was now some weeks past. Again Endicott felt a strange wave of affection for the man who evoked old memories of his father and childhood. He did not like to think of anyone drinking alone, not Bethyn and certainly not Conor. It made him imagine his father alone and lost, which was somehow worse than being dead.

He put those feelings to use when he grasped Conor's shoulder and sat down beside him. "Ho, Conor, what are the doings?"

Conor blinked at him owlishly or perhaps just drunkenly. His eyebrows scrunched. "Nimrheal alive! R-Robert? 'S that you?"

"Indeed it is." Endicott gestured to the bar lady for a drink. "I was out of town. What are the doings?"

The bar lady passed Endicott his beer stein and he handed her a copper knight.

Conor shook his head, more focused now. "A lot. The doings are changing so fast these days a fella don't know what to make of it."

Endicott nodded. "I hear they're building more elevators all over."

Conor tilted his head back, draining his mug.

"Do you want another?" Endicott asked as soon as Conor set down his empty mug, keen to keep him right where he was. "On me."

"Ha!" Conor said, smiling. "Watch this. No need for you to pay." He gestured to the bar lady, who raised her eyebrows at him. "One more. On his lordship's tab."

She produced a standard half-smile and poured him another big stein of beer.

"His lordship? Who's that?" Endicott pointed a thumb at the knights. "One of them Armadale fellows?"

"Nah," Conor waved his hand dismissively. "Them are foreign pot-lickers. Don't know 'em, don't like 'em."

"I'm not sure I'm a fan either," Endicott hedged, hoping Conor would reveal who his benefactor was, having eliminated the Armadale knights. Perhaps the conspiracy had no connection to Armadale after all. But now Conor went silent, staring into space and sipping his beer with an expression that could have indicated either deep thought or complete vacancy. After a few moments Endicott made another attempt to draw him out. "You sure do seem connected."

"To beer, anyways. The doings keep changing around here. I don't know what I got or where to go or who my friends are half the time." He hit his face with the heel of his hand. "Why can't things stay the same for five Knights-damned minutes? Just for five minutes!"

Endicott could not help feeling sympathy for the man who resembled his father. His emotions were trifurcated. One part of him was sad for the lost man beside him, one part was angry over the protests the same man was involved in, and a third part was confused.

Why would anyone protest positive progress like the New School's development of better varieties of grain?

And then there was a fourth, unemotional part of him that was very pleased that Conor seemed to be working himself up into a rant.

"Lost my sons to fever, and my daughters married away. Couldn't keep up on the old farm, and when the ox died, I sold the place. Sure enough, missed the market. Gots no luck 'cept bad luck. Since then, been a farm hand, but my paws ain't too good no more." Conor held out a shaking, beer-stained hand. Endicott didn't know if it was trembling from arthritis or from beer, but either way Conor did not look hale enough to withstand long days in the sun. "No one wants me, and these rich new farmers don't care a whit about anything but money and futures and how big a seed they can plant. New equipment's comin' too. It's gonna replace all of us. Then where'll we be, hey? Where will be then, if we gots machines for everything?"

Like for sewing?

The angry part of Endicott wondered if Conor might know something about who had damaged Freyla's stitching machines. Coincidentally he noticed Eloise on the other side of the room at that moment. She had stopped to speak with someone in the vicinity of the Armadale knights.

"You burned yer hand."

Endicott was surprised Conor was paying any attention to him, let alone enough to notice the small burn he had given himself during his explosive first attempt at cake baking. It was mostly healed. "I did. I've been working in a bakery."

Conor shook his head and slammed his beer stein down, sloshing a few suds on the bar. "We just can't get away from that grain! It's Knights-damned everywhere. It's a conspiracy of grain, and we're all going to drown in it, I tell ya. Drowned in the bin."

What?

"Oh. In the flour." Endicott raced to keep up with Conor's rapidly darkening mood. "I guess we're even drinking it now, aren't we?"

"Not here, Robert, we aren't." Conor put an arm around his neck and pulled him close. His breath was sour and reeked of foul beer and turnips. "The Spear only serves beer made from the *old* wheat. The true and ancient grains."

Conor let go of his neck, and Endicott took a sip of the beer. He hated the stuff. "That's why it tastes so good, I suppose."

"It's the taste of righteousness, Robert. Righteousness."

Endicott raised his stoup in a toast. "To the old ways, to ancient grains and righteousness."

"To Nimrheal." Conor clinked cups with him, his eyes fierce. He took a drink, then raised his cup again. "And it's not poison too."

Endicott nearly coughed out his beer. "Poison?"

Conor nodded. "That's right. You didn't know? The new grain is poison. It might not get ya right away, but it'll get you sooner as later."

That explained some of the signs Endicott had seen but not why such a ludicrous idea would gain any currency. "I didn't know that. How did you hear about it?"

Because I know you didn't conduct a scientific test of the nutritional value of the new triticale.

"Everyone knows!" Conor's shout was lost in the bustle of the crowd. "Ter said so. Froth said so. The old lady's baby wasted away to nothing. To nothing!"

"A baby died? From the new grain?" Endicott did not for one second believe the grain was anything less than optimal, never mind poisonous They had fed the new triticale to the cows and eaten plenty of it themselves. A hot anger rose in him. He found a use for that as well. "How?" His voice hardened. "Did you see it?"

Conor put a hand on his arm. Endicott realized he had been halfway to standing. "Calm down, young fella. That temper of yers."

Be slow. Be patient.

"Tell me you're joking, Conor."

"Not on yer life! Wish I was. I saw it me self. It was all long and blue, which a baby should not be. Starved to death."

Babies do not eat grain.

Conor took another gulp of his beer while Endicott stewed. "The demon comes for a reason."

"What was that?" A chill had run through the young man.

Conor stared at him with the awful intensity of a man deep in his cups. "The demon comes for a reason," he repeated pregnantly.

The old man's pronouncement reminded Endicott of something he had heard at the trial. It was a misreading of an old poem about Nimrheal. He struggled to recall the poem and where he had heard it. Then suddenly it came to him. It was called *Price* and it went:

> "We may have paid a price
> That does not make it right.
> Take heart in your battle,
> Against Nimrheal's evil.
>
> **Rage against the demon,
> Enemy of reason.**"

It was part of the liturgy of the Steel Castle. If attendance there had not bored him so much, he might have recognized echoes of the poem the first time he saw the protestors in Nyhmes. It made him want to slap himself that he had failed to make the connection when Davyn had mentioned Jennyfer Gray's recital of it in his story of the terrible night.

The demon comes for a reason, does it? Conor, consciously or not, was making a mockery of the religious poem. His slogans were thematically inverse to it.

"Those are our words," Conor said into his beer. "You remember."

Endicott remembered Conor speaking about Nimrheal. He remembered the protestors shouting, *"Have you paid the price?"* Conor was *not* an agent of Armadale. The Armadale theory had never made any sense, at least as far as Conor was concerned.

Our words. Our words?

His mind jumped. *There is a church of Nimrheal! A cult. Conor is one of them, and the other protestors too. They have their own words, their own poem— their own liturgy— constructed in morbid opposition to that of the Steel Castle.*

Could there really be such a cult?

This was not the first time he had thought about Nimrheal, but the notion of worshipping the murderous demon was impossible for him to understand or appreciate. The idea was anathema to Endicott's whole attitude to the world, to his lifelong trajectory as well as his current circumstance. It flew in the face of every plan and hope he had for the future. The perversity of praying against change, against progress, fueled both the angry part of him and the confused part.

Am I so naïve?

He wanted to cry, but he also wanted to rage against the stupidity of it, against what might possibly be his own stupidity. If he was naïve, Endicott realized he was not the only one. The Nyhmes registered seed riot had been investigated, the bald sign carriers had set up shop for months outside the New School, and he and Gregory had informed the constabulary of everything they had observed about the protestors, but no one had done anything to address the counterculture that made such actions and protests possible. It was not right to arrest people simply for having a different opinion. But what else could have been done?

All this thinking is out of step. They have their own poem, and he thinks I should know it. I must act now. I must think quickly.

Endicott rearranged and inverted *Price* in his mind, making a few guesses at half-forgotten words and taking some liberties with meter. As he worked, he checked on Eloise again and saw a bit of a crowd gathered around her. People were staring at her but, he assumed, more in admiration or lust than suspicion. Everything about her was striking. If they knew her, they would be even more impressed.

Now she was talking to the armored men of Armadale.

Does she know that Freyla Loche does business with the ambassador's household?

He tried to recall if he had told her that. Then he remembered that Conor was probably waiting for a response. He turned back to the counter. Sure enough the old bum was staring at him expectantly. His chance was not lost. "I've been out of touch with the ... church for a while, but I remember our words going like this." He paused as if gathering his thoughts and recited the doggerel he had cobbled together:

> "Have you paid the price?
> We will make it right.
>
> We take heart in battle
> With Nimrheal 'gainst evil.
>
> Raging against moral treason,
> The demon comes for a reason."

Conor was staring at him, wide-eyed. He rubbed at his face and eyes. "That's beautiful. I've never heard it quite like that."

"I may not have remembered it right," Endicott hedged. "It's been so long since I've been to a meeting. I don't even know where or when they meet."

Conor patted him on the shoulder. "Don't worry, brother. I'll help you pay the price. Next meeting is in five days. On Heyday. It's in the basement of this building." He took a big swig of his beer, draining the stein. "We'll have something to talk about then, believe you me."

Conor carefully disentangled himself from his stool. "Gotta see the privy." He wended his way slowly through the crowd.

Eight Knights! Was that good enough?

Endicott felt buoyed by Conor's apparent enthusiasm for his improvised guess of the kind of hymn a Church of Nimrheal might use to mock the Steel Castle. He was optimistic that Conor would divulge a lot more now.

Who is Froth? Who is Ter? Is one of them the "lord" who covers Conor's bar bill?

Endicott wondered if the baby of Conor's crazy story had actually existed and, if so, how it had really died. His ruminations were interrupted by a loud female voice.

"But *I'm* Freyla Loche! Who are you, giant? You must be a man dressed as a woman!"

Endicott looked over to see two blond women locked in some sort of wrestling pose. It was Freyla Loche grappling with Eloise!

Freyla was a very tall woman, but Eloise was taller still—and stronger. Of that Endicott had no doubt. He was less sure about what Eloise might do. Her cover story was ruined, and it was difficult to imagine any positive way out of the predicament. In unconscious mimicry of Conor, Endicott slapped himself in the face. How could he have been so stupid. First he had missed the distorted echoes of the Steel Castle in the protestors' signs. And now he had never questioned Eloise's plan to impersonate Freyla in a tavern the seamstress was highly likely to frequent.

Freyla and Eloise were still locked in their strange embrace. Neither seemed ready to risk breaking their hold. Then Freyla's eyes suddenly widened. "I know you! You're from the N—"

Eloise silenced her with one audacious stroke. She pulled her startled opponent close and planted a long, deep kiss on her lips. From his own recent experience

Endicott knew Freyla was not going to get away from that very easily. The seemingly passionate kiss between the two striking blond women aroused far more attention than their wrestling had. Grappling, arguing, and shoving were probably not unusual in this place. Kissing evidently was.

What would Bethyn say? And what else can go wrong now?

"We know Freyla Loche!" It was one of the armored men. He was pointing a gauntleted finger at Eloise. "Who are you?"

Eloise did not hesitate. She broke her lip lock but not her arm lock, using this to spin Freyla around and fling her at the Armadale knights so hard that two of them hit the floor. Freyla had barely made contact before Eloise wheeled and crashed through the crowd on her way to the doors. The third knight took a step forward in pursuit, but Gregory emerged from the crowd, and blocked his path.

"These foreign pigs are making free with our women!" he shouted, pushing the knight as hard as he could. The armored man was not as tall as Gregory, but he was heavy, and he was not eighteen years old. He was a full-grown man with the heft and solidity of maturity. He kept his footing and even took a step forward. His colleagues were still trying to untangle themselves from Freyla and get to their feet. Standing up in full armor after falling is not easy.

"They ripped her clothes!" Endicott shouted, pointing at the long revealing tear that had opened down the side of Freyla's dress. Most of those now watching had not seen the action from the start, Endicott included, and for those now trying to make sense of the hubbub, it looked bad for the foreigners. For the pot-lickers. Freyla was trying to hold a shoulder strap in place but was jostled by one of the knights as he finally lumbered to his feet with the help of a broken chair leg. She fell sprawling to reveal one long, bare leg. The rising knight froze on one knee, unsure if he should help Freyla or leave well enough alone. Gregory picked up a chair. "He's attacking her! Help her!" he cried as he swung the chair at the kneeling knight, who brought up an iron-cased arm to block it. There was a moment of shocked silence after the chair exploded.

For a moment Endicott was not sure which way things were going to go, but the crowd reacted like an avalanche. One second still, the next like a huge wave as everyone fell onto the foreign knights, fists, chairs, and beers flying. A platter heaped with mushy peas spun sideways into the face of one of the knights, smearing him with the green goo and temporarily blinding him. He went down in a heap under three much smaller, but enthusiastic, men.

Gross.

Endicott was not a fan of mushy peas.

Latecomers to the fight made new opponents by randomly lashing out at other fighters. There were hardly enough knights to go around, but once the chaos began, it developed a life of its own. There was no stopping, controlling, or understanding it. And when Endicott saw Freyla, who had struggled to her feet with a distressed and confused expression, knocked staggering by two unshaven pugilists who struck at each other with one hand while holding their beer steins aloft with the other, he waded into the fray.

He knew that drunks acted with self-centered intensity. He had observed their stupid, stubborn ranting, their maudlin confessions, and their self-absorbed willingness to abandon all restraint in the form of combat known as barroom brawling. Men hit men, men hit women, men hit men with tables, or hit men into tables, or with forks or spoons or whatever was to hand. As soon as the chaos began, hitting and hurting whatever or whoever was unanimously declared acceptable. He could not abandon Freyla to this insanity, especially since it was his fault that she found herself in the center of the fight. He never considered that helping Freyla might jeopardize his anonymity; he had stopped thinking.

Endicott dodged a pitcher as it flew by trailing foam and beer and knocking over two idiots as they thrashed at each other with wooden pepper shakers. As he passed these fools, he saw that the one who had ended up on top was grinding pepper into the eyes and face of the other. Stifling a sneeze Endicott elbowed aside a brawler who was pulling at the boots of his opponent, apparently seizing the opportunity to acquire better footwear, and reached through the remaining bodies to grasp a dazed and floundering Freyla by one hand. "Let's get out of here," he shouted over the din.

Her eyes widened again, but she clung to his hand as to a lifebuoy in a storm as he yanked her through the hurling bodies, trying to avoid getting caught in the mayhem. One grimy fellow about Endicott's size grabbed Freyla around the waist as they passed, burbling something and pulling her towards him. Freyla elbowed him sharply in the face, and he reeled back, stunned. In a flash of rage Endicott picked the man up by belt and shirt and threw him bodily into the crowd. Freyla grabbed Endicott's hand and led them to the door and through it.

Once outside Endicott took the lead again. "This way," he whispered, leading Freyla down an alley that was the shortest route to the next main street. Then he remembered Freyla's torn dress and stopped. Taking off his cloak, he wrapped it around her, hoping that restoring a measure of her dignity would help her to feel comfortable. She was still breathing hard, and her eyes still stared wildly. He took her hand again and led her as gently as he could to the spot where Gregory, Eloise, and he had agreed to rendezvous. As they waited there, Endicott realized he was still holding Freyla's hand. She pressed up close against him and her breathing slowed.

His stomach knotted. He felt wrong enjoying the feel of her hand in his, just as he had felt guilty about his enjoyment of the crushing embrace Eloise had given him and Gregory earlier. He knew it was natural for his young body to respond to physical closeness with a visceral exuberance that had little to do with conscious thought but still wondered why his love for Koria should not immunize him against the reactions he had to other women. It was not the way he thought he should be. He also had to admit that he felt an honest affection for Freyla. The two of them had made an improbable and exciting exit from the Black Spear, and the shared adventure increased his feeling of closeness to her. It also reignited that chronic feeling of love that seemed to work in symmetry with the rage he felt whenever he encountered women being abused. For this love Endicott felt no guilt; he knew it was honest and without any selfish intention. He did not want to confuse Freyla or take advantage of her trust.

Yet there was no denying that he liked the feeling of her hand in his and her body leaning into his. He knew he had to let go. Autonomic reaction or not, willing erection or not, Endicott was still in charge of *some* of his functions. He smiled and said, "Sorry, Freyla, I better give you back your hand." He released those soft, warm fingers and shuffled a half step away, feeling both better and worse. Freyla's mouth turned up in a tentative smile. "Robert, it's—"

"Are you cheating on me already, Freyla?" Eloise materialized in the alleyway, marching rapidly towards them.

Endicott blew out a sigh of relief. Seeing Eloise safe was thrilling, and it saved him from further potential embarrassment with Freyla. Freyla, however, was not as happy to see Eloise. Her hands came up reflexively as she stepped backwards.

Eloise smirked. "Sorry about throwing you, dear. After kissing you, I had run right out of things I could think of doing."

"Wh-why did you say you were me?"

Endicott could not tell if Eloise was going to be nice or not, so he stepped into the question. "You've seen the protests across from the Apprentices' Library?"

Freyla nodded.

"We were trying to find out who's behind them. There is a chance they are connected to what happened to your stitching engines." Endicott pointed at Eloise. "But my tall friend here is rather remarkable looking, and we worried she might be recognized as a student, which might have jeopardized what we were trying to do. So we decided that if anyone asked, Eloise would pretend to be someone from the neighborhood—you. Even though you are a student, we thought they would accept you."

Freyla frowned. "You never thought I might be there myself?"

"You tasted like flowers." Eloise blew her a kiss.

"Stay away from me."

Endicott put up his hands in a conciliating gesture. "Nobody is kissing anyone, Freyla. Eloise just likes to tease." He looked at his classmate hard. "A bit too much."

Freyla pulled Endicott's cloak more tightly about her. "I don't even go there very often. The guards invited me last time I delivered to the estate, and I thought it might be nice to go out."

"That makes sense. We obviously put more effort into jumping into the situation than thinking about tactics. Sorry." Endicott pursed his lips. "That said, maybe steer clear of there for a while, Freyla."

"You think those Knights of Armadale have something to do with damaging our machines?"

Endicott knew Eloise was watching him intently and realized that his tall friend had not found out anything at the tavern except for how far she could throw Freyla. "I don't know about them specifically, but I do think some of the people who patronize the Black Spear did. Until we understand more, please stay away from there."

Gregory charged around the corner into the alleyway. He looked behind him and seemed reassured. The tall young man was winded, his tunic stained with wine, and his hair like a mare's nest. He had a large red mark over his left eye and looked very, very relieved to see his friends.

"You started a fight for me!" Eloise grabbed Gregory and squeezed him in a long, tight hug. Gregory looked around Eloise's shoulder and nodded to Endicott.

Yes. That shield is going to be the perfect gift.

"I think *you* started it when you used Freyla here as a quarterstaff," Gregory said sheepishly after Eloise had finally released him. "But Lord Justice at your service." He stood conspicuously taller and then flourished a low bow.

Endicott laid out what he had learned from Conor on the way back to Freyla's shop.

"Froth might be Alfrothul Gudmund," Freyla speculated.

"Who's that?" asked Eloise.

"He is the ambassador's right-hand man from what I have seen. He wears polished silver chain mail with a black ship on the back."

Easy to recognize at least.

They swore Freyla to secrecy before leaving but promised to keep her informed. "And for the time being maybe send one of your employees to the ambassador's house when something needs delivering," Endicott suggested as they parted company.

It was a cool late summer night, and Endicott had forgotten to get his cloak back from Freyla when they dropped her off. But the three Knights of Vercors put on a good pace as they made their way back to the New School, and he scarcely noticed the hint of autumn in the air. For a long time, no one said a word.

"She must eat parsley," Eloise suddenly observed.

Gregory almost stumbled. "What?"

Why on earth?

Eloise's smile was wicked and only grew more sardonic during the long moment that passed while Endicott and Gregory waited for an explanation. "Her mouth tasted delicious. Not like tooth soda at all. She must have eaten parsley before coming to the Spear."

Chapter Eight

Perfect Knowledge

For the next day and a half, Endicott's class worked in a frenzy, as if the fate of the world depended on the perfect, fluffy consistency of their cakes. Endicott sent another letter to the constabulary but had no time to meet anyone to discuss what he had learned at the Black Spear. He knew that nothing Conor had told him was actionable and that he could only persuade the authorities to act if he pressed the issue personally. He did not lack the time because of the ongoing cake project. By this point he had mastered at least three ways to reach the correct temperature safely, but Gregory and Heylor had not, and Endicott could not let them be held back over it.

Heylor had enough raw ability, or affinity in the jargon of dynamics, but as in almost all things, the skinny man lacked finesse. Heylor could light a fire, freeze a block of water into ice, call a dice roll, and sometimes even make the dice come up double tens, but he was inconsistent and inaccurate. The only thing he always did well was his curious trick of tunneling objects into his pocket. One second the object would be on the table, the next in Heylor's hand. Endicott guessed that this was how Heylor stole things and that his affinity for that one habit was so high that he sometimes did it subconsciously. More worrying, Heylor also had a habit of trying to emulate Endicott, which often saw him rushed to the hot pool to steam, burning out a case of hypothermia.

Gregory was an even bigger challenge. His affinity for thermal manipulation had improved but was still the poorest in the class. And whenever the tall young man saw Eloise succeed in making ice or fire, he would tense up, push himself too hard, and end up in the hot pool.

In the same way that Endicott had unhesitatingly taken Freyla's hand and led her out of the Black Spear, he poured himself into helping his two classmates. Koria and Gerveault both seemed to approve, though Koria professed to be skeptical.

"I'm not sure men are really capable of baking a cake," she said, shaking her head.

"Tell that to Davyn," Endicott rejoined before turning back to Heylor. "Let's go through the scales again."

The scales exercise was a mirror-image of Gerveault's ice-freezing technique. Endicott had a hunch that the act of cooling was intuitively confusing for Gregory and Heylor. Instead he had them focus on heating: water, then cake batter, and in Gregory's case, small ingots of iron. Although the exercise was thermodynamically identical, simply changing the desired output of the thermal exchange to something more easily imagined made a difference. Gregory and Heylor were soon able to heat an ounce of water, a cup of water, a quart of water, a gallon of water, and a barrel of water, and then scale down from larger to smaller. Endicott made them repeat the exercise again and again until they could do it even while bored and disgruntled with having to do it again. Then, and only then, he made them attempt the exercise with cooling as the objective.

"Let's go spar, stupe," Eloise demanded, hands on hips, as evening approached on the day before the cake test.

Endicott kept his eyes on Gregory and Heylor as they readied the next round of scales. He could see Gregory trying to pretend he was not watching Eloise while he made his final pre-manipulation temperature measurements. "I would love to get beat up by you, but these two aren't ready yet."

Eloise shrugged. "I keep telling you that you can't save everyone, stupe, but you never listen." She thrust her chin in Gregory's direction. "He's already good enough for cake."

Maybe. But not quite ready for your shield, Eloise.

Endicott hid a smile. "We'll find you at the sandpits in a little while, giant. I want to see you try tossing Merrett the same way you did Freyla the other night."

As soon as Eloise was out of sight, Endicott nodded to Gregory, and his tall friend began again. The last exercise of the evening involved a thermal push-pull experiment with two ingots of iron and one trough of water. Heylor's task was to melt the bar, freezing the water. Then Gregory would freeze the molten iron and heat the water. Then they switched. Back and forth and back and forth until both young men were shivering again in the hot pool.

THE CAKE TEST WAS NOTHING IF NOT ENTERTAINING. ELEANOR CAME TO WATCH, WHICH was a rare pleasure for the class. Her absences had become frequent, and they had begun to miss her. Elyze Astarte and Vyrnus also arrived, intent on the results for reasons that only Endicott, Gregory, and Koria could guess.

Eloise's cake was slightly burned in the middle, but she shrugged it off, saying she preferred it hot. This produced a chorus of eye-rolls from the ladies present, even Eleanor, but seemed to make Gregory uncomfortable. Bethyn's cake was rough around the edges from operator artefacts, but she cut a sinuous design on the outside and top of the cake, which disguised the imperfections and filled the cuts with whipped cream to beautiful effect. She finally added chopped strawberries in a D pattern for dynamicist. Her work was received enthusiastically by everyone except Eloise. Davyn claimed the D stood for Davyn and ate some of it.

When Davyn's turn came, he produced his whipped cream in a chilled bowl first, eating a large spoonful of it to, he said, get warmed up. He then used the radial transform to bake his cake with minimal artefacts. He smeared the cake with a little too much whipped cream and declared the whole thing a masterpiece. Which it was, if you happened to like whipped cream. Heylor's cake had an arcuate pattern of raw and burned sections caused by a fat choice of support. One small piece near the center was missing. Endicott assumed it had ended up in Heylor's pocket.

Gregory produced his cake using an idea that he and Endicott had thought up the night before while looking in on the forges. He found an old iron woodstove, which he kitted out with a thermometer and a set of iron ingots in the fuel compartment. Then he heated the ingots dynamically until the oven reached the desired temperature and baked the cake in the conventional way, declaring it dynamically baked. Gerveault shook his head but gave the operation a pass.

Endicott had several choices about how to proceed. He did not want to steal Davyn's radial transform approach, though he knew how to execute the idea. He *did* want to impress Koria, whose twentieth birthday was that day. He decided on a stepwise method that he had worked out by experimenting with the empirical cooling history of the batter as he had taken it through various stages of temperature. He described the method as he worked.

"I am baking the cake in twenty ten-second intervals. In each interval I will heat the cake partially, starting with bigger steps but using smaller ones as I proceed. The average increase will be just under five degrees. Outgassing will occur during the ten seconds of rest between each manipulation. I have chosen an extra-fine level of support and have accounted for thermal cooling through each rest period, though it is negligible. Prepare to eat cake in precisely four minutes."

He executed his plan, starting with a ten-degree jump and ending with a very fine adjustment of the temperature of the batter. He added one touch he did not explain and that few could have understood unless they were watching very closely. Immediately after each heating step he probability-manipulated the edges of the cake to round them, and by virtue of an operator-apropos shape, obtained almost no artefacts. Any risk of explosion was contained by the many small steps and short outgassing opportunities. The results were outstanding. Endicott completed the cake with a whipped cream and strawberry design in the shape of the number 20 and passed the finished product to Koria to inspect.

"Delicate work," she said softly, which earned a shared wink.

There was no opportunity to follow up on Koria's hint. The affinity tests followed immediately and were administered one student at a time. They were not particularly interesting to Endicott, being little more than a repetition of the tests they had already been performing with only a few modifications. Elyze Astarte and Vyrnus assisted by recording each examinee's temperature. Eleanor did her part by recording the predictions and results. Gerveault conducted the tests and kept time, beginning with versions of the heraldry and dice-based probability tests, only with more dice and much less time between manipulations. A similarly modified version of the thermal tests followed. Though uninteresting from a theoretical point of view, the tests involved an incredible amount of dynamics in a very short amount of time. Every single student, even Koria, ended up in the hot pool. Endicott suspected that the tests were meant to continue until each and every student experienced hypothermia.

"Wow, Robert. High affinity at everything. Off the charts at probability dynamics." Elyze Astarte leaned on her elbows over the edge of the hot pool, ignoring hard looks from Koria and Eloise. She had materialized by the hot pool as soon as Endicott arrived and had been talking with him from her perch on the outside of the pool since he got in the water. "Heraldry is one method of predicting the future, but a more perfect knowledge comes from *making* the dice come up the way you want."

"Koria was better at heraldry," Endicott said, feeling more than a little uncomfortable. He knew Elyze was trying to use him, though for what he was unsure. He did not like the idea that the answer probably waited on the other side of the Castlereagh Line.

"What do you want, skank?" Eloise said, unable to contain herself any longer. The ugly word reverberated off the stone walls. Koria nodded her approval and slid up behind Endicott, putting her arms around him.

"Don't you know?" replied Elyze, smiling sourly. "Why don't you ask your little friends? It's happening soon." She got slowly to her feet with an arrogant, exaggerated casualness and sauntered out of the room.

"Even *I* think that was creepy," Bethyn said under her breath.

"I-I didn't m-mind it," shivered Heylor, craning his neck to see if Elyze was still in sight.

Deleske shrugged. "She just wants some help with her wheat-breeding, and no class has graduated in years."

"Breeding, my big, beautiful bum!" shouted Davyn, possibly enjoying the echoes. "There's something we don't know going on here."

Eloise punched Gregory in the shoulder. He had been shivering and trying to absent himself from the discussion by staring at the ceiling. The tests had shown his affinity to be modest, but he had scored better than anyone expected, almost certainly thanks to the extra work he had done with Endicott.

"That skank was talking about your conspiracy, wasn't she?" Eloise thrust herself in front of Gregory, hands on her hips and feet planted wide. No one could have ignored her, least of all her tall young admirer. She was wearing a shirt this time, but Gregory's eyes flickered over her in what Endicott could see was an effort not to stare at her breasts. "It's time you stopped lying to me about what you and your favorite stupe are up to."

Gregory surprised everyone by refusing to cower. He threw his shoulders back and stood tall, as he did most of the time with everyone except Eloise. Then he gently put his hands on her shoulders. "You are going to find out soon, Eloise. Can't you just be patient and reasonable for once in your life?"

"I better find out *very* soon!" she bellowed. "I won't be left in the dark!"

Endicott wondered if Eloise was just toying with Gregory or if their budding relationship was really going to be as volatile as it appeared to be right now.

"Professor Eleanor will see you now," Vyrnus announced from the doorway. As Endicott, Gregory, and Koria left the hot pool, Eloise called after them, "You better tell me soon."

▽

"Congratulations," Eleanor said, looking carefully at each of them in turn. They were alone with her in the picture room. "Don't be so hang-doggish, Sir Gregory, you did fine. This is the best class we have ever had." She had an odd smile as she continued. "So you want to know about the trip to the Castlereagh Line with Elyze Astarte, and you feel that now is the time?"

"Yes," said Koria. At the same time Gregory and Endicott both said "No."

"We do want to know about it," amended Endicott, "But we have another, more immediate problem we feel you should know about."

"The shield?" Eleanor hazarded.

Gregory shook his head. "Of high blood and humble talent though I be, my more talented friend and I are planning to solve that problem in the next forty-eight hours."

"Thanks for the rare metals, though," Endicott chipped in.

"So no. What is it, then?"

Koria smirked in a way that was both patronizing and disapproving. "They have had an *adventure* that has given them some concerns you should know about."

Endicott and Gregory related the story of the Black Spear, trying to focus more on the information and less on the brawl. Eleanor listened with an increasingly astonished expression. "We heard about the fight from the constabulary, but nothing was said about the pepper shakers," she said with mock solemnity. Then she sat down and looked at Endicott. "So you want to go to this meeting of the Nimrheal worshippers?"

"Yes," Endicott said firmly.

"You have my blessing," Eleanor replied. "I will see that the vice constable has men in the area to back you up if you need them. He will expect your detailed report after the meeting." She tapped her chin. "Perhaps he can even put a few men in civilian clothes into the tavern itself."

"Are you surprised?" Gregory asked. "About the Nimrheal church?"

Eleanor suddenly looked even older and frailer. She also looked more like the duchess. "People never stop complaining. I have learned to expect that. They have their own strange ideas and unforeseen dissatisfactions. I have even come to realize that the more the possibilities of success in a person's life, the greater the chance they will find something to be angry about. So no, I suppose I am not surprised. Nimrheal is a terrible being to worship, though."

You can say that again.

Gregory remained more task-oriented than philosophical. "How do you want us to bring you Lord Brice's shield?"

Eleanor stood up. "Why don't the three of you and Sir Eloise Kyre bring it to the Citadel when it's ready. We can speak about the agricultural mission in detail then."

It was the first time Endicott had heard Eleanor refer directly to her real home and true identity. It made him feel sad. He took Gerveault rather for granted. The old man was always around, but Eleanor had become, by her frequent absences, genuinely missed. For some reason her willingness to reveal who she was made him suspect he would be seeing even less of her.

Before Eleanor could leave, Endicott took her into a hug. It was not the crushing, forced intimacy of an Eloise hug, but it was a solid one. "Am I going to be able to call you Eleanor for much longer?" he asked as he let her go.

The old woman stiffened momentarily, perhaps shocked at Endicott's freedom. But she did hug him back, her frail bones evident to the touch through her thin skin. "Perhaps not, but whatever you call me, you're still my boys." As she said this, she looked at Gregory, including him. Then she turned to Koria. "And my girl."

▽

Much later that night, Endicott lay awake wondering how Koria felt about the Black Spear and about Elyze Astarte, her mission, and her interest in him. He was in Koria's bed, and her head was resting on his stomach.

"Was this much of a birthday for you?" he asked quietly.

"I enjoyed the delicate work, and having you close," she whispered closing her eyes. "Sometimes that is as much as one can hope for."

"Did you herald the brawl at the Black Spear?" he asked.

"Yes."

"That's why you asked us to take Eloise." He snorted. "As if we would have been able to get away without her."

"Two for two, Robert. You really are very good at probability manipulation. Though I didn't foresee that Eloise was going to be the cause of the trouble."

Endicott frowned and looked down at her. "What about the agricultural mission? And me going to the Nimrheal meeting? How do you feel about those?"

"About the same as my chances of stopping the moon in the sky."

Endicott was conflicted. He had agreed to go to the Line and felt he *had* to go to the Nimrheal meeting. "How can I make it feel better for you? How does it look when you herald it?"

Koria opened her eyes. "I am no longer objective enough to herald reliably on some of the truly important things, Robert. In the absence of perfect knowledge, I am going to have to dream that you are simply ... ready."

Chapter Nine.

Kairos

"Do you think we are ready?" asked Gregory, sweat pouring off him. The forge certainly was ready, and it was blasting the two young men with heat.

Endicott tilted his head, considering the question. They had made a trial run late yesterday right after the meeting with Eleanor. It had taken three attempts with a much cheaper and simpler alloy before Gregory hit the cooling mark, but the third attempt had produced their prototype. It had been easier to make, and it could be more easily destroyed, but it was still two and half times stronger than conventional shields. Entropy is imagined most often as the black nothingness of chaos, but entropy in steel shines like the moon illuminated by the sun. Entropy in an alloy of metal is like magic. The prototype's luminescence was bundled away in a corner under a blanket for the moment. As good as it was, the young men had their minds set on something even better now.

The full-formula attempt would be much more difficult. The finished shield needed to have extremely high tensile and compressive strength and a high yield strength, while still being flexible and resilient. It must not be brittle. This was the most difficult challenge: giving the shield an elastic behavior that would act to distribute the force of impact. Being resistant to one kind of physical test was not very rare but being resistant to virtually *every* test was virtually impossible. There was one saving grace. The shield did not require a cutting edge. For all its difficulty, it was still a simpler task than making the knife that Endicott wore at his hip. Adding an edge to such a hard object would have been impractical anyway. There was no substance he could obtain, apart from his knife and Gregory's sword, with which he could even hope to sharpen an edge on the shield if they made it correctly.

A diamond would do it. But the budget did not run to diamonds.

"Everything we have done so far has helped make us ready," Endicott said at last. Even the cake exercise, he reflected. For all its triviality, the delicacy it required was also needed here, but in spades. "And we'll miss the season if we don't do this now."

"You're thinking of taking one of these into that cult meeting?" Gregory's eyebrows leapt up in alarm.

"No," Endicott laughed. "That would be a waste. I'm thinking about my heraldic dream and the cloaked figure. There weren't any leaves on the ground in the dream, Gregory. Eloise must have that shield before the leaves start to fall!"

Gregory was silent for a moment. "Well, let's get started then." He wiped a rag across his sweat-soaked face. "I'm boiling away what little talent I have here."

"Being a little hot at the start is a good thing." Endicott turned back to the forge and saw that the tungsten was fully liquefied at last. He achieved the greater breakdown and purified the liquid metal through probability manipulation; the impure elements suddenly found themselves in the fire. Holding precariously on to the lesser breakdown, Endicott quickly pulled on gloves and took up the tongs. He poured half the tungsten into one of the two six-element mixes that sat on the secondary heated trays. At first the liquids would be partially immiscible. The hammers were ready. The tongs were ready. The huge square anvil was ready. They would begin with the shield for Sir Kennyth Brice.

Endicott envisioned the complex random-not-random structure he wanted the elements to take on in the alloy, and simultaneously, on an entirely different scale, he took hold of the image of the finished shield. The composition of the alloy would be slightly different from the one used for the swords, and its molecular arrangement was a secret he had from his grandpa. There were many kinds of alloy and many flavors of entropy. This particular combination had been discreetly tested on a maul back on the farm as well as on five critical bolts in the elevator. It was unique and extremely difficult to hold probabilistically, particularly in something the size and shape of a shield. It also happened to be exceedingly expensive and difficult to test. Endicott could only hope that they would succeed on this first attempt.

"Are you ready?" he asked through gritted teeth.

"Set." Out of the corner of his eye he saw Gregory, gloved and tensed, holding his tongs in front of him and staring intently into the forge.

Endicott performed the probability manipulation that would set the molecular arrangement and the overall shape of the shield. "Now!" he cried.

Gregory executed his own thermal manipulation, rapidly cooling the liquid while Endicott held the shape and arrangement probabilistically. The liquid alloy now had the form of a small heater shield, pointed at the bottom, flat on the top, and gently convex. It remained massively hot, still glowing and malleable.

"Hold it with the tongs!" Endicott called.

Gregory quickly pulled the shield onto the anvil, and Endicott took up a rounded hammer and struck the shield. The blow had to be just so, hard but not too hard.

Bang. Tap.

The tap was the sound made by the minor impact of the hammer on the anvil as Endicott rested it between each blow on the shield. This was necessary to give Gregory time to move the shield.

"Now rotate the shield with each blow."

Gregory rotated the shield.

Bang. Tap.

Endicott had to time each probabilistic manipulation to coincide with the hammer blows. Bang. Tap.

The shield's shape was becoming more distinct.

He struck and manipulated the alloy again, and the handles began to form. He struck and manipulated again, and then again. The two young dynamicists worked quietly, building a rhythm together,

Bang. Tap. Bang. Tap. Bang. Tap.

Each manipulation clarified the shape and refined the composition, finalizing the small holes near the handles, smoothing the lip, and always, always reinforcing the entropic molecular arrangement. Endicott's arms and shoulders ached but did not spasm. The probability manipulation felt natural, and he kept it fluent, parsing it out with the best specific preparation he could. He had developed his talent for metalworking under the expert eyes of his grandpa, but the cake exercise had helped to fine-tune the delicate control he needed for the shield. The work with the cake, the heat, the hammer blows, and the first rapid reordering, reshaping, and cooling made all the smaller modifications seem almost easy.

Bang. Tap.

But the effort was adding up. He could feel his temperature falling as expected but also a strange sensation of psychological resistance. After a hundred hammer blows his mind began to fight him as much as his forearms and shoulders had.

Almost there.

"Ready to freeze it?"

"Ready."

He added one final, minor touch as the alloy froze. The final procedure lasted a dynamically unusual two seconds, but it was a tough two seconds since most manipulations happened instantaneously. The molecules wanted to arrange themselves in a lattice. They fought for it, they wanted to slide ever so slightly in the direction of their preferred sense of order, and Endicott spent the last of his energy denying them this freedom while Gregory cooled them into place.

"One b-block of ice and o-one h-hopefully unbreakable shield," cheered Gregory, shivering. He dropped the finished shield into a water bath.

Endicott was also shaking, hard.

Thank Elysium it's so hot in here.

"L-let's see it."

Gregory pulled the shield onto the workbench and they examined it.

"N-nice V, R-Robert. Fit for a duke-to-be." Gregory traced the large, capitalized V for Vercors that Endicott had placed in the center of the glassy, shimmering surface as a last touch.

Endicott achieved the lesser breakdown and examined the shield's molecular arrangement. He nodded in satisfaction to his tall compatriot. "Get the b-big hammer." Gregory took up the long-handled five-pounder in both hands and held it aloft over the shield. The shield was laid out convex as if facing an opponent. "I can't," Gregory mumbled, hesitating. "W-what if we b-break it?"

"B-better to know now than later," Endicott replied dryly. He surprised himself by yawning. Was it an autonomic response to thermodynamic shock? "B-besides, my f-forearms are shot. It h-has to be you. N-now g-give it everything you h-have."

Gregory closed his eyes and swung.

Bwwwaaahhhh.

The shield reverberated loudly, and the hammer jumped violently back, almost smashing Gregory in the face and dragging the startled young man backward, stumbling two or three paces. Endicott ignored his tall friend's chagrin and reexamined the shield. No sign of metal fatigue. The force had been contained entirely within the elastic limits of the alloy. The hammer itself, back under control now, was slightly damaged, the head wobbling a bit on the handle. Endicott silently resolved to repair it before they left.

"I-is it w-well?" Gregory asked, even though he could see the shield's perfection for himself in the Empyreal Sky.

"Both y-your arms and b-both of mine would break from h-holding onto it before the shield w-would."

"So it c-could be b-broken?"

"Sure," Endicott smiled wryly. "But if you got hit h-hard enough to break this, it probably wouldn't m-matter anyway. You're a-arms would collapse like an accordion, shield or no shield."

"Let's m-make Eloise's t-then!"

Endicott insisted they wait a full hour while standing close to the forge before trying a second shield. Even with the heat from the forge, making the first shield had pushed their temperatures too low for safety. In a perfect world he would have suggested the hot pools, but he did not want to leave the heated metals unattended. He knew one thing as he started the second shield.

This is going to hurt.

And it did. The second shield would have the letter K at its shining center, signifying Eloise's last name.

Kyre.

Koria.

THE TWO PERFECTED SHIELDS AND THE PROTOTYPE WERE LAID OUT ON THE EDGE OF ONE of the hot pools as Endicott and Gregory slowly recovered in the steaming water, still shaking despite the heat.

Some might say we should have waited longer.

Endicott knew that Bethyn had been right, that Koria had been right, that Eloise had been right, and Gregory too. He *did* labor under a dream of doom, a probabilistic story of some near future that he could not accept and desperately wanted to change. He *was* sometimes reckless and foolhardy. But the future his nightmare foretold was coming. Every day the cloaked figure did *not* appear with an indestructible spear and murder on his mind was a day closer to the one in which he *must* arrive. And so, although he knew Gregory and he had pushed the boundaries of risk, he was sure they had done the right thing. Time and events do not always wait on readiness, comfort, or safety. The seasons turn and the world changes with or without permission. When the kairotic moment finally did come, no excuse would matter.

Darkness found the two young men bearing gleaming, reflective shields on their arms and the only slightly duller prototype on the taller man's back. Their plan was to cover them when they reached campus and hide them in the spare boys' bedroom of the Orchid until they were ready to present them to Eloise and Lord Kennyth Brice. They mounted the Academic Plateau wearily, but Gregory could not stop grinning. From the outside at last, Endicott saw how affecting real enthusiasm was.

Is this what I am like? Is this how I affect others?

"You look like a street dancer," Endicott said, deciding not to be serious.

"What?"

"That big smile. I can see all your teeth."

"Good."

"Does it hurt to smile that wide?" Gregory did not answer, so Endicott relented. "I like it, Gregory. Be happy." Endicott stumbled in exhaustion. "But it may give you away. She's already suspicious."

A jolt of something hit him. Every muscle in his body seemed to spasm.

The ground began to shake, and a roaring sound followed quick on its heels. Instinctively Endicott made the lesser breakdown. He observed, not far off, a rent into elsewhere. If the angels had torn a hole in the sky to a place of infinite power, it would have looked like this, a narrow funnel into an unimaginable, omnipotent infinity. A singularity. He tried to follow the funnel but failed. No words, no imagination, no mathematics could encompass the blazing white, unbounded energy someone had accessed.

I know what it is.

Endicott had seen it once before. On the terrible night when he accessed the powers of Elysium himself. *Then* he had been operating entirely on instinct, focused only the vileness of the two brothers and the impulse of retribution. He had not considered or observed what he was doing. Looking on from the outside now, he saw that accessing such power depended on reaching into a frightful, endless potential. On the terrible night, thanks to Eloise and Koria, he had left all that capacity where it belonged. Whoever was doing *this* felt no such constraint.

A flash of light exploded only a few streets away followed quickly by a concussive blast and a wave of heat. The smell of ozone rolled over him and he stumbled.

If I can feel the heat here, what must it be like there?

Endicott and Gregory looked at each other and without a word began running towards the light.

Is this it, our turning point? Is this him?

"All or nothing!" Endicott yelled as they charged around a corner. He readied himself to try the empyreal sky again. He was spent but that hardly mattered now. He never questioned the wisdom of charging in.

At the far corner of the next block, a two-story building was on fire. Its *bricks* were burning. Two figures stood there in the smoky distance, one much taller than the other. The tall one wheeled, cloak flaring, and ran off to the right.

That cloak!

"It's him!" Endicott roared.

Endicott and Gregory by instantaneous and mutual consent turned right and ran in parallel to the tall, cloaked figure. Endicott held his sword hilt in his right hand, shield in his left, and sprinted, not wanting to miss the opportunity of ending the threat he had anticipated for so long. They passed an intersection, and from the distance of a block away, the cloaked figure turned his head, and he and his pursuers, for an instant, looked one another in the eye before the figure leapt around another corner.

The pursuit continued down this street, which was narrower and darker than the first. Endicott had by this time gained three strides on Gregory, who was laden down with two shields. The street ended in a square, into which the figure disappeared, and Endicott arrived just in time to see something flash towards him. Automatically he raised his shield to cover his face.

Bwwwaaaahhhhh. Psht.

Whatever it was that had flashed out from the darkness hit the shield with tremendous force. It propelled Endicott backwards and sideways off his feet, but his arms were unbroken. By slipping out from under him, his feet had given his body a way of absorbing the impact. He raised his head, poised for the next blow, but the cloaked figure had disappeared into the night.

"Hati damn it!"

It was Gregory's voice. Endicott turned and understood what must have happened as soon as he saw his tall friend. Gregory's face and chest were peppered with cuts, and the long black haft of a spear lay on the ground to his right. The spear head was spread across the pavement in a cloud of broken, shining fragments. The cloaked figure had thrown a spear with such savage power that it had exploded on Endicott's shield and showered Gregory with shards of metal. Endicott scrambled to his feet and rushed to his friend, who seemed frozen in shock. There was a fair amount of blood from a great many small cuts. Most were on his forehead but none seemed serious.

He must have tucked in his chin just in time.

Gregory crouched on his knees, silent and trusting as Endicott examined the damage. Tiny bits of metal stuck out of his forehead. Blood ran into his eye sockets, which Endicott smudged away with his thumbs so that he could see Gregory's eyes. He thanked the Knights that none of the metal had gotten in there or, he quickly ascertained, had reached Gregory's throat. A few pieces had pricked the side of Gregory's neck and his chest, but they were all as tiny as the ones on his forehead. The failure of the spear point had been exceedingly brittle and explosive.

"Stay here." Endicott clapped Gregory on the shoulder and stood up to resume his pursuit of the cloaked man. "See if you can collect some of the bigger pieces of that spear head," he called over his shoulder as he headed across the square.

"I guess that means I'm all right," Gregory called after him, but Endicott did not hear him over the sound of his own panting breaths.

He knew where the spear had been thrown from and ran in that direction, only realizing how close he was to the campus when he passed the location where he had spoken to Conor and where Koria had followed him. He could just hear the fire crackling behind him and distant shouts, probably from people trying to fight the conflagration. Usually the sound of fire was soothing for him, associated with control over the environment and with comfort. It took on a wholly other meaning now. Not to mention the fact that brick was burning when it was well known that brick did not burn.

He ran down the block, closing on the Apprentice's Library. There was no sign of the cloaked man, no sound, no trace of manipulation in the Empyreal Sky. His quarry had escaped. Or Endicott had.

"Out a little late, aren't you?"

Endicott felt a thrill at the sound of Koria's voice. Part of him wanted to keep running—a large part—but that would have meant ignoring Koria to chase … nothing. The cloaked man was gone. Endicott turned and saw that Eloise was there too, armed with the sword Endicott's grandfather had sent him. Both girls wore their New School tartan skirts and blouses. Koria had a sweater draped over the blouse. She smiled archly at him.

I could ask the same about you two.

But he did not. He was too desperate to find the cloaked figure, too tired to argue, too used to being followed by Koria, too aware she might be pursuing her own means of control over the future, and lastly, too smart to try to tell either woman what to do. He did wonder how they knew to be out here so close to the scene of some … crime. He kept that question to himself as well.

Heraldry?

Koria may have said she could no longer reliably herald his future, but she had not said she had stopped trying.

"Did you see a man run by? In a cloak?" But Endicott knew the answer. He hardly needed to see the two girls shake their heads. If they had seen a tall cloaked man run by as if murder were on his heels, they would have greeted him very differently. There would have been no jests.

"What. Is. That?" Eloise's incredulous voice rose in pitch with each word.

Endicott wordlessly motioned the girls to walk with him and handed Eloise the gleaming shield. Eloise enthusiastically took it, tracing out the "V" in the center, and then buffed the black smudge that the spear had left with her shirt sleeve.

"It's like Gregory's sword!" Eloise sang, swinging the shield. "I want to keep it." She hugged the shield.

Ha.

"It is a gift for Kennyth Brice," Endicott said, concealing a smile and nearly having to wrestle the shield back from Eloise. He did not want her to feel she already owned one when Gregory eventually gave her another.

"A princely gift, Robert. Why—"

"Is that blood on your hands?" Koria cried out, interrupting Eloise and grabbing Endicott's hands. She started patting him down for injuries.

"No," Endicott said. "It's Gregory's." He held up one of his stained hands to forestall Eloise, whose face had hardened. "He's okay."

Endicott tried to explain what had happened as he led the girls back. The whole sequence of events was already taking on a surreal feel in his mind. This was not improved when they found that Gregory was gone. So were most of the spear fragments. Endicott picked up the spear haft, which had been abandoned.

"He left a blood trail." Eloise's voice was flat, and she seemed torn between following the drops of blood on the cobbles and scowling at Endicott. "How could you have left him?"

"You know why, Eloise. The cloaked man was here. Gregory was fine. He must have headed back to where we first saw the bastard."

Eloise maintained her scowl. "You left him."

"*After* I made sure he was okay." Endicott was tired enough to resort to a scowl of his own. "After. Aren't you the one always telling me that I have to toughen up and stick to task?" He thrust himself up taller, pushing his chest out and slamming his hands on his hips in his best Eloise impression. "You can't save everyone, stupe. Heh, heh, heh. Every decision is easy for Eloise Kyre, superwoman, but not for you. Stupe. Heh, heh, heh."

Koria rolled her eyes but could not help smiling. Endicott could not read Eloise's expression. It was full of bottled-up potential. The tall woman stared at him fixedly and followed that up by staring at him some more.

"Ha," she finally spat out. "I guess you finally learned something. I *am* super."

Eloise let out a softer breath. "You're sure Gregory's okay?"

Endicott turned and continued walking. "He's fine." He shook his head. "If only I could have caught the cloaked man. These decisions would all have seemed better."

Koria stepped in front of Endicott and put a hand on his chest. "Do you really think you alone were in any way ready to stop him?"

Endicott thought of the display of power that he had witnessed from afar. It was well beyond him dynamically. The spear throw was well beyond him physically. The cloaked figure wholly outclassed him in every way that mattered in the dark of night. If Endicott had not happened to have Kennyth Brice's shield, he and Gregory would likely have died then and there. Worse yet, Endicott had no idea who the man in the cloak was, what other strengths he might have, and if he had any weaknesses that could be exploited.

"No," he admitted.

It would not have been my moment.

Chapter Ten.
Crowd

KORIA SEEMED CONTENT TO LEAVE IT AT THAT, AND EVEN ELOISE SEEMED TO RELAX ever so slightly. They followed Endicott without asking where he was leading them, but the destination did not stay a mystery for long. The flickering light from a fire showed them where they were going, and the sounds of a huge crowd of people grew louder as they approached the glow. When they rounded the corner and saw the fiery mess, Eloise raced ahead, her speed creating a wake of roiling smoke. She had not been so sanguine about Gregory's situation after all.

It looks like a grinder. A dark, cloudy mill.

All mobs resemble a cloudy, dark mill, Endicott reflected. They all act, one way or another, to grind. They are all driven by a terrifying mass exigency.

A group of people ran to and fro with buckets. A long spray of water shooting out from somewhere in the crowd told Endicott that someone had found a two-person hand pump. Smoke billowed chaotically, darkly opaque one moment, eerily lit by yellow flames the next. A surging ring of other people seemed to push on the crowd, shaping the churn around some shadowy central area.

It's the constabulary.

As they approached the human maelstrom, Endicott found Koria's hand in his, and he began to understand that there was more than one exigency at work here. Eloise's concern for Gregory was obvious, and it had lifted Endicott's spirits. He had not been sure how the tall, fierce woman really felt until he had seen her reaction to Gregory's blood. She was not a lady who could be impressed by flowers or poetry, but blood seemed to speak a language she appreciated. The ad hoc fire brigade's exigency was also easy to understand. They lived in the vicinity. It was their homes and businesses that were in jeopardy. That the constabulary should arrive and attempt to take charge also made sense and was as it should be. The heavens had been split; fire had been called down. The constabulary surely were needed. What Endicott had trouble understanding was why all the other people were there.

All around the action, not assisting the firefighters, outside of the ring of constables, on the periphery, stood a vast crew of gawkers. Some were dressed in long nightclothes, others in the clothes they had worn the day before, and some perhaps in the only clothes they owned. They pressed aimlessly towards the constabulary, some dully curious, others with manic, almost gleeful expressions.

What is their exigency?

Endicott and Koria held up their medallions and were allowed to pass through the ring of constables. Ahead of them they made out Gregory sitting on a curb talking to a knot of officers. He was holding a cloth to his head. As they approached, they saw Eloise arrive, snatch the cloth from him, and begin aggressively dabbing his face with it. Thin clouds of smoke rolled slowly past him, but he seemed unaware of them. Perhaps the combination of questioning by the constables or the painful dabbing from Eloise put the smoke a distant third in terms of sensory input.

"I got most of the bits, Robert," Gregory called out when he saw Endicott and Koria. He had used Eloise's shield to hold the fragments of the shattered spear head. The prototype shield lay under it. In the surest sign of love yet, Eloise had not rifled through the stacked shields, but continued her aggressive dabbing of Gregory's blood. Among those questioning Gregory, Endicott spotted Chief Constable Eryka Lyon. Endicott had not seen her since the trial, but her long red hair and bright green eyes were unmistakable even in the smoke and half-light. The group turned to Endicott as he approached.

"Sir Robert, I am glad to see you. I've been briefed on your written reports by my vice constable. Sir Gregory here has been telling us that you gave chase to the person who did this. I am relieved to see that you are still with us," Eryka said, her green eyes less welcoming than her words.

Hopefully it is the job and not me.

It was not difficult to imagine that from her perspective the young Knights of Vercors could be more of an irritant than an asset.

Too many blacksmiths in the smithy.

Endicott had no intention of backing off, but he wondered what could be done to put the chief at ease. "He was too fast to be caught. Chief, how can we best help you?"

Eryka's brow went up, perhaps with unconscious skepticism, but she answered readily enough. "Well, let's first see if we can get the narrative straight. Sir Gregory tells us that a cloaked man did this. That he fled the scene when the two of you arrived."

Endicott described the chase, the size and speed of the cloaked figure, and the enormous power with which he had thrown his spear. Eryka nodded along, scribbling rapidly in a hardback notebook. "Anything else?" she asked.

Endicott frowned, noticing that something had changed. "Where is the other one?"

Eryka squinted, though Endicott did not know if it was from the question or from the smoke. It looked like the firefighters were getting the better of the situation; the fire would soon be out. Men and women were still running back and forth with buckets, damping the smoldering building, and wetting the ones beside it. As the light from the last of the flames dimmed, Eryka's long red hair began to look almost black. "Other one?"

Endicott pointed towards the brick building. "There was a second figure there. The cloaked man ran, but the other one stayed behind."

Eryka snapped her fingers with impressive force and motioned Endicott and Koria to follow her. Eloise grabbed Gregory's hand and heaved him effortlessly to his feet, and the two of them pursued Endicott and the chief, leaving the shields and spear fragments on the curb. "Do you mean this man?" Eryka pointed to a body laid out on the ground, partially wrapped in a long coat. He was a man of plain looks but rich clothes, perhaps in his late thirties as best Endicott could guess, given that half his face was obliterated. It looked as though a spear had passed right through his mouth, teeth first. There may have been other wounds, but the coat hid them.

That could have been me. Or Gregory.

"Or this one?" She stepped closer to the burned-out shell of the building. The bricks had not burned as Endicott had thought. They were severely heat-glazed, though all the extensive wooden trim on the wall and around the windows was scorched or burned away. Parts of the wall looked like they might collapse at any moment, and several constables were keeping the gawkers away and out of danger. They were also keeping folks clear of the second body. A soaking-wet, charred skeleton was sprawled against the wall. It was so badly burned that Endicott thought that a little more water from the fire brigade might wash it entirely away.

"Well?" she said.

Endicott thought about it. He turned and looked back at the body in the coat and the charred skeleton. "No. It is *not* well. We never saw this person." He pointed at the charred bones. "But this one," he walked back to the first body, "this person was standing over there." He pointed to the far end of the building. "He has been moved. Gregory and I saw the manipulation that started the fire. I would hazard that the cloaked figure burned this other person first—"

"Burned?" interrupted Eryka incredulously. "How was he burned?"

"It was a wizard. The cloaked figure is an extremely powerful wizard."

"Like you and your friends?"

"No." Endicott half smiled. "*Not* like us. An order of magnitude more powerful at least. See these bricks, how they're glazed? See the charred corpse? None of *us* could do that."

Koria had been silent throughout, but she suddenly pulled Endicott's sword out of its scabbard and approached the blackened heap of bones.

"Don't disturb the evidence!" Eryka shouted, reaching for Koria. Endicott, without thinking, intercepted her hand. Eryka turned her head sharply to say something, but Endicott got there first. "Trust us, chief. Please."

Koria crouched close to the charred bones, holding the sword with two hands. The tip of the blade slipped into the soupy ash and pulled up a deformed looking chain. A slagged chain with a medallion on it. She leaned forward and examined it. "It has been flash melted, but I am certain this is a medallion from the second class." She slowly let the chain back down and wordlessly handed Endicott's sword back.

Eryka rounded on the group of them. "Thank you. It is helpful to start on the work of identifying the body, but from now on please ask us if you want some item examined. I realize you are experts in … certain things, but I assure you this is *our* expertise."

Endicott, Gregory, and Koria nodded their assent. Eloise just glared.

"Carry on with your story," Eryka commanded.

"Immediately after the thermal manipulation," continued Endicott, "we saw him with that man," pointing to the first corpse. "Killed him already, I guess, but somehow left him standing up. That's when he saw Gregory and me and ran." Endicott looked around. "But someone moved the fellow."

Eryka's face matched her hair color. She wheeled on Gregory, voice level despite the anger in her eyes. "Is that correct?"

Gregory had mostly stopped bleeding, thanks to Eloise, but one trickle still ran down his face from his hairline. It encountered his left eyebrow, ran along the brow, and then trailed down the side of his eye. He nodded sharply. "No question about it, chief constable."

Eryka turned to the crowd of constables as if looking for someone. "Lynwen! You were the first one here. What happened to my crime scene?"

A tall, younger woman straightened into a salute. "Chief! The vice constable thought we should take the body down. Too upsetting, sir! Too many eyes, sir!"

"Well, I am the one who is upset now, constable." Eryka closed her eyes. "Is everyone here intent on destroying the integrity of my scene?"

"Sorry, chief!" She stood so stiffly that she visibly quivered.

Eryka opened her eyes. "That was a rhetorical question. Now. How was this man," she pointed at the fellow missing his upper teeth and half his face, "standing?"

Lynwen swallowed. "He had a spear … in him."

"In his face?"

Endicott found himself liking Chief Constable Eryka.

"No," said a visibly uncomfortable Constable Lynwen. "It was shoved … thrust through his … anus and up through his body."

"And you thought that small detail should be left out of your report?" Eryka's incredulity had reached a new height.

Endicott felt his gorge rising. He knew that image. It was depicted in chilling detail in the original edition of *The Lonely Wizard*. Gerveault's book. He glanced nervously at Koria, Gregory, and Eloise. They had all read the book. None of them could have forgotten the dead knight that the Lonely Wizard had found in the Ardgour Wilderness. None of them looked as horrified as Endicott felt. Perhaps they just did not want to think about it.

Constable Lynwen spent the next few moments explaining her actions. The spear victim had been laid out so that the pole sticking out of his anus was not immediately obvious. The coat had been placed to hide that grisly detail, and the hole that the spear had originally been planted into had been ignored in the darkness, smoke and confusion.

"Lord Justice! Lord Justice!" A gravelly voice interrupted the grim consideration of the corpse and of Constable Lynwen's well-meaning attempt to cover up the worst parts of it. It was an old woman, straining ineffectually to get past a big constable. "Please, my lord!"

There was no way Gregory was going to ignore someone calling him a lord, so he walked over to the crone. The lady had thin, scraggly hair and was missing her two middle front teeth. She was an eye-catching sight on a night of eye-catching sights. No one spoke as Gregory approached her. When he got close, her hand lashed out and she gripped his wrists. Gregory appeared too stunned to push her away.

"You saw *him*!" she cackled. Gregory's face screwed up involuntarily, possibly from a wave of bad breath. "You saw the Lord Nimrheal! He left you a gift, he did! Don't worry none about catching him. None escape him that he touches so."

"Eight Knights, old woman," Gregory cursed, disentangling his hands. "Did you see the man who did this?"

"In my dream." She pointed one gnarled, shaking finger at her own head. "I dreamed him here. You will see him again, Lord Justice. Twice more shall you see him."

Visibly shaken now, Gregory demanded, "What? Where?"

The old lady cackled. "You will be blessed thusly, thrice. Finally you shall pay the price. Rejoice! For when the third time finally arrives, he'll mount you up on that sword you so prize. You will become a sign for all to see, the cost of the Book of Nature perceived."

How you react when an old lady of exceedingly poor hygiene predicts your death at the hands of a transcendental being depends somewhat on circumstances. How you react when she predicts your death by sword up the ass depends entirely on your individual nature.

Lord Gregory Justice seemed to recover himself. "Damned peasant!" he sneered under his breath. Denial seemed to bring out a flash of the lord in him. It was a glimpse of the lord that Gregory might once have been. He turned his back on her. Eloise would probably have thrashed the pathetic old woman if fewer constables had stood between them or if Gregory had not effectively turned right into her. Her hands were clenched, and a vein stood out on her forehead.

Chief Constable Eryka reacted with a very slight, very weary look. "Get her out of here," she instructed a tall, angular constable. Koria's eyes went wide with alarm. She elbowed Endicott in the side.

"Chief," Endicott whispered. "She might be part of a group that could be of interest here. That Nimrheal cult I wrote to the vice constable about."

"Hold on a moment, Kayne." Eryka turned to Endicott, sighing. "I *saw* your letter, Sir Robert. We did discuss it at HQ. But even if there really is a cult of Nimrheal, I doubt she could be in it. She's touched. People like her are always drawn to this kind of thing."

"People like her are likely the ones drawn to a cult too," Endicott retorted. "Either of us could be right. Why can't we hold her and find out?"

"I'll beat it out of the hag," chipped in Eloise unhelpfully.

Really? The hag might be as pitiable and ridiculous as her prophetic chant, just a lost person seeking attention and importance by making grim pronouncements. If so a beating would be both cruel and pointless. And if the hag was more than just a delusional old woman, a beating was unlikely to make her reveal her secrets.

But who can tell when Eloise is being serious?

"There is another reason to hold her," said Koria softly.

They all looked at Koria. She was almost always serious, and her comments were almost always respected. The chief seemed to sense this and listened intently.

"Robert is going to a meeting of that cult in less than two days. She has seen him. She has seen the constables here, and she has seen Sir Gregory and Sir Eloise. You have to hold her at least until after the meeting."

"Right." Eryka pointed at the old lady, whose dark eyes had flickered between the speakers throughout the conversation. "Take her to a cell, Kayne. A private one where she can't see or speak to anyone else. Hold her incommunicado until further notice."

Endicott took Gregory and Eloise aside. "Why don't the two of you wander through the crowd? See if there is anyone here you recognize from the Black Spear."

Eryka had been finishing her own instructions to the various constables, but now she turned back to Endicott and Koria, pointing at the spear victim. "If the victim by the wall was once a student of the New School, then who is this poor wreck?"

"That is Konrad Folke. I have known him for seventeen years. He was a student in our second class and was a dynamicist working for me."

The speaker was Gerveault. He had arrived quietly with Vice Constable Edwyn Perry. Perry was the man who had ordered Konrad's corpse taken down. Endicott and Gregory had spoken to the vice constable on a few occasions, and he had seemed professional enough at the time, so Endicott decided to reserve judgement on the corpse debate. Perry was short and heavy with an oddly long neck a little out of keeping with his otherwise stolid build. He had a tendency to hang his head forward off that long neck, especially when he was thinking.

"Excellent," declared Eryka. "Both from the second class and one of them already identified. That is some progress at least. Don't go anywhere, if you please, sir. I will have more questions for you."

She smiled death at Edwyn Perry, who was looking outwards at the crowd. "Why ever did you order the scene disturbed, Edwyn?"

"You wanted me to leave that scarecrow up?" Edwyn's voice was dry.

A short but tense discussion ensued in which the value of unadulterated evidence was weighed against the apparently fragile state of mind of the citizenry. Edwyn maintained that such a gruesome scene should be hidden from the public and from the posts. He pointed at the crowd of gawkers still milling about on the outside of the ring of constables and suggested that the scene must have already been compromised. Eryka clearly disagreed. Endicott flirted with a darker theory.

It certainly looks like Nimrheal did it. But why make it look like that?

Endicott knew that simply invoking the name of Nimrheal did not mean much, but Konrad Folke's body had been deliberately arranged in a way that viscerally evoked Nimrheal by someone of immense physical and dynamic capability. That meant something.

Clop, clop, clop, clop, clop, clop.

A half-dozen horsemen rode into the alley. Endicott recognized Sir Christensen and Lord Kennyth Brice among them.

"This is bad," whispered Edwyn Perry. "Committees don't solve a lot of crimes, Sir Robert." Endicott had not noticed the vice constable work his way closer to him. Endicott did not reply, fascinated by how quickly Lord Kennyth Brice now took charge of the scene. Four of his guards joined the bulk of the constabulary in pushing the onlookers further back, while he and Sir Christensen took a moment to assess the situation for themselves.

"Let's have a report then, shall we?" Kennyth Brice said, standing up after a cursory examination of Konrad's corpse. Endicott found Eryka looking at him.

She must trust me a little.

He nodded a go-ahead to her. Eryka laid out the scene, showed Brice the bodies, the injuries as they understood them, and then passed the narrative to Endicott and Gregory, who described what they had seen, the chase they had attempted, and the spectacular way in which the pursuit had ended. They left out the moving of the body and the argument they had just endured over it.

Endicott hefted the shield and showed it to Lord Brice. "Without this I would have been killed for sure." Kennyth's right eyebrow leapt up as he stared at the gleaming work. "I'm glad you had it, then. What on earth is it made from?"

Endicott put a hand on Gregory's shoulder. "Sir Gregory and I just finished smithing it, Lord Brice. It is an amorphous alloy of tungsten. Strong, hard, and elastic. It's actually … for you. *Professor* Eleanor had us make this. We were planning to give it to you at the Citadel." Endicott thrust it out to Kennyth. "But why don't you take it now?"

Lord Brice took the shield in his hands, marveling at it. "It's an Endicott, all right," he said, both eyebrows raised now. "Perhaps you should keep it for yourself until you visit me, Sir Robert. The campus has been somewhat less safe that I would have hoped."

Endicott shook his head. "It's yours."

Kennyth handed the shield to Sir Christensen, who held it close.

"We know it works," added Gregory. "The spear point exploded off it like nothing I have ever seen. Actually I did not see it, but I caught some of the pieces."

Lord Kennyth Brice laughed, patting both young men on the shoulders before turning his attention back to the serious problem lying on the ground in front of him. "So. What happened here, do you suppose? Who did this?"

"It was a wizard."

Koria's soft voice came abruptly out of the night, momentarily silencing everyone again.

"Why do you say that, Lady Koria?"

"We all felt two distinct manipulations, possibly one by the deceased, Konrad Folke, and the other by the murderer." She pointed at the brick wall and the charred corpse. "They could only have been performed by an extremely powerful wizard. The energy required to incinerate the first victim and glaze the brick wall was enormous. The wizard is likely male, given the height Sir Robert and Sir Gregory observed. He—"

Edwyn Perry interrupted with a smile and a hang-dog look. "What about your friend, Sir Eloise? *She* is that tall."

Eloise *was* that tall, and she had joined the group when Brice arrived. Now she was clenching her fists again. Endicott wondered for a moment if there was going to be another murder, this time with an excess of witnesses.

Koria did not miss a beat. "Eloise is unusually tall, that is true, but she was with me. The murderer is *likely* a man and certainly a very strong and fast one. So he is probably young, in his twenties, thirties at most. We should be looking for a tall, strong, young wizard."

"That could be right." Edwyn Perry smiled again. "Another possibility is that Konrad Folke was the only wizard involved. He fought the cloaked man and tried to burn him but killed the other man instead. Then, after that mishap, the cloaked man, who was just a man, killed Folke, ran away and threw the spear at our two young knights here."

Eloise made a spluttering sound. It echoed what Endicott was thinking. Edwyn's theory was not very good.

Brice turned to Gerveault. "Could Conrad Folke have made such a fire?"

Gerveault did not hesitate. "No. Few could."

Endicott spoke before thinking. "Fewer still could have read your book, Professor Gerveault."

"Any scholar of Nimrheal knows that staging, Robert," Gerveault said wearily. "Most wizards would know it."

Eryka's eyes narrowed. "That still cannot be a great many people."

"Okay, so the cloaked man had to be a wizard," said Edwyn, head down and hand up, abandoning his hypothesis and switching to Koria's smoothly. "We are closing on some of the what. How about we think a little about the why?"

Eryka nodded and looked over at Gerveault. "The two deceased were both formerly students of yours. At least one of them also worked for you. Perhaps the why has to do with that."

"The question of why might relate to the staging as well," Koria added. "The staging is the most troubling element of the crime."

"More than the fire?" asked Eryka. "More than the fact that we have had two dead bodies on our hands?"

"Yes."

Gerveault nodded his agreement, and Edwyn took the opportunity to justify himself again. "That is why I had Folke's body taken down."

Kennyth Brice put his hand up, halting the conversation. "There are three things that I need to say: first we are in this together." He looked slowly around at the entire gathering. "I like how we are all coming at this from various perspectives. *How*, *why*, and *who* are all equally important questions. Keep that up. Second this is a horrific crime. It appears to have been perpetrated by someone of terrifying power. We must approach this rationally and very, very carefully. We must look out for each other. Keep the investigation as tight as you can within this group. Third," Kennyth smiled sheepishly, "I think I may have missed something here regarding this staging issue. Let us take a step back for a minute and go over the significance of the staging."

Eryka went over the bare details of the staging again and then passed the initiative to Gerveault, who added the historical observation that the demon Nimrheal was said to have three archetypal positions in which he would leave his victims. The spear through the face and bowels was the most fearsome of those.

"So we are back to the murderer being a very powerful, well-educated wizard," concluded Kennyth Brice. "Either that or Nimrheal has returned."

No one laughed at the joke.

"The motive may have been political," Endicott offered. Everyone looked at him. He saw Koria nodding. "A murder of two former students. Executed by a wizard to look like Nimrheal. It is an enemy of the New School. And what it stands for."

Eryka frowned. "Your Nimrheal cult."

Endicott shrugged. "Everything, including the old lady, screams Nimrheal, but right now we can't really know. If it was the cult, where did they find a wizard? Could it be a wizard from Armadale?"

Lord Brice gave Endicott an encouraging look. "I *have* heard about your theory tying our eastern neighbor to the protests. Armadale is no friend to the New School. But we cannot very well raid the ambassador's estate without hard proof of complicity. It would likely mean war."

Gerveault's jaw clenched. "They may have the wizards for this. *Maybe*. But I would not bet a war on it." He looked off at the glazed brick wall. "This is certainly very serious, but let us not rush to judgement and make it worse. We need evidence. Facts. We need to take one step at a time."

"Indeed we do," agreed Kennyth firmly. "What does our constabulary say?"

Eryka looked at Edwyn Perry, who shrugged, head down. "Like Sir Robert said, we can't really know. Our young knights have put together an interesting collection of ideas but little hard evidence."

"Perhaps if we had some help, we would have more evidence," said Gregory facing off with Edwyn, who put up his hands placatingly. Endicott thought Gregory was being too sensitive. It looked to him as if Edwyn was simply being cautious.

Eryka stepped between them. "You will get that help. Clearly we have to take the idea seriously." She turned to Kennyth, lowering her head. "I regret not taking the cult theory more seriously before this."

Kennyth Brice smiled wryly. "There aren't many crimes we solve *before* they happen, chief constable. As I hear it, Sir Robert's theory is highly circumstantial, and we do try to avoid arresting our citizens based on hunches and coincidences."

Endicott heard a muffled sound from Eloise, who was standing behind Kennyth now. She was laughing, one hand over her mouth.

Lord Brice continued. "But now circumstances have changed."

"Timing matters. Sometimes," agreed Eryka.

"I am going to a meeting of the Nimrheal cult in less than two days," said Endicott. "Undercover," he added sheepishly. "If they are involved, it is bound to come out at the meeting. We have already spoken with the vice constable about support from the constabulary."

Eryka exchanged a glance with Edwyn before speaking. "We *were* planning to put a couple of shadows in the Black Spear."

"But as you said, things have changed," Edwyn added.

Gregory scowled. "So now you don't want to help him?"

Edwyn and Eryka looked at each other again. "It's not that," Edwyn said.

Kennyth put a hand on Gregory's arm. "What is the concern?"

Edwyn scratched his scalp. "Before, when Sir Robert's theory was … more theoretical, we weren't so concerned about him going into the Spear. But two persons are dead now, and in a spectacularly gruesome way. What if the young man is right? If there actually is a cult and it is involved in this crime, the danger, especially for … an amateur, is extreme."

Endicott had not realized how little his ideas had been believed until now, and how much of the involvement of the constabulary may have been simple appeasement.

"Going undercover is very problematic," Eryka added, looking at Brice. "We don't often do it with trained officers, let alone with the untrained."

Endicott fought the sudden urge to laugh. He and Gregory had struggled on the knife edge of thermodynamic death for a good part of the night to make the shields. He had worried over the death of love and friends in his heraldic dream for so long that he could not remember *not* worrying. The cloaked man had come within a thoughtless instant of putting a spear through his skull. He had a lengthy list of things to be more afraid of than Conor and his friends. "Thank you for your concern, vice constable. I am going to that meeting."

Edwyn shook his head on his long neck. "I know you're brave, Sir Robert. But you're barely more than a child. You don't know how badly this could go."

Endicott smiled sharply. "I can see that you are looking out for me, but this won't be the first terrible thing I have seen. Or the worst."

No one had anything to say to that.

"Do it, then," affirmed Kennyth. Then he looked straight at Eryka and the vice constable. "But keep my young knights safe, will you."

Gerveault cleared his throat. "We should pursue all leads and all investigative methods available to us. I will see if we can get Keith Euyn on his feet to perform retrograde heraldry on this. He may well be able to see exactly what happened, perhaps even by whom."

How sick is *he?*

Endicott had not seen the old man in weeks. He admired Keith Euyn but had never really grown to like him personally. Nevertheless he was devastated to think that the great man could be so unwell. He shook his head at himself. Gerveault was still speaking.

"—Novgoreyl is still here in Vercors. Their delegation could include such a formidable wizard."

Kennyth held up his gleaming new shield. "Please let it not be them. We have enough enemies right now, and that is one I do not understand."

Gerveault laughed mirthlessly. "From Novgoreyl, only questions."

"Let's keep Novgoreyl and as many of the other details as we can out of the posts," instructed Kennyth Brice. "Find the murderer." He once again passed his gaze slowly over everyone. "Work together."

IT WAS A WEARY GROUP THAT MADE ITS WAY BACK TO THE ORCHID. GREGORY WAS LUGGING the two remaining shields, inner surfaces facing each other and wrapped in a blanket to protect the spear fragments. Somehow Eloise's shield had stayed hidden during the lengthy conversation with the constabulary and Kennyth Brice.

At least one mystery is a happy one.

"News of this will be all over town by morning," Koria said softly.

Gregory redistributed the weight of the shields while trying not to spill any of the metal fragments. "Which news? Of the fire, the burned man, or the speared one?"

"Or the duke-to-be coming down to look at it," added Eloise.

Endicott's head felt stuffed with sawdust. He was that tired. His forearms ached from swinging the hammer all day and then withstanding the impact of the wizard's spear. It seemed like they had smithed the shields a week ago, though it had only been a few hours. Yet he would rather have had to make two more shields than worry further about the gruesome events that had taken place in the alley. That he had a clear role to play going forward was his sole comfort. "We will have a good chance to uncover the truth at the Black Spear."

"Whose truth?" Koria's soft voice did not carry far into the darkness. "The truth for the murderer? The truth for the murdered? How about the truth for the crowd?"

"Dead is dead," said Eloise, her stern face shadowed and softened by her long hair.

"Even so, every person has a narrative," murmured Gregory.

"I hope not," said Endicott wearily. "I'm with the Lonely Wizard on this one. I want a single, objective truth."

Chapter Eleven

Optimist

"*There was one thing to which they gave no thought:*
The might and friends of Robert Endicott."

"I love that part!" exclaimed Conor. The only good thing about Conor's statement was that it signaled the end of his enthusiastic but horrific attempts at singing along. The grubby man had a hoarse, flat voice. Unlike the fool of childhood stories, Conor had yet to demonstrate some unexpected but heartwarming secret talent. Other than looking like Endicott's long-dead father.

Endicott did not join in the singing. He did not like his name in the song. He did not think he was quite the hero it made him out to be. He worried that if he did sing along in praise of himself, he might die of terminal irony.

Today the crowd in the Black Spear was less pugilistic but every bit as loud and pungent as it had been the last time Endicott had been there. He had not been sure the meeting would still be on, but he and Davyn had found Conor almost at once and on exactly the same bar stool. Conor accepted Davyn readily enough once the big man tipped a beer back with him. While they waited, Conor talked. His stories always started reasonably enough but rarely ended there as he regaled the two younger men with increasingly deranged tales of poisoned grain and elaborate conspiracies that went, as he was fond of repeating, "all the way to the top."

Endicott had his own conspiracy to get to the bottom of and was willing to let all manner of insane and irrational declarations go by if a few hours of patience would get him there. The older man's resemblance to his father failed this time to soften the young man's feelings. Homes and livelihoods had been destroyed in the fire, and people were dead. Endicott's tolerance was exhausted. Would an angry, impatient, intolerant Endicott fit in with the crowd at the Black Spear? Koria had thought so.

As usual she was right.

Taverns attract every kind of person, and Endicott's persona, "Robert," was known by Conor to be temperamental. Endicott looked over at Davyn, who was dressed in dirty, ripped clothes from the unclaimed items bin at the New School. The outfit was set off by a ripped leather hat with a loose chin flap that hung off the side of his round face like a losing bet. The big man somehow managed to keep smiling as he slumped on his barstool and listened to Conor's ravings, but Endicott knew Davyn was just as angry as he was. The world had begun to change for all of them on that terrible night. They had learned that terrible things could happen. But now with the arson attack and murders, a sinister pattern had emerged. Everyone had seen the protests over grain, but most had dismissed them as ephemeral and harmless. Even the assault on Syriol, as horrible as it was, could be rationalized as an isolated incident.

Perhaps that is just what we wanted to believe.

The protestors were not as harmless from up close, as Endicott's experimental heraldry had shown that day with Davyn. And as Jeyn Lindseth had implied, Syriol's experience was far from unique. Endicott wondered how many times he would have to be taught before he learned. Part of him, he recognized, did not want to learn some lessons. Part of him wanted to remain the eternal optimist.

Preserving his natural optimism had become a struggle, and innocence was a depleting commodity. His buoyancy had been jolted too many times. The murders in the alley were not even the most recent shocks. Just before leaving for the Black Spear, news had arrived that two men had died while attempting to burn down the Vercors registered seed office. One of the men had been beaten to death by a security guard. The other had leapt into the river to avoid capture and drowned. Apart from the crazy old lady detained on the night of the murders, the constables had no one to question, and the old lady had been no help, her hold on reality tenuous at best. The constabulary was jittery—fearful of what might come next and primed to descend on any suspect with overwhelming force.

That afternoon the protestors had set up again across from the Apprentice's Library. There were even more of them than before, audacious considering what had occurred at the registered seed office. They had the usual collection of signs about price, cost, and Nimrheal. The most off-putting had been new signs directed at the school. One, uncharacteristically literate, read:

"There can be no knowledge without sacrifice.

Knowledge belongs to the Empyrean, not man."

Others were even more hostile, threatening "innovators" with all manner of ghastly comeuppances from Nimrheal. One sign even invoked the old legend of Sir Seygis. It said,

"The Ninth Knight

Would eat YOU

Rather than the grain."

Everyone reacted differently to these new signs. Gerveault wanted to close the New School down for summer break even though it was still a week off. Bethyn agreed with him. The optimistic part of Endicott wanted to go down and debate with the protestors, but only Davyn had supported that idea. Heylor wanted to make up his own sign protesting mathematics and join the line. Gregory wanted to wade in and pluck out the original two bald protestors for questioning. Eloise argued that the signs constituted an explicit threat that called for immediate action to eliminate the danger. The chief constable and her crew tended to agree. They proposed arresting all the protestors then and there regardless of the violence that might ensue. Endicott demanded that they at least wait until he had attended the Black Spear meeting and learned more about who was behind the protests. Lord Brice sided with him, which had settled the matter for now. "Why do you care so much?" Bethyn had asked Endicott incredulously, as if she thought ignoring the protestors would make them go away. Evidently Endicott's heraldic dream meant nothing to her. Deleske acted as if he agreed with Bethyn, though he never said anything one way or another. He stayed in the Orchid with a book.

Endicott knew that answers had to be found and was determined that he and Davyn had a role to play in this. As they endured yet more foamy beer and flat singing, he thought again about the events that had led to Davyn of all people teaming up with him in the tavern of the Nimrheal cultists.

"Davyn will go with you, Robert." Those were not the words that Endicott had expected Koria to greet him with that morning.

What?

"To breakfast?" he asked.

"You know where!" She hit him with a pillow.

Endicott wrestled her and her pillow, finally gaining the high ground and holding it. "Why?" *he demanded, looking down at her head peeking out from under the pillow with which he held her in place.* "Davyn can't fight. He wouldn't fight even if he could. Gregory would be better, don't you think? Even Heylor would make more sense."

Heylor certainly wanted to go with him to the Black Spear. He had spent the better part of the previous day asking. But there was no way in Hati's Hell that Endicott was taking excitable, impulsive Heylor to a meeting where discretion was called for.

"Because you're angry and Davyn isn't."

"I'm not angry."

"Yes, you are. You don't know what's going on or why, and your response is anger." *Koria's green eyes had their own hard, angry look.* "You'll fit right in with the protestors."

Endicott's stomach sank. Is she right? *Memories of the dream, of Koria covered in frost and stabbed by the spear that broke Eloise's sword beat on his happiness every day. He could not live with the memory and fail to be angry. Or fail to do something about it.*

Yes, I am angry.

Being angry did not equate him to the protestors. How could it?

I am not ignorant. They are.

Personal criticisms had never had much an effect on Endicott, but he always took Koria seriously. Even so, it was time to move on. "Gregory should come with me." *He tried to smile.* "He has a cool head." *And a sharp sword.*

Koria looked back at him, unblinking. "No. Davyn will go. I've never seen you die in the presence of Davyn."

His stomach dropped again but not from fear of death. She had been heralding again! The intimation that Koria had seen him die with many of their other friends—possibly every other friend—was disturbing enough on its own. The implication that Koria continued to suffer heraldic dreams for his sake was worse.

This is what she does when I am inside the fence. She heralds.

It was an awful realization. And the end of the argument. Endicott was not going to defy a woman who suffered on his behalf, particularly Koria.

Davyn agreed to come with him on condition there would be no prejudicial violence on the part of the constabulary.

Endicott wondered how well the big man's pacifism would fare or how certain the promises of a frightened, angry constabulary would be if things went bad. Vice Constable Edwyn Perry had taken care to remind them how dangerous undercover operations could be.

"This is a bad idea," Edwyn said, shaking his head.

"All in all, I would rather be baking a cake," Davyn boomed.

Edwyn Perry's head tilted sideways on his long neck. He looked decidedly confused.

"It's a long story," said Endicott.

"Whatever. Look. We will have plainclothes constables right outside. I will be inside with a few others. We'll have your back. You'll have to be alone with them in the basement, but just blow your whistle and we'll be right down."

Davyn held the tiny whistle in his chubby palm and stared at it with a bemused expression.

"Don't hesitate." Edwyn looked off into some distant memory. "Listen. Things can happen fast in these types of situations. It doesn't matter who you are, how you are trained, or how smart you are. Things go wrong faster than you think they possibly could and in worse ways than you can imagine."

"Good pep talk!" Davyn boomed. "Hew, hew, hew. Any actual practical advice?"

"Look everyone in the eye, but not for too long." Edwyn looked Davyn in the eye for about three seconds before looking at Endicott. "Make it even shorter if the other guy looks angry. And remember, some of them will stink, and I mean reek. Others will be in poor physical or mental condition. Do not cringe away from them no matter what. Talk to them, but not too much. Keep it short if you can. Short and polite. But polite doesn't mean high talk as if you're visiting the duke or answering questions in one of your classes. Listen carefully, but don't react emotionally to what they say. Don't take any of it as a personal insult even if it feels pretty personal."

"Great." Davyn did not look great. His face was red. "Don't take anything personal. Short, polite, but not too high. Now I'm ready. Easy as mathematics. Got it. Why am I doing this again?"

"That's your best question so far, kid," Edwyn said flatly.

Endicott frowned at the vice constable and put a hand on Davyn's arm. "You don't have to do it. Maybe you shouldn't."

Koria is going to kill me.

"But you're going, Robert."

Endicott laughed softly. "I was always going."

"Why?"

"Because I need to know. Because this might get us some answers with less violence and mayhem than the constabulary will deliver if we don't."

Or because I'm frustrated and see a chance to do something? Anything. Because I see a chance to take control?

Because my heraldic dream demands it.

Edwyn Perry paused as he adjusted his nightstick inside his grubby clothes. "We are as violent as we need to be to keep people safe. No more than that."

Endicott and Davyn both looked at the thick-bodied, long-necked man. In addition to the nightstick strapped to the inside of his heavy coat, he had a knife hidden in his left boot and heavy iron knuckles in his right pants pocket.

Violence is the last refuge of the ignorant.

"Right. Violence only when strictly necessary." Davyn raised an eyebrow with the same skepticism that Endicott felt. "Any other advice, constable?"

"Don't go."

But they had to go. Davyn was still a pacifist, and Endicott hoped he could remain an optimist. Until the issue was decided, he would act like he was.

"You ain't looking so good, young Robert. What's the doings in your head?"

Conor's croaking voice pulled Endicott away from his memories. "I was just thinking."

Conor took another long swig of his beer, looking at Endicott over the rim of his stein. "Bout what?"

About arresting you and all your friends. About throwing you in jail and forgetting about you.

"My dad. He's dead." Endicott had no idea why he had mentioned his father. He had needed to say something, and that was what came out.

Conor put a hand on his shoulder, his eyes suddenly moist. "How did he die?"

"I don't know." Endicott was going to leave it there, but both Conor and Davyn were staring at him. Conor wore an uncharacteristic expression of patience and compassion. Davyn's expression was unreadable. "It was on the farm. I was young. Someone told me recently that my father died from carelessness."

"Don't you believe it, young Robert!" Conor slammed his beer stein down. He was red in the face now. Endicott had struck a nerve. "It was those rich farmers. Same as with me. They got him, they did, and they blamed it on him. That's the way of it, all right. He did their doings, and when their doings did him, they went and called it carelessness. They did it. Their doings. They were the careless. Them and their doings. They killed your father. Murderers."

Endicott kept his expression level through Conor's wild, escalating rant, and he knew better than to ask who "they" were. Conor's abrupt shift in mood was not out of character and made Endicott consider the morality of the situation. Conor was his only way of accessing the cult of Nimrheal, if it existed, which meant he wanted Conor to remain sympathetic to him. But going along with Conor's paranoia seemed wrong. The falseness made Endicott feel nauseated.

Conor patted Endicott's shoulder, once again misreading him. "We will avenge him, Robert," he said in a calmer tone. "We'll make it right. Those pot-lickers took my daughters, you know, and they took your dad. We'll make it right." He drained the last of his beer, tilting his head to the left and then to the right as he contemplated the undeniable emptiness of the cup. "Let's go."

Endicott caught Vice Constable Perry's eyes as he stood up. Perry was resting his head sideways on a table not far away as if drunk. He had a grease smudge across his nose and right cheekbone, and his belt was made of dirty twine. It was a convincing look.

Conor led Davyn and Endicott through a swinging door into the backroom of the bar. The barmaid said nothing as they passed her. She was probably glad to see the back of them. Conor managed a nearly straight line around barrels and boxes of bottles until he came upon a set of stairs going down. Instead of descending, he suddenly stopped, and Davyn, who was close behind, could not avoid colliding with the old man's back.

"Almost forgot," Conor said and turned right, away from the stairs towards another door.

"Sorry for bumping into you," boomed Davyn. "I thought we were going downstairs!" Davyn practically roared the last sentence.

Will Perry hear that? Over the clink of bottles, the crude scrape of knives on plates, the intractable voices of the dogmatic, the guffaws of the drunk, and the loud declarations of the ignorant? Endicott guessed that he would not.

Conor winced. Davyn had practically yelled into his ear. "Change of … vew-voo…new—" Conor explained, fumbling with the unaccustomed word.

"Venue?" Davyn bellowed into his other ear.

"Venue! Change of venue." said Conor. He opened the small door and led Endicott and Davyn down a narrow hall to yet another door. This led out the back and along a high fence to a storage shed. A man stood there in the shadows. He opened a door in the fence for them through which they exited to an alley. Endicott looked left and right, disoriented now, trying to make out the street where the troop of constables, along with Eloise and Gregory, were supposedly watching the Black Spear. He saw only more shadows.

We needed more constables.

"This way," Conor waved to them. Both Endicott and Davyn had been lagging behind, hoping to be able to signal someone surreptitiously. It was not to be. Conor walked across the alley towards a nondescript wooden door. It opened into darkness immediately after he knocked on it, and they proceeded inside. Endicott got one good look at Davyn as they passed into the shadows: the big man's eyes were huge with fear.

We aren't in the building we're supposed to be in. No one knows where we are. I am proven to be an optimist again. Or a fool.

Chapter Twelve.
Call Me Nimrheal

THEY STEPPED OUT OF THE DARKNESS THROUGH ANOTHER DOOR INTO A LARGE, SURprisingly well-lit room crowded with people of every description, though by their cloth mostly poor. Endicott could not immediately take stock of everyone, but he quickly observed about as many women as men and noted that a few of the men were armed with swords. He saw one reflection off chain mail somewhere in the crowd. A central space had been carved out from shelves and wooden crates, which were scattered out from that space in every direction.

A warehouse.

A wheelbarrow was parked near the door they had come through. Two short-handled shovels rested in it, their handles hanging off the end. There were more barrels and crates than he had ever seen anywhere before. A few of the barrels had been rolled out and used as platforms for serving food and drinks. The aromas of bacon and fresh bread filled the air, almost obscuring the less welcome odor of dozens of unwashed bodies.

"Bacon!" Davyn boomed, stepping eagerly around Conor and making for the nearest barrel top.

Endicott shook his head and shared a smile with Conor. A short, thin, brown-haired woman in a long wool skirt and shawl approached them. "Conor Karryk! I am glad to see you after last night." She looked at Endicott with soft, liquid, brown eyes. There weren't many lines around those big brown eyes. Endicott guessed she might be in her late twenties. "And you brought friends. Is this the young man you mentioned?"

Conor beamed, nodding as if proud of his recruit, making a drunk's best effort to conceal his inebriation behind gentility. "Robert, yes. Pot-lickers killed his dad."

That's not what I said!

Endicott held out his hand. "Robert Height."

The lean woman's brows furrowed in sympathy. "Your dad? Robert, I am sooo sorry to hear that." She surprised Endicott by stepping forward and hugging him. "It's okay." She had a very soothing voice. It was similar to the voice Endicott used on the farm when speaking to a skittish horse. She was, except for her eyes, plain-looking. Her kindness was unexpected. "You're with friends now. I'm Cyara Daere."

"And I am Davyn!" came a loud voice from behind her. He held out one slightly oily hand, then saw its sheen of bacon grease and quickly rubbed it against his pants before offering it again. Cyara took the large, soft hand in both of hers.

"Who do we have to thank for the food?" asked Endicott.

Cyara Daere glanced around. "It was sponsored by one of our longstanding members. We have found that people feel more comfortable meeting and talking if they are warm and have food. Not everyone here feels accepted in society, so we have created our own feeling of inclusiveness."

What is really going on here?

So far the meeting was not at all what Endicott had expected. He caught Davyn's eye and was rewarded with rapidly widened eyes in a signal that portended *something*, but like so many things in the room, exactly what it meant was unclear.

"That is very sensible, Cyara. Is it the same sponsor at every meeting?"

"About half of the time. I don't see him here yet, but when Ter gets here, I'll introduce you.

The name almost made Endicott jump. Conor had mentioned Ter, and Endicott again wondered if Ter could be Terwynn, the agent of Lord Glynnis that he and his uncle had seen at the Nyhmes Registered Seed Office. The agent, he recalled, who had stomped off angrily when Aeres Angelicus had refused Lord Glynnis's offer to purchase her business.

If you can't have it, destroy it?

Now all we need is to find Froth. Or Alfrothul Gudmund of Armadale? If I am right, our chief conspirators will then be here!

A new thought put a chill on Endicott's excitement.

Will Terwynn remember me?

"I should show my appreciation of the food," Endicott muttered by way of extracting himself from Cyara Daere and Conor. He approached a barrel topped by a heaping platter of shortbread cookies. He ate one slowly and looked around. While he nibbled, a well-groomed man stepped around him. He was only a few years older than Endicott but wore a rich-looking blue tunic and seemed to take exaggerated care to avoid coming near Endicott. He placed his cookies on a linen handkerchief and stepped fastidiously away.

A dark-haired, middle-aged woman in a motley grayish dress approached and fumbled absently with the cookie plate. Looking closer, Endicott saw that her dress was made of a great many small pieces of cloth—rags in fact—that had been haphazardly assembled into one long, lumpy garment.

It's probably warm at least.

Then it struck him. He knew this woman! He had seen her protesting earlier in the day from across the ring road. She had held one of the more disturbing signs. It read:

"The pain of knowledge is like the pain of birth,

except there is no life after."

He nodded to himself. He was in the right place.

Endicott took a vanishingly small bite of cookie and scrutinized the other guests. A tall, heavyset man at the next barrel also looked familiar. He had been there protesting as well. His sign had been even more disturbing than the grayish woman's. "Death is the antidote to discovery," it had read.

Are all the protesters here? I wonder where they left their signs.

On the far side of the room he saw one of the bald men. He craned his neck and saw the lantern light reflecting off *two* bald heads. He walked slowly in their direction, pausing at another barrel. This one had no platter, just someone's handkerchief and an abandoned cookie.

"Why are you following me around?"

Am I discovered?

Endicott's heart pounded and he whirled round in alarm. It was the well-groomed shortbread snob! "What?" Endicott said, confused and relieved in equal measure.

"You keep following me. H-how can I eat my cookies with the likes of you practically attached to me?"

Endicott could see that the fellow was agitated. "Go ahead and enjoy your cookie," he said as normally as he could. "There's plenty of room here."

Shortbread's brows furrowed in a short, rapid contractions. "But *you're* here!"

Endicott ignored him and surveyed the room again.

Is everyone here an idiot?

He had expected ignorant. He had expected volatile. *This* was worse. Endicott considered Conor and his rapid changes in mood, his proclivity to rant. He had forgotten that Conor had been barely comprehensible when they had first met in Nyhmes, that the man who looked so much like his father had not only been socially unviable but clearly mentally ill then. And that Conor could be so again. Cyara Daere's solicitousness was well-placed. Her hug and big moist eyes made better sense if she thought that Endicott might be emotionally unbalanced too.

What next?

He reacquired his sight line on the bald men. They were indeed the same two who had started the protests across from the Apprentice's Library. They were talking with someone else near a stack of crates, an enormous, heavyset man who towered head and shoulders above them. Today the bald men wore swords on their hips, and their faces were grossly animated as they spoke, like those of stage actors, though not very good ones. Endicott could see every turn and twist of their sneering expressions from across the room. He did not need to hear their words to know they were whining about the New School and its innovations. Were they also mentally unbalanced, or were they the most cynical of agents, preying on the troubled minds of the most vulnerable?

How about both?

Endicott turned to the dainty snob again and stepped back, raising his hands placatingly. "I'm sorry. The barrel is all yours." Only a few seconds had passed since Shortbread had griped at him. There was no way this man could be anyone's agent. Endicott wended his way slowly through the crowd, taking care not to jostle or disturb anyone.

"Come and join us, young fella."

The speaker was a short, dumpy-looking, gray-haired man. He was standing at another barrel with a thin man in a purple hat. A bacon-filled skillet dominated their barrel top. Endicott nodded to them and reached out a finger to touch the massive iron pan.

Still hot.

"Go ahead, have some. Don't let Reynald bother you none," he added softly, gesturing to the cookie snob, who continued to stare at Endicott from his barrel.

Endicott carefully fished out a piece of crisp bacon, trying not to scatter grease on himself. "Where'd this come from?"

"Next door probably," said the dumpy man.

Endicott chewed on the bacon. "It's pretty good!"

Purple Hat slapped his pant leg with his hand. "Hah. Usually we only get some biscuits, but this meeting's gonna be special."

"Why is that?" asked Endicott, licking his thumb and index finger.

What do you know?

"Don't know," said Purple Hat, reaching for a piece of bacon. "Can't say that we care that much." He winked at Endicott. "Don't tell on us."

"Why are you here, then?" Endicott tried to say it softly, but it came out a little more aggressively than he intended.

Dumpy frowned. "Why not? Friends here. Food's here. Do we need any more reason for our doings than that?"

"Do your doings always have reasons and make sense to you?" added Purple Hat.

"Yes, they do," Endicott responded automatically and instantly regretted not thinking before he spoke. They both looked at him skeptically, though still in a friendly enough way. He thought about all the things he had seen that had surprised him, including these two fellows. They did not seem crazy at all. Or even volatile.

"Truthfully," Endicott responded, smiling sheepishly, "there seems to be an endless list of people, interactions, and things that I don't understand. It can be quite frustrating."

"Well!" exclaimed Dumpy. "You came to the right place, then."

Excellent.

"To get answers?" Endicott said.

"No!" Dumpy and Purple Hat both stared at him like he was crazy. Endicott nodded to them with what he hoped was a dubious expression and moved on, working his way back to where he started.

What is going on here? Every time Endicott tried to puzzle out the situation, complexity reared its baffling head.

Davyn, Conor, and Cyara Daere were still talking. "—Oh no, Davyn, everyone gets a chance to speak at our meetings, and we encourage everyone to say what's on their minds. All are heard here." Cyara Daere smiled enigmatically at the big man. "As today is your first meeting, you and Robert will *have* to speak."

A trickle of sweat ran down Davyn's forehead, missing his right eye by a fraction of an inch. His eyes were huger than ever now. Endicott cut in. "You are the leader here, Cyara. What are your goals?"

Cyara laughed and shook her head. "There are no leaders here, Robert. We don't want any. I am just helping out."

"Just helping out?" Endicott did not feel he needed to tread as carefully around Cyara as the others he had spoken to. He also suspected she had the answers that others lacked. "Without leadership, entropy has free reign and no purpose can be served. These cookies did not get here without some effort. This group did not put itself together without a plan. I can see you played a part in that, Cyara."

"Where *do* you come from, Robert Height?" Cyara's smile was not completely gone, but she was watching Endicott more sharply than before. "*Entropy*. I haven't heard talk of entropy in quite a long time." She reached out and gently touched his arm. "Yes, I help organize the meetings, but I don't want to be a leader. I would go so far as to say I don't want there to be a leader here at all."

"Why not?" Endicott took in Davyn and Conor standing on either side of Cyara. Their reactions were in sharp contrast. Conor was smiling widely like the cat that brought in the fat mouse, and he kept smiling as he turned his head from Cyara to Endicott and back. Davyn was less pleased. The big man was subtly shaking his head. His hairline was damp with perspiration.

Davyn wants me to shut my big mouth.

Endicott could not do that. He could no more stop himself from indulging his curiosity than Davyn could stop himself from eating another cookie. The big man was naturally curious himself, but he had priorities.

Cyara also clearly had a mind of her own. She took no umbrage at Endicott's question, only smiled enigmatically and spoke softly. "A leader would imply an external goal."

"And you have no goals? That is ... interesting, Cyara, and if true it would be truly unique. Please tell me what is really going on? Why am I here?"

Both Cyara Daere and Conor smiled. "You'll see soon, young Robert," said Conor with patronizing and exaggerated satisfaction. "It's about to start."

"Everyone needs to be heard, Robert." Cyara Daere's hand was on his shoulder. She was trying to comfort him again. "Everyone needs help sometimes."

Cyara's compassion still confounded Endicott. "I thought this was about Nimrheal."

"Nimrheal?" she frowned.

"Yes," Endicott persisted. "This is the cu—group that worships Nimrheal."

"No," Cyara Daere sighed. "Oh, no, not at all. This group is about more than one thing, Robert. It is more imp—"

"Let us begin, Cyara!" called a new speaker from the far side the warehouse. Endicott remembered that arrogant voice. It was Terwynn. In a frilly white shirt, a wide black belt, and a hat with a feather in it, he strode confidently across the open center of the room, smiling beneficently. This was not the sour-faced would-be buyer Endicott remembered from the registered seed office. He was just as silly-looking in his frilly white shirt and out-of-place headgear, but the foiled, sullen, supercilious agent had been replaced by a happy and condescendingly generous, even supercilious master of ceremonies. He had found his room full of fools to feel superior to.

"Let us begin before we run out of bacon and cookies."

"This is not what I expected at all," Endicott muttered to Davyn under his breath.

"Let us count the ways," Davyn replied, eyes still wide, sweat still running down his florid face.

Terwynn spun theatrically in the center of the room, one arm outstretched. "The product of man's conceit, Nimrheal fights to defeat."

"The demon comes for a reason!" someone yelled in a thick, country accent from across the room. No one else spoke. Terwynn's dramatics seemed to have fallen a bit flat.

"Yes, he does, my friends, yes, indeed, he does," said Terwynn, grinning fiercely, not put off by the crowd's tepid response.

As if a demon coming would be a good thing. As if Nimrheal attended clown shows.

"He came just two nights ago and killed two from the New School. They were wizards, they were grain-makers, and he mounted them up on his spear of black!

He smashed the engines of evil a month ago. There are eight stitches, one for each of the Knights, and none of them are meant to be made by a machine! He is coming again and very soon to punish more who sin against Elysium."

"Fer a reason!" someone else yelled.

Cyara Daere walked out and stood beside Terwynn, her expression uncharacteristically closed. She waited until the yelling subsided and held a hand sideways towards Terwynn. "Let us thank Lord Terwynn for his support of this group. Thank you for the place to meet and the food to eat, Lord Terwynn."

There was clapping, some of it wildly enthusiastic, some weak and unconvincing. It was a strangely uneven crowd.

Terwynn smiled and slowly ceded the center of the room. Endicott watched to see where he went, wondering if he would stand with the bald men. He did not. Terwynn ended his short, smiling journey only a few feet away from Shortbread, who this time seemed unperturbed by another's close proximity.

Cyara Daere continued. "For we all need a place to speak, we all need a place to be heard." Cyara motioned for a short young man to come out of the crowd. He was about Endicott's age and carried a dog-eared, hardback notebook. There was something vaguely familiar about him.

"And what you say shall be recorded," Cyara continued in her soothing voice. "You know you will have been heard. Evyn will take the minutes of our meeting."

Evyn opened his book on an empty barrel top and began writing at once. Endicott caught his eye, and the young man's eyes widened as if he was afraid.

Cyara scanned the crowd. There were at least a hundred people in the room. "Our first order of business, as always, is to welcome new members and hear their stories. There are quite a few fresh faces today. We are not surprised, are we? The times are tough. It is easy to feel lost, to *become* lost in an ever-thickening forest of the new. We must help each other out of those woods. One of the new young men asked me why we are here. It is to speak and to hear. To listen and share. So let us listen to each other and thereby find our way through the wild new woods of today together. Who wants to go first?"

The room was so silent that Endicott could hear the candles sputtering in the lamps closest to him.

The awkward silence persisted. Cyara would have to pick someone. Davyn tried to hide behind Endicott, but it was like a bull trying to hide behind cat. He stuck out everywhere. Cyara smiled and passed them over. "Alannah. Come forward. Tell us your story."

A dark-haired woman slowly worked her way through the crowd and shyly took the center of the room. She was the woman with the dress made of rags, the protestor! Cyara returned to stand near Endicott.

Alannah hesitated, her face strangely blank. "You want me to speak?" She uttered this in the dullest, most monotonic voice Endicott thought he had ever heard.

Cyara nodded encouragingly. "Just say what brought you here, Alannah."

"My baby died."

Alannah said it like Endicott might have said he had dropped his pencil, except he knew he would have spoken with more interest about his pencil.

"And how did that make you feel, Alannah?" Cyara asked softly, but the room was quiet enough to make every word audible.

"Don't know," Alannah said in her strange, affectless voice. "Bad, I guess."

"It was the bad grain, the new grain!" called a voice from across the room. Terwynn's voice.

Alannah shrugged with all the subtlety of the truly uncaring, which is to say, barely at all. "Suppose. Lost my job. Freyla Loche said I was too slow on the new machines. I was slow. Had nowhere to go."

"That bitch!" It was yelled by Terwynn, but not only by Terwynn. "Nimrheal take her and her store!" The shouts and protests went on.

Another voice called out, "Who are you?" Endicott could not tell who called it. It may have been Terwynn.

Cyara held up a hand. "Let Alannah speak, please."

Alannah stood stock-still for a long moment. A few voices continued to call out sporadically. "Tell us," some said, while others just repeated, "Nimrheal!"

Alannah's words were not to be rushed. When they came, they came slowly and with inhumanely level tones. "Who am I? I am sad."

Alannah looked down at her grubby, unshod feet. "I am Nimrheal."

Nimrheal?

Endicott's heart pounded. He had seen and heard enough to build his own story of Alannah and what was going on with her at this meeting.

How can they use her like this? His teeth ground and his neck grew tense.

He felt deeply sorry for Alannah. He believed her of course. He believed that *she* believed at least. He believed that she was hurting, that she was so ruined by the loss of her baby that she had gone someplace beyond emotion, and that these people were taking advantage of her helpless condition, filling the void in her reason with their own purposes. Instead of helping her, they were manipulating her. Endicott's hands shook with rage.

"Robert." It was Cyara, whispering. She had crept close to him while he had been engrossed by Alannah. "Be calm. She is *not* Nimrheal."

Endicott looked incredulously at Cyara, more confused than ever.

Is this or isn't this the Nimrheal cult?

Terwynn clearly wanted it to be, for his own reasons. Cyara denied it. He wanted to ask her what was really going on, but she promptly left his side again and approached Alannah at the center of the room. She spoke soothingly, yet loudly enough to be heard by the room, addressing the crowd as much as she did the melancholy woman. "Thank you, Alannah. Remember everyone, we are here to listen, not to tell." Cyara turned from the room and held Alannah's limp hands. "We are here for you, Alannah. You are not alone. You are heard," she told her, but still meaning to be heard by all.

Alannah let Cyara hold her hands for a moment, but as soon as Cyara released them, those hands fell back limp and dead at her side. She shuffled off to the far side of the room, the sounds of her passing as muted as her words had been. Cyara sighed, watching her. Then she placidly scanned the room again. After a moment she settled on someone. "Dylan, will you please come and speak to us now?"

Dylan turned out to be one of the bigger men Endicott had spotted earlier. He was not quite a giant, being a couple of inches shy of Eloise's height, but he was tall and muscular, and he looked mean.

"Don't call me Dylan," he said aggressively, eyes bulging. "Call me Nimrheal."

Here we go.

"I'm glad that bitch Freyla Loche's machines got smashed! You heard what she did to Alannah. She might as well a killed her baby outright!"

The timing and causal relationship sounded more than dubious to Endicott, but he felt that asking clarifying questions might be unwelcome.

Dylan's rant continued. "I am Nimrheal all right. It's that or let them shrink me too! Like her baby! They are always trying to shrink me."

"It's that grain!" someone yelled. Endicott thought this might again have been Terwynn who, he realized, was about as subtle as a sledgehammer.

"You shut up!" Dylan yelled back. He clutched his head with both hands. "And stop following me. Someone's always following me. Stop it."

Dylan let go of his head and pointed aggressively at the crowd. "I won't be changed. Everything is changing! I don't want to be changed! Who gave them permission to change things? Who?"

He lowered his finger and stopped talking for a moment. When he started up again, his head was lowered. "Why are we so arrogant? Do we consider what we lose when we change things? It's not so great now. If it's not so great, why did we do it in the first place? Do we care what we lost? The bread's not the same. The beer's not the same. Farms aren't the same. Family's not the same. It's a war on all things old! New equipment's changing the doings. Isn't it sad the doings can't be the same? Why can't they be the same? Why can't I be the same? I wish Nimrheal was here. I wish *I* was Nimrheal."

This time no one yelled. Dylan was sobbing now.

Cyara walked towards Dylan but stopped several steps short of him. She did not fold him into a hug as she had Endicott, but her red face and eyes spoke her feelings well enough. "Thank you, Dylan. You have been heard."

Heard, but not necessarily understood.

Cyara did not move while Dylan looked around him as if dazed and then shuffled out of the center of the room. She watched him until he was settled on the edge of the crowd and then turned to Endicott and Davyn. "We have two other newcomers. Robert and Davyn. Who wants to go first?"

Davyn, who was still unsuccessfully attempting to hide behind Endicott, gave him a shove towards Cyara. Endicott pursed his lips, shook his head, and walked towards her with slow, measured steps. As he walked, he debated fiercely with himself about what he should say.

He had been looking for a chance to address the protestors since he had first seen them. His rage at their unreason demanded expression, but being asked to speak now gave the young man pause. More than anything he wanted to demand an answer to the question of why they were doing this, but he was no longer certain there was any single reason in the room. It was clear that the cult was made up of people with a wide variety of motivations and personal situations. He was very certain that some, like Terwynn, were simply out to manipulate others for their own advantage. He suspected that others had rational motives of their own, though he could not fathom what those might be. By their own admission, at least a few, perhaps many, were there only for food and company. And still more were there because they were truly unwell. There was no single, simple answer to the question of why.

Can I reach them? Should I try? What should I say?

The third from last refuge of the incompetent is not even trying.

I must try. I must be as honest as the circumstances allow.

He had wanted to talk to the protestors often enough before. He could not, at last, refuse.

"My name is Robert Height. I come from a farm originally. I have heard your frustration, and I want to tell you that ..."

That you are a pack of fools. That you need to grow up, enlarge your horizons, let go of your fears and prejudices, and stop trying to enslave everyone else with them as you have enslaved yourselves. You are nothing like me, and so I really have nothing for you but scorn.

It would have been a short speech if Endicott's anger was all that he had, if the anxiety and terror from his heraldic dream were all that defined him. Part of him *was* angry and wanted to hang on to that simple, pure anger, to that simplistic reduction of the people around him. But another part of him felt very differently. He often felt two things at once, and now, though he was full of hate and disgust, he also felt sympathy and compassion. The part of him that loved, and loved to express his love, felt sick at his anger. That part told him that Koria might have a point. Was he like the protestors? Could he have been one in different circumstances? Was he not exercising his own heedless initiative in coming here to oppose, to expose, them?

Eight Knights, I hope I am not like them.

"… I am just like you. I am also frustrated. I am also angry." Endicott saw Conor nodding and others looking on with interest or sympathy. "Sometimes I am afraid of what I might do with that rage."

I am not confused like *them. I am confused* by *them. Confused enough.*

"I am confused. Like you."

Endicott took a breath and looked around the room. He saw Evyn taking down his speech in his tattered book. He met the eyes of Conor, saw the big encouraging nod from Cyara Daere, the attenuated listlessness of Alannah, the attentive expressions of Purple Hat and Dumpy, and others he could not fully read but hoped were receptive.

"And why shouldn't I be angry and confused? The world has changed. It started with both my parents dying. I didn't need *that* change, I can tell you. The world keeps changing. People do things that I don't understand for reasons I don't respect. I've listened to what's been said. I hear not just anger but fear also. Fear of the future, fear of what is lost and fear of what is coming."

He saw again the image of Koria covered in frost. *I do fear what is coming.*

"I am also afraid."

Endicott paused, struggling to set aside the unwelcome intrusion of the heraldic dream.

I must change it.

"Here I am, not quite nineteen years old, and like you I am worried about my future. How am I different from you? We are all human beings in a world where the future is struggling to emerge from the past. What about *our* future? Everyone at every age wants to think about their future and imagine that it is alive with promise, friendship, and with purpose. At eighteen years old this matters, at fifty-five this matters. We, every one of us, need a purpose. Without it we lack hope. Without purpose we are lost in the woods. But what should our purpose be? What?"

Endicott looked around the room again. He saw heads nodding along with him. Cyara's big brown eyes were locked on him. They were expecting something, a catharsis.

What is the message?

The cloaked figure from his dream could not be Nimrheal, but he looked like Nimrheal, and he acted in Nimrheal's stead.

I must kill the idea of Nimrheal.

"I have heard some here say that they are Nimrheal. It is a call to the past." Endicott nodded, and a few nodded with him. "It is a call to stability." He nodded again, and a few more of them nodded. "It is a call to certainty." He nodded, and still more nodded with him.

"And maybe I understand it. I am going to say something now about that. Will you be patient with me?"

Endicott saw Davyn then. The big man mouthed "no" to him, shaking his head silently, eyes big.

Yes.

"Some of you say that you are Nimrheal. I invite you to consider something else. Consider that while we may feel fear and uncertainty, what we do in response to those feelings is the critical question. We cannot make the oppression of others our purpose. Our purpose cannot be the destruction of others, of their goals, their hopes, or their dreams of a better future."

A few in the crowd frowned, but Cyara Daere and Conor kept nodding encouragingly.

"Our hope cannot be a forced yesterday for everyone else. We must strive for a better, freer future. Nimrheal killed invention not because invention was wrong. Nimrheal was a demon who killed what is good and best in us. This happened for all recorded history right up to the end of the Methueyn War. Some say that there is no justice without crime, and so Nimrheal must have been an agent of justice who redressed evil. This is not true. Nimrheal was a demon, not an angel. Any action of his must be ethically inverse."

Endicott raised his voice to emphasize his next words. "Nimrheal was not punishing evil, he was suppressing good." Now he brought the volume of his voice lower, almost to a whisper, hoping to pull the audience along with him. "We used to know this back when the sacrifice was so obvious." Surprised and happy that they were still listening, Endicott continued in a more normal tone, "But now we learn new things easily and cheaply and we wonder at it because we are used to a history of paying for every innovation. But just because a price was paid does not mean we owed a debt."

A murmur started to rise, but Cyara Daere put her hands up and called, "Let him finish." Evyn kept writing.

"What about the misfortunes of us in this room? Have we done wrong to deserve them? Did Alannah do something wrong, and so her baby died? Did Conor do something wrong? What did I do that my parents should die? Nothing. We have been confusing punishment with crime, both Nimrheal's and the misfortunes that have befallen each of us. You are not punished because horrible things have happened to you! You aren't lost in the woods because you did something wrong! It is easy, too easy, to think that all that happened because of some evil other. Sometimes terrible things simply happen and there is no cosmic justice behind them. Let's not turn our misfortunes and our fears of an uncertain future into a yoke to oppress ourselves or others."

Endicott caught Terwynn's eyes locked on his. Lord Glynnis's agent was frowning, perplexed, suspicious. Endicott wondered if he was starting to remember that they had met before, and worse, where and when. He raised his voice, hoping there would be time to finish the argument he had started.

"Freyla Loche is one of us. She is a hardworking member of this community. She employs people here. And yet we speak poorly of her. And yet someone—possibly someone in this room—tried to destroy her hard-earned business. Is that what we are? Do we only feel good destroying what others have created? How does that help us? How does it help anyone? Absent the abuser, do we abuse? Absent the devil, do we do his work? We cannot go back in time; we cannot make tomorrow a retrograde yesterday. Time only marches in one direction, and no matter our fears, we too must march in that direction. People here have said, *I am Nimrheal*. I tell you now, that I am *not* Nimrheal. I want to be better. I am *not* Robert Height either. I am Robert Endicott!"

Endicott had hoped his speech would be considered calmly. He hoped he might have gotten through to some of those in the room, that even if they could not agree with what he said now, they might think about it later. He hoped there would be no violent storm with him at its center. He expected an impassioned response but hoped for a reasoned one as well. He was still optimistic. But he also wanted to live out the night, so in the silent and still seconds at the end of his speech, he calmly but quickly pulled out his whistle and blew it as hard as he could.

Will anyone hear it where we are now?

Splughhhrrh.

The whistle did not whistle. It was a dud. The room exploded.

Chapter Thirteen
The Fry Pan

Terwynn screamed, "He's one of them! Grab him!" His words barely rose above the other screams of "Nimrheal fuck you, Robert Height!"—apparently many had taken his self-identification as Robert Endicott in the same metaphorical vein as they employed in calling themselves Nimrheal—or the shorter but no less eloquent, "Fuck you!", and many variations on the same theme that seemed to sum up what was in the offing. The crowd closed on Endicott.

"No!" It was Conor's voice. "He fought with me against 'em!"

The crowd ignored the old man, and a sea of hands grabbed at Endicott, jostling, scrabbling, and scratching.

"Stop!" This time it was Cyara. "We don't hurt each other for speaking here. Let him go!"

They *did* stop. For a long moment, no one moved. Endicott was stuck, unable to move an inch in the now-paused press of hostility, unhurt for the moment but trapped by the mob. His right leg was jammed painfully against a barrel. Oddly enough a big pan of fragrant bacon sat undisturbed on the barrel, its long, iron handle poking into Endicott's hip.

He had never even considered fighting after the whistle failed. He had no weapons on him, and applying dynamics was out of the question; there was no way he was going to indiscriminately burn everyone in the room. He might have tried the whistle again, but it had fallen somewhere and was likely crushed underfoot by now. He also wondered if his words might have gotten through to some of those who heard them. Angry as he had been at times, he did not want to raise a hand when words might be stronger. But now, he reflected, it was probably too late. Without dynamics there was nothing he could do with this small sea of bodies all around him.

"Let him go!"

Thank you, Cyara.

Like a slavering guard dog hauled short from mauling an intruder, the crowd reluctantly stepped back a pace and then another. Cyara Daere and Conor pressed through. Conor came and stood beside Endicott. He put his arm around his shoulders and glared at the mob. "I don't agree with everything Robert said here today, but it sure does makes me think. It makes me think on my doings. That ain't bad. Sometimes I'm not sure in my own head, so it ain't bad to think."

Conor hit his forehead with the palm of his hand. "Robert's one of us. He fought them pot-lickers at Nyhmes. By my side he was and took injury there. I say leave him be!"

Oh, Conor.

"I saw him there as well." Terwynn stepped forward, face haughty. "I'd forgotten him until now. He was there, all right. Fighting on the *other* side. He was one of the leaders. He held the shield for Aeres Angelicus. I heard his name. He's called the Elevator Baron of Bron. He *is* Robert Endicott!"

WWHHeeeeeeeeee! WHEEEEeeeeeeee! WHEEEEeeeeeeee!

About Knights-damned time!

It was Davyn's whistle, but unlike Endicott's, it actually produced the loud, piercing sound intended. Endicott could not see Davyn, but he could just imagine what had happened: his big friend fumbling around for the whistle in the voluminous pockets of the lost-and-found-bin jacket he wore, juggling the tiny thing in his big hands, and finally blowing it.

The sound produced a startled silence. Endicott leapt into it, shouldering a space from the slackening crowd for himself. "I *am* Robert Endicott. Terwynn *did* see me there, but I *saw* him too. He was negotiating to buy the registered seed office for Lord Glynnis. Aeres refused, so now he's trying to destroy the project. He isn't trying to help you. He's a shill. He's using you to make money for himself!"

With a roar Terwynn lunged at Endicott, but the younger man was much stronger and even angrier. He slapped Terwynn's hands aside and pushed him away. There was a tearing sound, and Lord Glynnis's supercilious agent stumbled back into the crowd, his face red and one of his frilly sleeves ripped the entire length of the arm.

The mob heaved uncertainly, a confused, seething mass of shouts and gesticulations. Conor, who had stepped to one side after hearing Terwynn's story, was hitting his own face with the palm of his hand, but harder this time, and repeatedly. Cyara was staring at Endicott in shock. Evyn was still scribbling madly, despite being jostled repeatedly by the press of bodies moving in chaos.

WHEEEEeeeeeeee! WHEEEEeeeeeeee!

Davyn's whistle tore the air again, but someone lunged at him and the big man stumbled and swallowed the thing. He staggered back, choking.

Whesplurgh!

"He is liar!" roared one of the bald, stocky men in his thick accent, pointing at Endicott. "We'll beat the truth out of him!" He stepped forward and began drawing his sword.

Cyara rallied from her shock. "No one beats anyone here!"

His bald, stocky companion pushed Cyara roughly, and she stumbled backwards into the crowd. This was too much for Endicott. His heart leapt, and without thinking, he grabbed the heavy iron bacon pan and swung it, bacon-outwards, at the thug who had struck Cyara.

Gong! Glahhr!

Bacon, grease, and pan connected ferociously, and as a unit, with the man's rotund head, knocking him heels over cartwheeling head to the ground. His sword clattered to the floor. The other bald man came on, lunging with his sword. Endicott turned the blade aside with the pan and tried to step back, but he stumbled over Purple Hat, who was arguing with someone else behind him. The swordsman saw his opportunity and rushed forward, sword raised for an overhead strike, but stopped short with a puzzled look on his fat face. Something had caught hold of his foot. It was Cyara. She had him by the ankle in a surprisingly strong grip.

Gong! Glahhr!

Endicott struck him in the face with the pan before the swordsman could kick Cyara loose. As his attacker fell back, Endicott looked for Cyara, but she was hidden by a shift in the crowd. Then he saw Davyn. His big friend was surrounded by a group of people who were trying to help him cough out the whistle. Endicott almost laughed and was about to return to the two bald protestors when he was savagely struck on the temple by a blow he did not see. He staggered sideways, falling towards the grimy floor but was pulled up, dizzy and nauseous, by the massive left hand of some gigantic man. It was the fellow who had been talking to the two bald assailants. There was something familiar about him. He was young, only a few years older than Endicott, but anger had aged him. His eyes were thickly hooded, and he breathed in honking gasps through his mouth. He reached down with his free arm and pulled Endicott's chain out of his shirt. His eyes widened.

"Haghh. He *is* one of them!" he roared between his weird honks. He tore the medallion off Endicott's neck with colossal strength. "Hughhh. He is a wizard sent from the New School!"

With a start, Endicott realized why the giant seemed familiar. He was about to say something to the big man, but new movement caught his attention. The first bald man that Endicott had panned had recovered his sword and now came limping over. His face was a mess of blood and bacon grease concentrated most heavily between his nose and forehead. A hunk of bacon drooped from his left ear. He drew back for a thrust.

"Wait! Let's gut him together!" The other bald idiot was back, similarly greased, baconed, and bloodied. They stood side by side, smiling bestially and looking more like two demented, hairless twins than ever.

New screams distracted them as they pulled their swords back to strike.

"It's Freyla Loche!"

Endicott did not know who had shouted, and the words made no immediate sense to him. He had more pressing concerns, such as collecting his wits before the two protestors murdered him. He was still dizzy from the blow to the head he had taken, but he struggled to break free of the giant hand around his neck. Nothing. He could not find the strength or acuity he needed.

A commotion swept through the crowd like a wave, and the two bald men froze in confusion, sword blades still pointed at Endicott. A flood of constables was pouring into the warehouse, laying about with nightsticks.

The two bald men took in the oncoming constabulary and looked at each other. Perhaps the sight of bacon grease and blood in the mirror image of each other's mangled faces was too much to bear, for they simultaneously snarled anew and, in perfect symmetry, wound themselves up to strike overhand at Endicott.

Eloise burst out of the crowd, her entropic sword reflecting yellow in the lantern light.

"It's Freyla Loche!" someone screamed. "She's come for her revenge!"

Eloise swung her glassy sword hard at the closest bald man's blade. It whistled as it cut the air and rang like a bell as it caught the other's sword edge on and parted it. The point and last third of the blade flew past Endicott's head, missing him by inches, and hit the honking giant on the shoulder. Eloise swung her sword again and split the bald man's head to his chest. Brains, blood, and bacon hit the floor.

"Gahhh!" The giant fell to his knees, blood streaming from the chunk of sword blade now embedded in his right shoulder, but he was not finished yet. With his left hand, he flung Endicott into Eloise with enough force to knock her staggering. Endicott found himself crouching with his face in Eloise's stomach, still disoriented from the blow to the head he had taken.

Blood streamed from the enormous man's shoulder, down his arm and into his hand. He held the hand up to his eyes, honked "Hughh" again, turned, and ran, shouldering a constable into a crate as he thundered by.

"Halvar!" the surviving bald protester screamed, stunned at the grisly sight of his twin's split head. "Murderers!" he screamed, and then a stream of incoherent curses as he hurtled towards Eloise and Endicott. Eloise, juggling her sword in one hand and Endicott's head in the other, was in no state to respond, but was saved by Gregory, who emerged from the crowd at a run and barged Halvor's accomplice with his shield. The bald man was thrown off his feet. He slid along the now blood-soaked floor into a barrel. Cookies rained down on his grease-glistening head, but instead of pressing his advantage, Gregory slid his shield to Eloise, who had dropped her sword and was trying to lift the still-dazed Endicott up.

"What's wrong with him?" Gregory called as he drew his sword to face the bald man, who was lurching to his feet. The blade rang out as Gregory moved it to guard.

Eloise squinted, looking at Endicott's eyes. "Blow to the head. Heydron! A bad one."

The bald man had regained his feet now, something clutched in his off hand. He threw a cookie at Gregory's face and charged. Gregory flinched from the cookie and misjudged the heavyset man's thrust, taking a sharp cut to his left forearm.

"Knights!"

Blood dripped on the floor.

The bald protestor screamed and swung hard at Gregory, who caught the blow near the tip of his own sword, shearing off four inches of metal from his attacker's blade. The shard went flying off into the crowd of constables, but the follow-through almost took off Gregory's face. He managed to lean back just enough to keep skin, teeth, and nose. Both men stared at each other, wide-eyed at what had just happened.

Gregory swore again and pressed forward. His burly adversary was wary of losing more sword, so he thrust instead of slashed, and Gregory was unable to catch the stocky man's weapon directly enough to break it. Eloise scowled, still juggling the floundering Endicott with one hand and Gregory's shield with the other. "Quit playing with him, Gregory!"

Gregory let out a breath and seemed to steady up.

The bald man struck again, but Gregory's ringing parry took off his bacon-soaked left ear. He screamed and blindly charged his taller opponent, sword overhead. This time Gregory's blade shattered the bald man's completely. He lost his balance and stumbled past Gregory towards Eloise. She positioned herself in front of Endicott with Gregory's shield now firmly in hand, calmly raised the shield and brought it down with a resounding clang on the bald man's head. The edge of the shiny metal cut a line through his forehead and into his brain. The stocky man convulsed on the floor, eyes fixed and wide, making wet "yughh" sounds as he thrashed.

"Shut up, fucker!" Eloise screamed and kicked him in the stomach.

"Freyla Loche killed Iver!" Endicott could hear Dylan's voice from the crowd. "She killed them both!"

Thwack, thwack, thwack.

Endicott turned his head as the room swam dizzily around him and thought he glimpsed a group of constables beating Dylan with their night sticks before his vision went dark. He regained awareness to see Koria kneeling in front of him, holding a bag of ice to his head. Eryka, Eloise, and Gregory were huddled together a few feet away, talking excitedly.

"H-how did you find us?"

Koria gently kissed his throbbing forehead. "I saw the barmen bringing food here while we were waiting outside the Spear. My conclusion was a bit too inductive for Eryka, but she put a few of the constables closer by just in case it meant what I thought. That's how they were able to hear Davyn's whistle."

"Thanks for being so clever."

Koria just smiled.

How many times is it now that you have rescued me?

"Sir Robert," said Eryka, "Is the murderer here?"

Endicott shook his head, but the motion nearly made him vomit. "No. I don't think so. He was never here."

Edwyn Perry approached and knelt beside him. "You sure, kid? What about these two?" He gestured to the bodies of the two bald men.

Endicott snorted. "Not them. They're at least a foot too short and certainly aren't wizards."

Edwyn laughed. "Yah, well, they won't be telling us anything about the Armadale ambassador either."

Eryka squinted. "Dead or not, they might tell us something."

Maybe.

"We heard you fought them both with a pan by yourself." Edwyn shook his head wistfully. "Swords against fry pan, that's a new one. Heard you were doing real good too, until you got sucker-punched by a third man. A real big fella, about a foot taller than the other two."

"Robert." Eryka was now crouching beside Edwyn. "Could that big man be the murderer?"

There was *something* about the big man, but Endicott could not remember what it was. His head ached. The giant was … strange.

"I don't think so. He seemed … simple, just angry. I don't think the man that Gregory and I saw fleeing the alley was simple."

"Huh" said Edwyn, disappointed and looking away.

"He took my medallion." Endicott felt the absence of the chain around his neck. *Knights damn it.*

"It's okay, Robert," Eryka smiled sympathetically. "We will find it. Someone that big won't find be able to hide from us."

"Where is Conor?" Endicott tried to find Conor from his sitting position, but there were too many people surrounding him. "Where's Cyara?" He tried to stand up but needed help from Koria and Eryka.

Conor was gone. Terwynn too. More than half of the cult had been captured, but a worrying number had escaped. Even though Eryka had taken Koria's advice and put constables on the warehouse, the bulk of the constabulary had still been in or around the Black Spear when Davyn blew his whistle.

Cyara had stayed though, offering no resistance. She sat on the floor now, alone amongst a mess of overturned barrels, spilled bacon pans, and shattered cookies. She looked up at Endicott accusingly. "You really fooled me, Robert."

Cyara was a pathetic sight. Her nose had a wide cut across the middle. *Broken?* Her accusation woke Endicott up, shocking him back into alertness. "I had to."

"I was *so* worried for you." Cyara shook her head. "I thought you needed help. I thought you worshipped Nimrheal and needed to be saved, but I misread you completely. You have another master."

"Coming here was *my* idea. Blame my conscience."

Tears ran down Cyara's face. "Your conscience? Fine. I'll do that, but what good will it do anyone? My group is broken. I won't hold it against your conscience if your conscience finds a way to look after all these people now."

"I was trying to find a *murderer*, Cyara." Endicott knew he had acted properly, but he could not look at Cyara and feel good. Her eyes were teary and red, and she slumped as if all the life had gone out of her.

"I still don't know what this was supposed to be. What was the point?" he demanded.

"I was trying to help them, Robert! How could you have missed that?"

Endicott crouched down beside her, fighting the stiffness in his body and the lingering dizziness in his head. "I know you were trying to help people, Cyara. That was obvious, but it was also futile. There was another subset in the group—Terwynn and others, more than a few—who weren't. *Those* people were inciting murder."

Cyara looked at him as if he were simple. "Should I have stopped trying to help everyone else?"

Chapter Fourteen.
The Legend of Freyla Loche

"Should you stop helping crazy people just because they are crazy? Good question!" Davyn's voice remained a little hoarse from gargling his whistle, but he still managed to hold the title of loudest talker in the room.

"Do you think she knew about the attempt to burn down the registered seed office?" Kennyth Brice sat in a chair beside his mother. Duchess Eleanor Brice was dressed in her robes of office, which included a thick, dark wig. Her face was also heavily powdered. She was barely recognizable as the same Eleanor who had taught Endicott's class. Beside the duchess sat the duke, gray-haired and bluff. He was the quietest of the three but had a more practical way of speaking and lacked the smooth and diplomatic cadences of his son.

"Would she have cared?" the duke asked in his usual down-to-earth manner.

They were in a small audience chamber in the Citadel in private conference. Endicott did not remember travelling to the Citadel. He had never been inside the great fortress, and now he found himself there with nothing more than lost time to account for his presence. That and a savage blow to the head. Koria, Eloise, and Davyn were in attendance as well, along with Chief Constable Eryka Lyon, Vice Constable Edwyn Perry, and Gerveault. Koria held a fresh bag of ice to the side of Endicott's head, which if anything was hurting worse than ever. But it was not bleeding, which was more than Gregory could say for his lacerated arm. The tall young man was the only one of the group who was absent, instead keeping company with a surgeon and the old-style stitching engine known as needle and thread.

"We don't know who attempted that arson, Your Graces," said Eryka matter-of-factly. "As for tonight some are dead and some escaped. Of those captured most have yet to be properly interrogated. What Sir Robert got out of Cyara may not be what *we* get out of her."

The duchess gave Eryka an unreadable look before smiling at Davyn. "You have always been a good observer, Davyn, and you stayed out of the center of the action as much as you could. What do you think?"

Davyn did not hesitate. He jumped to his feet. "Cyara Daere is no murderer, Your Grace. I doubt that she would willingly be involved in *any* violent crime. But she was not the only one there."

"She was the leader, was she not?" asked Kennyth.

"She claimed she wasn't," replied Davyn loudly. "In fact she rejected the idea of there being any leadership at all."

The duke scowled. "How could that work?"

Davyn shrugged. "Didn't seem practical to me either, but it may have been the intellectual mechanism she used to form a working arrangement with certain others who had vastly different motivations. Particularly Terwynn and the bald gentlemen from Armadale."

Edwyn Perry snorted.

"Let's not rationalize," said Eryka with the same disgusted expression as Edwyn. "She willingly allowed those people into her circle. What kind of person does that?"

An optimist?

"Hmm, hmm." Gerveault cleared his throat and shifted in his chair. "I can tell you at least *who* she is. Cyara Daere was once a student at the New School. An arts student. She left us over two years ago. You took a notebook off a young man named Evyn? I believe he is another student."

The duchess's eyes widened. "I don't know the boy, but I *knew* Cyara. I just did not recognize her name until now."

"I have not thought about her either since she left. She just dropped out without giving any reason or any notice." Gerveault looked down at his hands.

"We can get to the bottom of this pretty quickly," asserted Perry. "She doesn't look like she'll stand up to any kind of rough questioning. And the other kid will fold like a piece of cheap paper."

"No," Endicott said flatly. Flat was all he had thanks to the way his head was spinning.

"I agree," boomed Davyn, still standing. "Cyara tried to help Robert when the fighting started. I would have helped, but I was struggling with this more-swallowable-than-loud whistle at the time."

"Right," Eloise huffed, turning from Davyn to Endicott. "Are you in love with her too, stupe? You do realize you almost died in there, don't you?"

Edwyn Perry was just as exasperated. "These aren't nice people, kids. That journal from Evyn—"

"The minutes," said Davyn loudly. "He was keeping the minutes of the meeting."

"Right, the minutes. Thank you so much. I wonder what program he's in?" Edwyn smiled. "Those minutes showed people cheering the destruction of private property. Perhaps that's no big deal to some, but they were cheering on a couple of murders too. And promising more. They want the duchy in ruins. And you don't want to ask them a few tough questions?"

Pain shot through Endicott's head, but he heard Davyn's response. "They weren't all cheering."

"Well, that's a relief," huffed Perry. "Thank the Knights they weren't *all* cheering."

Eryka cast an inscrutable look at her subordinate. "It hardly matters who cheered for what. The very kindest interpretation we can apply to Cyara Daere is that she turned a blind eye to conspiracy and treason. Maybe to murder." She shook her head. "Can we be practical here? The only two possible connections to Armadale that we know about are dead. Several suspects escaped, including the murderer if he was there." Eryka looked at the ducal family pleadingly. "We need to delve those we have, and hard."

Koria squeezed Endicott's hand and jumped into the fray. "I don't think either Sir Robert or Davyn are saying you should go easy on everyone. They are asking for some discretion for Cyara. Just because some people in the cult wanted to do harm doesn't mean they all did."

"She was just trying to help," Endicott added, wincing through the pain in his head and trying to open his eyes all the way. The light hurt. "I would have died if not for her."

Edwyn Perry exchanged a hasty glance with Eryka. "What, so we can't touch her? Even if she is as blameless as all that, she might know something indirectly, kid."

Kennyth Brice leaned forward in his chair. "That is *Sir* Robert to you, vice constable."

Edwyn put up his hands and bent his long neck in submission. "I'm sorry. I respect what you did, Sir Robert. It was brave. But we have to get at what she knows."

Endicott nodded slowly at him and Eryka, taking no offense, and turned to the duchess. "We can just *ask* her. Ask her. If we ask nicely, she will talk to us."

"Ask an accessory to murder nicely?" Edwyn returned.

The duke leaned forward, frowning at Endicott. "I don't think so. I don't feel as charitable about the episode as you do, Sir Robert," he said, but as he spoke his expression transformed from a sneer to a grudging smile. "I would think you would want justice more than anyone, considering what happened to you."

"She's no murderer," Endicott said as loud as he could, which was not very loud at all. "Most of the people there weren't acting out of malice."

The young man winced as he stood up and looked both duke and duchess in the eyes. "Let's not punish the mostly innocent we have in hand because the truly guilty got away."

The duke glanced at his wife wryly.

"Two of them didn't get away," interjected Eloise with an evil smile.

While some of them chuckled at Eloise's shot, Endicott shuffled over to the duchess, kneeling carefully on one knee in front of her. He looked at Eleanor as he spoke, all other eyes on him. "We are conflating several very different things."

Remembering all the different forces that had been at work at the meeting, the young man was sure of that much. Terwynn had *wanted* the issues mixed and confused. It served his ends. It seemed to serve the ends of Armadale too. Their efforts at confusion and conflation had worked because there were other, *genuine* issues not being addressed. When Endicott had spoken, he had tried to address those real issues. He remembered what Koria had said about there being little difference between the cultists and himself. It was a terrible thought, because if true it denied him an easy enemy.

I can't be like them, can I? He was never going to like their signs or agree with the content of their protests. He was never going to applaud their ignorance. *Never.* But setting aside Terwynn, setting aside Armadale, there were *real* people in the cult. *They care. Like me.* Endicott reached for clarity. "We are partially responsible for what's happened," he breathed, realization rather than pain making a whisper of his words.

"Really?" The old duke's voice rumbled out the question. "How exactly is this a problem of our making?"

Endicott stayed kneeling in front of the duchess but met her husband's eyes for a moment. "I'm only speaking in a general sense." He closed his eyes from the throbbing pain in his head, wobbling in place before Eleanor. She reached out to catch his shoulder and steady him. Edwyn Perry moved as if about to take advantage of Endicott's involuntary pause, but Kennyth Brice gestured sharply at him.

The young man eventually managed to smile at the old woman before him. "I appreciate the New School more than I can put into words. I feel like I have a second home and a new family here. I am deeply grateful. The school is necessary. It is an act of leadership enabling progress. But progress on a scale never seen before, is it not so? Never. We are creating our *own* change on our *own* people. From a world that could not progress to one that *could* but did not, to one that now, finally, *is* progressing. I didn't see the problem at first. I couldn't sympathize with the protesters. I couldn't appreciate the shock of it for them. I grew up with change being possible, with the New School being out there. My family was part of the change. We profited from it. I never questioned its value, and so I didn't have much patience for the protestors. Honestly I still don't. But after being with those people, I have realized that the scope and pace of change is genuinely discomfiting to many, genuinely hurting others. It is not a joke, and it is not just because people are crazy."

The duke frowned through this but did not try to stop Endicott from speaking. When the young man paused again, Kennyth Brice and the duchess smiled at him, which he took for encouragement to proceed.

"The problem exists neither because we have done anything wrong nor because there is something wrong with those who are having trouble with what we have done. It is simply a phenomenon, Eleanor."

Endicott did not see the raised eyebrows of Eryka and Edwyn when he called the duchess by her first name. "We need to try to help some of the ones who aren't doing well because of the changes. There were things going on in that meeting that the constables need to get to the bottom of even if that means tough questions and hard boots. But some of those people just need to be helped. And helping them will solve part of the problem."

Eleanor put a hand on Endicott's head, looking at the bruise that spread from his temple into his hair. "Still the romantic even now?"

"I'm trying."

She pursed her lips. "What do you want to try now, Sir Robert?"

Endicott wobbled on his knee. "I don't know."

"We could do what Cyara was trying to do," Koria suggested. "Have meetings. Provide counsel. But without the other influences."

Endicott smiled wearily. "Yes."

"Sit down before you fall down, Sir Robert." The duke's voice was gruff. "You're making me jealous kneeling in front of my wife like that." As Endicott took his chair beside Koria again, the duke looked hard at his duchess, then back at the young couple. "Besides, you and Koria are playing into my wife's hands. Eleanor has brought this kind of idea up before. Many times."

He shook his shaggy head and suddenly erupted. "By the eight Knights!" The bluff old man's right hand thumped down on the arm of his chair. "I would tell you to shut the hell up and get out of my throne room," the duke added, "though probably not so nicely. *Except* you bled for us. *Except* you saved Syriol Lindseth." He looked at Kennyth. "*And* my son keeps talking about how you plucked a pen right out of the air before it could hit my wife's eye. So your soft sounding words earn some consideration from a grumpy old man." His eyes bulged. "Some."

The duke pointed at Eryka Lyons, his eyes still a little hard. "You and your men will treat Cyara Daere carefully. And any others that do not appear to be of the murderous variety. Take Sir Robert—no, he's barely hanging on to the stalk. Take Davyn with you to determine who we sift hard and who we don't."

He turned a scowling face back to Endicott and Koria. "The larger ... philosophical question is more difficult."

Eleanor put her wrinkled hand on his. "The question can go to council."

"This mud will only get deeper," the duke said, looking put-upon and still vacillating at the crossroads between amused and angry, though holding Eleanor's hand now. "But fine. If *you* sit in on the meetings, my dear. When you work it all out, make sure you tell me how we are going to pay for all this, considering our … other recent commitments."

"The economics are there, Your Grace," said Gerveault. "In the full season."

Endicott was still dizzy and in a fair amount of pain, so he was pleased to have someone else take up the argument.

The duke may have been less pleased. "The full season?" he growled skeptically. "I've heard that before."

"Mathematically speaking, the costs of arson, murder, and criminality are high. The recovery of someone lost to the productive workforce is worth the investment. Viewed in the long term, it will cost less to help than it will if we do not."

"I would like to see that math," said Edwyn Perry dryly.

"You sure you would understand it?" rejoined the old man.

"No," laughed Edwyn easily. "But Eryka probably would."

"Hmmf. Feel welcome to come by for a lecture."

Davyn shook his head at them in a silent warning.

Gerveault continued, pretending he did not notice the big man's obvious pantomime. "Back to the main point, which is that there are other benefits as well. Why—"

"It's the cost of controlling the narrative," interrupted Davyn.

"Can we please just take a minute here?" Eryka scanned the room, both eyebrows up. "There has been a double murder. There has been an attempted arson. We have some indications of a conspiracy, possibly involving Armadale. Is this the time to talk about therapy and narrative?"

"Therapy for the criminals," Edwyn amplified. "Ridiculous."

Koria pursed her lips. "The therapy is not for the criminals, constables. It is for the everyone else."

Eryka rubbed her eyes. "Knight damn it! Are we really discussing the problem as some kind of mass psychological malaise instead of murder?"

"We had better if we want to prevent a lot more of it," said Koria. "Hear me out." She raised a hand high. "Without bounds, we cannot solve many of our mathematical problems. We *need* bounds. People's minds are the same. The ethics that guide them must be defined and bounded. When they perceive those bounds are gone, they become upset. They become as unbound and intractable as my mathematics."

"Unbound?" exclaimed Edwyn shaking his head. "Like a formula?"

"Intellectually," supplied Davyn, pointing at his head.

"This isn't a classroom," Eryka replied sharply.

Kennyth Brice started to rise, perhaps irritated, but the duchess put a hand on his arm. She smiled and in her gravelly voice said, "Eryka is right. We have not caught the murderer. We still have a problem, and we are not going to stop working on it. You are not going to stop working on it, chief constable. So you are right, Eryka. We must be practical. There are clearly some very malicious forces at work here that need to be stopped." She paused. "But Koria is also right. Even if we had caught everyone involved in all the crimes committed so far, we would still have a problem. There would be another crime committed by someone else. And another one after that. We must solve the murders, break down the conspiracy—if there is one—but ultimately we must solve the root problem. We cannot allow this ... *unboundedness* to develop further."

"And how are we going to do that?" asked Eryka with exaggerated care.

Koria fixed the chief constable with a flat stare. "We have to bridge the cultural change. We must do what Cyara was trying to do. But better."

"I am super stoked!" shouted Davyn excitedly.

Edwyn Perry's face was a scrunched-up picture of skepticism. "And here I thought we were just going to bust a few heads and catch the bad guys," he said sardonically, then shrugged. "But I think I understand." He looked at Eryka, who was frowning but nodded to him. "I guess it isn't every day that we decide to create a new social organization."

The duke's deep, rough voice filled the room as he spoke. "Do not think for one moment that I have missed the fact we have just gone in a circle. And speaking of doing the same thing again and again, does the Steel Castle not already do this kind of social thing?"

"Yes, your Grace, it does" Gerveault replied, speaking carefully. "The church prides itself on helping the poor and the homeless, and it certainly has its own story to tell."

"Perfect," said the duke, jumping on an easy solution. "Why don't we just use them?"

"You cannot." Koria's soft yet determined voice surprised the plain-spoken old duke. His eyebrows rose in silent enquiry. "You cannot depend upon the Steel Castle to promote the virtues of learning new things," Koria explained.

"They aren't our enemy!" The duke's face was red.

The duchess put her hand on his again. She reminded Endicott of a rider, holding back two horses, her optimistic son on one side and her dour husband on the other. "They may not be our best friend, at least on this issue."

Edwyn nodded his head on his long neck. "Yah, well, as uncomfortably academic as this has all gotten, I have to agree that the bishop won't any time soon be giving too many lectures suggesting *change* is a good thing."

Kennyth Brice pointed at Edwyn, one eyebrow raised. "Change is not a moral issue at all, vice constable, and it is going to continue to be a part of everyone's lives. As such it is something we must recognize and manage. I am convinced. We cannot fail to address this."

The duchess smiled and looked up at the ceiling. "Narrative. It would be nice to have a more positive narrative on our side, one that people could relate to more easily."

Even simple-seeming issues can be frustratingly complex, Endicott reflected, as the discussion continued. Eventually the duke declared that the conversation had outlasted his patience and that the wagon was stuck too deep in the mud to dig out today. The subject was to be tabled, along with the allegations of Armadale's malign interference in events. The former problem would be scheduled for another set of meetings by the duchess, while the latter would wait upon further investigation by the constabulary. And the quiet, slow preparation of military powers. They moved on to other matters and pleasantries.

"We haven't thanked you, Sir Robert. Or you, Davyn." Kennyth Brice's modulated voice was a startling contrast to his father's. "It turned out to be a bit more of an adventure than we expected."

"Too much of an adventure for my tastes," said Gerveault. He looked up, light eyes flashing from his dark face. "I do not like my students putting themselves in harm's way like this. I do not like them mentioned in the posts. I especially do not like them getting hurt."

Kennyth leaned back, smiling. "Ah, so you would not be happy if we chose to formally recognize them tomorrow in open court? We *do* wish to recognize the gift of my shield."

Gerveault raised one finger to the ceiling.

Here comes a lecture.

The old man seemed to think better of it. He lowered his finger and just said, "Please do not. Not tomorrow at least. I would like to get them all out of the city for a few days while we ascertain exactly what has happened, round up the ones who escaped, and give the posts a chance to lose interest."

"What do you think the news will be?"

"Well," Gerveault hesitated, "I heard some of the witnesses to the scene talk rather excitedly about Freyla Loche and some act of vengeance she took on the cultists."

Confusion was plain on the faces of the ducal family. "The student Freyla Loche that Robert and Gregory helped? The one with the stitching engines?" asked the duchess.

"That's me!" said Eloise triumphantly.

More confusion.

"It's a bit of a ... narrative," explained Davyn with a grin. "Would you like to hear the dramatic details?"

"Later, Davyn." Gerveault waved him down. "We cannot be sure what the posts will say, but you can count on Freyla Loche—Eloise, that is—being prominently featured, and Robert Endicott of course. There will be another tavern song at the least from this one."

"I want to hear the story," said the duke, sitting back and looking more relaxed.

"The Legend of Freyla Loche ... Me too," added Kennyth.

"I think I do as well. But first where do you want to send our students?" asked the duchess.

Gerveault affected a sly look. "We have a couple of water projects they can help with. On the engineering side. Being seen to be involved in something that everyone will benefit from will help build that positive narrative about the New School we are looking for. And it will be perfectly safe."

Chapter Fifteen

Unsafe Practices

"Don't worry, Robert. You have the number one team!" Heylor seemed improbably chipper for a man who did not know the first thing about sitting on a horse. His skinny legs stuck out from the side of his mare like straw from a hay bale. Heylor had not learned to use—or did not like— stirrups, which made little sense given the pounding his bony behind was taking from his shoddy horsemanship.

He's lucky it's a short way to Aignen.

"The best!" Davyn roared, a study in physical contrast to Heylor. The big man looked a lot more comfortable than his scrawny friend but was equally excited to finally be out of the big city. He had acquired a straw hat from somewhere and reminded Endicott a little of his grandma riding their donkey.

"Yah," said Bethyn, holding a finger in the air and rotating it in a small circle.

It had taken two days to organize the excursion, though Endicott had done very little to help. Koria had not let him get off the couch or move far from a bag of ice. Instead it had been all her and Gerveault organizing the horses, sending out messengers, and arranging lodgings. When that was done, Koria had gone ahead with Deleske, Eloise, and Gregory to the city of Eschle, while Endicott had been given the task of working in the nearer town of Aignen along with Heylor, Davyn, and Bethyn. They had been given the shorter ride and the easier task so that Endicott could recover from the blow to the head he had taken at the Black Spear.

"You're the number one bunch of idiots I've ever seen." Merrett rode jingling close beside Endicott, as he had apparently been ordered to. The large, heavyset man rode his dark horse easily, reins held in one gauntleted hand. He was dressed in a long blue tunic over full chain mail, with a sword at his hip and a bronzed helmet on his square, upright head.

"Let's hope not," Endicott said, one hand on his new medallion. He was not bothered by Merrett. If the big soldier had been solicitous, Endicott would have been concerned. As it was, his head was feeling far better already. Gerveault had warned him off attempting any serious dynamics and advised him to think of the trip as a holiday.

Holiday?

Endicott did not know how to relax except perhaps with Koria. Even the couple of days recuperating on the couch had almost been too much for him. He had never been able to sit still with nothing to do. He looked over at Heylor bouncing in his saddle and wondered if they were really so different.

Am I a clown?

Endicott was not sure. He contemplated once again his tendency to plunge into problems without taking the time to fully understand them. Usually he could acknowledge this fact with some equanimity. He knew and accepted that everyone sometimes had to respond to situations with an imperfect understanding of them, but he had woken up with a darker view of matters this morning.

His first drink this morning had been from a bottle called idealism. There is no more bitter drink, he reflected. It *should* slake the thirst of those wanting to improve the world, but in reality it tended to poison the drinker, producing an ever deeper and thirstier dissatisfaction. Today Endicott felt like he had drunk the whole bottle and with each sip remembered events more sourly.

Since coming to the New School, he had started a feud with Lord Jon Indulf over a problem that a less impulsive person such as Koria would have handled easily. He *may* have helped save Syriol but was certain that he would have killed himself without Koria and Eloise's intervention. He had helped create a remarkable shield for Kennyth Brice, but he may well have stirred up more enemies to test it with in his blunderings at the Black Spear. He had betrayed Conor, who had thought he was a friend, and destroyed the humanitarian efforts of Cyara, who had only tried to help him. Even his repairs to Freyla Loche's stitching engines would have been a disaster if not for Gregory's good advice.

He shook his head slowly. *Clown.*

Why do I feel so sad?

Although Endicott was unaware that his rising feelings of melancholy and unbalanced idealism were largely the result of head trauma, his reaction was more typical of him. He wanted to do better at this next task, holiday or not. He wanted to do better at the real problem in front of him.

But how?

He felt trapped. On the one hand he had to prevent the murder of Koria and Eloise that his terrible heraldic dream foretold, but on the other hand he felt demoralized by the repeated errors he had made in rushing to prevent that dream from coming true. He had hoped to improve himself and his skill at dynamics in order to change the future, but for the most part dynamics was not the problem; being ignorant was.

What I need is better information.

The town of Aignen rose in the distance. Endicott could see the stonework of its two reserve water towers on the gentle hill behind the town and the collection of big stone houses that spread out from the foot of the hill. At some distance from the houses sat the stockyards and grain storage array. If the registered seed office in Vercors had burned down, the array in Aignen would have been catapulted into importance. As it was, Aignen remained an idyllic satellite city of Vercors, an easy place to do business for local farmers who did not want to venture into the big city.

"Ride on, Robert!" called Heylor, bouncing along roughly at a trot. "Let's go build some good feelings!" Davyn spurred his horse and caught up to the skinny man. Endicott watched them both pull ahead and away.

"I can see you are in a thoughtful mood," said Bethyn softly. "But do you think it's a clever idea to let Heylor and Davyn act as our ambassadors?"

Merrett snorted. "That's just what I would want if I were a hardworking farmer depending on the water station in town: two runaways from the circus."

How aggravating could they be?

Endicott did not have to ponder the question for very long. "I guess we can't have Heylor stealing the keys to the city, can we?" He gave his horse some rein so it could catch up to its equine friends. Unfortunately Heylor and Davyn had started singing once they had the lead, and as Merrett, Endicott, and Bethyn overtook them, they raised their voices louder.

"There was one thing to which they gave no thought:
The mighty friends of Robert Endicott!"

Endicott gritted his teeth and hoped no one in town could hear the singing.

"That's us, Robert!" crowed Heylor, raising a fist over his head and nearly falling off his horse.

"He's excited to finally be out with you on one of your grand adventures," whispered Bethyn, looking at Endicott's stony face sideways. "Go easy."

"Heylor!" Endicott shouted.

The skinny man jumped like a scalded cat, and Endicott reconsidered what he had been about to say. "Glad you're feeling so positive, but I think we should try for a lower profile, don't you? There might be some of those Nimrheal cultists in town."

"Really?" Heylor's eyes were wide.

"They had to go somewhere."

Heylor nodded slowly and rode over to rejoin Davyn, with whom he engaged in a loudly whispered conference. Davyn turned around and winked at Endicott when Heylor was not looking.

"Maybe we should send him after them," Merrett grumbled, posting and pulling at the mail under his butt.

The big stone-and-wood inn that Koria had booked for them was called the Ninth Knight. Its sign depicted a black knight, referring to the story of Sir Seygis, the murderous Methueyn Knight of the old times. A red-haired woman in her early thirties waited for them in the cobblestone foyer. She patiently watched them ride up, a wry smile on her freckled face.

"Sir Robert Endicott," she said in a clear, firm voice as she reached for his reins. "Bethyn Trail, Heylor Style, Davyn Daly, and Bat Merrett." She nodded to each of them, still holding Endicott's reins. "You have been well described," she laughed. "I am Adara Torrinton, chief engineer here. Let's get you off those horses and checked in."

Adara was funny, smart, and had clearly been given very explicit instructions on how to handle the group from the New School. She had a big table in the dining room set aside for them, and after they had stowed their gear, she had the staff hopping to their dinner orders. The chairs were comfortable, the room bright with many windows. The inn was transparently new and smelled delightfully of cedar. The great mural of Sir Seygis over the fireplace jarred Endicott. It was a true avaunt guard touch to use such an obscure, though horrific, figure as a brand in the modern establishment. *His story is so old, it's lost all coupling with its meaning.* The disconnection acted to deepen Endicott's dark mood.

Naturally, Davyn and Heylor almost immediately engaged Adara in an elaborate retelling of the terrible night. They told it from every perspective: theirs, Bethyn's, Syriol's, Koria and Eloise's, and lastly Robert and Gregory's. "What did you have in mind for tomorrow, Adara?" Endicott asked to end the uncomfortable, never-ending story.

"Well," she said, clapping her hands firmly together once. "I thought we would spend the morning touring the town. We have a new neighborhood with beautiful estates. It is largely populated by rich merchants out of Vercors."

"What about farmers?" interrupted Davyn loudly from a very full mouth. "Any of them selling out and moving into town?"

"A few," she smiled at him. "In the afternoon, the mayor and city council would like to meet you and talk about the New School. After that she would like the five of you over to her house for dinner and a small party."

"Tours, dinner, and a party?" Endicott tried to smile, but his poor disposition made it a little lopsided. "Adara, I thought we were being sent to help you with your waterworks."

"Uh, yes, of course," she said, lips tight. "But I was told not to load too much on you right away."

Bethyn drained her third or fourth cup of wine. "Load me with another glass of wine, would you?" she asked a serving man.

"And I can see you still have quite the bruise there." Adara pointed to Endicott's temple.

"I'm fine," said Endicott. Good manners made him add, "Thank you for your consideration, Adara, but my friends are eager to get started." He reached for Bethyn's refilled wine glass and passed it to Merrett, who downed it in one gulp.

"Hey," called Bethyn, reaching for the glass an instant too late. She put her chin in her hands and stuck her tongue out at Endicott.

"They would really hate to be held back because of me," Endicott finished, ignoring Bethyn's mostly mute protest.

"That's all true," chimed Heylor. "Keep us busy."

"Dinner with the mayor sounds nice," mused Davyn. He looked over at a grumpy-looking Endicott. "*After* we fix whatever it is you need fixed."

Adara put a hand to either side of her plate and raised her fingers. "That's fine. I was hoping for some help with a leak somewhere in our infrastructure. Probably a series of leaks, actually."

"Caused by what?" Davyn's voice filled the busy dining room. "Subsidence? Tremors?"

"I doubt it, Davyn," Adara said. "It is more likely just tree roots."

Endicott thought about that. "How deep are your aqueducts?"

"Mostly eight to ten feet below ground level, but it's a town." Adara smiled. "There are a number of places where the pipes have to be briefly at surface, and of course we have an entire system of them exposed at our filter station and reserve water tanks."

Expensive to dig up everywhere else.

Heylor pulled a fork out of his pants pocket and placed it carefully beside his plate. "How are we supposed to help with that? We won't even be able to see the pipes!" He reached into his other pocket and pulled a knife out of it.

Davyn frowned at the knife and pulled his plate a few inches away from Heylor. "You mean you never tried heraldry with your eyes closed?"

"We can do that?"

"Sure," said Davyn. "It works just as good with your eyes closed as long as you know where to look and what to look for."

"A lot of things are better with your eyes closed," muttered Bethyn, drinking from Heylor's wine glass, eyes closed.

Adara spluttered, laughing. "Not just that either."

Endicott waited for Adara to stop laughing. He ignored Bethyn's giggling, which did not stop. "So we should have maps of the aqueduct rights-of-way for everything below ground, and something to mark the locations with leaks."

Desert and a few details later, Adara bid them all good night. Endicott noticed Bethyn staring at the red-haired woman's ample behind as she left. He did not say anything, unsure if he could be of any help to her in his dark mood.

"I was thinking about our conversation yesterday," Davyn declared.

Bethyn craned her neck back to the front, refilled her wine glass, and slurred, "I understand it was very long and boring."

"Not at all!" Davyn boomed. "We were talking about how people struggle to accept that the world can change more quickly now. And that resistance to change is a phenomenon of the mind."

"Yup," Bethyn declared, hand slapping the table. "Boring. They just need to grow up and get over it."

Davyn smiled at her. "I was talking with Jennyfer Gray. She said there is a theory of the mind that says some people become unfalteringly and literally attached to what they believe is the way things should be done. Then naturally they get upset if *the right way* is changed."

"Huh," said Bethyn. "What kind of things?"

"Well," said Davyn, "take the cutlery here. Heylor has been playing with it all night. That would be upsetting to such people. They expect the knife and fork to be placed just so on the correct side of the plate every time. If it isn't, they get anxious."

"Ha!" pronounced Heylor, his forks and knives transposed so they were each on the wrong side of the plate.

"What's your point, Davyn?" Bethyn leaned to the side, out of balance. "You're talking about crazy people."

"Actually," Davyn declared loudly, "the principle applies to everyone to some degree."

Bethyn stood up, swaying a little, and started walking away. "Good of you to apologize for them all."

"Is she mad at me?" Davyn asked, for once in a normal tone.

She's having a different conversation than you, that's all.

"She's having a bad night, gentlemen," Endicott said humorlessly. "Why doesn't one of you go sit with her and make sure she's okay."

"I'll do it!" Heylor sprang out of his chair and bounded after her. Davyn followed a few moments later.

When they were gone, Merrett approached Endicott. "Robert." His face was dark. "You, sir, are an idiot."

"Of course I am," Endicott muttered. "Why am I an idiot this time?"

"Always take a break when it is offered to you. It's best practice."

▽

"Prove it." Adara held up a coin between her index finger and her thumb. "I am going to put this somewhere in my desk. You tell me where it is."

"It's in my pocket!" exclaimed Heylor, winking at her.

"No, it isn't. It—" Adara's eyebrows shot up. The coin was gone. Heylor fished it out of his pocket and handed it back to her. "How in the—?"

"He used to be a street clown until it got him into too much trouble," growled Merrett, wrapping one heavy mailed arm around Heylor's neck and dragging him to the far side of the room. "Now hide it," he called.

"You three go stand by Heylor and the rest of you turn around," Adara instructed. She opened each of her desk drawers and rummaged around randomly before placing the coin and carefully closing all the drawers. "Okay. Come ahead and tell me where the coin is."

"Not you," Merrett said in a low voice, glaring at Endicott. "The old man said no unnecessary anything out of you."

Endicott shrugged. He would have been annoyed the day before, but it did not seem as important to him now. Besides he had already opened himself to the empyreal sky and knew exactly where the coin was.

"It's right there," boomed Davyn, pointing. "The far corner, bottom drawer."

"I *can* see it," Heylor said, smiling at Adara.

Bethyn smiled briefly. "It's showing knights."

Adara pulled the bottom desk drawer open and retrieved the coin. It was knights up. "That is a very useful skill," she said grudgingly.

"It's the least we can do!" crowed Heylor.

Adara squinted at him. "Perhaps it's the least you *should* do, hmm." She walked over to a map rack, pulled out a tube, and unrolled the map that was inside it. "This map shows all the pipes in town, starting from here."

"Why is it twinned?" asked Davyn

Adara pointed at two circles. "See this? These are our two identical tanks. You saw them just up the hill. They were originally meant to serve as both hot and cold reservoirs. Some of the houses, including the municipal buildings and the mayor's house, are fully set up to run from either tank through separate valves. Most of the rest of the houses either pull from only one of the tanks, or pull from both but only have one valve."

Heylor gestured dismissively, his eyes on Adara's red hair. "We have all that at the Orchid."

"Then you should know it is very expensive and that you are very lucky," replied Adara. "In any case either pipe could leak, so look at them both, please." She walked over to the door and opened it. "Okay. Two of the crews are here already. They have stakes, hammers, and shovels. Just point them to the spots with leaks and have them start digging. *You* don't dig. That's their job. You can work ahead of the crew provided you have one crew member with you when you stake the next site. Heylor, why don't you work down the hill towards the new development? Davyn can go the other direction from the sand filters back towards the main line. Meet back here at lunch and mark off the breaks on the map, okay?"

And just like that, Heylor and Davyn were off.

"I'm sorry I was in such a bad mood yesterday," Endicott said contritely. He was feeling remarkably better, barely remembering why he had been so sour the day before.

Merrett growled, "Never apologize."

"I wasn't speaking to you, Merrett. Mood and manners are wasted on you, sir." Endicott bowed his head to Adara and Bethyn. "But I could have been nicer to you, Adara."

"You were perfectly nice," Adara said, sitting down behind her desk. "Everyone knows how serious Sir Robert Endicott is."

"Seriously wound up," added Bethyn, sitting on a corner of the desk and smiling at Adara. She seemed to be doing fairly well considering how drunk she had been the night before.

"Finding the leaky pipe is going to save a lot of time," said Adara, dimples showing.

"We can do better than that," said Endicott. "We can identify metal fatigue and even point out sites that are probably going to break."

Adara raised her right eyebrow. "As easy as that?" Her face slowly smoothed as she closed her eyes and sighed. "What I could do if I had your gifts."

There was a knock on the door.

"That will be your crew, Bethyn." Adara straightened up and pointed at her map. "They will take you to the old-town section. Go from here to here. Let the crews do the work."

"Do you even have a crew for me, Adara?" Endicott asked once Bethyn had departed.

Adara shared a glance with Merrett before responding. Her freckles seemed to grow extra dark. "Just me, Sir Robert."

"The conspiracy is a little transparent, Adara." Endicott crossed the room to the door and opened it. "Why don't you show me the sand filters and the reservoirs?"

The sand filter was an enormous cylindrical stone vessel set on the very top of the hill. The water technically came from a higher elevation in the hills further north, but there was a small hydrostatic head to be overcome in reaching the vessel. Adara proudly showed Endicott the slow sand filter, its water-purifying biota, and set of pipes.

"I graduated from the New School myself," she said as she led him to the two large reservoirs set not far below the sand filter. They were more wide than tall, but each had a metal ladder bolted to the side and a heavy steel access hatch built into the top. They stood close together, perhaps only three feet apart. One of the reservoirs had a copper base and stonework set on the ground underneath it. Endicott guessed this might have been rough preparation for heating, though it was not apparent what the fuel source would have been.

"When was that?"

Adara's freckles turned red again. "Oh … more than a decade ago now. I look at you, young as you are, and I still see myself."

Merrett cleared his throat. "Thank the Knights you don't look like him."

"Or act like me, I think," added Endicott, taking no offense from Merrett's remarks. "I doubt you were ever a naïf. Look at you now. You're in charge of all this." Endicott gestured at the pipes, filter vessel, and reservoirs.

"That's me," Adara smiled and looked down the hill towards the town. All the stone houses, stockyards, and grain arrays could be seen neatly laid out below.

In the distance they could see Vercors, and even a suggestion of the Academic Plateau. "I like it up here. I can see everything I'm responsible for. My job and my life unfold below just so."

It was a pleasant view. Endicott took a few slow breaths through his nose. He could smell the end of summer approaching, and looking hard, he could see just a hint of yellow in a few leaves.

They'll start falling in a few weeks. Sooner, if the weather turns.

Fear rolled through Endicott in a sudden, irresistible wave. It did not last, but it unsettled his easy mood and undid his momentary repose. He opened himself to the empyreal sky and began examining the pipes for metal fatigue. Adara must have seen his eyes defocus, for she took a step towards him and seemed about to say something. Merrett intercepted her, taking her arm and shaking his head. Looking for problems in metal had always been easy for Endicott. It was a simple task, and the metal did not lie.

"This shut-off may fail," he said, pointing to a valve set in a bend in the pipe just below the sand filter. "It was not good practice to put this here. I would replace and resituate it."

Adara's brows went up. "I'll see it done." She pulled a black chalk stick from her jacket pocket and circled the valve. "I was told you could even herald a failure happening in the future, like you heralded the terrible night. I have to say, I am *very* jealous." She turned around, gesturing at the hill, the reservoirs, the pipes, and finally the town. "If I knew *everything*, I wouldn't have to worry about *anything*."

"If you knew everything, Adara, you *would* worry about everything." Endicott closed his eyes. "You would worry about it before it happened, and you would blame yourself after the fact. But I don't know everything. Just ask my biggest fan here." He pointed at Merrett.

"Hmmm," Merrett said. The heavyset man had a hand on his sword hilt and was peering suspiciously at the trees on the far side of the hill, the tanks, and the pipes. He retained his chain mail, gauntlets, and apparently his stoic attitude. Merrett's lack of commitment to the conversation did not surprise Endicott; the soldier had always picked and chosen his moments.

Endicott shrugged. "The song fails to mention that I only heralded the terrible night *after* it happened. Which is worse than unhelpful. You see, I don't know everything. Just like with your work, you only know what you examine carefully *when* you examine it. Heraldry is like that, and it isn't even certain. We only see probabilities of what might be. Heraldry is like a memory of the future. Think about that. The might-be possibilities feel just the same in your mind as the actually-was. Sometimes we see the events we desire or fear most of all, which can make heraldry more nightmare than dream, and just as subject to subconscious bias. Even without bias and the burden of memory, heraldry has other issues. No one heralds far enough to know even the result of one action to the end of all its possible consequences, and even if you were the furthest herald there has ever been, you would only know what *might* be, not what *will* be. What do you do with a possibility anyway? You can't act categorically in response to what *might* be. It is one thing to reach across facts to find meaning and project a reasonable course of action. It is quite another, a hell, to see only fearful, threatening possibilities and be unable to see clearly what it means or what to do about it. In some ways, heraldry is the worst burden of all."

Adara's dimples showed again as she somehow smiled and frowned simultaneously. "So it's not perfect. I guess you're just stuck in the real world with the rest of us, Sir Robert." She turned back to the view of her town. "I don't like to hear anyone complaining about an informational advantage, though. You really are very fortunate."

Endicott stood beside her to share the view. "On balance you're right, and I hope we prove helpful to you, Adara. This is the best kind of job, you know. Pipes, fittings, the straightforward physics of flow rates, the biology of filtering. Nothing subject to bias, interpretation, or competing narratives. The heraldry and future-memory of a pipe has no associated emotional burden."

"If one of my pipes breaks, you can bet there is going to be an emotional burden." Adara said, smiling again. "But you might just be a little too sensitive, don't you think?"

Right.

"Were you talking last night about an old plan for hot and cold running water?"

▽

"Knights alive! That would be sooo awesome!" Heylor exclaimed, looking at Endicott's calculations. Heylor had been the last to return for lunch and the least tired from the work. The skinny man had a speck of dirt on his nose and a streak of it under his right eye. "Wouldn't that be a surprise if the mayor had hot water for the party tonight?" He beamed at Adara. "She would give you a promotion, Adara!"

"Oh sure," Adara smiled, looking up from her pipe map. "Promotions all round."

"That's the life of the engineer in the modern world," amplified Davyn, breadcrumbs falling out of his mouth from the sandwich he was eating.

"Excuse me," Heylor said in a loud whisper. "I have to go, you know …" He jumped up and hurried across the room, exiting through the side door.

Bethyn was looking at Endicott's math. "How carefully did you do this work? It *looks* good."

"Yah," boomed Davyn as he jammed a pickle into his mouth. "How— Hmmf, that's good … Careful …"

Endicott shared a look with Adara. "Well, we measured the water salinity, temperature, depth, and volume in each tank twice. Then I made the calculations with a fine sampling and even used Davyn's radial transform."

"So you're going to do it?" Bethyn asked, tapping her finger on the paper.

Adara and Endicott looked at each other again, very serious now. Abruptly they both broke up laughing. Adara hit the leg of her heavy pants with one hand. "No!"

Bethyn frowned, possibly more annoyed at their laughter than genuinely interested in the calculations. "Well, why the fuck not? Heroes and medals and all that."

Davyn rushed over and put a big, meaty hand on each of Bethyn's shoulders. He grasped her as if he was holding her down. "I think I know the answer to this, but first let me help my esteemed colleague. What she means to say is: why ever not?"

"We would have to audit all the valves up and downstream of the reservoirs," Adara explained, still smiling. "I am not sure about the pressure tolerances, and we would have to think about closing the system first as well."

Endicott held up his mug of tea and gestured towards his mathematics. "Those calculations call for an extreme thermal change, probably too much of a change if you were really going to do it. And of course dynamics happen fast, a lot faster than this infrastructure is built for. It's a bit like the cakes."

Adara's nose scrunched up in confusion.

"I get it now," said Bethyn. "It could be like that first day when both your frozen and heated mugs exploded."

"Except a whole lot bigger!" laughed Davyn.

CRRRK! WWHHHMMMP!

Their discussion was interrupted by two thunderous reports from outside.

Heylor!

Endicott found himself charging out the door, Adara close behind him. They rushed towards the reservoirs, where the noises seemed to have originated. A scene of chaos awaited them. Heylor was on the ground, unconscious and shaking. His pants were wet around his groin. Beside him both reservoirs showed signs of damage. The so-called hot water reservoir was missing its hatch— a hundred-pound vented steel disk—and steam was whistling out the top. On the side of the other reservoir two bands of narrow cracks glinted near its equator. Adara stood on her toes and reached up to run a finger along the cracks.

"It's damned cold. But not leaking. Yet," she noted coolly.

Ice.

Endicott scrambled up the ladder of the cold reservoir and opened the hatch. He could make out a shining layer of ice a few feet below the top of the water. He called it down.

"I heard a sound from the filter vessel," said a member of one of Adara's work crews, who had rushed over from their lunch spot nearby.

Adara put a hand over her mouth but quickly pulled it away. "That must be from the pressure wave." She looked at the man. "Go get Sorin Kype as fast as you can. Tell him to bring his masonry equipment. Quickly! We have to fix this before the ice melts enough to start springing water." She turned to another man. "Kyle! You and your crew go close all the downstream valves. When you're done, go upstream and do the same."

Think fast.

Endicott focused on what needed to be done to save the waterworks. He did not think about why Heylor had acted as he had or even whether the young man was too far gone to survive. He pushed out of his mind any speculation about what would happen if the reservoirs fell completely apart. He thought only about what needed to be done right now and how best to do it. When he spoke, his voice was calm and even. "Adara, we can fix this. Let us help."

Adara's mouth was tight. Her eyes searched his. "Let's hear it," she said through gritted teeth, glancing nervously at the cracked reservoir.

Endicott nodded, eyes locked on hers. "Bethyn and Merrett, take Heylor and figure out how to deal with his hypothermia before it's too late." He pointed at the cold reservoir. "I'll repair the cracks in this tank."

"Meanwhile," he added, taking Adara's hand to reassure her, "take Davyn with you and check along the lines to see if anything else is damaged."

"Gerveault told us you weren't to do any heavy manipulation, Robert!" Bethyn said with uncharacteristic concern.

Adara stepped in between her and Endicott. "What do you need?"

"A hammer."

"I'll help you," boomed Davyn. "We can fix the cracks together while Adara starts flagging other problems."

Endicott knew Davyn was his equal in intelligence. He was less sure if the big man had an affinity for his smithing method. He *was* sure Davyn had never tried it. In fact, other than his grandpa, Endicott was not aware of anyone else using that particular style of specific preparation for dynamics.

Do I take another chance?

"Best if you help Adara. We can't leave this place worse than when we arrived."

Davyn nodded but stayed put.

Merrett said nothing. The big man had already picked up Heylor and carried the shivering, skinny man over to Bethyn like a baby.

He's literally in their hands now.

Endicott left it at that. He turned from them, considering the fractured reservoir in front of him. "It's a tensile fracture," he observed.

"And it's still iced up, you said," continued Davyn. "So the wall is still under tensile stress from the expansion. Let me start on that." The big man walked round the side of the tank, shouting at the work crews to bring the tools he would need for his part of the operation.

Someone pressed a two-pound hammer into Endicott's hand. "Hurry," Adara said into his ear. "You have until my mason gets here or the reservoir falls apart. Whichever happens first." Then she was gone.

Endicott opened himself to the empyreal sky and examined the cracks. He had made an extensive study of the reservoirs with Adara earlier as part of his preparation for the heating calculations, but he needed another look before he dared attempt to change the poured stone of the walls. He gathered that Gerveault had impressed the prohibition on his use of dynamics on Davyn, Bethyn, and Heylor as well as on Merrett, and brought some other form of pressure on Adara and who knows who else in town. The old man must have thought that the head injury would either affect his abilities or make it too dangerous to exercise them. Endicott knew this was not the case. His abilities were fine. It was rarely a question of ability. Reasoning and preparation almost always mattered more, although this time there was very little opportunity for either. As for the danger to himself, that was another matter, one he could not afford to consider now. If the reservoir burst, it would not only be a disaster for the whole town. It could undo the change in narrative they were attempting and damage the reputation of the New School beyond repair.

He had a pretty good idea of the temperature in the hot water reservoir, but he checked that before he swung back his hammer and put steel against stone.

Bang.

Just as he had done with his grandpa back at the farm in Bron, as he had done when repairing Freyla Loche's now-famous stitching machines, and as he had done when he created the shields, Endicott manipulated probability at the precise moment that he struck. The hot water reservoir made the perfect heat sink; it was close enough to draw from easily but not too close to prevent a full, clear, powerful swing of his hammer. Yet probability manipulation was by far the toughest of the disciplines within dynamics. And the first attempt would be the most dangerous.

I don't know the cost.

Luckily Endicott knew that he did not know the price, so he worked around the problem by over-borrowing energy from the hot water tank.

Knights.

The cost turned out much higher than he expected. There was almost no leftover energy. His manipulation was also not as precise as he had hoped, and this cost him some of his own precious internal heat.

I must swing harder. Much harder.

Endicott shivered as he examined the results of the first blow. Six inches of crack on either side of his hammer was repaired. That section was now smooth and perfect. He looked up and saw that Davyn and two crewmen were now at the top of the reservoir. In their hands were what looked like either spears or some kind of gardening poles. With these they began hacking at the ice inside, trying to break it up.

Good. It must be a thin layer.

Endicott raised the hammer again, pushing it as high and as far behind him as his arms could stretch. Then he steadied his footing and struck dynamically in perfect time with the steel.

Bang!

The impact made a tremendous clang. He wondered if Adara had heard it wherever she was and what she must be wondering, or dreading.

This time Endicott's grasp of the process was sharper, his assessment of the cost more accurate, and his hammer blow stronger than the first. The superior preparation meant he spent less internal energy for the same effect. Out of the corner of his eye he saw Davyn begin to climb down, apparently satisfied with his ice-breaking, but he pushed his big friend out of his mind. He would have to trust that Davyn had accomplished his part and would now carry on with checking for other damage to the system.

The stone wants to be smooth and strong. In his mind Endicott built a powerful image of the reservoir as it had been. He gripped that idea as firmly the hammer, and with both he struck again and again and again.

"Eight Knights! It's Darday'l. Hammer and scroll." The awed voices of the workmen barely registered. Endicott continued working, developing a rhythm as he hammered the cracks whole. The rhythm morphed into the two-beat hammer sound he had adapted from the shield work, though the second tap was more muted due to the lesser elastic properties of the stone.

BANG-tap, BANG-tap, BANG-tap.

Endicott's forearms ached, but his shoulders ached more. He had to reach high to hit the cracks, and the strain began to tell. He ignored the pain. He ignored the gathering crowd of crewmen and their exclamations. He focused on holding firm to his mental image of the reservoir and asserting it each time he struck.

BANG-tap, BANG-tap, BANG-tap.

Even with the heavy hammer and ferocious swings his specific preparation was not as good as it could have been. Cold-poured stone was less likely to flow whole than heated metal, so the thermodynamic toll on Endicott was extreme. All that practice with Koria now proved essential, making what would have been a suicidally difficult task merely agonizing.

Or maybe not. I am getting colder and colder. When will I pass the point of no return?

BANG-tap, BANG-tap, BANG-tap.

Endicott considered asking Bethyn or Davyn to heat the crack just ahead of his probabilistic manipulation, but he knew they were too busy. Although a group of crewmen had gathered to watch him work, Endicott sensed the buzzing activity of Davyn, Bethyn, Adara, and others somewhere in the background. They had their own urgent issues.

BANG-tap, BANG-tap, BANG-tap.

By the time Endicott had almost finished hammering, he was shivering so hard he could barely grip the hammer, and he could no longer see or hear beyond the task, the pain in his shoulders, and his own shivering tremors.

"Just let it go." Somehow a single voice penetrated his concentration from somewhere off to the side.

Let it go?

"Let it go, Robert." It was Adara. She was trying to take his hammer away. "My mason is here. He can take care of whatever is left."

"Grab him, Bat!"

Awareness flowed back, and Endicott found himself being dragged by Bat Merrett towards a rain barrel. "L-let g-go of m-me, M-Merrett!" he said.

The big man ignored Endicott's stutters, picked him up over his head, and tossed him into the barrel, barely avoiding catching his legs on the rim. "F-fucker." The water was delightfully hot. Endicott closed his eyes. When he opened them, he saw Heylor in another barrel not far away. The skinny young man was staring at him with red, feverish eyes. Merrett leaned against a tank behind Heylor, watching silently, his face some combination of amusement and disgust.

"You made it," Endicott called wearily to his classmate.

"Thanks to Bethyn." Heylor looked down. "She saved me from my stupidity. You too. She's pretty smart, you know. Smarter than me."

"Merrett helped you too."

Heylor sloshed water as he jerked around to look at the soldier.

Merrett spit sideways. "Don't bring me into this, Impulse Control."

"No," Heylor said. "Thanks, Bat. Really."

Merrett didn't move, but his voice was thick with sarcasm. "There's still time to burn down the town when you're done soaking your nuts."

Heylor's eyes screwed up. "Wouldn't you stop us?"

"That's not my job," Merrett snorted. "Just keeping you idiots alive while you do what you do. That's my job."

"Tough job, hey? Maybe it's better not to be able to do wizard stuff." The skinny man turned ungracefully in his barrel back towards Endicott. "I understand you saved the town."

Now is the time. We can't have this happen ever again.

He wanted to let Heylor have it, but new thoughts occurred. Memories rose unbidden in Endicott's mind, layered one upon the other like thin paper over bold ink, leaking their message from memory to memory. They stopped him from initiating the angry lecture he had planned.

He remembered walking with his grandpa, working with him, and all the silent time that would pass before ideas found voice. Grandpa never lectured him right off. Lesson always followed silence and time spent. He remembered working with Uncle Arrayn in the fields and then riding home with him in the wagon. Quiet but together. Endicott remembered the long, happy moments alone with Koria in her room, when between reading or manipulating the Empyreal Sky or kissing, thoughts would appear of themselves and pass between the two of them. The inner observations, questions, and secrets of youth and the world did not reveal themselves when called. Truth came forth only in the space of silences and the moments between actions, when family or friend was present but not speaking, not demanding. Communication flowed of its own accord with patience and specific preparation.

And so Endicott stifled his instinct to scold and said nothing, allowing the silent space to work.

"I'm sorry, Robert." Heylor said finally.

"I know."

"I didn't mean to do break everything."

"Clearly. You did something you thought would be harmless. Not small, mind you. What I don't understand is *why*, Heylor?"

"I wanted to be like you, Robert."

"Next time be a *better* me. You don't have to repeat *all* my mistakes."

"Huh." Heylor snorted, looking down. "I thought that bringing the hot water to the mayor's party would make for a ripping good story. I wanted to be the one who did it for once. I wanted to make Adara … like me." Tears streamed down Heylor's face. "I wanted *you* to be proud of me."

What should I say to that? What do I say to someone who is the cautionary example I should be learning from?

He took a moment to distance himself from the problem and decided that too much sympathy was not the answer, but nor was too little. "Worrying about the opinion of others is a hole that cannot be filled, Heylor. Ever."

Heylor nodded, face miserable.

"You nearly killed yourself. You might have killed others. That would make for a pretty shitty story."

"S'pose so."

"Slow down next time."

"But you're always pushing the bounds!" Heylor cried.

"Yes," Endicott answered after a moment. He shuddered, not entirely from the lingering effects of hypothermia. "We are both impulsive. But I've been pushing for a specific purpose, Heylor. To prevent Koria and Eloise from dying like I dreamed. That's different from what happened here. Can you see that?"

"Yah." If Heylor were a dog, his ears would have lowered.

Endicott visibly, with exaggerated slowness, let out a long breath. "If you want to emulate someone, choose a wiser model. Koria, for example. She watches and considers and then acts with such subtlety that most of the time you don't even know she has been at work. She *chooses* her moment." Heylor nodded and looked away. "Better yet, don't emulate anyone. You are fine the way you are, brother. When you use this muscle." Endicott pointed at his head. He thought about saying more, but sometimes *less* provokes thought better than more. He kept quiet, and the two of them resumed their silent vigils in their separate barrels. Silent time enveloped them once more like the warm baths that surrounded them.

▽

"Come look at this!" Davyn's voice was unnervingly loud in Endicott's ears. Louder than ever.

Oh. I fell asleep.

Heylor was gone. Endicott was pretty sure his impulsive friend would not take Merrett up on the suggestion of burning down the mayor's house, but not so sure that he didn't call Merrett over to help him out of his barrel. He was reminded of *The Lonely Wizard* when Feydleyn and the wizard had first approached the Line, only in the book the difficulty of climbing unassisted out of a water-filled barrel was never discussed.

Merrett and Endicott walked up the hill towards the sand filter, both dripping water. Heylor, Bethyn, and Adara stood on top of the big stone tank peering down into the open hatch. Endicott climbed up, briefly put an arm around Bethyn's shoulders, and whispered, "Nicely done with Heylor," and looked in.

Davyn pointed at the walls and ceiling all around the hatch. The biota from the top few inches of the filter had been pressure-blasted by a pulse of water from the downstream reservoirs and was now splattered all around the walls of the vessel in a gross-looking, greenish-black ooze.

"I did something like that to a privy once," Davyn said thoughtfully. "On a smaller scale."

"Nice," muttered Bethyn, scrunching her nose.

"We'd best shut off flow to the filter until we can get this cleaned up," said Adara shaking her head. "It's pretty gross," she added with a queer smile.

"How are we otherwise?" Endicott asked.

"We found some fatigue in three valves, but we will have them all replaced by tomorrow night." Adara blew out a breath and smiled, freckles brightening and dimples showing again. "It was a good recovery." She looked at Endicott. "What you did to those cracks was frankly amazing, Sir Robert. I have never seen or heard the like of it. You changed the nature of reality. Instantly. It was like the power of gods and angels." She put her hands on her hips. "You know, I think I have realized what your problem is. You are so Knights-damned talented you think you should be able to control *everything*. You aren't challenged enough."

If only that were true.

Endicott wondered when it was that he had ever lacked challenges, but he let the comment pass. "I suppose that is the least of what we deserve. And you know, Adara, you change the nature of reality every time you put in a new valve, groom the filter tank, or repair a pipe. You just do it … differently. And probably through a more considered process."

"Do you think?" Adara exclaimed. "Well, even when we do make our *considered* decisions, the outcomes are a lot slower to arrive. A less sophisticated bunch than my crew," she smiled sardonically, "might be a little scared if they thought you and your *mighty* friends were going to run around loose doing whatever you want whenever you want."

Endicott started shivering again as he dripped onto the tank. There was no arguing the point. "I'm sorry about this. Is there anything else we can do to make life more difficult for you while we are here?"

She snorted. "How about finding the missing hatch?"

Missing hatch?

Endicott remembered the hot water reservoir and its missing stopper.

"Is that party still on for tonight?" asked Davyn. "I hope the hatch hasn't gone through the roof of the mayor's house."

It was not until late the next day that the heavy metal disk was found in a farmer's field nearly a mile away.

Chapter Sixteen.
Empirical Tests

THE SUN SANK TOWARDS THE HORIZON- RED AND SWOLLEN. HEAVY EARS OF WHEAT SWAYED gently in the slight breeze. An old, crumbling tower rose to the right of the setting sun, casting a long, deep shadow. A group of people were scattered about the field, speaking in the quiet rumble of relaxed conversation. A man cried out suddenly from somewhere in the trees, but Endicott could not hear what he said. He wondered why the man's voice was pitched so high.

Suddenly a terrible, rotten-meat smell filled his nostrils, clogging them, almost stopping his breath.

What?

The world spun.

A bloody hand lay, absent an arm, on the dark cobbles. A ringing sound reverberated in Endicott's ear. Someone breathed loudly in a manner that seemed strangely familiar. A man screamed and ran by, his cloak on fire. Koria stumbled into view, the heel of one of her shoes broken and half hanging off her foot. An enormous cloaked figure stepped forward from under a broken gate.

Koria!

"Robert!"

He woke, terrified and confused. Koria was shaking him, her frightened eyes hovering above his.

"Knights!" Endicott swore, holding the image of Koria tight in his gaze.

She is okay. She is okay. She is okay.

"You're okay." She clutched him while he repeated it again and again.

"I know it feels like the only thing in the world," Koria whispered, arms around Endicott while he sobbed. "That it is everything; that it is forever, that it is *all* of your forever." She held his head with both her small hands and looked into his reddened, weeping eyes. "It is *not* your forever, Robert. It has not happened. It is only a *maybe*. The pain will pass. Just breathe it out."

Endicott tried to do that. He labored to let the heraldic dream go, but there was a problem with the whole idea of letting go. When the pain has a causal connection to your future, you cannot rationally afford to forget, which makes letting go of bad future-memories nearly impossible.

What am I doing to myself?

Is it better to forget what hurts you or to talk about it? How much worse is it to talk about a harrowing memory in detail, to hammer those memories into immutable shape, reinforcing their power and durability? If it were only an event from the past, no detailed examination of the memory would be helpful, but when it is a memory of the future, there is a rational motivation to mine the details. And so it becomes the worst combination of the rational and irrational mind acting together to destroy emotional equilibrium.

There was no question that Endicott would go over the details of what he had seen with Koria. There was no question that he would relive the dream. He told her everything he could remember, hoping for some advantage to offset the cost of memory.

"You have to see it as a gift, Robert." Koria said firmly.

"A painful one." Endicott felt no shame in saying this. Koria knew what heraldic dreaming was like.

"It's *information*, Robert. You know that. *Potential* information." She made him lie down on her bed, looked him up and down for a moment, and promptly straddled him. "Separate yourself from how you feel about it. You didn't *make* yourself dream it. You aren't the *cause* of it. Those feelings are not helpful, but the information is. It's a gift. Let's use it."

"Ha! If that's true, I don't know whether I should be upset that you woke me from it before I learned more, or happy to have avoided seeing the rest." He wiped his eyes.

Koria sat astride his stomach looking down on him, her hair draping her small face like the branches and leaves of a tree. "Maybe we should be happy you avoided seeing more."

"How so?"

She smiled sadly. "Because you saw enough. Seeing the outcome was not important. What was critical was the affirmation of the threat. It still exists."

"Apparently," Endicott rejoined. "Which means that nothing we have done—including the fiasco at the Black Spear—has gotten rid of the cloaked figure, whoever he is. He's still coming for you."

"And coming soon," added Koria, staring intensely into Endicott's eyes. "The wheat was ripe, but the trees still had leaves. That will be very soon. Though we should keep in mind that the two parts of your dream may not have been contemporaneous."

"Do you think I can get out of the trip with Elyze Astarte?" Endicott asked, but even as he spoked, he doubted he would ask to back out. He had given his word.

Koria looked up at the ceiling. "We lost Konrad and Rendell. They were both on the agricultural project."

"Rendell?"

"The other dead dynamicist from last week. The burned one. The death of two key people is motivating Elyze Astarte to have you there even more. She was already very strangely attached to the idea." Koria's eyes narrowed. "And then there is the deal with Novgoreyl in play as well. I have a hunch where Eleanor at least is going with this and what sort of plans she has for you."

"What?" Endicott asked. As usual, Koria knew more than he did.

"Go get dressed, and we will find out for sure. We are all due at the Citadel in a few hours."

THE TRIP TO THE CITADEL WAS NOT AS SIMPLY DONE AS ENDICOTT HAD AT FIRST IMAGINED. Bat Merrett, Eoyan March, and Jeyn Lindseth arrived in full chain armor and surcoats to escort them. Jeyn had a longsword on each hip. It was quickly apparent that everyone was expected to dress their best. This proved a challenge for Heylor especially. So soon after the trip to Aignen, he had very little in the way even of clean clothes, never mind formal wear. They did have a sword for him, though, hastily borrowed from the military school. The skinny young man still couldn't swing it safely in company, but its scabbard and belt did help dress up the unkempt package that was Heylor.

Eoyan, by prior arrangement, had taken charge of the shield that Gregory had hidden first in the Orchid and later in the Lott. He carried it concealed under a soft blanket in the school colors, a quirky, lopsided smile pasted on his face. Gregory wore his entropic sword and, like Endicott, his formal, blue-and-gold Knight of Vercors cloak. Tall Eloise flanked him, similarly armed and cloaked, but wearing the blue-and-yellow tartan skirt of the New School, her long, muscular legs and unmistakable Armadalian features drawing equally intense, if differently motivated, glances from both men and women as she passed. Davyn, Deleske, Bethyn, and Koria went unarmed in the New School colors. They knew who they were and did not carry weapons.

Endicott found himself walking beside Bat Merrett, who had a hand on his sword and appeared quite tense. The heavily built young man's attention was all outward, except for an early head shake at Endicott as they fell in together.

"What?" Endicott asked.

"Why didn't you keep a better sword?" Merrett pitched his voice low, eyes on the streets. "Or make another? You had the time."

Endicott looked down at the old nicked sword belted to his hip. It was the one he had used when they worked with real iron at the military school and was something of a relic. Various possible answers went through Endicott's head, including the fact that making entropic swords was difficult, dangerous, and expensive. One answer stood out. "I never had a dream where I needed one." He gestured to Eloise. "But I had a dream where she *does*."

"Hmm."

"Why did you say my father died of carelessness?" The question popped out without any warning, surprising both of them. Once it was spoken, Endicott realized he had been harboring it for some time. Merrett gave only one small sign that the question bothered him, just the slightest tightening along his jaw. He kept silent for a few moments, until Endicott began to wonder if he would have to ask again, and more forcefully.

"I was told to." Merrett said this almost in a whisper, and he did not look at Endicott as he spoke.

"By Keith Euyn?"

Now Merrett did look at Endicott for one still second before facing forward again. "No."

Endicott's eyebrows shot up. He did not ask the obvious question. Instead he said, "Well, at least we are all saved from an awkward moment by your policy on apologies."

Merrett's face remained forward but his eyes slowly rolled sideways towards Endicott. "That depends. Do you trust Eleanor and Gerveault?"

"I do."

"Then you don't need an apology."

▽

THE CITADEL WAS AN ANCIENT, BEAUTIFUL STONE CASTLE SET IN THE HEART OF VERCORS. It was well maintained and as clean as stone could be. Its thick walls were largely granitic, though some of the floors had a layer of polished limestone. It was a castle of towers and elevated walkways, of gates and stone balconies, sky bridges and secret vantage points. For all that complexity it had a single massive, wide entrance with stairs that went directly to the heart of the edifice. The grand entrance was both inviting and deadly. It was called the Fool's Way. The Fool's Way stairs had eight heavy iron gates set deep in granite. Each gate was set far enough apart that the top of the first gate was below the bottom of the second gate and so on, and each gate was secured by entirely different structural elements. Once those gates were closed, ingress was only possible from the elevated walkways, narrow corkscrew stairways, and well-hidden iron doors. Attackers faced an impossible geometry of towers and crenulated sky bridges and could be held at bay indefinitely until worn down with gravity-accelerated assaults of iron, oil, and wood. It was a dauntingly expensive setup to sustain, as expensive as only something built never to change could be.

"I never imagined I would be invited here," said Heylor loudly enough for Endicott to hear him from three strides and more away. "It kind of makes home seem like a sty."

"It's probably drafty," rejoined Bethyn under her breath. Deleske snorted.

Lord Arthur Wolverton, commander of the military school, walked towards them down the Fool's Way, his polished boots clicking on the stairs. Endicott had met him on a few occasions at the school. It was Wolverton who had assigned

Bat Merrett, Jeyn Lindseth, and Eoyan March to train the class. He was heavyset but starchily upright and composed in the fashion that the old Engevelen nobility was noted for. Now he was flanked by two other armed officers Endicott did not recognize, one of them a dark-haired lady only a little taller than Koria. The other was a man of about Endicott's height, who shared the distinctive coloring of old Engevelen with Lord Wolverton.

Polite greetings were exchanged, though Lord Wolverton's task-oriented professionalism made them seem more pro forma than heartfelt. "The gentleman on my left is Lieutenant Vaugn Somne," he announced, "and the lady on my right is Sergeant Eirnyn Quinn. Please file up by twos with Lady Valcourt and Sir Robert in the front followed by Sir Gregory and Sir Eloise."

"Please walk with me, Bethyn," Jeyn Lindseth said in his unassuming, gentle tones. His thoughtfulness made Endicott smile.

"And you can go right in front of me, Heylor," said Merrett, slapping two massive paws on the skinny man's shoulders. Heylor's knees buckled. "Don't steal anything, and don't try heating the water here."

"Basically, don't do anything," added Eoyan March, whispering in his ear but smiling.

"The acoustics are excellent!" said Davyn with implausible volume as they ascended the second flight of stairs. Wolverton turned and frowned at him, but Davyn just winked back. The stairs seemed to go on and on. By the eighth flight Davyn was huffing and puffing beside an incredulous Deleske.

"So tired!" he exclaimed, pausing and bending over, hands on his knees. Endicott knew Davyn was putting on a show. He had seen the big man bound up the hill at Aignen without breaking a sweat.

They passed down a long, wide hallway. The floor was a sealed and polished travertine with a series of mottos carved into it. The first one read:

> "KNOWLEDGE AND WISDOM ARE NOT TWINS,
> BUT THEY MAKE GOOD COMPANIONS."

This made Endicott chuckle despite its obviousness. He had been to the Citadel once before after the fiasco at the Black Spear, but he remembered nothing of the Fool's Way or its etched mottos. The second motto was less obvious, and it chilled him as he read it.

"Know the cost."

Endicott recalled the protestors' signs.

How different is this motto from some of what they proclaimed?

He was more comfortable passing over the well-known mottos of the eight Methueyn Knights. Darday'l's scroll-on-hammer symbol reminded Endicott of the hill at Aignen. It was the name some of Adara's crew had shouted as he repaired the hot water reservoir. It was also the same symbol as the one on his replacement medallion.

At last they reached the vast iron-bound double doors that led to the formal audience chamber of the duke and duchess. Eight guards stood outside the doors, four on either side, all in full plate armor. Lord Wolverton led the group past the guards and motioned everyone to pause just inside the door. A herald stood there, though of a different kind than Endicott normally associated the term with. As this officer resonantly announced each pair, they stepped forward and down the long, carpeted pathway to the throne. Goose bumps broke out on Endicott's skin when he heard his and Koria's names ring out. He looked back to see Bethyn's and later Heylor's reactions to being announced. They both blushed. Deleske only smiled a little smile as if he had a secret. Davyn waved enthusiastically and unabashedly to the crowd.

The room was nearly full. Endicott recognized very few of the people lined up on either side of the carpet. Most were dressed in rich, formal clothes, including Lord Jon Indulf and a smiling Jennyfer Gray. He almost missed Adara Torrinton, who stood beside the more elaborately dressed mayor of Aignen, Gwendolyn Holt. They both clapped as the students went by, a relief to Endicott considering the mixed results of their visit to Aignen.

Syriol stood below the thrones, smiling at them as they approached. Endicott held her eyes for an extra moment, genuinely pleased with her apparent ease at court. She winked at him and made a small hand gesture to Lord Wolverton, who then stopped five steps or so from Kennyth Brice's throne. The thrones were arranged much as they had been in the more private audience chamber that Endicott had previously visited, with the duke and duchess sitting side by side on the highest level and Lord Kennyth Brice one step down. Gerveault once again stood at the side of the duchess, as he so often had when the she was simply Professor Eleanor of the New School. Further to the left stood the tall armored form of Sir Hemdale. Endicott had not seen Eloise's uncle since the twenty-four-hour test.

Syriol turned to the duchess, and in a loud, careful voice that trembled almost imperceptibly, pronounced, "As commanded, Your Grace, here are your Knights of Vercors and their friends from the New School and the military school."

"Thank you, Syriol Lindseth," said the duchess in her gravelly voice. Endicott found it difficult to reconcile this stately figure in wig and dark powder with the friendly, down-to-earth professor, but the raspy voice was familiar and soothing. She stood up slowly and carefully in her majestic blue and yellow gown. "Thank you, Lord Wolverton. You and your soldiers may stand to the side while we address our students."

Wolverton, Somne, and Quinn were escorted away by Syriol, who came quickly back and resumed her position on the step below Lord Kennyth Brice.

"These, our students at the New School, have rendered us great service," the duchess called out in a louder voice. "Some have wondered at the expense and usefulness of our facilities on the Academic Plateau. Certain foreign powers have worked to deride the value of our studies and our students. We accept all questions asked honestly and without malice. We understand that some feel frustration over the many changes to our duchy during our reign. We understand that there are questions to be answered. We advise two things. First make peace with the new world. It moves and changes faster than the old one, but the duke and I, and our son Kennyth Brice, believe in our people. We believe that everyone can thrive in this dynamic new world, but to do so we must all take an active part in change. That is why we have supported the New School. We are confident it will help guide and assist all the people of this duchy. We have also supported the New School because we want to ensure that the changes that come are ones we choose and understand. Which brings me to the second thing that I advise: come to us for help."

She looked at her husband. He stood up. "The New School and some of its students and faculty are being made available to help its citizens and leaders in public works projects." The duke spoke in gruff tones, eyes scanning the crowd. "Applications should be sent to Lord Latimer. All will be duly considered on the basis of merit and need."

"For example," added the duchess, gesturing at Endicott's class, "these students have recently returned from Eschle and from Aignen, where they aided both cities in important public works, which included assessment and repairs to the series of cisterns in Eschle and to the waterworks in Aignen. These projects significantly reduced time and expense for both cities. As a token of our gratitude, each student will now receive these capes signifying their recognition by our court."

Several pages emerged carrying glowing blue and gold capes. They were handed out to Endicott's class as well as to Lindseth, Merrett, and Eoyan March. The soldiers did not put theirs on, but Endicott removed his cloak and donned the cape. It was decorated with beautiful hand-stitched work and a gleaming metal clasp with the scroll-and-hammer of Darday'l. Heylor beamed, clearly delighted with his cape. As the assembled nobles clapped their approval of the gifts, the skinny young man wept. Endicott was not unmoved either, but he knew that this gesture was part of the new ducal narrative. As he looked about at the assembled nobles, wealthy merchants, and others, he wondered if the politics of the proceedings were as transparent to them. Gerveault caught his eye, giving him a subtle nod.

Narrative.

"We have one other piece of business to conduct," said Kennyth Brice in his highly modulated voice. He leaned to the side of his massive chair and pulled up the shield that Endicott and Gregory had made for him. It had been hidden by a silk cloth, and when he stood with it, the shield seemed to blaze as if amplifying rather than just reflecting the light that struck it. "This indestructible shield was made for me by Sir Robert Endicott and Sir Gregory Justice. It required heroic effort and courage. I wish to personally thank them for it." Kennyth Brice's posture was perfect and his smile proud as he shook hands with Endicott and Gregory.

The nobles clapped again.

"May I speak, Lord Brice?" Gregory requested in even tones, bowing to the duke-to-be. Kennyth made a small hand wave of assent, and Gregory turned to face a suddenly startled Eloise. Eoyan March removed the cloth covering from the shield he carried and passed it to Gregory. It shone as strongly as Kenneth Bryce's, silvery and almost liquid. Eloise's eyes grew wide.

Gregory went down on one knee. "I also helped make this shield for you, Sir Eloise Kyre, as a gift and as symbol of my regard and interest in courting you." He held the shield out to Eloise.

She took it and replied almost curtly. "I accept your gift. And interest." She turned to the assembly and held the shining shield high, smiling as widely as it seemed possible for a person to do. This time the applause was thunderous. Someone in the crowd yelled out, "Kiss him!" Eloise obliged immediately, though only with an un-Eloise-like peck on Gregory's cheek.

That was incredibly drama-free. Endicott felt a little disappointed.

I thought Gregory would be pregnant by now. He had to look more closely to see that both pairs of hands were shaking.

Ah.

The court was quietly adjourned, and the students ushered into the duke and duchess's private audience chambers. Before the doors had even closed, Eloise shoved Gregory so hard he stumbled into Merrett's broad back. "So that was your big secret, stupe?"

"I told you something was going on!" Davyn exclaimed. Everyone ignored him, their attention riveted on Eloise and her suitor.

Gregory glanced at Endicott with a look of mock exasperation before answering the tall, blonde woman. "Are you not happy with the shield, Eloise, or with me?"

Bethyn had both arms crossed and was nodding her head. "Ya," she muttered under her breath. Endicott could not be certain, but thought she might have added "bitch" to the end of her barely audible comment.

Eloise ignored Bethyn, keeping her hard-eyed stare solely on Gregory. "Hrmmff." She glowered at him a bit longer before shrugging. "Both are acceptable. *I* prefer to do the surprising." She hoisted the shield up to get a better look at it. "Is this exactly the same as Lord Brice's, or is it more like yours?"

Sir Hemdale stepped in between them and grasped the shield, staring at it. He tapped the hilt of his sword against it.

Brrrrrraaaaa.

"It rings," he said in his deep voice.

Gregory shot an appeal at Endicott, and his friend stepped into the discussion. "Yes, Sir Hemdale. It has some unique elastic properties." He glanced around the giant, armored man at Eloise. "It is supple yet resilient, with superlative toughness and impact strength. When Gregory and I made it, we built it with a special set of elements in a particular brand of disorder. Please have a closer look."

Eloise's eyes defocused for a moment. Sir Hemdale watched his niece. Her eyebrows went up. "It looks a little like my sword. Is it the same?"

"Yes," said Gregory.

"And no," added Endicott. "The shield has a different purpose. It doesn't have to hold a particularly sharp edge, though it has a reasonable one. Our process was considerably more involved than even the one used to make your sword."

"What do you say, wizard?" Hemdale was looking at Gerveault, who stood off to the side but had been carefully watching and listening.

"I'm no more a wizard than you are," the old man complained. He gazed appraisingly at the shield. "It looks good, though as young Robert implied, goodness needs to be tested by use. I would prefer to examine it in the lab before saying more."

"Can't you just say yes or no?" Hemdale rumbled. "Is it a good shield?"

"To your first question: no. I am a dynamicist, not a sock puppet. If you want a simple answer, ask something simpler." Gerveault accented his response with a quick contraction of his brows. "To your second question, its molecular arrangement speaks well for it, though I have not seen this precise formulation before. If the shield is as strong, or somehow even stronger, than that oversized Endicott sword you wear—which, given its purpose and provenance, it may be—then it could have the highest toughness of anything I have ever seen." He held up his hand imperiously. "But to a physicist, empirical testing is necessary before rushing to some easily digestible narrative and declaring it the best shield in the world."

Hemdale smiled, though Endicott could not guess what this portended.

"It's *far* better than even my shield, Eloise," Gregory added quickly, obviously not sure if Gerveault and Hemdale were really arguing or not. "And *exactly* like Lord Brice's, except yours has your initial on it."

Endicott was reminded of Eloise killing Iver, the bald protestor, with the edge of Gregory's shield. "It actually was empirically tested once," he suggested.

Gregory's right eyebrow went up fractionally, and he rubbed at a still healing scab on his face. "That's … right. Kennyth Brice's shield—the identical article—stopped and shattered a thrown spear." He pointed at the scab. "The one that did this."

"A shield fit for a duke. Welcome, nephew!" Hemdale grabbed Gregory in a rough hug that Endicott guessed must have been intensely uncomfortable given the obvious force the old knight put into it and the sharp plate armor that he mashed against Gregory. The young man's feet left the ground for a long and awkward moment that made Endicott and everyone watching wince. Gregory stumbled when Hemdale let him go but did not get a chance to straighten himself out before Eloise wrapped him in an equally fierce, if presumably less painful, hug. "No more surprises," she growled as she let him go and patted his chest.

"This is sooo romantic," cooed Davyn loudly. "Toughness, empirical tests, and surprises. Where will this all end?"

"A beating behind the woodshed?" Bethyn whispered.

"*Something's* going on back there," Deleske added in a sarcastic stage whisper.

"Uhh," Gregory mumbled. "There is one more surprise."

Eloise's scowl and potentially violent response was forestalled by the duke, who announced from his throne, "We see that everyone is here." His deep voice dropped lower yet. "It is time we moved to the next item of business."

Endicott looked around and saw that the private audience chamber was, except for the ducal family on their thrones, standing room only. Lord Wolverton and his soldiers, as well as Merrett, Lindseth, and Eoyan March, had joined Endicott's class.

"Lady Gwenyfer has been murdered."

Eleanor's hoarse announcement froze everyone. Endicott felt his stomach drop. He remembered the administrator well from his first day at the New School. Koria slipped through the press and found his hand.

Why would anyone wish to harm her, let alone kill her?

Endicott's immediate instinct was to assume the murder had been perpetrated by the cloaked figure, the Nimrheal wannabe, but on reflection this made no sense. Even the best administrators were seldom truly innovative. They ordered, organized, and ruled, at best facilitating innovation rather than initiating it. They were systematic and served the system. Lady Gwenyfer was, in Endicott's limited experience, all these things. She served Eleanor's system. So even if the cloaked figure pretended to be Nimrheal, he would not have been following Nimrheal's rules properly if he were the killer.

"Was it Nimrheal?" Heylor blurted into the spontaneous moment of silence.

"There is no Nimrheal." Gerveault said with a sneer as he went to stand beside the duchess's throne. "Not in this world."

"Might as well be Nimrheal," growled the old duke.

"Do not say that!" admonished Gerveault sharply.

The duke was not put off by Gerveault's boldness. "That is what the posts will say."

"Not without reason." Kennyth Brice leaned forward in his chair. "Witnesses spotted a large cloaked man, consistent with the perpetrator that Sir Gregory and Sir Robert saw fleeing the other murders." He looked back at Gerveault. "He also had a spear, though Lady Gwenyfer was immolated."

There was another moment of silence. Heylor did not interrupt this one, but Endicott reluctantly did.

"I should tell you something," Endicott said. He described his abbreviated heraldic dream of that morning. A shocked silence followed.

"Are you all right?" asked Bethyn, brows scrunched. Eloise's mouth was open, Gregory looked mournful, Davyn curious, Heylor excited, and Deleske unreadable.

"Yes," Endicott said. He glanced at Koria. "I have been advised to view it as information."

"That is very good advice," said Gerveault. "Hang on to it. It is common for a person who has one heraldic dream to have more, and a person who has two heraldic dreams *always* has more."

Eleanor had been wringing her hands, apparently unconsciously, for she suddenly seemed to notice what she was doing and abruptly let them go. Endicott could see the twisted dark blue veins under her thin, powdered skin. "Thank you for telling us, Sir Robert. Whatever happens, you have done well in passing this along."

"Here, here," affirmed Kennyth Brice. "Thank you, knight. This is useful information."

"Should we assume the cloaked figure in Sir Robert's dream is the same person who has been murdering our people?" Eleanor's hands came together again. She gazed at them for a moment, then settled them on the arms of her throne.

Davyn's hand shot up. "Sounds the same, looks the same, murders the same. Same enough for me to run away from."

"Is running what we should be doing?" asked Jeyn Lindseth softly.

"Yes!" said Davyn. Bethyn and Deleske nodded. Heylor's eyes were as big as saucers.

"You *should* run, Davyn. Please do if you see him." Kennyth Brice smiled ruefully. "Give the constables time to catch him."

"Can they?" asked Endicott, thinking of the burned corpse the cloaked man had left, and his impossibly hard spear throw.

"We discussed the same thing earlier this morning, Sir Robert." Kennyth's left hand rose, palm up. "We wondered if he is *beyond* our constabulary. It is a reasonable question. If the cloaked figure is a powerful dynamicist, they will need help. That is why we have attached Sir Christensen to the constabulary until the matter is resolved," Kennyth added. "That should make the problem more one of time than capacity."

"Perhaps," said the duke. He stood up and impatiently paced the room. "I hate sitting so much," he muttered before continuing. "I am not content to sit passively and wait on time," he said in a louder voice. "I know we made adjustments, Kennyth, but this new dream of Sir Robert's bothers the hell out of me." He made an abrupt chopping motion with his hand. "It makes me think we are failing. Are we doing enough?"

Endicott observed that if you hold counsel with people, if you seek out their opinion, they will give it to you. And so there followed a longer, more open-ended discussion of the murders, the cloaked figure of Endicott's heraldic dreams, the threat he represented, the still missing fugitives from the Black Spear, the constabulary's frustration at failing to make the city safe, and what should be done to help them. Many opinions were forthcoming, but nothing was resolved.

How can anything be resolved while the cloaked figure is still out there?

"We could adjourn the New School tomorrow or the next day," Eleanor suggested at last. "The end-of-summer break is almost here, and the constables need more time to catch the murderer. Meanwhile I want my kids safe." She looked at Lord Wolverton. "Move the trip across the Castlereagh Line up a few days. Can you be ready to leave the day after tomorrow?"

Wolverton nodded. "Yes. Our planning was complete some time ago, so making ready will not be an issue. I had planned on sending Lieutenant Vaugn Somne, Sergeant Eirnyn Quinn, and ten soldiers to guard Elyze Astarte and Vyrnus Hedt. I would like permission to give them more support in case Sir Robert's fragmentary dream does pertain to some unexpected risk."

"You have it," said Eleanor. "Anything reasonable. As you know, Sir Robert and Sir Gregory will be joining them, along with Eoyan March. Be aware that they will be outside your command structure."

What does that mean?

The duchess swung her gaze to Endicott and Gregory. "Assuming you are still willing to go?"

"A deal is a deal," said Gregory. Endicott nodded.

Eloise bristled. "Deal? When was all this decided? Who knew about this?" She put her hands on her hips and bored into Gregory with her fierce eyes. "You can't propose to me and leave the next day, stupe!"

Koria and Endicott exchanged a look. Gregory's face turned red, but he faced up to her. "Yes. I. Can." He pointed at the shield Eloise held on her arm. "That shield came with a price, Eloise. We agreed to go on this trip in exchange for the very rare and expensive materials needed to make your shield."

"But we would go anyway," Endicott added. "The duchess has asked us to do something, and we will not deny her."

"Fine," gritted Eloise. "*I* will come too."

"Me too!" yelled Heylor.

"Not me," Deleske whispered just at the edge of Endicott's hearing.

"No," interrupted Gerveault. "I don't think so. I do not want all my students in one place, and part of the motivation for making Eloise's shield was so she could protect herself and Lady Koria. We are going to stick to that."

"This has been quite a conspiracy," Eloise spit out. "You've worked everything out. But who's going to look after these stupes?" She pointed at Endicott and Gregory. "What the fu—"

Sir Hemdale put a firm, gauntleted hand on Eloise's shoulder and squeezed hard enough that she stopped mid-curse. "Enough. I am going with your fiancé as well. You will go with Lady Koria to her estate and protect her." Eloise scowled up at Hemdale, but she was looking at someone who could out-scowl even her. She locked eyes with her uncle for a moment and then sighed, seeming to accept Hemdale's decree.

"What about me?" asked Heylor.

"You can come with us," Koria said. "Everyone can if they want to. It would be safest."

Deleske crossed his arms and shared an unenthusiastic look with Bethyn. Endicott could understand Deleske's lack of interest in being a guest at Koria's estate. He had always acted slightly outside the group and probably did not consider himself in real danger. Bethyn was another matter. She might have been irritated at being treated like an afterthought, but Endicott guessed that she simply did not want to holiday with Eloise. She hated the tall girl. Or loved her, perhaps.

Kennyth Brice's eyebrows had been half raised through the entire discussion, but he finally smiled sympathetically. "Perhaps if we explained exactly what is going on, everyone would appreciate the situation better." The duchess nodded to him, and he continued. "There is more at play here than this horrible series of murders and the unrest we have been experiencing." He paused, taking in the room.

"Some of you are aware that we have been working for some time on a treaty with Novgoreyl. That treaty cedes the former Ardgour County of Novgoreyl—now known as the Ardgour Wilderness—to Vercors. The agreement has finally been ratified by our own emperor, Laureate, and goes into effect immediately. There are some interesting challenges, however. One being the skolves, who will certainly defend what they see as their territory. The other is a performance clause in the treaty. It states that if we fail to substantially reclaim the Wilderness within a certain time period, we will lose our rights to the county, which could then be ceded to Armadale."

Davyn's hand shot up. "But why? Why would Novgoreyl make a deal like this with us? Why cede territory at all, and why put us on a schedule?"

"We don't know." Kennyth spread his hands. "But the opportunity is too good to ignore. We must try. And the years will go by very quickly."

"Strange," muttered Bethyn.

"Let me count the ways," Endicott whispered. Koria was saying nothing, which was not unusual, but it told him she likely knew more of what was going on than he did. Also not unusual. "I take it that you have a plan that somehow involves the New School's modified grain."

"Very good! We have *two* plans, Robert," said Gerveault. "The one with the grain is called Lighthouse and involves less military exposure. Rather than risking our soldiers, it uses the modified grain to fight the skolves. I proposed the first plan, and your trip across the Line is part of an empirical test of Lighthouse."

It cannot really be a new idea, then. Nor can it be a small plan.

Davyn's hand shot up. "Thank you for realizing that *I* do not want to go out and play with the skolves. Heaving myself back and forth across the Line is not a pretty image in my head, I can tell you. If you must send any of us, you are right in sending Robert and Gregory rather than me."

Gerveault frowned. "I sense a question is coming."

"You don't need to be a herald to see this one," Davyn said with a sharp gleam in his eyes. "Why send *any* students with less than a half year of education and training out there? You have more experienced dynamicists. Why them?"

"Do you want a list?" said Gerveault.

"Yes," boomed Davyn.

"My question was rhetorical," Gerveault replied.

"I still would like an answer."

Gerveault pulled a letter out of his belt. "Even a long-term plan can be short of time, Davyn." He waved the letter briskly as if underlining a point. "Both plans call for dynamicists, but in different roles." Gerveault waved the letter again. "We have lost two very talented members of our team, and we have had to accelerate our training." Gerveault continued waving the letter to punctuate each point as he made it. "Now we want to give Sir Robert and Sir Gregory some of the seasoning we think they need. Sir Robert has become too well known and controversial in Vercors; we are uncomfortable with the level of threat to him if he stays here *or* if he goes home. We believe the agricultural trip is safer than the other alternatives. And lastly," Gerveault said, waving the letter once more, "we have had some heraldry suggesting Robert and Gregory need to be there. Elyze Astarte swears she dreamed it. But we have also heard from the most astute herald this side of Keith Euyn. Finlay Endicott says that both young men must go. He wrote us a letter saying so."

Davyn looked at Endicott and Gregory. "I guess you're going," he declared. "*Grandpa* says so."

"Who would my grandpa even write to?" asked Endicott. Hearing his grandpa's name shot a thrill through him, but Gerveault's revelation was hard to believe.

"Me," Gerveault stated evenly. "I have known Finlay for a very long time."

I think deep down I knew that.

Endicott reached for the letter, hoping to see it for himself, but Gerveault quickly put the paper behind his back. "This is not it. Well, he wrote this letter too, but it is for Sir Gregory to hold on to until your birthday. That is next week, correct?" He handed the letter to Gregory. "Give this to Sir Robert on his birthday. Finlay Endicott says that you will both be on the other side by then."

Chapter Seventeen

The Lonely Wizard

When most people go home, they feel relieved and at peace. The precise feelings vary from person to person, for we are all ultimately alone, but the human condition ensures that everyone needs a home and the reassuring feelings associated with it. At home people relax and feel safe. Home summons memories of family, of half-remembered formative moments, of familiar smells and comforts. It is the upward continuation of the accumulation of a multitude of fond and soothing memories. Home is all things familiar; it is a taste, a smell, a touch. It is all these things much more than it is ever a rational calculation.

I smell no memory, taste no dream, and feel no remembered comfort. I know none of those things of home. I see only the bare, denuded stalks of wheat in front of me. I approach the edges of the Wilderness and see that the skolves have eaten all the heads. Only about a score of miles to go. The time will pass quickly. I will run the rest of the way. I *am* running, fast, smooth and easy, deep in the equilibrium of my certainty, in the state of being that is orthogonal to both thinking and feeling. No memory, emotion, or association interferes with the perfect simplicity of my being. I achieve this space in my mind, and I live there. It is a space where home is unnecessary.

If Feydleyn was with me, he would have commented on the gravel road and perhaps the crunching sounds it made as his feet sped over it. It would remind him of something else he had experienced, and without a doubt he would want to discuss this at length. He would mourn the people of Ardgour, now scattered or dead, his face grieving and possibly tear-streaked. Feydleyn is the kind of person who carries home with him wherever he goes. He effortlessly imagines home, conjuring it into a sort of existence.

Feydleyn could still be described as the sort of person who lives in the moment, just not a focused moment. I live in the moment too, but differently. For me time flows in a series of simple, single instants of instantaneous intention. Feydleyn lives a hundred lives in every moment. If a bird flew by overhead, Feydleyn would track its progress and smile, taken up with the journey and life of the bird. If he saw a flower, he might forget the bird. If he saw a frog, he might forget the flower. He is easily distracted.

He might have enjoyed the journey across the Ardgour Wilderness if he could have survived it. There is indeed a stark beauty even in the crumbling ruins of old foundations. New undergrowth pops up among the stones in the myriad patterns defined by the Book of Nature, sometimes as bland gray-greens and sometimes, when the weeds flower, as a riot of colors.

A glint of something at my feet. I stop and pick it up. It is a rusted iron whistle. It is so old, crimped, and corroded that I do not understand how it could have reflected light, though somehow it did. The whistle lies at the edge of a small grove of cherry trees. Strange, so far north. An image flashes through my mind of children playing here. They are spitting out cherry pits, and one is blowing a whistle. Gone now. No sounds of laughter, no whistling, no children to be seen or heard. Feydleyn would have loved it. I pocketed it for him.

Clanggg.

A sharp ringing not far away. It is not some old child's toy but something harder and sterner. It sounds again and again, rapidly. I pocket the whistle and run through the cherry grove across a small stream and up a rise towards the sound. The staccato din of sword on metal is closer now, but I also hear the low autonomic growls of skolves. Expectation howls as I draw it from its scabbard and surmount the rise to see hell unfolding.

A tall knight in smoky armor hacks at a mass of swarming skolves. They converge on him like water rushing in upon a thrown rock. Some howl as they charge. The bodies of skolves lie strewn around the knight, suggesting this is the pack's second attempt to take down the tall armored man. Heads, claws, and crude, poorly maintained iron weapons are scattered about. The knight leaps aside just as the collapsing wave front of skolves hits. He breaks the circle of their advance and cuts one of the beasts in two vertical pieces that, held at a deadpoint, seem to adhere, then fall slowly, almost gracefully, apart.

But skolves are fast.

Two of them spring at his legs as he moves through the parted carcass. He stumbles to his knees, slashing desperately around him, and manages to regain his feet, but another wave front of skolves engulfs him and he disappears under a pile of thrashing fur and flashing teeth. I run down the small hill towards the writhing mass, but suddenly it breaks apart. The knight is on his feet, throwing the skolves off, but his helmet is gone, lost in the chaos. A rusty sledge cracks him in the head and he spins, falling. Some of the skolves leap on him while others turn and propel themselves towards me.

I cut the first skolve in half with a wide lateral slash through its spine, step past its separated, levitating pieces and rotate my wrists and shoulders to cut vertically through another skolve's head to its breastbone. I step forward and kick the twitching body into a third skolve, which frees my sword and bends the third skolve at the waist from the force of the collision. I drive my left hand like a spear through its eye socket and into its brain. It convulses and drops off my blood-soaked glove. Six others rise at once from the fallen knight to face me. They pause just long enough for me to make a rough set of calculations. The empyreal sky breaks like my hand through the skolve's eye, and I innovate a sharp exchange of heat from three of the creatures to the other three. One trio burst into flames, while the other freezes solid, cracking in a beautiful and complex pattern.

A rime of frost covers the ground, the denuded wheat, my face, my feet, the knight, and Expectation. I rub my eyes to free the lashes from the cold rime and see two new skolves emerge from the wheat stalks and make towards us. The young knight springs to his feet. His left eye is full of blood, but it is also half crusted with ice. I imagine one of the skolves in pieces and borrow heat from the other to make it happen. Both skolves explode, though for different reasons.

"You ate my dinner. Why march so far when the price is low?" It is the knight. His accent is all Armadale, but the sense of his words escapes me. I squint at him. He is just a boy, perhaps seventeen, though very tall. He is near my height already. He points his sword at my chest. I sheath Expectation, realizing something is wrong.

"You have to come to the church with the bridge and the hammer. The price has been paid but the candles are lost." He thrusts his sword sharply at me, though he does not make contact.

He is a Deladieyr Knight of Armadale. That much is clear. I study him. He studies me. Blood thaws, leaking from his distended left eye like half-frozen tears. Many would tell me he is an enemy combatant, that I should kill him or take him prisoner. But this man is a Deladieyr Knight. He is on a mission either of his own devising or that he has sworn to others to accomplish. Not even the King of Armadale can order a true knight to do that which he judges unworthy, though I hear he has sometimes tried to do so. I choose to keep faith and not kill or hinder the knight. But still, his words make no sense.

"I cannot understand you, sir. What bridge?" An idea occurs to me. *Is he searching for the Tree?* "Do you mean the Methueyn Bridge? Have you just Risen? Do you seek the Bifrost?"

He puts a gauntlet to his forehead. "The principal bridge! Where the gate has been *brought*. If we go there, we can dance on the door and unpay the price."

"You are not making sense, sir. You should come with me until you feel ... more yourself." I reach out for his shoulder, but he brushes my hand away.

He motions me to come with him, his feet rotating half away from me. "The price is too low, the prose too long. We must not retire from the floor."

"I do not understand you, knight."

He seems unfazed by my confusion and only smiles expectantly at me. "You dreamed it. The floating towers saw the cost."

"Do you mean a heraldic dream?" I ask. "I had no such dream."

"No!" He said, shaking his head. "*You* dreamed it. When you were the furthest herald."

I feel my teeth grinding. Usually I know exactly what to do. If he is searching the Wilderness for what was lost at the end of the Methueyn War, I should accompany him. At the very least I should stay with the knight until he recovers his senses. But I have no time. And no idea where he is going or why. Indeed I do not know if *he* knows, though it seems he *thinks* he does and will not be denied. I hold one finger up to him and he nods, waiting, while I find his helmet. I hand it to him. "I would come with you, sir, but my mother is dying."

The young knight nods again. "The cost is high." He puts the helmet on and sheathes his sword.

I make another attempt to help him. "Come with me instead. Until you are feeling better."

He shakes his head, another gob of blood rolling from his eye, trailing down his face. "I hope you get there before dinner," he says sympathetically. With no more than that, the young knight waves, turns, and walks rapidly in the direction I came from.

I thought I knew what hell was, but something rare has happened. I have changed my mind. Is the young Knight's reason gone, or is he simply unable to express it? We are born alone. We dream alone, remember alone. We love in the separate half spaces of our individual minds—if we are capable of love at all—imagining that on the other side of the line, there is the same feeling. But there is not. No two people can feel the same way. Subjective and unique, our experience is as isolated as tiny, single-masted ships in a wide and empty sea. Yet sometimes we manage to convey a flimsy, one-dimensional representation of our many-sided feelings through shared words. If we are skilled or determined enough, we can communicate an imperfect projection of self. This is a comfort, at times, to lonely intellects. This man, this knight, has lost even that.

I take up the run again. The day is late, but I may yet arrive before dinner is served. The Castlereagh Line rises ahead. I sprint towards it. The ground is level here, with scattered dead trees and fully denuded stalks of wheat. Skolve tracks are everywhere, but the beasts know me now and hide. A tower rises crookedly to my right, but I ignore it as I rush to the stone of the Line. A soldier calls down from the wall, pointing at me. I ignore him and hurdle to the top, landing smoothly beside him.

"It's you!" he says, eyes wide, craning his neck to look up at me. He is a good foot shorter than me.

"Did you see another knight pass this way today, but going out into the Wilderness?" I ask.

"No one has crossed the Line today but you, sir." He steps back uncertainly. "Will you stay with us at the tower?"

"No."

I leave him and his questions and leap off the wall. Home is only six miles away now.

The town sits in a broad saddle between three large crescent-shaped sloughs. I pass over a small stone bridge. It spans the narrows between two of the sloughs and is barely wider than a wagon. Past the bridge, sunset's long rays illuminate an empty street in amber and red. I pull the old whistle from my pocket and hold it in the palm of my hand as I approach the stone house of my parents. It will not blow; it is too bent and squashed. The air cannot pass through. No sound can escape.

The house is empty. They must be at the tavern, our town hall. It squats at the end of the lane. I see amber lights through its windows and shadows of movement within. A breeze picks up a thin curtain of fine dust as I approach. I feel it upon my skin, gritty and dry. I pass along the lane like a shade and come to a set of wooden stairs, which I vault up on quiet feet. I could have gone in through the tavern's ground floor door but prefer this way. At the top of the stairs I pause before a narrow door for a moment, then push it open and step inside.

The room is lit all in a strange amber, a pale yellow-orange that illuminates the relief in the grain of the wood. It reminds me of sunlight behind a thin, wispy cloud, almost there but not quite. No one sees me. I step to the wooden rail and look down on the crowd. My father is there. My sisters too. My mother is there, lying on a table with a blanket over her. Villagers, some familiar, others not, stand around raising mugs of beer towards her. I gaze at the grain of the rough old timber of the table behind my father. Little filaments of wood stand up like hairs on an arm. They glint in the golden light of the many, many lamps. I say nothing, entranced by the filaments and the color.

My father stares straight ahead with the limitless desolation of the bereaved. There is no love, familiarity, or warmth in his eyes. Those feelings have been burned away. His bereavement is an emotional singularity. It shocks me. Its power and capacity are frightening. The pain of loss is an endless wave. It always surprises me when I feel another person's emotion, even when it is the second, third, or fourth time. Nothing can prepare me for it. I did not know there was such pain in the world. Or that there could ever have been enough love to fuel it.

Both the pain and the love are foreign to my experience. The love is not for me in any case. I am an outsider. I have not been here in years, and even when I lived here, I was as unreachable and incomprehensible as a star, infinitely far away and cold.

On some instinct, my father looks up and sees me. He does not look at me as a father should look at a son. There is no friendliness or comfort in his gaze, no instantaneous and autonomic relief at seeing me. No happiness or consolation attends my presence.

"You're too late," he calls up at me.

Many people say that home is the place where they never feel misunderstood, and never misunderstand. Home is the place where they never feel like a stranger. The words sound like some trite cliché, but home is where I also experience certain feelings most strongly. I am always and everywhere strange, always and everywhere apart. But home is where I feel it strongest.

Home is where I feel most truly alone.

Chapter Eighteen

Specific Preparation

"Does anybody actually *not* know your grandpa?" Gregory asked wryly. Endicott only shook his head and increased the pace. Sir Hemdale had known Finlay. Gregory's father had known him as well. Finlay had made the rare, expensive probability swords for them. "Apparently not." He stopped suddenly. "You know, he doesn't talk very much. He's just a quiet, quiet man. But I would have thought he would have said something more about being a student here with Gerveault back in the early days."

"Maybe you just weren't paying attention," quipped Gregory.

"Knights. Quite possibly," admitted Endicott ruefully.

"*I* don't know him," said Eoyan March, smiling. He was still wearing his full chain mail surcoat, and like Merrett, kept a hand on his sword. Unlike Merrett he was smiling, but then Eoyan March smiled almost all the time. All the same there was a studied quality about the way he looked at the world that suggested to Endicott that this jokey man's smile was all on the outside. Something else, Endicott sensed, was going on in the interior.

"Well, he seems to have a lot of pull for someone from a small, far-off town," Gregory grumbled.

"Hey!" Eoyan exclaimed, off hand raised, "You're talking about the Elevator Baron of Bron. You should have expected it."

Endicott squinted. "How did you hear that term?"

"It's all over the place. Everyone knows it, Sir Robert."

Endicott's blank expression betrayed his confusion. Gregory looked equally clueless.

"You don't know, do you?" Eoyan stopped walking. "They didn't even ask you?" He put his off hand half over his face.

"What?" Gregory asked.

"Come with me. This won't take us far out of our way." Eoyan marched them purposefully to Mathematics and Physics Square and its monument. He pointed at the sheaf of papers posted there. It was a copy of the minutes Evyn had taken at the Black Spear. The title at the top of the first page was in a different hand. It read, "Sir Robert Endicott defends the New School."

Endicott's heart seemed to stop dead for a moment before resuming very loudly. He did not regret what he had said at the meeting, but at the same time he would have wanted a chance to consider his words again before they went on to live some life of their own.

The context has been lost.

"Why?" Gregory said, echoing Endicott's anxiety.

Eoyan smiled wryly. "You know why, and you know who. *Narrative.* It's been posted everywhere."

Gregory settled in beside Endicott and read the document. Eoyan turned his back on the two young men and scanned the square, watchful. Minutes passed.

"Are we at war? It's like we are in some kind of strange war," Gregory mused.

"Yes," came Eoyan's voice, his back still turned. "I think we are."

"A war of words?" Gregory suggested, staring from the pages to Endicott and back again. "Better words than swords, though, hey?"

Endicott leaned back, looking up at the top of the monument. "But if it's a war of words, is anyone listening? Without listening to one another, how will the war be resolved?"

Eoyan turned his head. "Give it time."

"Yes," Gregory agreed, clapping Endicott on the shoulder. "Not everyone is a combatant."

Where is my faith in dialogue?

Another thought ran like lightning through Endicott. "Take us to where she was killed."

It was where they had been heading in the first place, and as Eoyan March had said, it was close. He led them to the narrow pathway behind the administration building and stopped at a spot where the grass was scorched. A black stain spread out from the grass and up the stones of the building. On the ground a wide halo of discolored grass surrounded the stain. A second halo surrounded the first a pace further out. Eoyan pointed at the central scorched area. "We think he burned her and that she stepped or ran three paces back and then collapsed against the wall. She … rolled to the right and the left. That's why it's so wide there."

Gwenyfer.

Endicott felt his eyes sting as he crouched to examine the grass and the stonework. The roots of the grass were not burned. Not even in the very center. He looked up at Gregory, whose eyes were red rimmed too. "It's different."

Gregory frowned uncertainly, and Endicott pulled him down and pointed at the roots of the grass. "But what does it mean?" Gregory asked.

"The fire was not nearly as hot this time." Endicott turned to Eoyan. "She had a chance to run, even if it was just a few steps into a stone wall. She rolled. Twice. She was not nearly as badly burned as the other one, was she?"

Eoyan shook his head. For once he was not smiling.

"It's been so long!" Annabelle Currik exclaimed from her desk. She smiled broadly, and her eyes seemed to sparkle. "And you brought a new young man with you."

Gregory introduced Eoyan to her.

"Well, I'm glad you came by. I hate the way we lose contact with you until the next year." If anything Annabelle's long hair was even longer than it had been. The chalkboard in her office was covered in formulae and diagrams, but her eyes were on her guests rather than her work.

"We have some questions for you," Endicott began. "Have you read *The Lonely Wizard*? The original edition?"

Her happy open expression deflated. "Long ago."

"Okay," Endicott said. "If you remember, at one point the wizard says he sends a wave of fire or plasma in a semicircle through a large number of skolves, instantly killing them. Is that possible?"

"Which part?" Annabelle asked, standing up. "That air can ignite in a fireball or that skolves can be instantaneously lit on fire?" She wiped her chalkboard with a cloth and began drawing a graph. She labelled the lateral axis temperature and the vertical axis time, then drew a curved line across the graph, giving the curve a vertical asymptote on the left. "You are talking about autoignition, gentlemen. All materials are different, of course, but you should think of liquids quite separately from solids. Flammable liquids burn when they exceed their flashpoint, that is, when they give off enough vapor for the vapor to be ignited. Solids will burn too, if they are flammable, but require more time and hotter temperatures."

"The Lonely Wizard burned the skolves instantly," Gregory repeated.

"I will skip the lecture about works of fiction versus works of physics," said Annabelle, her face becoming animated again. "How would a dynamicist do it if it could be done? That's your question, correct?"

Endicott nodded.

"Tell me this, first," she asked. "How fast are dynamic operations?"

"*Really* fast," said Gregory, gesturing rapidly with both hands.

Endicott thought about it. He had always considered dynamics to be instantaneous, but during the cake-baking exercise he had been forced to think about the rate of the innovation. "I think that thermal changes happen in a range of about a quarter second to a second. Yes... the slowest I was ever able to make an innovation happen was just over a second."

Annabelle hoisted her chalk. "Well, in that case the temperature would have to be high. *Extremely* high." She pointed her chalk to a section of the curve in the asymptote. "But bear four things in mind, gentlemen."

"Yes?" Gregory and Endicott said together.

"Okay, the most obvious first. When I study autoignition, I am studying a sample with behaviors related to volume and heating method. You dynamicists are either heating the air all around the object or the object itself. That should move the whole curve to the right, but how much? The other three points are subtler but just as important. First you need a source of energy that you understand. Air likely doesn't have enough heat energy. Second forget about a fireball. You will not get air to burn sustainably at any temperature unless you vastly change the oxygen content first. Lastly, if the Lonely Wizard really made the air turn hot enough to become a plasma, he would likely have killed himself either by thermodynamic losses or operator error."

"So how did he burn the skolves?" Endicott muttered to himself. They were back at the site of Gewnyfer's murder.

"I know I am just the dumb soldier here, sirs, but this is very confusing," Eoyan March mock-sneered, pursing his lips. "Are we talking about a book or are we talking about these murders?"

Gregory scratched his head. "I am more upset than confused. A woman *died* here, Robert, and we are talking about *The Lonely Wizard*."

Endicott frowned, irritated now. "Don't you see? It's all connected!"

"The book?" Gregory's eyebrows were raised. "The plot? The characters? The theme?"

"No. Well, I hope not the theme," Endicott said more levelly. "The *physics*."

"I don't want to piss on your crop, gentlemen, but as the good professor so gently suggested, you are talking about a work of fiction." Eoyan smiled wryly.

"I know that" said Endicott a little sharply. "But who *wrote* the book?"

Gregory's eyes widened. "Gerveault! A man who couldn't write bad physics if his life depended on it."

Eoyan smiled again, but in a crooked-mouthed, leading manner. "And …?"

"You know, you aren't fooling anyone, Eoyan. You're as smart as any of us," Endicott retorted impatiently, then caught himself and took a breath. "There is more than one reason for this exercise. Look, the thermal innovation used in the first murder—or at least the first murder by immolation—resulted in temperatures at least an order of magnitude higher than in the murder of Gwenyfer. That suggests two murderers."

"Or," put in Eoyan, hand still on the hilt of his sword. "One murderer refining his method."

Gregory added, "The witness descriptions sound like the same person."

"They do," Endicott admitted. "So we have two different, unusually tall, cloaked murderers. Both of whom happen to be powerful dynamicists. Hmmm. Or we have one murderer who is learning. That makes more sense. There aren't that many dynamicists around. That fact is one of the big problems with the Lighthouse plan. It has to be part of the reason so much expense and security have been mobilized for our training."

"And here I thought it was because you were all so special," Eoyan quipped.

"Oh, we're special all right," replied Endicott, giving Eoyan a sharp look, "but let's stick to the cloaked figure and his methodology ... If he's still learning, that makes him a younger man. An experienced dynamicist would surely have a better idea of what temperature was required."

"How do you think the constables will take all this?" Gregory said sardonically.

"What?" Endicott rejoined. "I am *very* popular with them."

"Let's go then, Mr. Popular," said Eoyan. "We don't have a lot of time to spare given we leave for the Line day after tomorrow. We must look at horses, armor, food. And we have to talk with Somne about all those things and see what we need to add."

Endicott shook his head ruefully. "We have to go to the Bifrost first."

Eoyan shook his head like a duck throwing water. "We have to go to the bar and get liquored first? Is that what I heard?" He scowled at the two dynamicists. "Are you out of your minds? The laboratory? Gregory needs to go and see what is really going on in Eloise's head first. Unless you think the last time we saw her she seemed pleased and full of... I don't know... patience. And... what is the word I'm looking for? Oh, I know. Passivity! No, you should definitely put off talking to Eloise for a while. Heck, maybe wait until *after* the trip across the Line. Or if you put it off that long, why not wait until after you're married. *That* ought to work out fine. Come *on*, gentlemen. You're supposed to be geniuses. Prioritize!"

"Maybe you *should* see Eloise, Gregory," Endicott admitted. "I can go to the Bifrost by myself."

"No," said Eoyan flatly. "You can't."

"Well, *someone* has to go there." Endicott knew that Eoyan would not immediately understand why. "Remember I said there was more than one reason to investigate the murders? Beyond simple decency and a desire to help? Well, I would also like to help prevent anyone else from being burned alive. Especially my classmates, especially Koria and Eloise, who I have seen lose a fight to this cloaked... person. I saw Koria resist immolation in my first heraldic dream, but she did not do it efficiently. If we can pull together some more accurate data, we can help her resist better."

"But how?" asked Gregory.

"Remember that day with the dice when I interfered with your rolls?"

"No," said Eoyan.

"You weren't there, skolve, but Gregory was. To stop him, I had to understand the cost of his manipulation."

Gregory frowned. "That was just a dice roll, Robert. Now we're talking about stopping an *enormous* thermal manipulation."

"Ahhh," said Endicott smiling. "It is all just physics. Dice rolling or thermal manipulation, it is all just mathematics and physics. If we know the cost, we can buy the outcome."

"I retract some of what I said," replied Eoyan, smiling again, though his eyes still gazed outward, watching. "That actually sounds reasonable."

"But not easy," cautioned Gregory.

"What is?" countered Endicott. "But there is another element to this work I want to develop, and it concerns all three of us. The Lonely Wizard repeatedly destroys large groups of skolves, twice using thermal innovations. If we are across the Line and skolves come, I want to be ready. I want to use this … evil for some good." He looked at Eoyan.

"Are you saying you could actually use what you know about baking cakes and boiling water to do battle with skolves?" the soldier asked incredulously.

"Possibly," Endicott answered carefully. "I know we don't have much time, but we should at least try to be ready."

"If you expect me to argue with that, prepare to be disappointed. I'm all for preparation," said Eoyan, surprising Endicott. He turned to Gregory, expression turning deadpan. "I know you also like to be ready for anything, Justice. You're marrying Eloise after all."

"Are you jealous?" Gregory shot back.

"Yes!" Eoyan smiled and gestured to Gregory and Endicott to walk with him, presumably towards the Bifrost now. "It's a good thing I've been told not to let you out of my sight."

"So you can mock us?" Gregory growled.

"That too," said Eoyan. "Primarily, my friends, it's this. When we go across the Line, I want to be able to work with whatever dynamic or wizard stuff you're planning. I need to know which way the cake blows. Don't think you're going out there fully loaded and ready to burn down the county and I'll just tag along not knowing how to back you up or where to stand so you don't crisp *me*."

Huh.

"We haven't practiced any of this in class," Endicott said.

"To my knowledge no one has, at least not here at the school."

"Heydron herself!" Eoyan swore, swiping frost off his face and raking ice out of his hair with the fingers of his off hand.

"I'd swear too if I could only see," said Gregory. His eyelashes were covered in ice, and he could not open his eyes. He waved his sword dangerously close to Endicott, who nearly tripped jumping out of the way.

"Help Justice, Robert," Eoyan warned.

Endicott carefully took the sword from his tall friend and gently rubbed his eyelashes. "At least we burned the scarecrow this time."

The scarecrow was an adult-sized dummy made from old bags of oats, rags, and wood. It was planted on a large earth-filled basin in the old thermal testing hall. They had taken the soil from the greenhouse. The scarecrow was burned and looked ready to fall apart.

"I'll go get another one from the aggies," Endicott said, leaning Gregory's sword against a stone trough.

"T-take your time, Robert." Gregory muttered. "See—that's what life is like here in dynamics, Eoyan. Robert is always burning, boiling, or detonating something, usually at us. Did I ever tell you about the time he—"

Endicott was happy to have walked out of earshot. He was sick of the cake story and needed to think clearly about what he had learned so far. It had been relatively easy to determine empirically the temperature at which the scarecrow would burn based on his first innovations using water as an energy source. It was far trickier to estimate the amount of energy he could get from soil and match it to the requirements for burning the scarecrow. The soil's heat capacity depended on how wet it was, how packed it was, and of course what its mean temperature was. Endicott had learned a certain amount from observations made during the first breakdown, but actual testing was necessary for calibration.

Trickiest of all was how to treat the problem tactically. Without more care and testing, someone could either be killed by the error wave, the resulting heat wave, or their inability to see or fight if they were compromised while enemies were nearby. But there was so little time.

We need to try this outside on real ground.

"Well, that was fun," Eoyan declared a little later. The new scarecrow was thoroughly burned. Eoyan no longer seemed to care. He pulled at his chain mail. "I think I need to oil this now. Thank you very much, by the way."

"C-can we go now?" Gregory was shivering. Endicott had made him try a few attempts at immolating the mock-skolve, and he had succeeded, but not efficiently or safely. Even Endicott was starting to become dangerously cold himself.

"Let's go sit in the hot pool for a few minutes," Endicott suggested. "Then you two go back to the Orchid. Eoyan's right—you better go talk to Eloise before night falls on your proposal. Send someone to get me later. I have a few things to try yet."

"I'll send Merrett if he's there." Eoyan smirked. "He hates coming here."

"W-what are you going to d-do?" Gregory asked.

"Oh, I'm going to change the oxygen content around my skolve." Endicott smiled. "Then, I'm going to burn him."

Ha.

"Great!" Eoyan clenched both fists high in the air in celebration of victory. "What could possibly go wrong?"

▽

IN THE END EOYAN HIMSELF CAME BACK. THE EXPERIMENT HAD ENDED WITH MIXED RESULTS. Endicott had succeeded in sustaining a fireball in a small glass bulb by enriching the oxygen with air from another, connected bulb, but in open air the operation had proved more dangerous and difficult to manage. Eoyan arrived just as the last trial was ending and seemed genuinely curious, but as they approached the Orchid, he suddenly went off on a strange and unwelcome tangent.

"Ahem ... and, er, so it's a thing, Robert. I heard it from the arts students. It's called self-sexual suffocation. Usually people do it with a rope or a belt, not by changing the air like you. Er, that's what I hear anyway."

I didn't completely pass out. But what was the point of saying it?

Endicott missed Merrett's stoicism.

They started up the stairs. Endicott could see Lindseth standing outside the door to the boys' floor and was anxious to prevent Eoyan from resuming his bizarre monologue. He decided to risk taking Eoyan seriously.

"But Eoyan, I didn't *do* that. I've never even heard of it until now. When you arrived, I was just a little ... off from low oxygen."

Eoyan hit Endicott on the shoulder. "Sure you were, Robert. You can tell Uncle Eoyan anything, you know."

"I can tell you to shut up. And don't start lecturing Koria about this *thing* either."

"Okay. It's just between us." Eoyan winked at him. "Invite me next time," he whispered.

"Don't let him bother you, Sir Robert," Jeyn said as they approached him. "He can't help himself."

"That is entirely true," smirked Eoyan. "Robert here is a very interesting fellow, you know." He patted Endicott's shoulder and continued in a more serious tone. "We need to quantify our tactics a little. Let's work with some measuring cords and chalk tomorrow."

Endicott nodded, not completely surprised by Eoyan's sudden serious turn. It had been on quiet display all day despite the tall young man's banter. He stepped past Lindseth, waving over his shoulder, and entered the boys' common room. Jennyfer Gray sat on a couch across from Davyn. She had her notebook out and seemed to be copying details from the original edition of *The Lonely Wizard*.

"Hello Jennyfer," Endicott said. "Still working on the poem?"

Jennyfer put the book down and looked at Endicott. "Do you ever wonder what would have happened to the Lonely Wizard if he had looked at his sisters instead of his father?"

"The possibility is null."

Davyn's hand shot up. "Ha! That is exactly what I said. *Exactly.*"

"Speak human, please." Jennyfer shot mock disgust at both Davyn and Endicott. "What is that supposed to mean?"

Davyn and Endicott shared a look. Endicott made a little head gesture at Davyn, and his friend leaned forward. "There is no chance that the Lonely Wizard would have looked in a direction where support would come from, even if part of him wanted it. Looking for comfort was completely against his nature. Every choice he made through the entire book was towards loneliness." Davyn put his hands on his hips. "He wasn't exactly an optimist. So the question must be discarded. If he could have looked at his sisters, he would have, and yes, the outcome would have changed, but it would no longer be the story of the Lonely Wizard." Davyn sat back, a big, satisfied smile on his face. "Mathematical terms are so much more compact than this crude language." He pointed at the book.

Jennyfer laughed. "Now I know you are pulling my leg, Davyn. You *do* value the lyrical. Syriol tells me so. She says—"

"How is the poem coming, Jennyfer?" Endicott interrupted, not sure either that he or Davyn wanted to hear what Syriol had said about her relationship with Davyn.

Jennyfer threw her hands up. "You're in cahoots." She tapped her writing feather against her lip. "But I must tell you, gentlemen, that I am on the edge of deciding that it won't be a poem after all. Every time I try to fit the message to rhyme and meter, I end up butchering the theme."

"So blank verse maybe?" Endicott asked. "Or straight prose?"

Davyn's hand shot up. "How about mathematics?"

Jennyfer did not rise to the bait. She looked pensive. "Well, that was the wizard's problem, wasn't it?"

Ouch.

At the door to the baths Endicott stopped and turned. "Davyn, where are you going while we are at the Line?"

Davyn grinned. "I will be doing nothing Jennyfer here would approve of, I can assure you. I've been assigned to work on a little mathematical problem at the Citadel." He winked at Endicott and glanced sidelong at Jennyfer Gray. "On that long-term project. They even have chambers there for me."

Endicott nodded, relieved that Davyn would be safe, and stepped into the baths. But as he washed up, he felt a strange anxiety creeping over him and found himself scrubbing up a little faster, and then a little faster still. By the time he got to his dental paste, he was rushing, and droplets of paste were flying about. He closed his eyes and listened to his heart accelerating. He tried to avoid remembering his heraldic dreams—he had worked hard to push the images to the furthest reaches of his mind—but they could still creep out of the shadows at unexpected moments

Be slow.

He took the stairs two at a time to the girls' floor, nodded to Merrett and stepped into the common room. It was empty, and all the girls' doors were closed. Endicott had hoped to catch Bethyn at least and reassure himself about her plans, but her closed door and the imperative of seeing Koria put that idea in abeyance. He crossed the room to Koria's door and knocked gently. When he heard her answer, he opened the door, trying to stay calm. But as soon as he saw her, his heart raced again.

Be slow.

Koria was at her desk, pen in hand, expression serious. When she saw him, her face softened a little. She was as task oriented as he and had been working on her own problems. As the moment lengthened, the set of her eyes changed.

She sees the state I'm in.

She did nothing and said nothing, simply waited, wise, patient, and very Koria-like. One choked sob got away from Endicott, sounding incongruously like a hiccup. Then a single tear escaped. He rushed to Koria and embraced her. Her arms came around him. "What's wrong, Robert?"

In the familiar emotional and physical half space of Koria, he relaxed a little. "We visited the site where Gwenyfer was murdered and spoke to Professor Currik about the fire. We came up with some pretty good ideas on the temperature of the fire. I'll lay them out for you later. They might be useful in your preparation of a dynamic defense." He shuddered. "But how she must have suffered." His arms gripped Koria even more tightly.

Not you, not you, not you.

"Then we went to the Bifrost and tried to work out potential tactics with Eoyan. But there's so much to consider and work out in taking dynamics out of the lab and into the field. I don't know anything about skolves. I don't know how fast they are, how resilient to fire, how many really come when they do come, if they do, and how best to respond. In the time available I don't think I have a hope of coming up with a response that might not just make things worse, like maybe killing our own people. Each component, if defined, would be solvable, but there simply is no unique definition. And not nearly enough time. I'm just not fast enough. *I'm too slow."*

Koria's hands moved slowly over his shoulders. "So you can't solve any of the major problems as you see them? You can't stop the sun in its tracks or keep the earth from spinning?" She pushed his shoulders so she could see his face. "You've seen a glimpse of the future through a mirror but don't know where the reflection comes from. You fear what could happen but also fear doing the wrong thing if you try to stop it." She paused. "You aren't in complete control of anything, are you?"

"No," Endicott whispered, relaxing.

"Me neither," she said, smiling sadly. "But not having *complete* control is not the same as having *no* control. We've both made progress. We just have to keep working."

She pushed him a little further away. "I have a great idea, though."

"What's that?"

Koria stood up. She took Endicott's hands and led him to her bed. "Two ideas, actually. One is to ask Gerveault to help you at the Bifrost tomorrow. If he really is the Lonely Wizard, he should be able to help you clarify your tactics and hone your specific preparation."

"And the second idea?"

Chapter Nineteen.
Signals and Simple Solutions

BANG-bang, BANG-bang, BANG-bang, BANG-bang

"That sword of yours is more nicked than my old practice shield and less sharp." Eoyan had been the last of many to suggest that Endicott do something about the old weapon he had picked up at the military school and hung at his belt. Even Koria had made it clear she wanted him to have a better one before he left for the Line.

Time's up now.

It was near the end of the day, and Endicott had finally found a few spare moments. Gerveault had anticipated him, ordering the forge fires to be ready when he had visited in the morning. The old sword was nicked, scratched, and generally beaten up. It had been the last one in the barrel, and no one had missed it, for good reason, but as soon as he achieved the first breakdown, Endicott could see that its steel was not bad. The carbon content was reasonably high, though he wished he had some other elements to work with. There was a small amount of phosphorus in it, an impurity that most metallurgists would have preferred not to see, but Endicott thought he might have a use for it. Less useful were the many voids and dislocations, a hundred microscopic defects for every nick that was visible to the naked eye.

The sword was hot now, almost melting. Endicott knew he could not make a work of art like Gregory's sword, its alloy blade so perfectly suited to its use that it was almost magic. People spoke of it as if it *was* magic. Eloise's sword was almost as good. It certainly looked as good, and she could swing it more expertly too. In the battle at the Black Spear, both weapons had proven themselves paragons of metallurgy and classic exemplars of the art of dynamics, while Endicott had made do with an umbrella and a greasy iron pan. The improvised weapons had served him well enough at the time, but he could hardly take them across the Line with him.

He raised his hammer and opened himself to the Empyreal Sky.

BANG-bang, BANG-bang, BANG-bang, BANG-bang

"Knights damn it!" Eoyan swore. "That's the eighth time today you've blasted me with oven and ice, Robert. For the love of Leylah, can you not warn me when you are going to execute? My sword's going to be as rusted and ugly as that thing you wear before we're even done practicing."

Eoyan walked away, looking again for a dry towel to wipe his sword with. And his face. And the rest of him.

"I look like I pissed myself, by the way. Thank you for nothing, Mr. Wizard!"

Endicott only grinned and shook his head, wondering at how the tall soldier's use of the vernacular seemed to grow more picturesque with every trial they executed.

"You know, he has a point, Robert." Gregory was less disheveled. Unlike Eoyan he had learned to keep one eye on the empyreal sky and time his movements better. "You need to say something before you innovate."

"How?" asked Endicott. "Once the fight is on, matters will be moving a little too fast for anyone to benefit."

"True," admitted Gregory, rubbing at a patch of frost on his forearm. "But we're mostly just practicing the set pieces here. A bit of advance warning might help us get the hang of things."

Endicott frowned. "I have sometimes spoken while innovating, but for less ... primal work."

"How about a hand signal? Something simple and easy to see?"

Yes.

Not much later, a drier and less irritated Eoyan March helped Gregory and Endicott work out a very small selection of hand signals adapted from the military school's standard repertoire. In addition to the advance warnings for calculating and innovating that Eoyan had requested, they included signals for stop, charge, attack ahead, move up to my position (but behind me), and fall back. The innovating signal was a high clenched fist. The response was to brace and close the eyes for one second. The calculating command, a rotating, raised hand, was both a sign that an innovation was imminent and a command not to alter relative position with the innovator.

BANG-bang, BANG-bang, BANG-bang, BANG-bang

As the phosphorus and carbon found their optimal positions, the voids, displacements, and cracks disappeared, and the battered old blade grew more and more mirror-like. It was a simpler reordering to disorder, given the uncomplicated nature of the alloy and the superheated condition of the metal. The effort came easily to Endicott. His hands felt strong, and having some time at the forge was a welcome break after all the business of this last day before travelling to the Line. The simplicity of the task was a relief. Dented and scarred as the sword was, it really had no hysteresis and would carry none of the damage from its past into the present. The hammer, the heat, and Endicott's mind beat it into perfect form.

"Not bad, gentlemen." It was Gerveault, arriving at last. The old man had a bright, knowing smile on his dark, normally more opaque face. "Elyze's people are complaining that you have made off with all their spare wheelbarrows and stakes."

"We are trying to figure out how to work together when we are in the field." Gregory's sword rang as he sheathed it. "In case Endicott's dream was correct."

"He did not see much, gentlemen." Gerveault rejoined.

"We should still get ready!" Gregory exclaimed.

Gerveault held up a hand. "I did not say you should not. It is a clever idea. Eliminate one point of the triangle —time— through preparation. That and the good and proper use of physics are how a dynamicist succeeds."

Endicott chuckled, remembering the old man's notional triangles. "Then you can surely help us, Professor. In your book, the Lonely Wizard makes plasma. How did you do it?"

"How many times do I have to tell you the book is fiction, Robert?" Gerveault's blue eyes blazed. Endicott stared back calmly, refusing to back away from the question. Eoyan's lips pursed and Gregory took a deep breath. Finally Gerveault shrugged. "Plasma requires nearly two orders of magnitude more energy than you are manipulating here, Robert. It requires more energy than you can get almost anywhere except directly from Elysium."

It did not surprise Endicott to hear that the Lonely Wizard had so easily performed an extradimensional breakdown, but he had needed to hear the words. His hunch, once confirmed, made him curious about something else. "Will you teach me how?"

"I certainly will not, Robert." Gerveault's eyes were steely and calm again. "It would kill you. That particular breakdown is a thing I would hesitate to attempt." He gestured at the scarecrows. "What you gentlemen are practicing will be quite sufficient. Lord Wolverton is doubling the guard that will cross the Line with you. There should be no skolves about, and even if there are, you will be well protected."

"But keep practicing?" asked Eoyan wryly.

"Indeed. You can never practice too much."

Gerveault turned to leave, but Endicott cut him off. "Can I talk with you privately?" He waved Gregory and Eoyan away with the fall back signal. Gerveault saw them move off and raised his bushy eyebrows at his eager protégé.

"I realize now that it makes sense you knew my grandpa." Endicott let out a breath. "I should have thought it through when I was asked about my father on the twenty-four-hour test."

Gerveault sighed. "I am sorry about that, Robert. The question needed to be asked of you for reasons to do with you, but it was ... unjust to your father."

"You knew my father as well?" Endicott's voice rose a little at the exciting thought.

Gerveault noticed the change. "No, Robert. Finlay told me about him."

"And now you are going to tell me," Endicott declared.

"Am I?"

"It's only fair, Professor. You are the one that instructed Merrett to say what he said."

Gerveault's lips tightened. "I would rather talk about physics, Robert. It is easier and less subjective. Anything I say will inevitably be biased or colored. It could be more unfair."

Endicott smiled, thinking of the Lonely Wizard. "Let us agree to be charitable about the subjectivity of it all."

"And set aside the scholarly prevarication, hey?" The old man's expression was a cross between annoyed and amused.

"Right."

"Fine. Just remember this is not my story." Gerveault straightened his back, assuming an even more rigid posture than usual. "Your father is the reason Finlay allowed you to come here to the New School. Neither your father nor your uncle Deryn would come. It was before the duchess had a program, but we did ask them. They had no interest. Your father's death changed things. Finlay became worried. He thought you might be too much like your father. That is why he decided you needed ... different training."

The mind can run in many different directions at certain times, and Endicott's mind did this more than most. Gerveault's explanation raised a host of simultaneous questions, but one commanded attention more than the any of the others. He had asked Merrett this question in vain. Gerveault at least might know the answer.

"Did my father die because of his carelessness?"

"Knights, I dislike this," the old man muttered, looking genuinely uncomfortable for once. Endicott stared at Gerveault until he sighed and continued. "That is not what I was given to understand. Your father ... Meycal ... was in mourning, Robert. Finlay foresaw an array of bad outcomes for him, so he tried to keep him close, but Meycal was ... headstrong. Like you. All I know is that he became too ambitious while creating ... something and died of hypothermia."

"Creating what?" Endicott's hands were shaking now.

Gerveault looked sternly at the young man. Then a flicker of doubt seemed to pass across his sharp features, softening them for a brief moment. "I cannot say. The what does not matter as much as the how. The how does not matter as much as the why. Or the mindset. Your father's mindset was ... wrong at that time, Robert. He was distraught. He may have neglected elements of preparation. He was more focused on *what* he was doing and *why* he was doing it than on physics. He was too confused about his feelings, distracted by his grief. An emotional wreck, according to Finlay."

This did not make sense to Endicott. "But why did my grandpa not just herald it and stop him? Grandpa has heraldic dreams all the time."

"I thought we agreed to be charitable, Robert." Gerveault frowned at Endicott. "I am going to suppose that Finlay heralded as much as he could. We do not know what other possibilities were avoided. You know the dangers of heraldic dreams. They can be terrible. How many heraldic dreams did your grandpa have? As many as he could handle, I should think."

Endicott sat down on the edge of a stone trough. The story did not seem right; he did not want to accept it. To even consider the failure of his greatest hero was crushing. He had hardly known his father or his mother. His grandpa and grandma had been his parents, and it had seemed there was nothing his grandpa could not do. He was all-knowing, all seeing. He could do anything. He was wisdom incarnate. Yet he had failed to save his own son from a pointless death.

"Did Grandpa really tell you all that?" Endicott finally said. "Aside from what you have supposed."

"Not all at once," Gerveault replied with a smile. "Remember, I have known him far longer than you have been alive."

"A man of few words," Endicott mused. "Unlike me. I wish I could be half the man."

Gerveault sat down beside Endicott. "You are more like him than you think. You have the same talent. And the same moral compass as far as I can tell."

"How did he learn to handle the heraldic dreams so well?" Endicott looked down. "I've only had a few, and you know how they have almost undone me. And might still undo me." Before Gerveault could answer, Endicott continued. "I mean, I know he is more mature than me. Obviously. And far more stable. But can that really be all the difference?"

Gerveault said nothing, as if waiting to see what else his student might want to say, but Endicott merely gazed ahead, and after a few silent moments the older man broke the stillness, speaking slowly. "Wisdom is just a word, but it means a great deal, Robert. Finlay is certainly wise. He is very wise. He always was, even at your age. Love is just a word too, but I have never seen anyone love so ... big ... so generously as you. Maturity could be the key, but I do not think it is the entire answer. Look." Gerveault tapped the stone of the trough lightly. "Think about why heraldic dreams are so damaging. Think about what has happened with yours and what we have done in the background." Gerveault looked at the pensive young man and raised his eyebrows. "The dreams that hurt are the traumatic ones, and they hurt so badly precisely because they might come to pass."

"There are nice ones?" Endicott asked.

"So I have been told," said Gerveault wryly. "They pose their own problems. I mean when they do not come true. Disappointment and disillusionment. Frustration. But that is a topic for another day. The traumatic dreams are a problem because the trauma hurts you. Forget about that old saying, how does it go, whatever does not kill you makes you stronger?" Traumatic events hurt you, and the hurt can bend you off course. Painful heraldic dreams hurt so much because they feel like they *have* happened. They cannot be forgotten because you *know* they may yet come to pass. And you feel responsible for the outcome because you have been warned."

"Don't I know it," muttered Endicott, both relieved and disappointed to hear his own thoughts and words confirmed.

"You do. Those dreams can make you feel almost like you are the victim, and because you were warned, you might come to feel you deserved the outcome. If it happens. That is very hard on anyone." Gerveault smiled. "You know why I think Finlay handles it so well?"

Endicott nodded. He felt almost impatient now; it was his nature to anticipate and have trouble waiting.

Gerveault held a finger up. "Yes, because he has always been mature. He is as stable as any man or woman has ever been. Yet like you Finlay always looks further ahead. He is a far herald. He has always looked further, and he has always *acted* on whatever he saw. Usually his actions have been ... parsimonious, subtle, but I have seen him, with the most economical of means, avert the most extravagant disasters. Finlay has never been a victim, never acted as one. I think that is why Finlay handles the dreams so well. He takes control of his responses. He makes the dreams a gift."

The word resonated in Endicott's mind.

A gift, yes. Grandpa does effortlessly what I struggle so hard for.

Gerveault continued while Endicott's mind raced. "With you, he took some pretty overt steps, I have to say. Overt for him, at least. Why do you think Gregory has that beautiful sword?"

Endicott was startled. "But that sword was created years ago!"

Gerveault smiled with uncharacteristic enthusiasm. "Finlay is a *far* herald, Robert. Let us follow the path further. Why do you think Eloise has another one almost as good?"

"But I gave that to her," Endicott objected.

Gerveault shook his head in mock disgust. "I do not feel that I am introducing too much bias in suggesting that Finlay knew exactly what was going to happen when he sent it to you. I know it sounds a little fatalistic, perhaps even fantastic. After all Finlay failed to save your father. But I do not think he plans to fail you."

"Hmm."

"Now let us come to you, Robert." Gerveault looked Endicott in the eye. "You had one of the worst heraldic dreams I know of aside from Koria's. And though she is more mature than you, hers took some doing to get over, I can tell you."

Endicott remembered the stories he had heard of the old carefree Koria. He nodded.

"You may have broken down initially when you had your first dream, but what did you do when you came to your senses? What did you immediately *do*?"

Endicott remembered waking up in the girls' common room. He remembered needing to be assured that they were okay, that Syriol, Bethyn, Eloise, and Koria were okay. He still felt the pain and anxiety like a knife cutting through his mind and body when he thought about it. Then he remembered the beginning of a more constructive response. The beginning of a plan to deal with the horror foreseen in the dream.

"I worked out a plan. A way to get ready for the cloaked man."

"Yes!" Gerveault practically shouted this. "You took action, many actions. Not exactly like Finlay. Your grandpa kept his plans to himself whereas you sought out allies and helpers. But neither of you let your pain make you passive. Neither of you acted the victim.

Yesterday at court was a good example. You took the dream apart—you unpacked it—and attempted to devise an effective response."

"I had help from Koria."

"Yes," agreed Gerveault nodding vigorously. "You have had a lot of help. Eleanor, Kennyth Brice, and I smoothed over a few things for you with the constabulary so you would have that help. There is still a constable watching over Freyla Loche's store, you know. But you were always the driving force in your own recovery."

"Is that all there is to it?"

Gerveault's lips tightened. "No." He stood up. "Remember, I am a dynamicist, and so are you. Keep a cool head. Stay objective. Do not let subjective feelings become a part of your process. Take responsibility for your plan, but remember that you never control the outcome."

Endicott sighed. "It sounds a little algorithmic, Gerveault."

Gerveault started to walk away. He stopped and looked back. "What did you expect? Remember. Preparation, not inspiration; that is the way of the dynamicist."

Endicott watched his professor until he disappeared somewhere in the recesses of the giant warehouse complex of the Bifrost. Gregory and Eoyan were waiting. It was getting late.

I should fix this sword.

BANG-bang, BANG-bang, BANG-bang, BANG-bang

The old sword shone now. It was coming into its perfect form, gleaming and disordered. Superlatively strong. Endicott hit the sword one final time before innovating a near instantaneous cool-down, fixing the form.

BANG-bang

If only every problem could be solved so simply.

Chapter Twenty.
The Value of a Good Pair

"WELL, THAT EXPLAINS WHY YOU'RE ALL FOREARMS AND SHOULDERS," DECLARED Eoyan March. He rubbed his chin. "But not why you aren't blind. I have never seen a man beat his sword as much as you."

Endicott ignored Eoyan's coarse joke and held out the lustrous blade. "Good enough to stand with you now?"

Eoyan's eyebrows went up. "Definitely." He took his time gazing carefully down the sharp, liquid-seeming blade. "It looks completely different. Did you add some secret metals like you did for Justice or the shields?"

"*Looks* different, yes," said Endicott calmly, examining it one last time in the empyreal sky. "But I added nothing. What you see is simply a rearrangement of what was already there."

"That sounds really sweet, Robert." Eoyan smirked. "Uh, speaking of which, I should warn you that Gregory has gone with Merrett. Instead—"

"You get my company."

Endicott was startled to see Eloise standing in the doorway. He had not spoken to her privately since Gregory gave her the shield, which now hung on her left arm. Endicott was happy and a little relieved to see that Eloise was smiling radiantly. He held the sword out of the way as she marched aggressively forward and wrapped him in a hug, the big shield enclosing them both. Endicott's face was jammed into the top of Eloise's chest and neck. "Uh," he said after the hug went on a bit longer than he was comfortable with.

"I love it when you come around, Eloise," declared Eoyan. "I can never tell whether Robert looks like your child or more like something you plan to eat."

"You're the child, stupe!" Eloise released Endicott and glared at Eoyan. He smirked back at her. She turned to Endicott, smiling again. "I had to let my ex-fiancé down easy."

"Well," said Endicott, nodding and sheathing his sword, "Gregory is a good man, so I understand why you would prefer him."

"And look what he made me." Eloise held the magnificent shield as high as she could reach. It towered above his head, burnished and sparkling. "I know you were a big part of this, Robert. Thank you."

Endicott nodded and smiled. "The dynamic alloy method is even better suited for shields than swords, Eloise, so I was glad to help."

"But what am I going to do now?" Eloise cried, tears abruptly filling her eyes.

Knights!

Endicott and Eoyan stared, viscerally shocked by the strange, sudden change in her demeanor. Crying was the last thing anyone ever expected from fierce, forward Eloise. It felt like a betrayal, and becoming aware of this, Endicott felt guilty. Eoyan involuntarily backed up a step and almost burned himself on the forge.

Heydron, I hope she actually loves Gregory! Part of Endicott had always feared that Eloise might really be in love with *him*, that her jokes and teasing were not jokes at all. Endicott of course loved Eloise, but he loved her differently from Koria. And he loved Gregory as well.

"I love him, Robert, but what am I going to give him in return?" Now she was sobbing. "There isn't any conceivable gift as fine as this!" She hefted the shield again as the tears continued to run down her face. Endicott was amazed by the strength of Eloise's feeling, and relieved as well. It explained her strangely defensive—almost angry—reaction when Gregory had presented her with the shield.

Eoyan, looking almost awe-struck, wordlessly handed Eloise a towel, which she used to clean up her face.

"I might have used that to wipe off my groin," Eoyan whispered. When she looked sharply at him, he put his hands up and hurriedly added, "After all the practicing, Eloise! And it was my pants! You have such a dirty mind."

"Shut up, you," she said smiling weirdly through her tears.

Endicott thought fast. He had not previously known that both parties to an Armadalian courtship were obliged to give each other presents, but he did now. "It's not the expense or the uniqueness of the present itself that matters, Eloise. You just need to get him something that will really matter to him."

"Like what?" she asked with a curious mix of hopefulness and importunity.

"How about a scarf?" said Eoyan.

"He's not a little girl!"

Eoyan blanched. "For sweat," he said. "Across the Line," he finished lamely.

"A portrait of you?" hazarded Endicott.

Eloise's head tilted. "A boudoir portrait, do you mean?" She shook her head. "Where would he put it that you stupes wouldn't go perve at it? Anyway there's no time. You leave tomorrow, or had you forgotten?"

I can hardly think of anything else.

Endicott still had many things to do, but there was no ignoring Eloise. She might burst in tears again at any moment. Or into violence. Or violent tears.

"You could write him a poem," Eoyan said, reminding Endicott of the eerily similar conversation he and Gregory had had about Eloise, the conversation that culminated in the scheme to make her shield.

Eloise turned on Eoyan. "Shut. The. Fuck. Up."

"A song?" he asked, like a slow learner, cautiously circling around Eloise in the direction of the door.

"How about new boots?" Endicott asked, trying to give Eoyan a better chance of avoiding an imminent beating. He continued talking into Eloise's ferocious expression. "His boots are looking pretty worn. The practicing we've been doing in this enclosed space have taken a toll on them."

Eloise seemed to consider the idea. "He *is* going on a trip."

Yes. Boots. "Remember my boots from the terrible night? How they were ruined? Well, I was very happy when a new pair mysteriously arrived. I think it was Eleanor."

"It was," affirmed Eloise. "This is good. What else?"

Endicott thought about his heraldic dream. "How about a hand telescope? Professor Currik has a few for sale."

Eoyan March, who had not quite reached the door and was glad of an opportunity to make peace, announced that he had heard of a good cordwainer who worked not far from the Apprentice's Library, and it was decided to seek this craftsman out at once. Dusk was beginning to descend as the trio climbed the Academic Plateau and made their way there. An ice carriage sped by along the ring road. Endicott shook his head, thinking back to the days when he had wondered where all the ice came from.

There isn't going to be much ice next week.

He was so lost in thought that he did not notice heads turning in the small crowd waiting to cross the road. "Is that Robert Endicott?" someone called.

Endicott looked up in surprise. A boy of six or eight pulled his young mother towards them. "You're him!" the boy sang out, face wide-open and exalted. "You're the man who protected the maiden! You carried her off to Elysium on your white horse!"

Others were staring now. Some who had been about to cross had stopped. Endicott shared a look with Eloise. Eoyan March's hand was on the hilt of his sword, but he was not looking at the boy, who had taken a couple of shy steps forward and was staring up at Endicott, transfixed. His mother smiled apologetically. "I am sorry, sir, if we bother you. But are you Sir Robert indeed?"

Endicott wondered how forthcoming he should be. He wanted to avoid a scene but did not want to hide. "Yes," he said simply, looking from the mother to the boy. Then he crouched down and looked into the child's eyes. "I don't have a white horse. The maiden survived without one. She's not in Elysium. She's alive and healthy, just like you. That's a relief, isn't it?"

The boy frowned and took a half step back. "I don't know. It isn't as good a story without the horse."

These tall tales of the terrible night bothered Endicott. He did not feel that those events were a fit subject for stories or songs. He especially disliked the idea of Syriol's suffering being discussed by strangers. His distaste must have shown on his face, for the mother pulled the boy away. "Sorry to bother you, Sir Robert."

"Well, that didn't turn into much," declared Eoyan March. "You need to work on your storytelling skills, Robert. You looked so angry I was scared you might be about to thrash the little fella."

"Really?" Endicott was horrified by the thought.

"Yes. You were gritting your teeth the whole time." Eoyan still had a hand on his sword. "I thought you were going to pop a tooth."

Endicott leaned back, wondering how seriously to take his sardonic companion. He glanced at the Apprentice's Library on his left. The cordwainer's shop was just down the road. *Maybe I'm just on edge from all the rush to prepare.*

I probably need a minute to myself. "Why don't I take a break in the Apprentice's Library while you two go and get the boots?"

Eoyan frowned, clearly uncertain. Endicott smiled reassuringly. "I will stay right there, Eoyan, until you two come get me. It's only a few buildings away."

Eloise gave Endicott a strange, almost suspicious look. "Come on, Eoyan. There are some instructions I need to give you for next week. *Private* instructions concerning my two stupes."

"Instructions?" Eoyan said, a knowing smile on his face. "As long as it's you telling me what to do, Eloise, I'm listening."

She shook her head and turned away. "How do you make everything sound sick, pervert?"

"Ahh, you're not mad at Uncle Eoyan," Eoyan said at the limit of Endicott's hearing. "You just like to be the one to…"

And they were gone.

The Apprentice's Library was surprisingly busy, given that dinner hour was approaching, but Endicott managed to find a quiet booth. Lord Quincy Leighton was sitting at another booth nearby with Steyphan Kenelm. Endicott had barely given the two a thought since the day Gregory had parted Steyphan's sword and they had ended the feud with Lord Jon Indulf. It was strange and a little heartening that Indulf had subsequently become a kind of inherited friend through Jennyfer Gray and Davyn. Both men nodded to Endicott but did not approach him. Their two other tablemates, both slightly older ladies, stared curiously at Endicott.

He ordered a big pot of tea and three mugs and thought about the little boy and his silly, innocuous question. Syriol was still a very important person to Endicott. He had not really had a chance to speak with her since the trip to Aignen, though they had crossed paths and traded smiles at the Citadel. Endicott hoped he would have more time for Syriol when he returned from the Line.

Maybe—

Someone had abruptly and without a word sat down at his booth. Endicott looked up and was shocked to find Conor sitting not more than two feet away from him. His heart pounded. Conor's resemblance to his father often hit him hard, and the interval since the night at the Black Spear had not been kind to him. He had a wide, ugly, greenish bruise like a distended halo around his left eye, and his jacket was soiled and ripped. Endicott thought the darkened eye looked dead, like it belonged on a corpse. He wordlessly pushed one of the cups towards Conor and poured tea into it. The old man put two shaking hands around the cup and said nothing. His right eye was red inside and out, and the veins stood framed in weird convolutions on his nose and cheeks. Endicott poured cream into his tea and offered the carafe to Conor. They drank, saying nothing. Conor closed his eyes in enjoyment.

"I know you think I'm crazy, Robert." Conor took another sip of tea, closing his eyes briefly again. Endicott refilled his cup from the pot. "But I'm not. I am not crazy, Robert."

Endicott's heart was still pounding. The image of Conor—of his father—bruised and degraded provoked rage, but he kept the anger out of his voice, speaking carefully. He did not ask, "Who did this to you?" Instead he said, "How can I help you, Conor?"

"You can listen!" Conor hissed. "Yes, listen. Please just listen to me."

Endicott showed he was ready to listen simply by saying nothing. This was enough for Conor.

"I'll tell you two things, Robert. Two things, and both are true, but I must tell you two, so you'll believe the one. You're my friend, aren't you, Robert? You fought beside me at Nyhmes." He hit his face with the palm of his hand.

Out of the corner of his eye Endicott saw Quincy and Steyphan staring open-mouthed at them. He did not care. Endicott reached across and grabbed Conor's hand, stopping the older man from hitting himself again. "I was at Nyhmes, Conor. I *am* your friend."

"Yes," Conor said, tears leaking from red eye and black eye alike. "I told them you were. They didn't believe me, but you are my friend, Robert. My friend."

The more it was said, the truer it seemed to become.

Conor raised his mug and drank from it again. "There was a group pushing the protests here in Vercors. You were right about that, Robert. Terwynn was part of it. He's dead now, Robert. They hung him before he could talk to the constabulary."

Endicott's eyes widened. "Who? How?"

"Them foreigners! It was them! The black ship. They hung him there."

"On a ship?"

"No!" Conor spilled some of his tea. "Down by the Hanging Man. Thought it was funny." More tears flowed down his ruddy, stubbly face. "Go see. I'm telling the truth. I'm telling you so you'll believe me about the other one."

"I will look," said Endicott firmly.

"Good!" exclaimed Conor. "Just because the protests were pushed, don't mean they were wrong, you know." Conor looked down at his shaking hands. "There was a baby, Robert. A baby."

"What?" said Endicott, confused.

Conor lurched to his feet, bumping the table and spilling tea. "It cried Robert. It cried, and it starved!" He turned abruptly and clumsily, colliding with the table again and charged through the tavern towards the door. Endicott looked at the old man's ruined shoes. No piece of sock stuck out this time. Now the soles flopped loosely at a crazy angle to each shoe. The shoes were on the verge of coming completely apart.

Endicott sat for a moment, confused and struggling to connect Conor's comments about a baby to some rational and coherent idea. He remembered the story Conor had told him at the bar. It had been a better day for the old man than this one. He had been more lucid then. What had he said? Something about a baby starving because it could not digest its mother's milk after she ate the new grain. Then he remembered the woman at the meeting. Alannah.

Alannah's baby?

Endicott made a decision. He had allowed Conor to escape him too many times. He had been passive when more direct action might have helped. He found a couple of copper knights, set them on the table, and slid out of the booth with more grace but just as suddenly as Conor had. Ignoring his promise to Eoyan March, he headed for the door. Lord Quincy called over to him as he went by. "What was that about, Sir Robert?"

Endicott dismissed the question with a wave of his hand.

"Do you need help?" Quincy called after him, but Endicott was already halfway across the room. A moment later he burst out the door, head swiveling, hunting for Conor. There was no sign of him. He summoned up the memory of finding Conor here before, the direction he had gone in that time, the alleyway he had chosen. One hand on his reforged sword, Endicott sprinted down the street, found the alley, and turned into it without pausing. His hunch was right. He could see Conor at the end of the alley, silhouetted in lantern light at an intersection. He was talking to another man.

The man was armored head to toe in dark plate, his face masked by a closed helm with the narrowest of eye slits and a perforated vent tail. Those holes were the only things that suggested that a human being dwelt underneath the gleaming, black metal. As Endicott raced down the alley towards Conor and his companion, this armored stranger suddenly drew a sword and thrust it through the old man's abdomen. Conor cried out and fell, his rag-covered legs buckling under him. Endicott sprinted closer. The armored man raised his sword to strike Conor in the head or neck. He intended to decapitate the old tramp.

No!

Endicott imagined the sword missing and innovated, drawing heat from the air. The sword struck stone rather than flesh, and the knight stumbled, momentarily off balance. A wave of frost shot down the alley and rolled over an already shivering Endicott. He tried to draw his sword as he came on, but it was frozen to the scabbard.

Endicott skidded to a stop on icy stone as he arrived at the intersection. Another alley opened to the right. Conor was on the ground now, shivering and clutching at his stomach, groaning in agony, and the knight was no longer alone. Behind him two other plate-armored men had emerged from the other alley. They struggled to draw their swords as well.

Endicott had just spent the better part of two days practicing with this sort of problem. He crouched, bending his knees, and rapped the end of his scabbard sharply on the frozen cobbles, then pulled on his hilt again. The sword came free.

The first knight raised his massive sword and stepped forward. Flakes of ice fell off him in a series of small cracks as he moved. His sword blade was black with frozen blood. "Get out of here, boy. Unless you want to die for an old rummy." His voice sounded hollow as it reverberated behind the tiny holes of the vent-tail on his closed helm.

Giving the lie to this offer, the other two men moved to cut Endicott off. Shivering from the innovation, paying out a cost he had not calculated and could not have known, his heart pounding, Endicott looked down on the anguished face of his father and thought no thoughts but one. He felt no feeling but one.

The knight reared back for a mighty two-handed swing, but Endicott was faster. He had foreseen the gambit, though whether from instinct or an unconscious act of millisecond heraldry, he would never be able to stay. With a howl of rage he stepped in on the man and, with a speed that made the air whistle, twisted around and slashed his sword down upon the knight's gauntlet, shearing through all four fingers of his left hand and rebounding off the hilt. The digits exploded outward like beans off a drumhead, and the knight's sword flew out of his hands across the icy pavement.

Gahhh!

The knight clutched his ruined stumps. Urine steamed as it flowed down his frosted plate armor. Endicott roared again and swung his sword still more ferociously, speed making it sing until it hit the knight sideways through the lower half of his visor, denting it sharply into his mouth. Steaming gobs of blood spurted forth, and the man fell backwards, twisting crazily. Endicott caught a quick glimpse of the sigil on his backplate. A longship. The implications were not lost on Endicott, but he had more pressing issues to consider. His sword had rebounded from the destroyed helm into a position approximating guard as he turned to face the other two knights. One had finally unsheathed his massive sword, but the other still struggled with his. Their body language was hesitant, their movements cautious and crabwise, startled, blue eyes completely filling their tiny visors.

"Sir Robert!" The voices of Lord Quincy Leighton and Steyphan Kenelm echoed down the alley as they rushed towards Endicott and his adversaries. The aggressors' visored heads pivoted to each other and then they scrambled down the other alley, feet slipping on the ice, and were swallowed in darkness, only the clanging of armor marking their panicked retreat.

Endicott let them go. He crouched down beside Conor. The old man had stopped twitching and was breathing shallowly. Both his eyes looked equally morbid now. Endicott pulled the old man's bloody shirt up to examine the gaping hole in his abdomen. He had to swipe blood away to see it. The blood was turning brownish and flowing sluggishly. He put his head to Conor's chest. More blood seeped slowly across the cold ground, soaking the younger man's clothes.

Quincy, still moving fast, wrong-footed on one of the knight's severed fingers and slid roughly into the far wall. Steyphan slowed before hitting the fully frozen section of the cobbles. "What the hell…" he trailed off.

Quincy regained his footing and took in the situation, eyes popping out of his head. Then he knelt by the knight, listening to the desperate gurgling sounds that escaped from under the visor. "He's still alive!" Quincy shouted. He struggled to remove the knight's helm, but the visor was dented too far into the injured man's mouth, jamming the moving parts too tightly together. "Help me, Sir Robert. He's choking."

"No." Endicott stayed with Conor, not certain he was gone. He held the old man's hand as the amplitudes of his breathing attenuated to nothing.

Steyphan was with Quincy now, but neither of them could figure out how to pry off the deformed, bloody helmet. The gurgling sounds grew louder, and the knight's damaged hand thrashed about, clutching at nothing, stumps still leaking blood. His other hand clawed spasmodically at the cold stones.

The gurgling stopped. Eoyan March and Eloise arrived shortly after, though not before Quincy had finished retching. Steyphan was silent but looked just as sick. None of them approached Endicott.

"How dare you get in a fight without me, Robert!" Eloise exclaimed through the hand she clasped to her mouth as she gazed at Conor's torn, bloodied body. Eoyan walked around the scene carefully, eyes alert, silent for once.

Endicott was staring at Conor's floppy, wretched shoes when Vice Constable Edwyn Perry arrived. Quincy and Steyphan crowded the constable, talking and gesticulating. "Okay," Perry said, one hand palm out. "Thank you, gentlemen. Don't go anywhere." He turned to Endicott, still crouched beside Conor.

"Hey, kid." Perry's head tilted on his long neck as he peered down at Endicott, Conor, and the fallen knight. "Good to see you vertical," he added. He crouched down too, and his left foot slipped. "Kinda slippery here."

Perry examined the man in armor, using a dagger to move the head gently and very slightly to the side. He pulled on the knight's arm to expose his sigil and tried to peer into his visor. A small flow of blood leaked out of the crumpled vent-tail as he moved the man around. "I think I know who this is," he said, trying to pull the visor open. "I need to break these rivets," he gritted, failing to make any progress.

"My sword could cut right through them," offered Eloise.

"I don't want to lop his head right off," Perry muttered. By now a crowd had begun to gather, "Move those people back," he barked at a constable who had been standing aside, grimacing at the dead knight.

"Take this," Endicott said, releasing Conor's hand at last. He reached for his entropic dagger, which was sheathed on his opposite hip.

Edwyn took the dagger, pausing involuntarily as his eyes caught its uncanny, glassy surface before digging at the rivets. A moment later he was able to pull the visor away from helm and face. Once pressure was released on the buckles, the helm opened properly, and the whole ruined metal shell was promptly removed. The knight's blond hair was orange from blood that had pooled within the steel shell. He might have been fair to look upon before Endicott hit him, but his nose had been squashed flat. That was ancillary to the real damage. His jaw was hideously broken, along with numerous teeth. Some of them were floating in the thickening blood that still filled his mouth.

He choked to death.

Endicott felt sick. Not guilty, for he had no doubt about the ethics of the fight or who should have priority of care, but sick nevertheless. The fight was over. The price could now be assessed. It was high.

One half of Edwyn Perry's mouth came up in a smile. The other half was not a joiner. "This is Sir Colborn Vig that you killed, kid, a full Royal Knight of Armadale. Reputed to be a very strong, very dangerous man."

"Maybe he got too used to murdering old men," Eoyan said.

"Apparently that came with an unforeseen hazard," Edwyn replied, looking at Endicott. "The key point here is that he is, or was, the right-hand man of one Alfrothul Gudmund. Who happens to be the right-hand man of Armadale's ambassador. I know that's two right hands, but I'd like to see them try to deny the connection. You killed him pretty good," he said looking at Colborn's stumps and the wreckage of his jaw and helm. "And I hear he had two colleagues with him. I kinda regret pissing you off back at the Citadel last week."

"You never made me angry," Endicott said absently, trying not to shiver. He was very cold. "But I have to tell you a few things." He proceeded to describe his conversation with Conor, leaving nothing out. He recounted the fight in the alley dispassionately and ended with the need to follow up on the report of Terwynn's alleged murder.

"That's quite a story, Sir Robert," Perry said, shaking his head.

"Robert doesn't lie!" Eloise said stepping close to the constable, looming over him. "It's not a *story*."

"Whoa, hey." Perry put his palm out again. "I didn't say he lied. I believe him." The vice constable squinted up at the tall young woman. "You know I deal with people all day long. Some lie most of the time. Almost all the rest speak with, shall we say, a heavy bias. So I call everything a story. But I believe this story is the truth."

"What you need to do is find Terwynn's body," Endicott said evenly. "From what I gathered, it ought to be in one of the buildings near the Hanging Man."

"Oh, we'll do that, Sir Robert, don't you worry. I heard you." He glanced at Eloise. "And your *mighty* friends. This is more serious than I had imagined. A lot more." Edwyn put a hand to his head. "If all the grain ends up in the barrow, we might be escorting the ambassador out of the duchy before this is over."

Eloise tugged on Endicott's arm. "Let's go, Robert."

Endicott glanced up at her, thinking about how he had never seen the cloaked man in heraldry except around Koria or Eloise. They were still in danger, and it was looking more and more as if the cloaked man was from Armadale. "How long until all Armadale is gone from here?"

Edwyn squinted. "That's up to the duke, not me. Depends how willing he is to take us into war, kid. The politics of this have to be done right, have to *look* right. Could take a week, maybe more."

A week. Or more.

"Keep Koria at her estate at least that long, Eloise," Endicott said.

"Count on it," Eloise declared.

Endicott said nothing as he removed Conor's ruined shoes and put his good ones on the old man.

Chapter Twenty-One

Independent Command

Endicott, Eloise, and Eoyan were not able to leave the alley for some time. Before he could go home, Endicott had to record and sign a detailed written statement, as did Quincy and Steyphan, and Eloise and Eoyan could not abandon their friend. By the time the formalities were done, getting back to the Orchid was an urgent necessity. Endicott needed to travel the next day. There was no question of delay, especially now that legal and military action against Armadale loomed.

Lord Quincy Leighton and Steyphan Kenelm insisted on escorting the now shoeless Endicott back to the Orchid. The mood of the small group was discordant. Endicott's feelings were an odd mix of confusion and melancholy over what Conor had said and what had subsequently happened to him. Eloise walked in a slow boil over having missed the fight, while Eoyan was—if not angry—tight and even more alert for further trouble. Quincy and Steyphan were oblivious to these feelings. The horror they had felt at the gruesome deaths of Conor and Sir Colborn Vig was somehow transformed as they walked back with their heroic friends. Their discomfort at the brutality and gore of that evening was replaced by a feeling that they had been part of some grand and virtuous adventure. They had also never been allowed into the prestigious Orchid before and reveled in the experience.

As soon as everyone was safely inside, Eoyan said his goodbyes, anxious to get their mounts and gear ready for the morning. Quincy and Steyphan were like two horses out of the gate, competing in a rush to describe to the rest of the housemates what they thought had happened that night. Gregory listened spellbound, perhaps a little guilty about his absence from the fray, as the two described the Battle of the Bisecting Alleys to everyone. Endicott and Eloise sat in silence, absorbed in their own recollections.

"What I want to know," said Davyn at a volume just below a shout, "is what in Hati's Hell happened to Robert's boots? And you know," he crouched down to study Endicott's feet, "Robert's feet *are* kind of hairy. Though not as hairy as his a—Ow! Eloise, why are you always hitting people?"

"Why do you lot always act like stupes?" she shot back.

For his part, Endicott did not respond. He knew the big man was just trying to lighten the mood. In any case Eloise had hit Davyn rather hard, so there was no need.

"Whatever," Deleske said dryly, spinning a feather pen around his thumb and looking around lazily. "Eloise, you must be sooo pissed. You always do the killing around here. But now you have some competition. It's what, four to one now?"

Quincy and Steyphan had been smiling and laughing up to this point in the conversation. Now they abruptly stopped. Endicott could almost see them adding up the bodies in their heads and reassessing their feelings about the evening's adventure.

"It's going to be five to one if you don't shut up," advised Eloise.

Davyn, still rubbing his shoulder, gave Deleske his best stink eye. "In all seriousness we know that no one here goes out looking for violence. Right?"

"Really? For someone who doesn't look for it, Robert sure finds it a lot." Deleske stood up, patted Davyn on the shoulder, and went to his room. No one said anything for a few moments. They just stared at Deleske's closed door. Finally Endicott pushed himself up and walked to the baths.

"Thanks for your help today, gentlemen, but we all better get some rest now."

As he threw off his clothes, Endicott could hear Gregory politely seeing the two young lords out. He grabbed a handful of soap grains, and jumped in the big tub. The last of his hypothermia was finally dissipating. Davyn and Heylor joined him in the baths a few moments later. Davyn had a fresh set of clothes under his arm, which he placed beside the towels.

"Let me come with you tomorrow, Robert." It was the eighth time Heylor had asked. As he had done the previous seven times, Endicott did not answer. In the silence the three young men sat without speaking, Endicott soaking up the heat, Davyn sweating out the tension, Heylor jittery and dumbly pleading. After an uncomfortable few minutes Gregory, Eloise, Bethyn, and Koria entered the baths.

"Well, now that we have a quorum, we can start the meeting." Davyn's loud voice reverberated off the cold, stone walls.

Endicott sighed and looked tiredly at the girls. "As familiar and comforting as this situation feels, the first item of business has got to be privacy in the baths. You do know I'm naked in this tub, don't you, ladies?"

"Yes," said Bethyn and Eloise at the same time. "We can't see anything through the soap bubbles," Eloise added, peering intently into the water.

"Those aren't *soap* bubbles!" boomed Davyn.

Gregory frowned. "It does make me consider saying something I would not have expected to have to say. When Eloise and I are married, it will likely be at my family's estate. Yes, we still own it." He spoke in an exaggeratedly posh voice. "While you are there, *if* you are invited," he added, glaring at Davyn, "do *not* walk into my parents' baths. They will not take it well. I am mostly speaking to you, dear." He looked archly at Eloise. "But it goes for the rest of you as well. Our time in the Bifrost hot pools has perhaps made us a bit ... unconventional."

Eloise put her arm around Gregory's waist.

"Well, *I* feel comfortable," said Davyn, hands on hips and chest outthrust.

Ha.

"I can pack your saddle bags," pleaded Heylor, obviously preoccupied with an entirely different subject.

He still hopes I'll let him come with us.

Gregory's hand came down on Heylor's shoulder. "I have already done it, Heylor. You will have another job. While we are away, I mean. Remember? We are counting on you to take charge of it."

Look after Koria and Eloise. That was the task he and Gregory had given Heylor as a sop, but the jittery wannabe either did not believe Eloise and Koria needed help from him, which was probably true, or he thought that any possible trouble would inevitably come to Endicott, which was clearly not true. Either way the skinny young man remained fixated on being around Endicott. Missing another adventure had apparently only stoked his eagerness even further.

My adventures are not as free of cost as he thinks.

"Quincy never said who the old man was," Davyn said, almost as if he could read Endicott's mind. "It was Conor, wasn't it?"

"Yes," Endicott said, avoiding eye contact. "It was Conor."

Davyn seemed to wobble for a moment. Then he wiped a tear off his cheek. "Damn. I liked that old fool."

"So did I," said Endicott. The old man's face—his father's face—rose in his memory.

More than liked.

"Now kindly turn around, ladies, and allow me dry off. In return I will tell you the whole story."

The ladies decorously complied, with a few stifled giggles, and when Endicott had put on the fresh clothes Davyn had brought, he told them everything. Though she had heard it all on the way back from the alley, Eloise managed to listen almost patiently. Tale told, Endicott let his audience absorb the information. Gregory stared off at nothing, thinking. Then he said, "So it's been Armadale all this time. Behind the protests. Behind the cloaked man."

Koria frowned. "Perhaps."

Davyn looked unconvinced. "I would like to take 'mystery solved' for an answer, but this is a test in which the only acceptable outcome is a perfect score. I am not sure Armadale explains everything that's been happening. Or that we have *seen* happen. Who knows what else may have been going on behind the scenes?" he added, looking closely at Koria. "But if Armadale is truly the problem, the entire situation could de-escalate very quickly. If we can say that the risk of a war qualifies as de-escalation."

"Way to look on the bright side," Bethyn whispered.

"Regardless, let's all try to stay out of trouble for the next few days," Endicott said. "Go to the Citadel," he looked at Davyn and Bethyn. "Go to Koria's estate." He looked at Eloise, Koria, and Heylor.

"And we shall go to the Line," declared Gregory. "With a veritable army." He shook his head. "When we come back, it may all be behind us."

Heylor still had a pleading, almost desperate look to him. "That skolve Deleske shouldn't have laid it all on you, Robert."

Koria broke the ensuing silence, her face dark. "Deleske made a good point in his cynical way." She ran a finger along Endicott's arm lightly. "You do seem to attract more than your fair share of trouble."

When Endicott joined Koria in her room later, he found a set of outdoor clothes and armor laid out on her bed. "Try them on," she commanded softly. "I want to make sure they fit." Endicott obliged, donning the soft, flexible pants, undershirt, heavy riding boots, and sheepskin-lined leather jacket. Over this went hardened leather vambraces, greaves, and gauntlets. Each piece had its own set of laces protected by overlapping leather cuffs. Koria carefully tied each piece in place as Endicott savored the smell of fresh leather and wax. Each element was the highest quality, and each had the emblem of a tower etched into it. Endicott looked closer and saw that the towers were exact depictions of the Bron elevator.

"It shouldn't be too heavy," Koria observed, "but it will come in handy out there."

"This must have taken some planning," he said, testing his ability to move easily in the gear. "How did you decide on these pieces?" He looked down at the boots. They had an extra layer of stiff, floating leather plates on top, a bit like a sabaton.

How did you know I would need new boots?

Koria looked at him darkly. "I went to the library and learned what I could about combat with skolves. I also interviewed Lord Wolverton and Sir Hemdale. They have both fought them before. Do you know what I found out?" She grimaced as she pulled the laces on his last vambrace tight.

"What?"

"Skolves sometimes try to bite their opponents. Their elongate jaws are quite strong. So if you parry or remove their weapon, their next move could be instinctive. That's when you can use your greaves or vambrace."

I guess that would work. If the skolve doesn't just bite my face off.

"Full plate or chainmail would be better, of course" Koria added, as if reading his thoughts, "but I knew you wouldn't wear it."

"Thank you," Endicott said. "What do you think?" He came to attention in front of her. Koria sat silently on her bed for a moment. Her green eyes seemed to gleam more than usual as she stared at him, but Endicott could not guess what she was thinking.

Abruptly Koria jumped up and rushed at him, kissing him urgently, tongue probing. Her normally reserved demeanor was nowhere to be seen. Endicott was not unhappy, but for a moment he could not process this sudden, unprecedented sexual aggression. He almost fell backwards in shock but rallied just enough to keep his feet. For the moment.

Koria's urgent kissing continued. She pressed herself against him and began to slowly undulate, as if she wanted to absorb him into her, abdomen rhythmically thrusting and arms tugging. He could feel her hips pushing. He could feel they were open. The room spun, and then spun again as she roughly turned him around and shoved him back onto the bed. He sat up in time to receive her onto his lap. She rose up, kissing him on his face, in his ears, on his neck, running her hands up and down his body, along his arms, caressing the smooth new vambraces. She grabbed the hair on the back of Endicott's head and pulled it back, planting him flat on the bed.

"Be careful out there, Robert," she whispered as she began untying the laces on one of the greaves. Then she turned to the other and finally to his pants. She threw one vambrace aside and wriggled onto him, pressing her breasts against his mouth and her hips into his stomach. She slid lower, sliding her skirt up, grinding slowly, firmly.

LYING IN BED WITH THE WOMAN HE ADORED AFTER BEING THOROUGHLY, ENTHUSIASTICALLY, and assertively immersed in the physical act of love, Endicott did not ask why. Violence may be the last refuge of the incompetent, and sexual aggression the first refuge of the opportunistic, undisciplined and unimaginative. But when a woman of surpassing intelligence, sophistication, and self-control goes so much against her accustomed nature, questioning seems ... inappropriate.

He knew why.

Koria was every bit as sensitive and passionate as he was. She felt for Conor and for him. She felt the same horrible catharsis. She knew, like Endicott, that the conflict was far from over. She knew it was not just Armadale. More was coming. Koria was just as uncertain about the future as he was, and just as certain that it would unfold in a moment of ultimate kairos. Like Koria he had been working with all his strength to prepare for the moment, to be ready when the time came, and he recognized that she wanted to make sure their love had been expressed as passionately, as urgently, as possible before that moment came and the opportunity was perhaps lost forever.

Or she may just have really liked the way I looked in leather armor.

▽

As dawn crept across the Academic Plateau, the business of the day before was far from over. Runners had come and gone throughout the night with messages and questions from the Citadel. Only Deleske seemed to sleep soundly.

The morning was even busier. The Orchid emptied as, first, Davyn, Deleske, and Bethyn departed under heavy escort. Then Merrett and Lindseth came for Eloise, Heylor, and Koria. Watching them go, waiting for his own turn, Endicott saw each departure like that of a child leaving home for the first time.

Gregory, Endicott, and Eoyan were the last to go. They had a few details of equipment to sort out and a few more messages to pass back and forth to the Citadel. When they were finally free to leave, they found they were a good three hours behind Sir Hemdale, Elyze Astarte, and the rest of the expedition.

No trip should lack roadworthy conversation, and Eoyan seemed determined to make the most of the opportunity.

"So ... how do you like your new boots, Sir Gregory Justice? Is the fit okay? Pinching any toes?" Eoyan March rode expertly, hips into his saddle. On top of his full chainmail he had added a dark, iron breastplate, backplate, and gorget, and in addition to his sword, he had a heavy spear holstered in a saddle sheath. To no one's surprise he had also brought his sense of humor, inappropriate or not.

"They fit perfectly, thank you very much," replied Gregory. "Eloise knows my size." His big shield was strapped to his back. Endicott kept an eye on it, half expecting it to poke him or his horse as they bounced along. He had not made up his mind about armor other than his shield, but had stowed a shirt of chainmail in one of their bags.

Eoyan smiled as if he had been handed a gift. "Hooo! I recall she did say that she. Knew. Your. Size." He looked over at Endicott, waggling his eyebrows. "And how about you, Sir Robert Endicott? I see you have some wonderful new pieces of armor. Does Koria—"

"I am happy beyond words that the three of us have learned to work together so well," declared Gregory sternly, speaking over Eoyan. "But how are we to work with the other soldiers? What exactly is our role in all this?"

From the beginning it had felt to Endicott that their role in the expedition was being glossed over, that the importance of dynamics had been unexplained except as control for the grain. Whatever that meant. *Why* ever the grain was so important.

Get us out of town to somewhere safer while other matters are worked out. Can that really be the whole story?

Then he remembered the letter Gregory carried. The letter from his grandpa. There was more to it.

"That is a very good question," said Eoyan, seemingly unperturbed at having his next joke derailed. "I say that because I mentioned the very same thing to Lord Wolverton before leaving this morning." Then, unaccountably, he went silent as if focusing only on the road ahead.

When it seemed that no more would be forthcoming, Gregory squinted over at Eoyan. "And …?"

"Let's trot," said Eoyan, nickering at his horse and simultaneous flicking his reins and heels. "My role is clear. And quite simple: look after you two ruffians. And in particular try to keep Robert from running off and getting into some new mischief. Your jobs are a little … less clear. More … implied than spelled out." He posted his trotting horse smoothly and easily. "Actually I'm not sure you *have* a job. Just be there and get some … seasoning."

"Get some seasoning?" Gregory snorted, verbalizing Endicott's own thoughts. "Seasoning indeed. How does a dynamicist of Professor Gerveault's exacting and demanding demeanor tolerate such, er, vaguery?"

"You don't know Lord Wolverton well, but he is cut from the same cloth," Eoyan supplied. "But I don't let it bother me much."

"Why not?" responded Gregory with a trace of suspicion in his voice.

Eoyan smiled almost condescendingly. "Sometimes I set the agenda, but I am a student too, you know. I don't expect to be in charge every moment of every day. You dynamicists are always trying to control everything." He put his hands up in a gesture of surrender. "I know there are some extenuating circumstances in this case, but sometimes you just have to take things on trust."

I trust they have a reason. I would just like to know what it is.

Endicott's mind drifted with the rocking of the horse. He thought about the cloaked figure of his heraldic dreams. He thought about the knights from Armadale and about how easily Colborn Vig's helm had caved in when he struck it. Then he thought about how much easier Vig's sword had seemed to slide into Conor. He thought about Conor clutching at his guts in agony, covered in frost, blood slowly turning black. He thought about Conor's face, so like the poorly remembered face of his own father's.

I know Conor's face better than my father's now.

The thought only brought on another wave of melancholy.

Who did I remind Conor of? Was I truly a friend to him or merely a sort of projection created by the addle-brained, memory-jumbled osmotic association of a series of chance encounters? Is there a difference? He thought I was his friend.

And it may have killed him.

Like a musician working the scales, Endicott envisioned the complex, irregular set of causal connections that had brought him and Conor together, twice randomly at Nyhmes, then by yet another coincidence, at Vercors. The tones turned elegiac as he saw himself use a misremembered friendship to infiltrate the Nimrheal cult and reflected on how their feeling of connection brought Conor to the Apprentice's Library and finally, at the darkened end of sound and memory, to the alley where he was murdered.

"Sir Gregory may be making all the objections, but you, sir, look more upset." Eoyan's voice was low. For once he was not trying to be funny.

"I keep thinking of Conor's face."

At this Gregory turned in his saddle and looked searchingly at his friend. Eoyan maintained his sober, cool demeanor. "It's only natural," the soldier said, chainmail gently jingling. "He was your friend."

Endicott sighed, still wondering what sort of friend he had really been. Still feeling guilt. "He looked like my father. Or at least how I remember my father. Did I ever tell you gentlemen that?"

"You told me," said Gregory, looking stricken and agitated.

Eoyan shook his head. "That's a horrible connection. It must be like losing two people."

Gregory's brows furrowed. "He was not alone at the end, Robert. Remember that."

Everyone dies alone. In the last instant, when sight is gone, when the touch of a loving hand fades, when the scale ends and sound flutters away to nothing, when all perception narrows like a dark funnel leading nowhere, everyone is alone.

"That's right," Eoyan added, noting Endicott's haunted expression. "He was fortunate to have someone looking out for him." Before Endicott could reply, the soldier spoke again, perhaps trying to change the subject. If so he chose the wrong question. "What did your mother look like?"

Endicott remembered how Koria had tried to help him recover that memory after his so-called fight with Sir Hemdale during the twenty-four-hour test. They had talked for hours, but no amount of discussion had changed anything.

"I have no idea."

∇

"Where is the Inn on the Rill?" Gregory asked, staring down the lane. It was dark, and he had never been to the town of Kuiyp.

"Well, let me think," said Eoyan. "Down by the creek if I remember."

The Inn on the Rill turned out to be unmissable. It was the largest building in Kuiyp, bigger even than the grain storage facility. It was three stories of river stone and timber enclosing a spacious courtyard. Sergeant Eirnyn Quinn waited with another soldier and a boy of about ten at the porte-cochere. She smiled as they walked their horses into the courtyard.

"Glad you made it, gentlemen," she said, nostrils flaring. "Welcome to Kuiyp. Daeg here will settle your horses." She gestured towards the boy. "Private Rhysheart and I can help you with your bags and show you to your rooms."

Rhysheart was a man of about Endicott's height with light brown hair. He was dressed in chainmail and carried a short sword at his hip. He stared at Gregory with a curious, open look on his face. "You're Sir Robert?" he asked with a frank, plainspoken air.

Eirnyn nudged him as Gregory scowled and Eoyan laughed. Endicott was unfazed. He reached out a hand to shake Rhysheart's. "That is my friend Sir

Gregory. He has the look of a hero, private, and I rather think he is one, but I am Sir Robert."

Rhysheart shook his hand eagerly, as well as Gregory's, who was grinning now. Eoyan just nodded affably in his usual sardonic style.

"Sorry, sir," Rhysheart said. "You as well, Sir Gregory. You're just both so young. Boys really ..." He caught himself too late. Eirnyn was shaking her head at him in dismay.

"Private!" she barked.

Rhysheart almost clicked his heels. "Sorry again. I didn't mean ... That came out wrong. I never got the chance to meet you when we were getting ready for the expedition, but I've heard all about you. Remarkable things, I mean. We heard that you destroyed a whole column of Knights of Armadale last night. Are you—"

"Later, private," Eirnyn interrupted. "No one likes to be interrogated the moment they arrive on the stoop. Let's get their bags and get them organized first."

Eoyan, Gregory, and Endicott unpacked and rested briefly before joining the rest of the expedition in the inn's large common room. By then Lieutenant Vaugn Somne had apparently been apprised of Rhysheart's gaffe, for he took the trouble of presenting Gregory, Eoyan, and Endicott to all of the soldiers one by one. Many of them already knew Eoyan, and the tall young soldier soon found himself surrounded by a group of his old colleagues eager for the latest news from the capital. Endicott and Gregory joined Sir Hemdale, Somne, and Elyze at a big table near the fireplace.

"Robert," Elyze said, as if pronouncing the name of some rare element. "Gregory. I am so glad you have both made it." Her deep voice purred as she spoke, and her eyes seemed to twinkle as she watched them.

But not surprised? Endicott was curious about the heraldic dream she professed to have had, the latest claim she made as part of her escalating demands that he join the expedition.

"I understand you had a bit of trouble last night," said Vaugn Somne in a low, cautious voice.

"Yes, a bit," said Endicott. He felt reluctant to talk right away about the previous night's events and hoped this perfunctory answer might discourage further enquiry.

Gregory sensed this and stepped into the awkward silence that followed his friend's curt response. "He fought three Knights of Armadale. One of them a Royal Knight. Sir Colborn Vig."

"Sir Colborn?" growled Hemdale. Even seated, even without his plate armor, which could only have been left temporarily in his room, Hemdale was enormous. He was taller even than Eloise, and probably twice as heavy. Terse, scarred, and hard, he would have been intimidating at half the size.

"You knew him?" asked Gregory.

"Knew? Do you mean…?" Hemdale stopped himself and only stared at his nephew. After a moment he added, "I'm *from* there, nephew."

Gregory nodded. "Then you might be able to answer a question I have been harboring, uncle. Three Knights of Armadale murder a sick and defenseless old man. They are so sure of the righteousness of their action that they then engage in battle against a single man half their age. On another occasion, two maniacs from Armadale engage in a deceitful sham of a protest and later attempt to murder Sir Robert." Hemdale was momentarily speechless, and Endicott saw that much of the conversation at the other tables had dropped away as soldiers and guests leaned in to overhear the confrontation with Hemdale.

"What I don't understand," continued Gregory, one hand absently tapping the side of his beer mug, "is how from such a storied, honorable culture such dishonorable acts can come."

Hemdale's fierce, cold eyes were fixed on Gregory from under bushy brows. "That is why I left them," he explained with eerie calmness. "One of the reasons. Self-gratifying righteousness, ego-oriented righteousness, is a sham. It is an excuse to dehumanize and visit cruelty on those deemed dishonorable. What such *honorable* warriors fail to understand is that honor is a gift even the poorest persons can give themselves. All that honor costs is to abandon your own desire and the easy road. Its essence is the denial of your own gratification for the sake of a just cause." As he spoke, his voice rose louder but its pitch, low to start with, descended to a basso profundo, his eyes growing even larger as if they might burst from their sockets.

Gregory opened his mouth to reply, but Hemdale preempted him.

"What most call honor is a thing without integrity, a tool to direct others what to do, to make others do what they *cannot*, to give up or go without what they *will* not. It is an excuse to take offence at the slightest cause, especially if their own inadequacy or hypocrisy is threatened with exposure. True honor is a lonely, inward journey. It is not about other people. The so-called knights you met know nothing of it. They wear a suit of armor but forget to dress themselves in their own integrity. They are political puppets, not true knights at all."

It was a conversation-killer, asking Hemdale a question. No one anywhere in the common room was speaking now. They were all looking at the big, elderly knight, or more accurately looking near him. Most feared making contact with those cold, bulging, unblinking eyes.

"Still," Hemdale continued, taking an unnaturally loud drink of his beer, "Colborn Vig was a tough fighter. He has killed five different knights in tournaments in Armadale and murdered many more *actual* enemies in real combat." Suddenly he reached out and clapped Endicott on the shoulder, almost knocking the startled young man off his chair. "Well done, Sir Robert. To defeat a warrior of that caliber, you must have found some of that simplicity we once spoke of. As far as I am concerned, you are still family."

Another violent and unpredictable uncle. Yay.

Vyrnus Hedt chose that moment to enter the common room, winding around the chairs a little loosely and finally taking a seat, uninvited, beside Elyze. He grinned confidently at Gregory and Endicott. "Glad you made it Robert, Gregory. Heard you found some trouble last night." Vern did not seem to notice the silence of the common room or the fierce, big-eyed stare of Sir Hemdale. Instead he continued talking casually and a little smugly to the two younger men. "But now you're in the real deal. This is the task that is going to win us the Ardgour Wilderness. And you two boys get to be a part of it while still in your first year at the New School. Elyze and I have been looking forward to having someone do the grunt work. Isn't that right, Elyze?"

Elyze Astarte smiled but said nothing. Vern shrugged and leaned closer to Endicott. "You know what you get to do when we cross the Line, Robert? You get to count dog shit," he sniggered.

Sir Hemdale's beer mug exploded. Beer, suds, and shards of pottery flew everywhere, though mostly over the head and shoulders of a shocked Vern. "You seem confused, Vyrnus." The words were chewed like the glass the big knight probably ate for breakfast. "You are addressing two Knights of Vercors. Address them as sir, if you please. They are not boys, and they do not take orders from the likes of you."

Vern's face was as red as the hottest part of the fire he now stared wordlessly at, as if wishing himself in the middle of it. He leaned back in his chair, perhaps from a combination of fear and a desire to minimize the amount of spittle he collected as Hemdale barked at him.

"I was just teasing the young—"

"The likes of you do not tease the likes of them."

Vern put his hands up, voice breaking. "Look, I'm sorry. Please realize, this is just how we talk up here. That's the job we always give the new folk, the ones on the lowest rung of the ladder."

"They are not on the same ladder as you." Hemdale's hand slammed down on the table. "*Realize* that."

"Thank you, Sir Hemdale," Elyze Astarte said calmly. "No one should knock anyone else's ladders over. Please excuse Vern. He is normally much politer. He is simply... overexcited." She smiled at Robert and Gregory. "It's the thrill of having you here." She turned to Hemdale, who was still glaring at the unfortunate Vern. "We are very happy they are both here. However I must admit I am a little confused too." She tapped her index finger against her jaw. "I also thought Sir Gregory and Sir Robert were here to assist Vern and me. We need their help, and I have an extensive list of important things for them to do."

"If I may," interjected Lieutenant Vaugn Somne, "I was under the impression that these two fine young knights were to help my soldiers and me with the security of the expedition."

"You are both wrong," said Hemdale in a slightly gentler growl. He stood up. "They are knights. They are an independent command."

"Yours?" asked Vaugn Somne, unfazed.

"They are *knights*. Their own."

"Well, Sir Independent Commanders," Eoyan said wryly. "No one is going to bother you now. In fact I think they are all afraid to talk to you. Big mean uncle, you know."

They were back on the road, this time with the whole contingent of soldiers. Elyze occasionally rode beside them but only made small talk. Vern avoided them altogether, head craning around to keep track of Sir Hemdale, but only so he could ride as far from him as possible. Keeping track of the big knight was easy. There was no hiding nearly seven feet of plate-armored giant. Keeping away from him would be another matter if he decided to approach, but that seemed very unlikely.

"It's too bad, really," Eoyan continued. "I was telling Eirnyn and some of the lads about our tactical training using dynamics. They were interested in giving it a go, but now they're pretty much off the idea. Scared of getting crushed like a certain someone's beer mug."

Endicott thought about that. It would make sense to train with the others, but their alienation was not a thing that could be easily overcome. He turned his head to Gregory and Eoyan, leaving his reins where they were. "Okay, very funny, Eoyan, except it really isn't. Let's go speak with the lieutenant and— Hey, what is that smell?" A sharp, musky odor had suddenly filled his nostrils.

"That would be a humble skunk, oh high and mighty knight," said Eoyan.

Gregory's lip curled up and he coughed. The smell was getting stronger. "Yes. Definitely skunk."

They were close to the Castlereagh Line now, only about two days away, and there was a growing presence of wetlands and undeveloped land amidst the farms. It was not that the land was completely unfarmed, but it was certainly getting wilder. They had turned off the main road that led to the great border castle of Ardvaser that morning, so more and more wild country was to be expected. Apparently skunks came with wilderness. The smell was becoming almost unbearably strong now, but it was unavoidable.

Lieutenant Vaugn Somne balanced a small notebook in one hand as he scribbled something in it with the other. "You actually like the smell? Skunk? Really?" Between jottings he stared at Seargent Eirnyn Quinn, who rode beside him. Endicott exchanged looks with a puzzled Gregory and an elated Eoyan as they slipped in behind the two to eavesdrop on their conversation.

She shrugged. "Always have. Can't explain it."

Somne wrote something down, perhaps about his sergeant's strange olfactory preference. "Damned odd."

"Some people like liver," she replied, apparently unbothered by her companion's incomprehension.

"How about week-old dinner?" the lieutenant asked, smiling beatifically.

"Not me," Eirnyn replied at once. "But somebody somewhere. Probably." She looked up. "How about three-day old fish from the river?"

"Okay, that might work better." He smiled and scribbled another note. A moment later he started speaking again, this time in a singsong voice.

"Some like the smell of wet dog,
and some an old muddy hog.
My sergeant is partial to skunk,
or fresh-turned rusty junk.
The highlanders indulge in liver,
while downstream they take
three-day old fish from the river."

His voice resumed its usual formal tone. "Yes, I think that works well enough sergeant. I'll pound the meter down later. Thank you very much."

Endicott was uncertain what would be most polite in the circumstances: pretending he hadn't heard, joining in with a stanza of doggerel of his own, or leaving and never listening to these two again.

"Hmm, hmm," grunted Gregory pregnantly.

Eoyan, proving he had his own independent command, tried something else. "I don't know which is worse," he said with vast sincerity. "That Eirnyn likes the smell of skunk or that we brought along an amateur poet instead of a tough-as-nails lieutenant."

"It's nothing to be embarrassed about," rejoined Gregory in his lordliest tones. "Some of our best friends are poets."

The lieutenant jostled his notebook in his lap. "Gahh!" he cried, dropping it on the road. "I'm not really a poet," he added, equally piteously.

Eoyan leaned his head towards Vaugn Somne. "We know," he said archly.

Endicott had already leapt off his horse to retrieve the book from the dirt. He held it up for Somne to take, but the officer hesitated. "I am sorry about last night," Endicott said.

Gregory urged his horse around the two soldiers and pulled up in front of them. "Eloise, I mean *Sir* Eloise, told me that *Sir* Hemdale can be very literal. We know it can be... off-putting."

"It's not his literalism that bothers me," said the skunk-enthusiast. To Endicott she did not look like a person who would enjoy foul smells. She was strong-looking and seemed highly competent, pretty too. "It's the unequivocal threat of decisive and life-changing violence."

You got that right.

"Yes, indeed," agreed Gregory, more soberly now. "Imagine being part of the family though. The rest of them are like that too."

"Look," said Endicott, still holding the notebook out. "We know we have to work together with you and your soldiers. And we will. No one is better than anyone else. We are all just different."

"Unique little butterflies," sang Eoyan to a tune of his own, ignoring the scowls from Gregory and Endicott.

Vaugn Somne took the notebook from Endicott and straightened himself in the saddle. "Perhaps we can talk more about it tonight over dinner." He smiled wryly. "And we will just forget about those other two conversations."

▽

Sir Hemdale had other ideas.

"What separates you as knights from everyone else is your responsibility to your own conscience," he declared gruffly. He had a big mug of tea in his even bigger hand, and he held it high as he turned in front of the fireplace of the inn they had stopped at for the night. He had an audience again, though the soldiers seemed a little more at ease as they listened in on his lengthy lecture to Gregory and Endicott on the nature of chivalry and Knighthood.

"Sir Robert, if you could just grasp the simplicity of that principle *all* the time, you could be a Deladieyr. If you had been fully comfortable with your decision, you would not have just stove Sir Colborn's helmet in, you would have taken his head clean off."

Eirnyn Quinn looked askance at the big knight. "There's two things I don't get about that," she boldly proposed. Her voice carried well in the crowded room, a surprise to Endicott given her short stature. More surprising was her fearlessness in the face of the glowering mass of scars and two piercing eyes that was Sir Hemdale's gloomy face.

I can see why she's the sarge.

Hemdale did not have a fit, however. He just nodded at Eirnyn to proceed.

"First," she said, "I don't get how certainty equals 'head clean off,' and second, what about the law? We don't just decapitate whoever we want to. It has to be legal."

A few of the soldiers chuckled covertly. Others suppressed their amusement, or their fear, like a kettle holds steam when the water boils. No matter how hard they tried, a little bit got away from them.

Hemdale's eyes bulged for a second, but then he seemed to stop himself. He scanned the audience with a steely air. "Sounds funny, yes? I have a sense of humor. For example I can laugh when I lop off a head because I only do it when I am sure it is the right thing to do. Some sit in doubt when they pronounce ultimate justice, but a knight must *know*. He—or she—must be certain. With certainty there can be no regret."

Hemdale's declaration unsettled Endicott. It reminded him eerily of the Lonely Wizard.

"There is a strength that comes when you act in unity with yourself. When you are not conflicted, when you act within your own integrity, you are at your best. For one with the gift, there is even more strength. Sir Robert has it." He made a rocking motion with his hand. "Sometimes."

"But what about the law?" asked one of the braver soldiers. Endicott remembered being introduced to him. Corporal Ildrys, a stocky, dark-haired man probably in his late thirties. His hairy arms were crossed now, and his face was red.

"The law?" barked Hemdale. "It is the First Precept. It is what I have been saying to these two young men all night. A true knight is defined by his or her own ethics. Nothing more. Those ethics *are* the law. That is why they have an independent command. No rule made by others can stand between a knight and acting rightly." He glowered, turned, and tossed his tea into the fire. "But that goes over your head no doubt." With that he rose to his feet without another word and stamped out of the room.

It is possible that Hemdale was not stomping purposely, that he was just so big that it seemed that way to everyone else. In the moment of silence after his departure the pressure in the room seemed to change. It was like a storm passing. Some were simply relieved that Hemdale had left, some—like Rhysheart—seemed fascinated with him, and a few—like Ildrys— were angry.

This will not do.

Endicott shared a questioning look with Gregory. Eoyan winked at him, but Vern avoided his eyes. Elyze was watching him intently, brows raised as if questioning something.

And there is no more time.

Endicott stood up. "I cannot argue with Sir Gregory's uncle about how to be a knight, but I think the good lieutenant had suggested that we discuss ways of working *together*." He turned and tossed his tea into the fire.

Chapter Twenty-Two.

Dumping

"He was in the Ardgour Wilderness once. When he was first knighted. Eloise told me. Apparently all the newly Risen Deladieyr Knights used to do it." Gregory flanked Endicott, with Eoyan on the other side. They were due to arrive at the Castlereagh Line by mid to late afternoon, though they could not yet see it.

"That was what, fifty years ago?" said Eoyan glumly. "Sometimes I wonder if it would have been better if he had stayed there."

"He's not that bad, Eoyan. He just likes to be the center of attention," Endicott replied, trying to take an evenhanded position. He wondered if they would get hit by a late summer thunderstorm. The sky looked unsettled. *If the cloaked man shows up, Hemdale could be the difference.* Endicott could not imagine any force that could stop the old knight.

"I suppose no one can be. Though two nights in a row of alienating rants..." Eoyan chewed on this, "puts rather a strain on my sense of humor and natural equanimity, it does." He winked at Endicott. "You two did all right after he left. We are a still a long way from workable tactics, but at least you didn't make things worse."

Endicott was glad for even this faint praise, though he wondered what the innkeepers made of all the tea and beer that got thrown on the fireplace. Not one of the soldiers retired for the evening without throwing something on the fire in their best imitation Sir Hemdale swagger. Even Ildrys had joined in.

Endicott had suggested that he, Gregory, and Eoyan March should support the soldiers by performing some scouting in coordination with the lieutenant and sergeant. This way they could also observe Elyze and Vern's activities without becoming embroiled in them. The independent command would be an unobtrusive one.

"What else were we going to do about our undefined role," asked Gregory, turning to fiddle with a strap on one of his saddlebags. "It's a classic mistake. Knights-damned vague orders. I almost think they did it on purpose." He shook his head ruefully. "No wonder every subgroup in the expedition wants to roll us into their hierarchy. Of *course* the soldiers want things neatly under their authority. Of *course* Elyze and Vern want us to act as their lackeys. Of *course* Sir Hemdale want us to be knights."

"You *are* knights," laughed Eoyan, watching the heavy cumulonimbus clouds gathering above the hills. "You just aren't his fanatical variety. You're the little 'k' knights in the songs and poems." He turned, eyeing them both. "Listen to Uncle Eoyan; stay that way. We'll all live longer. Especially me." His brows furled in an exaggerated show of concern. "I think you are going to be all right, Gregory. Your head is on straight and your feet are on the ground. Well, your horse's are. But you, Robert, you lovely dreamer, are probably fucked."

Yes, I probably am. Thank you very much.

Endicott still felt the full weight of his heraldic dream and all the fears and more complicated feelings that went with it. It was heavier than even the most anvil-shaped of the dark clouds forming in the far air.

The small stone tower they had been expecting rose in the distance not long after. It was a little needle above the slowly resolving shadow that was the low wall of the Castlereagh Line. *The Tower and Line War.* The war Keith Euyn had fought in when he was young. Endicott could see how it got its name.

"I've been thinking about something," said Gregory almost in a whisper. "And I wanted to bring it up before we reached the Line."

"Uncle Eoyan likes women," declared Eoyan. "Mostly."

Gregory scowled but resisted the bait. He reached into his jacket and pulled out a letter. It was the one from Endicott's grandpa. "Your birthday is still a few days away, Robert, but perhaps you should read this now?"

Yes.

"No, Gregory," Endicott sighed. Tempting as the idea was, he had not needed to give it much thought. "Thank you, but, well, it's a present. And he doesn't write often, so it means something extra. Besides I can't know if I might be interfering with some specific intention he had, something important even." He closed his eyes. "I have to respect his wishes."

"Not very fun!" sang Eoyan, eyes still on the darkening horizon.

The tower rose out of a single-story, walled stone courtyard that contained a well, forge, horse pens, and storage sheds. The tower itself was only about forty feet across and, despite its appearance from the road, stood back from the Castlereagh Line further than its height.

"The commander would greet you herself, but she is seeing to the urine dispersal," said the seargent who greeted them with a totally straight face. He was in every way forgettably average, at least by way of first impressions.

Urine dispersal?

"Follow me and we will get you squared away for the night," he added. "I think we are going to get a little blow soon."

He was right. A furious though brief thunderstorm blew through not much later, but they enjoyed it under shelter. Gregory, Endicott, and Eoyan ended up bunking in a clean, plain room on the fifth floor of the tower with Vern and Elyze. Vern unpacked four copies of a gridded map and a set of writing quills.

"It's a mapping project," said Vern acidly. "Oh, didn't you know that? I would have mentioned it earlier except I was told you're too good to be spoken to."

"Careful, you're getting little boy tears all over your maps," Eoyan shot back, lip curling.

Elyze laughed softly. "I think we can all agree we were wrong-footed at the start." She tilted her head. "Hear that? The storm has passed. Come on, I'll show you what the expedition goals are." In a tone that Endicott thought might be either conciliatory or condescending, she added, "You too, Vern."

Elyze led them out of the tower, past a guarded gate to a set of stairs, then up the stairs to the top of the Castlereagh Line. The parapet was only slightly over fifteen feet high, though it was nearly as thick, with a crenellation on the side facing north into the Ardgour Wilderness. The stone was old, pitted, and in a few places showed signs of small-scale disaggregation.

Endicott was surprised at what he saw when he looked over the Line to the other side. He had expected a dark, forbidding landscape, full of the ruins and wreckage of its former masters: broken, rusted wagon wheels, collapsed houses, abandoned children's toys, perhaps even piles of human bones. Some of that might indeed have been out there somewhere, but all he could see in front of him were amber fields of wheat laid out neatly in well-marked squares.

"What on earth is this?" Gregory gasped.

"This," Elyze crooned, squeezing in between Endicott and Gregory, a hand insinuating itself onto each of their backs, "is how we are going to tame the Ardgour Wilderness. This is how we expand the duchy and the empire. This is how we—we dynamicists—will one day become lords. This is how we defeat Armadale." She shrugged. "In about fifteen or twenty years."

"You're planting crops," Eoyan said blandly. "That's your secret weapon?"

Elyze turned slowly and arched her back, thrusting her chest out proudly, perhaps even seductively, smiling at the younger men, who had to make an effort to look at her face. "Knowledge is power, gentlemen." She put one long, slender finger on the hilt of Gregory's sword. "You've been fighting with metal, while the real war is with the Book of Nature. I told you before; we are writing a new chapter here."

Endicott was a quick learner, but he was still missing crucial information. "How is making the grain bigger going to tame the Wilderness? The skolves are still out there."

"You don't know!" crowed Vern, taking one slow step back. "You really don't know!" He smiled at the young men, enjoying his secret for a moment. "The new grain is poisonous."

"To skolves," added Elyze, perhaps a little too quickly. "They don't come from around here. Maybe Gerveault or Keith Euyn know what hell the miserable creatures really crawled out from. It's not our field. Wherever it is, they don't have the same food as here. Skolves can barely tolerate anything that grows in this world. They'll bite your arm off, but they can't actually digest it." She laughed. "They cannot digest ungulates or chicken or hogs. Wheat, barley, oats, they can eat. Well, the old stuff. Our new wheat, they cannot. We are going to starve them out."

"You're going to push them out with ... new crops," said Endicott, goose bumps rising on his arms and shoulders.

"Eventually there will be no place for them here," added Gregory.

Eoyan's face was as white as ash. He stared slack jawed at Elyze. "Eight Knights, that is diabolical."

"It's *inevitable*. I'm glad you can see that," Elyze purred. "We are going to change the world." She smiled with a vast satisfaction and tilted her head back as if posing for a portrait. "I laughed every time I saw those idiots protesting about our grain. They were so right, just not in the way they thought. Some say knowledge is power. I say ignorance is the hell of fools. People who lack real knowledge of the world run and run around, so loud and furious, fighting and arguing like bees in a jar over things they know nothing about for causes that don't even matter. Without knowledge all errands are fools' errands, don't you think?" She reached forward and patted Endicott's cheek. "I always like teaching you boys. No need to thank me, but you're welcome. This is the seasoning that you've been sent here for."

She languidly pushed herself off the stone wall and sauntered down the steps and out of sight.

It's more than just about poison grain.

Endicott had come to appreciate how arrogant people could be, but he knew Elyze was right about the grain's importance. He considered his life since leaving home: the incredible expense and regulation of the grain exchange, its focus on the future cost of the product, how the price for the new grain increased so much in the near future, the fight at the registered seed office in Nyhmes, the protestors in Vercors, and finally the revelation of the vital role the grain had in the treaty with Novgoreyl. It suddenly all made sense to him.

The futures prices! Lighthouse's projected demand is buoying them!

It was about more than the grain. It was about arrogance and personal ambition of course, but also a vision of the future. It was a battle for untold future wealth through expansion of territory, all made possible by the grain. It was about more than the grain, but the grain was the commodity fueling the change.

And that grain is poisonous. To skolves.

"And here I thought *you* were full of yourself," Eoyan said to Vern.

"Well, she stole the harvest from me, so I won't bother trying to top her," Vyrnus said. "What would the point be? Honestly my part in all this has been ..." he sighed and held his index finger and thumb just slightly apart, "about *this* big." He turned to leave, but Gregory interrupted him.

"So what exactly are you trying to do here now?" asked Gregory. "What are you actually mapping?"

Vyrnus smiled tightly. Endicott wondered if he might even be embarrassed, perhaps unconsciously balancing his self-presentation with Elyze's.

"We are estimating the density of seasonal skolve feces in our new crops. An algorithm based on that tells us how many of them have been eating the grain." He hung his head and started walking away. "So, you see, we really *are* counting dog shit."

"I *told* you she was being condescending," muttered Gregory, looking sharply at Endicott, who found his own gaze drawn inexorably across the Line to the waving fields of wheat. The sun was going down on them, and the heads of the wheat glinted gold in the dimming light. "What do *you* think of her, Robert?" Gregory persisted.

"I think it's risky turning food into poison," Endicott answered, wondering again about Conor's story of a baby, remembering his grandpa's warning about invention going against intention in the elevator.

The bolder the innovation, the riskier the unintended consequences.

"Well, you don't know this yet," confided Eoyan, "because you're younger than me, but—"

"You're only what, two years older," protested Gregory.

"That's the two years that really count" Eoyan responded glibly. "Now if I can finish my train of thought? You don't know the arrogance people are capable of. Doesn't matter whether the person is a big success or not. In fact the most arrogant people I have met have either been right at the top or way on the outside. Some people are just full of themselves."

Endicott remembered Uncle Arrayn saying much the same thing when he had told him he was going to change the world. Endicott *still* intended to change the world. He still wanted to make it better, and he still hoped this could be accomplished without developing a case of megalomania. But changing the world was several notches of priority behind making sure Koria and Eloise were not murdered and that the cloaked man was stopped. In any case changing the world was best done, he had learned, by first understanding the world.

I need to know more. I feel like I'm still back in the elevator, on the leg going around and around.

Like the elevator leg, events proceeded at their own pace or at whatever pace was chosen by the person doing the pedaling. Endicott did not know who the pedaler was here, but the leg was definitely going around. His heraldic dream had given him a rather cryptic suggestion of trouble on the Line and a much more explicit picture of disaster back in Vercors. He had ignored the vaguer glimpse of danger in order, he hoped, to forestall the more certain one. He had attempted to take the initiative, to wrest control away from whoever was doing the pedaling. But he did not know enough to judge how well he had succeeded.

Have I done enough?

He considered Gregory's shield, which was on his young friend's arm now, and then the superior one he knew Eloise also kept close. He thought about the entropic swords that both Gregory and Eloise carried, and the rigorous practicing, both dynamic and martial, that he had done by himself, with Koria, with Eloise, with Lindseth, with Merrett, and with Gregory and Eoyan. He contemplated the temperature data he had shared with Koria in the hope it could help her fight the cloaked figure if it came to that. He remembered the knight he had killed and his lack of regret.

Am I ready?

"Think you youngsters are ready?" It was Corporal Ildrys with Rhysheart trailing after him. They had come up the stairs while Endicott was lost in thought. Ildrys scowled at them. "Ever been across the Line?"

"Never," confessed Endicott, "so as for being ready, probably not."

I need to make peace with my decisions and just get on with it as best I can.

"I am pretty sure we are going across, ready or not," Gregory added.

"It's our job," said Eoyan coolly.

"Not sure what kind of idiot that makes each one of you," replied Ildrys, crossing his arms. "But at least you're honest."

"I'm not sure you should talk that way to them," said Rhysheart diffidently.

Ildrys scowled at him. "Oh? The *mighty* friends of Robert Endicott going to toss me off the Line, are they?"

"Perhaps later," said Endicott, remembering his uncles. "But I think we would rather have your help. You have been there; we haven't. We have barely had time to *talk* about the Ardgour Wilderness. What should we expect? How should we act?"

"You can't learn everything in school," said Ildrys, spitting over the edge of the wall but nodding amiably enough. "I've been across, let's see, five times in all, but I don't know what's going to happen tomorrow. Hopefully a big bin of nothing. Hopefully you don't have to do nothing."

Gregory had been frowning at Ildrys, but now his hard expression softened a little as he asked, "What's this we hear about urine being dumped?"

"That's because of the skolves' noses," blurted Rhysheart. "They smell *everything*."

"That's right, blondie," said Ildrys, slapping a hand down hard on Rhysheart's shoulder. "Skolves can smell even better than dogs. Which is kind of important when it comes to keeping clear of them. But what's really gonna make your bread rise is their, what do you call it, terri… territory… territoriality," he finally pronounced triumphantly. "They cannot abide us in what they think of as theirs. And right now they think everything on that side of the wall is theirs. Which it kind of is, after all. If they smell us there, they'll try to swarm us. So we're gonna trick them."

"You're dumping urine somewhere up the Line from us so the skolves will go there instead." Endicott guessed.

"That's right." Ildrys beamed at him. "The entire contents of the septic tank here at this tower. Some down the Line and some up. They take our piss as a right awful offense and insult to their territory. Used to be, folks would piss over the wall to bait the skolves, but that … let's just say it didn't always turn out so good. Them skolves can throw a spear or a hammer pretty far. No one walks away from a ten-pound hammer in the chad. Now we use piss a mite more … intelligently. We attract the skolves *away* from where we're gonna be. Hopefully won't see a one of them."

"What if we do happen to see one of them?" Gregory asked.

"Run," said Rhysheart.

"Yup," concurred Ildrys, chuckling. "We run." He extended his arms and pushed himself away from the crenulation. "If there's only a few and they are far enough away, we run. Where there's one, there's always more and then more still. They keep coming." He nodded again. "But you run in good order and under our cover if you can. We are here to help even the *mightiest* of you. We'll slow them down some, and hopefully everyone gets out."

Endicott remembered the Lonely Wizard. That was how it had been in the story; the skolves had kept coming and coming. Until they learned to fear him.

Ildrys was still talking. "Yes, they are a little faster than us, a little bigger, and a fair bit stronger. If they come, it won't be like sparring. It will be fast and brutal and without mercy or hesitation. I'll leave you to think on that." He turned as if to leave, then turned back. "It'll be better for us working men if you don't wander off over there tomorrow. Don't string us out. We have to keep together."

Rhysheart smiled wanly at Endicott and Gregory before following Ildrys down the stairs.

"What does that tell you about that chain mail you've been debating over?" Endicott asked Gregory.

"Leave it behind," the taller man said, looking out over the Line. After a moment he turned back to his friends and reclined against the wall. The pose was similar, but at the same time nothing like Elyze's had been. "You've been unusually quiet," he observed, thrusting his chin at Eoyan. "You *are* a part of the military, aren't you?"

Eoyan looked at Gregory sharply. "Officer training. Special assignment." He smiled darkly. "Guarding stupes." Eoyan frowned and glanced down the stairs where Rhysheart and Ildrys had so recently passed. "I wonder who sent them? Lieutenant Lyrical or Sergeant Skunk?"

"We are a liability to them, aren't we?" Endicott asked.

"No. You're the mission. You two and the twin egomaniacs." Eoyan snorted. "I can't guess how this is going to work out with Elyze and Vern."

Gregory's lips curled. "I imagine they'll just ignore the good soldiers."

"Hmm. Everything the corporal said was congruent with what I've been told. I would strongly recommend following his advice. If you can." Eoyan turned and stared at the tower. "Do me and yourselves one other favor though, if you please. On your way out, and periodically throughout the day, glance back at the tower. Imagine how it looks and where it is. If you must run, best you know which way."

Chapter Twenty-Three.
The Other Side

"Is it the same?" Endicott watched Elyze closely.

"What?" Elyze had been watching the gate winch up. It rolled up quietly on a freshly oiled chain. Lieutenant Emyr Wynn, back from supervising the urine dispersal, was organizing the departure. Her eleven soldiers would augment Lieutenant Vaugn Somne's.

"The wheat," Endicott said evenly as the gate was locked in place. "Is the wheat you have been planting the same as the new Title Triticale that entered the market a few years back?"

The same Title Triticale that we tested on our farm animals.

"Yes. Why?" Elyze frowned at Endicott. "Is your mind on the task at hand, Robert? We are heading across the Line now. Are you ready in case we encounter skolves there?"

Endicott could see that Elyze was nervous. It was the first time he had seen her other than cool, collected, and consciously seductive. Her eyes darted about, and she kept swallowing. Her usual smugness was gone. Her words seemed rushed. Altogether she was very unlike the composed, arrogant woman that he had become accustomed to. But she was not the only one so evidently keyed up. Vern's lips were moving silently, perhaps in prayer. Gregory had his shield strapped to his left arm; his other hand constantly checked the hilt of his magnificent sword. Eoyan March had not referred to himself as Uncle Eoyan or made a joke or sexual innuendo in … minutes. He had armed himself with a heavy spear in addition to his now-usual sword, mail, breast and backplates, claiming he would rather negotiate with the skolves at more than arm's length if possible.

He is the best man with a spear at the military school.

Sir Hemdale looked the same as always, fierce, haughty, and ready for anything, but the rest of the soldiers looked as keyed-up as everyone else. They were certainly heavily armed. All wore mail, most carried spears as well as swords, and some had bows with extra heavy-headed arrows. The two groups of solders lined up carefully in front of the gate. There were no horses. Wynn nodded to Somne and gestured solemnly for the first column of soldiers to proceed through the Line.

"The skolves are not my biggest concern, Elyze." Endicott kept half an eye on the soldiers as they filed out. "You were probabilistically manipulating the grain when we first met you."

On the terrible night.

"For control, Robert. Just for control." Elyze looked irritated now. "The genetic form of the Title Triticale was finalized years ago by Konrad and Rendell. All I've been doing since then is ensuring absolute genetic purity in our seed crops. It's boring me to death, but it controls this experiment."

It was their turn to go. Endicott walked through the gate—actually twin gates set at opposite sides of the thick wall—and across the Line. He felt no different.

Did I expect to?

The air was the same. The ground felt the same. His leather armor was the same. He was the same. He turned and looked over his shoulder at Gregory. Lines of sweat ran down his tall friend's face. Gregory nodded back but said nothing. Eoyan's eyes passed over both of them, then focused further out. Endicott's hand encountered the first head of wheat. It had been partially eaten by something. He pulled on it and examined the kernels. They looked the same as the wheat he knew.

"That's why we need to map feces," said Elyze. "Birds, bears, ungulates all eat cereal crops too." Her voice was already losing its tightness. Somne's soldiers were now across the Line, guarding the rear, and Endicott guessed that since no skolves had leapt out of the tall stalks yet, Elyze was starting to feel safer.

Or perhaps she is just incapable of feeling anxious for any length of time.

On impulse Endicott heralded, looking ahead across the fields. The grain blurred, its unpredictable sway smudging its probabilistic appearance. The soldiers spread out like cards, left, right, and ahead. Elyze flickered, conferring with Vern one way, then the other. Controlled experiment or not, heraldry showed that she did not always map the area in the same way. The soldiers fast marched, flickering out into the undefined domains of the future. Endicott pushed further, seeing them disappear from sight deeper into the fields. He pushed further, past seeing anyone, enjoying the pastel yellow of merged and moving wheat. He pushed until the soldiers came back, their deck-of-cards uncertainty now exaggerated and discontinuous. They were single peacock feathers on different birds this time. Endicott smiled. No skolves.

He barely shivered as he emerged from the heraldry. His affinity and control were continuing to improve. He barely felt the need for tea this time and would easily walk off the drop in body temperature.

"What do you think you're doing, Robert? Were you heralding?" Elyze pulled on Endicott's vambrace to get his attention.

"Yes," Endicott replied calmly, pulling his arm gently but firmly from Elyze's grasp. "All the way to late afternoon. No skolves. Not a single probability."

"That far?" She looked startled. "Amazing. But do you realize that Skoll and Hati are still out here somewhere? Do you want to attract them to us?"

"Really?" Gregory asked. With Vern and Eoyan he crowded around Elyze and Endicott now. "I've never heard of that."

"Not in fifty years," said Vern thoughtfully, "and not from heraldry alone."

"But not a chance I want to take," rejoined Elyze. "Not even *he*," she pointed at Sir Hemdale, walking not far away, gazing intently out into the Wilderness, "could handle *them*."

Endicott looked Elyze in the eye. "I hear you, but I make no promises. I'll herald if I think I should."

Elyze snorted loudly. "At least *think* before you act." She looked pointedly at Endicott and Gregory and flipped open her map. Vern followed suit, but Gregory's hands were taken up with his shield and sword, and Endicott had already decided he preferred armed-and-ready to head-in-a-map.

"Perhaps tomorrow," Endicott said.

Elyze and Vern finished reviewing their plan for the day quickly enough, and each joined one of the columns of soldiers. Endicott had decided to follow Vyrnus and Sir Hemdale to start with, leaving Eoyan and Gregory with Elyze.

"You see," said Vern, holding up a dried, cylindrical piece of feces. "It looks exactly like dog shit."

From a very big dog.

Endicott walked with Vyrnus, watching how he located and jotted down the density of feces on his map grid. The first few pieces were interesting, but after that the exercise became increasingly mundane. It would have been completely mundane if not for the unknown elements of the Ardgour Wilderness. Heraldry aside, soldiers aside, Sir Hemdale aside, there remained the question of what could be out there. When all was said and done, it remained uncharted territory. Endicott looked back, straining to see the tower.

There are two of them!

Endicott could see the tower they had come from in the far distance to the south of him, the tower of the Castlereagh Line. But now another tower rose, faint and just resolvable, to the northwest.

What is that?

"This is where you find out who you really are, Sir Robert." It was Hemdale, towering, implacable, but speaking now in an almost intimate tone.

Endicott looked at the old knight, a little surprised but also more than a little curious.

"Out here beyond civilization and its rules." He looked down at Endicott as if examining him. "This is where you will find your authentic self. Only when no one is looking." He breathed in deeply, closing his eyes.

"I thought you were unaffected by the opinions of others," Endicott said.

"I am," his eyes opened. "It is you who are not."

Endicott decided that he might be able to get something more valuable from Hemdale than declarations of personal philosophy. "What is that structure over there?"

"An old castle," the big man said. "There are quite a few scattered around. Hundreds in fact. They are like the gravestones of a vanished people." He turned and gazed toward the tower.

Endicott jogged over to Vyrnus to check if the old castle was within the mapping grid. It was, though nowhere near the current day's area. He walked on. Time to check on the soldiers. They were fanned out in front, back, and both sides, forming a perimeter around Vyrnus. All had hands on weapons. Their eyes scanned the fields. Except for two of them. Seargent Eirnyn and Rhysheart were gazing earnestly at a pile of rocks slightly off the left of the column. Endicott approached them.

"What's the doings, gentlemen?"

Eirnyn's nostrils flared. "It's an old well. Smell that? Musty. There's moisture down there."

Endicott walked over to the pile and peered down into what looked like a crack at the top. All he could see were a few feet of tumbled rocks, dirt, leaves, and one stalk of wheat.

"Well, it's no skunk, but it doesn't smell too bad." Endicott winked at the sergeant as he said it. Her eyes glinted back at him.

"Better stay back, Sir Robert." Rhysheart held his hands out almost imploringly. "It could collapse, and then where would we be?"

"Right," Endicott said, touched by Rhysheart's concern. He smiled to himself and looked back towards the tower in the south, the one they were supposed to run to if the skolves came. It was at least a mile away now. He rejoined Vyrnus and got a closer measurement from the map. The tower was just over one and three-quarter miles away.

Much too far to run if skolves were right on us.

In the end the old well turned out to be the highlight of the day. Endicott started to sympathize with Elyze's desire to accelerate her replacement as poo-density mapper, though not with her arrogant attitude. Gregory seemed less bored with the proceedings. He was interested in the history of the place, if it had one, and the way the wheat had become self-sustaining despite its tough rachis. He even seemed to enjoy the minute details of the mapping exercise. Endicott guessed that his tall friend was enjoying this break from the grueling pace of most days at the New School.

At dinner back on the right side of the Line, Endicott found himself wondering again about Elyze. He did not trust her much, and he definitely did not like her smug arrogance or her seductive manners. He liked her apparent interest in him and Gregory even less. But he had an idea for something that he had not had a chance to try before this. Perhaps some questions could be answered whether Elyze wanted them answered or not. She caught him staring at her and returned a shimmering smile. "My dear Robert, you are staring at me," she said, hand at her breast in mock shock. "What will your little friend Koria say?"

"Right now, I am more interested in what you will say about something," Endicott said.

Gregory and Eoyan were both staring open mouthed at Endicott. Elyze pushed her smile to its limit. "Oh, just ask, Sir Robert," she cooed.

Ha.

"You swore to Gerveault that you'd had a Heraldic dream about this trip, and on that basis it was important that Sir Gregory and I come with you. So important that ... well, here we are." Endicott leaned forward. "What was it that you dreamed?"

Endicott achieved the first breakdown before Elyze could answer. He could monitor her body temperature, the blood flow to her face, even the contents of her exhalations. "That is not a very interesting question, Robert," she complained.

Liar. Her temperature and blood flow betrayed her.

"I really don't remember now," she continued.

Lying again.

"I had hoped you were going to ask something of a more ... personal nature," she stood up to leave.

Also... lying. I think.

Vern left not long after, and Endicott was able to describe what he had seen to Eoyan and Gregory. Rhysheart, Ildrys, and Eirnyn also listened in.

"That's quite a skill, Sir Robert," gushed Rhysheart.

"Useful in card sharping," added Eirnyn.

"You know," hedged Eoyan, "blood can flow to all sorts of places and it doesn't always mean you're lying." He rocked back on his heels and then rocked back forward, thrusting his hips forward just a little bit extra.

Eirnyn's head bobbed back, chin tucking in. "Eww." Gregory said nothing but only shook his head in disgust.

Eww indeed.

"Ever tested it?" asked Ildrys.

"No," said Endicott. "But I am pretty sure of what I saw."

Ildrys scowled. "You New School types. You don't live in the real world."

Rhysheart's eyes were big. "So let's test it. Ask us questions!"

Ildrys had a different idea. "Why don't you grab her little lackey, Vern, and *make* him tell you the truth. Hang him over the wall for a while."

This idea was given thoughtful consideration, with Eoyan particularly in favor or pretending to be. Endicott and Gregory had to argue in earnest that hanging Vern from the wall did not represent their values as Knights of Vercors, which made even grumpy Ildrys laugh.

Endicott resolved to try again, and the next day, he, Gregory, and Eoyan all escorted Elyze on her mapping assignment. Eirnyn saw this and maneuvered the guard duty so that her column went with them rather than staying with Vern. Endicott had briefly considered grabbing a map and helping directly, but he still remembered the few seconds of his latest heraldic dream and did not want to be distracted by the tedium of mapping.

The second trip across the Line was conducted as soberly and carefully as the first. The soldiers shared hand signals and nods with the same seriousness as before. There was a sincerity to it that struck Endicott. He could see Gregory take a deep, slow breath as he stepped under the first gate and sensed the goosebumps breaking out all over his taller friend. Even Elyze once more shed her confidence-alloyed armor for just a moment and clasped Endicott's shoulder. He was not absolutely certain she had been lying to him about her dream, or why she would want to lie, if liar she was, but Elyze was still human. She still feared the unknown.

Why are we most human when humbled?

Eoyan was dressed head to toe in chain mail, but this time elected to forego his breastplate. His eyes were alert, he carried his heavy spear again and kept his thoughts to himself. Emerging from the gate, Elyze put her hand up and waited for Endicott, Gregory, Eoyan, and her column of soldiers to form up. When they were all there, she pulled out her map.

"See this rectangular area?" she said, pointing to a location just northwest of the grid. "This is where we are going today. It has a small patch of the old triticale bordering the new. It's a control point we cannot miss."

Elyze had been over the plan twice already, but she seemed to feel that reinforcing her authority was worthwhile. Lieutenant Vaugn Somne and Seargent Eirnyn did not object. They nodded professionally and directed their soldiers. The two mapping parties quickly marched off in radically different directions. In a few moments the Castlereagh Line, the tower, and the group of soldiers that guarded Vern, including Sir Hemdale, were all gone.

Elyze's team assayed the skolve feces as they went, following a zigzag pattern. The sky was clear, and the late summer day warmed up quickly as morning passed. The buzzing of bees, chirping of birds, and the distant squeak of a marmot comforted Endicott with memories of home. Before going to the New School, he had been well accustomed to those sounds, ubiquitous reminders that nature was all around. He had missed that in the city. He breathed deeply, smelling the ripening wheat.

Maybe I understand now what Eirnyn means when she says she likes the smell of skunk. It reminds her of simple things, childhood things maybe.

It was an easy thing to think while *not* smelling skunk. Endicott felt a pang of melancholy thinking of his childhood, but the bitter part of the bittersweet moment did not last. He breathed in again and smiled. It was a beautiful a world.

"Daydreaming?"

It was Eoyan. He had come up close and spoke in a whisper, eyes still gazing outward.

"Just trying to enjoy the moment," admitted Endicott with a shrug.

"Ahh well, that's okay. Just try to keep your eyes open, okay?"

"Got it."

They walked on. Endicott turned his attention away from his memories. Eoyan was right. He needed to stay on top of things. Nothing stirred, but as the day matured, an arc of darkness teased the horizon. Endicott guessed they might see another set of thunderstorms later.

"I was thinking," said Eoyan ominously as he Endicott and Gregory drank sparingly from their canteens. "Maybe Elyze isn't lying at all."

Endicott said nothing. He did not want to encourage Eoyan to speculate.

"Isn't it possible she's just bored and wants some help, just like she said." Eoyan put the cap back on his canteen, looking at the far clouds.

"Possible," admitted Gregory. "She's always acting like she knows something we don't, though."

"Ahh," said Eoyan, smiling. "She *is* older than you two. She undoubtedly knows a lot of things you don't. On campus you gents are like two skolves in a glassmaker's shop. You might have intimidated her. Ever think that maybe she sees you fellows as the arrogant ones, and this is just how she's reacting?"

"No," said Gregory, frowning. Endicott was not fooled either.

Eoyan had a hand on the hilt of his sword, but there was a wry smile on his face. "Or maybe she just likes the stitch on your pants. Here you are, two young men in your prime."

"Shut it," said Gregory.

"Untried."

"We aren't entirely—" Gregory sputtered, but was interrupted.

"Eager."

Please stop. Endicott didn't bother saying it aloud. He knew Eoyan would never stop.

"Impulsive."

"Enthusiastic."

"There it is again," Endicott said pensively, cutting into Eoyan's unending innuendos. "The tower." It was coming into view to the north, a shadowy vertical line. It wavered in his vision in the moist heat of midday, but as they got nearer to it, Endicott realized it was quite close to their target area.

It turned out to be just by the northwest border of the grid section with the old wheat. It had broken down partially but was still perhaps sixty feet high. What remained leaned to the left and had an ominous fracture near it base. It might soon collapse completely. Piles of old rock lay around the base, either the remains of an old wall or, Endicott thought more likely, elements of the missing top section. A stand of trees grew further to the west.

Endicott checked the sun. It was starting to go down. They would turn around soon. With a chill he remembered his heraldic dream and the falling sun in it.

Is it so late? Not yet.

He signaled Eoyan and Gregory and led them at a slow run past a startled Sergeant Eirnyn and two other soldiers towards the tower. The old wheat parted easily. Most of its heads were missing. There was skolve feces everywhere. His heart beat faster.

Be calm.

They cleared the old wheat and entered the boulder field that surrounded the tower. A few small trees had sprouted among the tumbled rocks, but clear paths remained. Endicott bounded up to the old entrance to the castle. A bent and rusted iron gate hung half off its hinges. The sides failed to come together, leaving a rough gap in the middle. The gate did manage to mostly block an entrance that originally would have been about eight feet wide and high. He squeezed through to examine the rocky mess inside.

"Robert!" Gregory called. "What is it?"

"I think this is the tower from my dream," Endicott hissed, squeezing back out and returning through the boulder field again.

"You think?" said Eoyan, eyes darting about. "I thought you remembered those dreams vividly."

"I only saw it for a second," Endicott said, "and not from this position."

Sweat ran down Gregory's face. He regripped his shield. "So we aren't in the world of your dream?"

"Not exactly," whispered Endicott. "I think I should herald it."

"What about Skoll and Hati?" asked Eoyan, spear held ready.

Endicott shrugged. "That they can sense Heraldry? Sounded dubious to me." He opened himself to the empyreal sky.

The green of the trees blurred into a verdant pastel in the flickering, reverberating view of future probabilities. It shaded well against the amber pastel of the wheat. Both held true against the start-stop discontinuity of unpredictable humanity. The soldiers careened across time, space, and probability, moving about in a multitude of fantail paths. The sun alone did not vary. Endicott resisted the temptation to push deeper into its probabilistic nature. He saw it move towards the horizon, which is all he needed to reference against the far more urgent question. It happened sooner even than his fears had suggested. Skolves darted crazily out of the wheat and the trees, faster than he could have imagined, caroming into the soldiers before they could react. Blood flew, flickering, drenching the canvas of his heraldry. The stench of rotted meat clogged his nostrils.

"Knights alive," Endicott whispered. "Skolves! Coming from the trees. Lots of them."

"Stay here," said Eoyan, rushing through the boulder field towards the soldiers. Gregory, eyes huge, bounded after him with Endicott close behind.

"Skolves!" Eoyan roared, hands cupping around his mouth. He stood at the edge of the field. He shouted it again.

"How soon?" asked Gregory, hefting his shield and loosening his sword.

"Soon," Endicott replied.

"How certain?" Gregory asked again. Eoyan was still yelling at the soldiers, some of whom were staring at him, some walking towards Elyze Astarte.

"Certain."

Gregory looked back, straining to see the Line or their home tower. "If we run, we'll never make it back, will we?"

"No." Endicott was looking through the empyreal sky at the thermal characteristics of the ground, the boulders behind him, the trees, and the air. He rushed to make the necessary calculations. Given the tension and his uncertainty over time, Endicott was tempted to use a coarse level of support, but instinct told him his innovations needed to be decisive. Working under pressure, he kept the smaller sample size.

Will I have time?

"They have to come through here, Eoyan," Gregory said, his sword singing as he drew it. It joined his shield in reflecting the late rays of the bright orange sun.

"This way," Eoyan roared, taking a few steps closer to the soldiers and motioning urgently with one arm. "Run!"

Elyze started running, which both forced the soldiers to pick up their pace and gave them the license to do so. Eirnyn and her two soldiers reached Endicott and Gregory first, but the others were some distance back.

"Where are they?" Eirnyn yelled, more loudly than Endicott could have ever expected from the diminutive sergeant.

Gregory looked at Endicott, who was racing to finish his calculations. He spared a moment to glance quickly at the sun and answer his friend. "They will be here very soon. Momentarily. The tower may be defensible. I suggest you secure it."

"You come too," she said.

"I have to see." *I must be ready to act.*

A moment later, the long tally of transformational math was complete and he was ready.

Gregory gestured her towards the tower. "Go! There'll be no convincing him until he sees them." Eirnyn gestured with her head and the two soldiers followed her into the boulder field. Endicott assumed they had gone into the tower, but when he glanced back, he saw Eirnyn and one of the soldiers position themselves atop a couple of the larger boulders and ready their bows.

Elyze and the bulk of the soldiers, including Ildrys, were closer now. Vaugn Somne and one soldier lagged behind. They had been on the opposite side of Elyze when Eoyan had started shouting.

"Into the tower!" Eoyan roared, even though the soldiers were still outside the boulder field. "Don't stop and don't look back!"

There was more yelling between Eirnyn and Ildrys as Ildrys and his group got closer, but Endicott ignored it. He was fully immersed in the empyreal sky, considering which innovation to execute and which ones might kill soldiers, depending on where they were when the skolves came.

They did come. Fast.

Three skolves raced out of the wheat towards Somne and the soldier with him, so fast they looked as if they had been shot from a bow. They were a brown and gray blur against the gold of the field. The collision with Somne was sickening. The lieutenant was struck by something big, perhaps a hammer. He flew backwards. The sound reached them less than a second later like a flat, wet slap. The soldier who had been with him stepped forward with his spear and impaled the second skolve but was immediately hit over the head with a long metal bar by the third beast. He collapsed in a spray of gray and red.

Endicott noticed that both skolves had struck straight overhead, their motions solely in the vertical plane. He also noted that both strikes had been immediately lethal. Endicott's pounding heart slowed, his attention fixing and focused on the unfolding situation. The two skolves tore at Vaugn Somne and the other soldier for a moment. It appeared as if limbs were flying off the bodies.

They do bite. But they can't digest.

He looked at his vambrace but concluded that his arm would fly off just as easily as Somne's legs did if a skolve got its teeth on him.

Don't let them.

Five more skolves streamed through the wheat, joining the first two.

More always come.

AAAWOOO

They howled just as wolves would. It was just as loud. Just as haunting. As the skolves cried out to the sky, Elyze Astarte and the rest of the soldiers closed the distance to Endicott and began filtering past him under the direction of Eirnyn and Eoyan.

"We better go too, Robert," Gregory hissed.

The seven skolves stood together for a moment, then abruptly turned towards the boulder field. Over his shoulder Endicott could hear the soldiers bunched at the tower, struggling to get through the bent gate. He imagined getting caught there when the skolves arrived.

Two arrows flew overhead.

Will it be worth the risk?

Endicott made a quick decision. He had already made the longer, slower calculations. He held his hand up in the calculating signal. Gregory yelled it out. The skolves were charging as fast as a racehorse now. Faster. Endicott held up the innovating signal. Gregory screamed it, standing just to Endicott's side.

WHUMP.

Six of the skolves were within the area of the innovation. They burst into flames. It took a second before their eerie screams rang out, and then they careened about, two of them colliding and biting in a rolling mess of fur and fire, collapsing seconds later. The grass burned in a circle around them. Beyond that a wide ring of frost formed. The boulder that Eirnyn stood upon cracked, and he heard her curse as she fell off it. Other boulders also frosted over, their thermal energy totally absorbed into Endicott's manipulation. A wave of freezing air washed over him, followed immediately by a second wave, now searingly hot.

Shivering from thermal losses, Endicott drew his sword. His blade had barely cleared its scabbard before the seventh skolve shot through the roiling air towards him, leaving black and gray contrails in its wake. Its fur smoked.

My timing must precede its timing.

He waited for the precise moment, ready to lunge and thrust. Eoyan stepped forward to intercept the rapidly closing beast, but it dodged his spear thrust, sidestepped him, and raised its heavy-headed hammer high over its head. In the back of his mind Endicott noted that the skolve was taller than most men and women, about seven feet in height, long and stringy. It wore no clothes but was covered in coarse gray fur. Long front incisors and flat back molars gleamed darkly in its gaping maw, which was similar to a wolf's but far larger. Gregory stepped in from the side with his shield raised, and Endicott had to abort his lunge. The hammer came whistling down, just as it had on Vaugn Somne.

BRRRRAAAAA

The hammer stroke rebounded off Gregory's amorphous shield, the deflected blow smashing the skolve's snout. Bright red blood and long brown teeth flew in all directions. The skolve stumbled and folded, impaled through the back of its head by Eoyan's spear.

"More will come," Eirnyn shouted from behind. "Let's go!"

"Hell yeah, let's!" Eoyan yelled. Gregory and Endicott, with Eoyan guarding their rear, raced along the winding route through the boulder field towards the tower and its mangled gate. Eirnyn was still squeezing through the gate as they arrived, but Endicott heard rapid, lunging steps close behind him. He turned to see another skolve charging. It held a five-tined rusty pitchfork in its hands and tried to flow around Eoyan's spear exactly as the last one had, but this time Eoyan anticipated the move and shifted with it, striking the beast in the abdomen. His spear only penetrated shallowly, and instead of shrinking back from the sharp pointed edge, the skolve pushed forward and thrust its pitchfork rapidly at Eoyan's face. He leaned backwards, and it fell just short of his face. At once Gregory swung his ringing sword down on the creature's head, cutting its skull in half just above the ears. As it collapsed Endicott guessed what had happened.

Eoyan's spear caught on the skolve's heavy, oversized hip bone.

They squeezed through the gate, Eoyan coming in last, watching with big eyes over his shoulder for another skolve. An arrow flashed overhead, though Endicott could not see whether it hit anything other than dirt or rock. He looked around quickly, assessing the space. The room they were in was circular and perhaps thirty feet across, and the floor was uneven, littered with jumbled rocks of every size from a pebble to a half ton. A depression on the far side of the room may once have been a staircase going down, but it was now choked with rocks. A few feet to the side was a hole in the ceiling a little over two feet wide. A few rocks leaned up against the wall, making it possible to climb into the hole. There were no windows, but there was a narrow, chest-high gap in the wall at one point.

"I think they will eventually tear this gate out." Eirnyn's voice was a little lower now, though it still rang off the stone walls.

"Then what?" asked a female soldier Endicott had hardly spoken with. She was tall, almost as tall as he. Her name, he recalled, was Ida Yseult.

Then we die. If enough of them come at us in this much space.

There was no denying the strength and speed of the skolves, especially in the open.

Eirnyn shared a look with Eoyan. She gestured at the eight feet of empty space immediately behind the gate. "We have to build a barrier there."

"Why don't we just climb up?" asked Elyze, pointing at the hole.

Eoyan shook his head. "No. Not yet."

Eirnyn clapped her hands together loudly. "Rhysheart! Keep a spear ready at the open side of the gate. The rest of you start piling rocks on either side. They're coming, sure as the sun is setting. Let's set to work."

Chapter Twenty-Four
The Wrong Side of Sunset

GREGORY JOINED RHYSHEART BY THE GATE AND RAISED HIS SHIELD TO PROTECT THEM both, while Endicott assisted with the construction of the barrier. They had ten highly motivated, if badly frightened, soldiers and an abundance of sizeable fallen stones, so progress was quick, though their haste produced more of a mound than a wall, from which many of the stones rolled down and hit the rusty iron gate. The work was carried out in a kind of quiet desperation. No one could know if or when more skolves would come, and the uncertainly intensified everyone's anxiety. Endicott sensed that the silence was a reaction, the groping for a false sense of security even though they all knew they had very little control of what would come next. Behind the growing mound of stones Gregory and Rhysheart crouched, only their heads showing over Gregory's shield, eyes straining against the red glow of sunset.

AAAWOOO

The howl of the skolves pierced the artificial quiet within the tower. Everyone froze.

"Can you see anything, Rhysheart?" Eirnyn stepped forward and crouched over the two sentinels, peering past them.

"A fat lot of nothing," he replied. Gregory also shook his head. With a grunt he shifted his feet.

Eirnyn patted Rhysheart's shoulder. "Say something as soon as you see them. They will come quick," she instructed him quietly. Then she shouted to the others, "Keep piling, boys!" and took one long look around the circular room before turning away from her soldiers to consult privately with Eoyan.

"You should climb up to the second floor with me, Robert." Elyze stood out of the way of the laboring soldiers. "Their job is to protect *us*, not the other way around."

Ildrys hobbled by, both arms around a roughened cuboid block of stone that looked like it weighed a hundred pounds. "Heard you burned up six of them. Can you do that again?"

"No, I am not going up there, Elyze." He shifted his gaze to Ildrys. "Yes, I burned six skolves, and yes, I may be able to do it again if they just cooperate by bunching up where I can see them. But I can't do it too many times, so it would be best to spend the effort wisely."

He returned his gaze to Elyze. "If you did once herald something about my being here that is relevant to tonight, I would like to hear it now." Moving the boulders was helping to return his body temperature to normal, and because he had enjoyed the luxury of so much time to calculate his innovation, Endicott had not been badly affected. He could not count on the rest of the fight to provide the same luxury. His dynamic efficiency was likely to suffer.

Elyze's face was caked with dirt from somewhere. It wasn't from carrying rocks. She shook her head. "My dream was vague."

Really?

Endicott sighed and changed tack. "Can you help me thermodynamically with the skolves?"

"Not and live," she said in a smaller voice than he was used to hearing. "I am *specialized*, remember. All I've done for more than a decade has been to modify wheat."

Ildrys snorted. "That's not going to do nothing here for us." He already had another large rock in hand. With a loud groan he dropped it on the growing pile. "You New School kids. Get in the moment. You," he pointed at Endicott. "If you can burn more of 'em up, get working on that. You" he pointed at Elyze, "if you can't offer nothing else useful, how about carrying some rocks at least?"

"Look out!" Gregory roared.

BRRRRAAAAA

A thrown spear shattered on Gregory's shield like an explosive. Most of the pieces flew back and scattered against the bent bars of the gate, but some fragments burst upwards towards the ceiling of the tower and fell among the soldiers. A small piece of rusty iron landed in Endicott's hair. He shook it free.

"It works out better when you are the one holding the shield," Gregory said wryly, eyes flickering quickly to Endicott.

It also helps to see it coming.

"Are they coming?" Eirnyn asked, once more huddling over Gregory and Rhysheart. Eoyan moved up beside them, eyes squinting through the failing light. A faint flickering in the distance suggested a storm, but they heard no thunder.

Endicott joined them, opening himself to the empyreal sky, searching for the skolves. He knew from working with the dice that he did not have to see a die to affect it, but he had thoroughly understood the positions and properties of the dice in those experiments. He could not hope to deal efficiently with the skolves if he could not even locate them.

There.

A skolve crouched at the base of a small bush, perhaps a hundred feet from the gate.

It's just lurking there. Not moving. Watching. Waiting. For what?

For a moment he wondered again what his true role in the agricultural mission was supposed to have been. Had such a moment been foreseen by someone somewhere? Then he pushed away the speculation and refocused. He could not waste time second-guessing the decision to join the mission. The decision had been made, and what was past could not be changed. The only question was what to do now. The lives of his comrades, and his own life, depended on *that* decision.

How is this fight likely to proceed? How many skolves will come? What will their tactics be? How intelligent are they?

He had seen what a skolve could do out in the open. This was why he had directed everyone into the tower. Now that they were here, he was less sure they should stay entirely defensive. They had chosen a strong position and made it stronger, so patience was a reasonable strategy. But allowing an enemy so lethal to prepare without hindrance did not seem wise.

That skolve is still there.

There were quite a number of them out there now, mostly moving around, visible one moment in the empyreal sky and gone the next, but the first skolve just stayed put, crouching there, watching and waiting.

Be first.

Endicott made a calculation using the earth directly under the prone skolve, but this time chose to ignite the skolve itself rather than the air around it. He had never practiced a manipulation of this type with Gregory and Eoyan. They had never thought they would have an unmoving opponent. But as a process, he realized, it was something like the direct manipulation of a reservoir of water, which they had practiced often, though under controlled conditions.

"Calculating," he announced, taking his time to make the most of the opportunity. "Innovating." He unleashed his manipulation.

WHUMP.

The skolve ignited like a torch. It immolated with a bright, blue flame, burning so hot that it could not even scream. It died before it could roll, before it could move at all. The blue flame illuminated several other skolves, which scattered sideways into the boulders. The innovation had taken place so far away that the error wave did not reach them at the tower. Endicott's body shook, though, as it fought the thermodynamic losses.

"Th-that w-worked," he managed to say, shakily stepping back. He had chosen to make the prone skolve much hotter than the other ones; almost an order of magnitude hotter.

Now we'll see if it's true that skolves cannot be scared off.

"Eight Knights!" Rhysheart exclaimed, still crouching beside Gregory, spear at the ready. "There's nothing left of him but char!"

Eoyan was looking off to the side of the now smoldering carcass, watchful for other skolves, but he was smiling. "Even better than we practiced."

"Are you all right?" Gregory said, taking his eyes off the gate momentarily and adjusting his cramped feet again.

Endicott smiled wanly as he staggered back. Ildrys slapped him on the back. Cheers rang out from the tower into the dusk. Someone hugged him and started rubbing their hands on him. It was Elyze. He frowned at her, but she only smiled back. "There's no hot pool, here, Robert, so don't get too excited."

"I-I'm glad you d-decided to stay a-and help," Endicott stammered, still cold. "Why d-don't you go h-help w-with t-the lookout."

"Now I know why you decided to become a wizard, Sir Robert," declared Eoyan, coming back to look at him. He lowered his voice. "How many more times can you do that?"

"Zero t-times for a w-while," Endicott muttered.

Eoyan nodded and looked at Elyze. "Keep working him over." He did not use his pervert smile this time.

"I-I think I'll p-pile some m-more rocks," said Endicott breaking away from Elyze. He had too much youthful vigor not to enjoy being touched all over his body by a woman, even if it was meant platonically and just enough maturity to find another way of warming up.

"Let's keep a steady eye out," said Eirnyn to her soldiers. Eoyan was whispering something in her ear. Only half of the soldiers were still piling rocks. The others stood ready now with bow, spear, or sword behind the pile.

"None of them are sitting still out there now," whispered Gregory. Light from the still-distant storm flickered over his face.

AAAWOOO

Elyze rushed to join Gregory and the others. She stood on tiptoes behind him and peered over the rim of his shield. "They're coming!"

Rhysheart squinted. "I don't see them."

"You will in a second!" Elyze yelled, stepping back involuntarily.

She's heralding!

Endicott dropped the rock that was in his hands and drew his sword, readying himself.

Sp-aa-aak!

A spear came out of nowhere, rattled off one of the bent bars of the gate, and juddered through the air into the temple of one of the soldiers. Endicott could not remember the man's name. Despite having lost some of its force on the gate, the point still hit the man hard enough to throw him head over heels onto the rocky floor.

An instant later a wave of skolves smashed against the gate and pressing into it in a hairy, pulsating crush. One wriggled into the gap and lashed out with a sword towards Rhysheart. Gregory blocked the wild thrust with his shield, which rang out like a bell. Then he turned the skolve's sword to the side and, when he had achieved a good angle on it, raised his own sword and cut through the skolve's arm, just managing to avoid hitting Rhysheart and Eirnyn. The creature let out a terrible howl as it wriggled spastically and leapt back, colliding with the mass of skolves behind it. Gregory crouched back into covering position.

With a sudden, sharp metallic sound, the gate on the right flew backwards, hurled completely off its hinges. Another skolve rushed through the gap, snarling into the now open space, but Eoyan put a spear neatly through its left eye. Without hesitating, yet another skolve leapt over its fallen companion, only to receive Eoyan's spear, still dripping eye jelly, deep in its the snout.

"We need more light here!" Eoyan roared. It was almost dark now. Soon only the burning, yellow eyes of the skolves would be visible. Endicott had still not fully recovered from his last innovation, but he focused on an area about fifteen or twenty feet outside the gate, which included a tree.

"Calculating," Endicott said. "When I c-call it, cover your eyes." He checked his work. The ground temperature had barely changed since they had first seen the skolves; there was sufficient remaining energy to borrow. "Innovating."

WHUMP.

The tree lit up and with it three of the skolves at the rear of the pack pushing at the gate. They screamed horrifically, like tortured puppies, thrashed back into the flaming tree, and plunged out of sight into the surrounding darkness. Endicott imagined that they might yet survive, though not prettily. A wash of reverberating cold and heat shot into the tower.

Eirnyn was firing arrows into the backlit skolves while the tree still blazed, standing high on the makeshift stone wall. Three other soldiers joined her. A spear flew out of the silhouetted mass of skolves, deflected off the upper left corner of Gregory's shield, and just brushed the top of Ildrys's head. He yelled and went down, clutching his scalp. Endicott could not see how badly hurt Ildrys was. Too much was happening. With trembling hands he tried to find the right moment to use his sword without hitting the soldiers around him. Two spears shot past him into the skolves, followed instantly by more howling. Yells, groans, and desperate gasping for breath filled Endicott's ears from all sides.

Then, abruptly, unaccountably, silence. One second a snarling, howling, bloody scrum, the next only a gentle crackling from the remains of the tree as it smoldered. Lightning flickered again in the distance, and Endicott thought he could make out a distant, time-delayed rumble. His body shook, and he paced about, trying to generate at least a bit of the warmth he needed.

The intermission was short-lived. Skolves came again perhaps two minutes later, snarling, grunting, slobbering, and tearing at the one remaining piece of gate. Elyze was able to give them the same warning as before, which may have been the only thing that kept the soldiers from being overwhelmed in the opening seconds.

BRRRRAAAAA

A huge rock showered off Gregory's shield, fragments flying off it at every angle. The skolves rushed in behind the boulder, terrifyingly vital, horribly quick. The warning had helped, but the skolves came on hard. Without the narrow opening and the piled rocks, they would have been unstoppable. Even with the rock wall, they were on the verge of overwhelming the defenders.

"Heydron," Endicott muttered as he swung his sword at a skolve. It hit the axe the creature held in its elongate six fingered hands or paws or claws—Endicott could not decide how to think of them— and cut three quarters of the way through the haft. The axe head flew off on the skolve's next ferocious backswing, hitting another one of the creatures and making it howl. The first skolve gaped for an instant at its broken axe and, before the creature could move again, a spear soared through Endicott's peripheral vision and plunged into its ear. The skolve fell back out of the fray, either dead or gravely injured. Endicott could not tell and did not care.

Arrows flew past Endicott's ears.

"Look out!" It was Rhysheart's voice.

BRRRRAAAAA

Endicott heard Gregory's shield ringing but could not see what was happening in the chaos.

BRRRRAAAAA

BRRRRAAAAA

BRRRRAAAAA

Splinters of iron, pebbles, and chips of rock exploded off the shield in a staccato clangor. Gregory leapt up, angling his shield with both hands into the onslaught, while Eirnyn lunged at an oncoming skolve.

Endicott realized that the skolves' tough hide made them very hard to mortally injure unless they were hit with a weapon as sharp as Gregory's sword. His own sword was markedly sharper than most but not comparable to Gregory's, and in any case he was not as strong. He managed to deliver a glancing blow across a red-furred head, but this did not stop the creature and barely drew blood. Still, the blow stunned it just long enough for Ildrys to reach over Endicott's shoulder and put his spear into the intersection of the skolve's jaw and neck. The creature bucked and thrashed sideways and was lost in the fray. Not dead perhaps but at least out of commission for the time being. Another skolve lunged up the stone mound, snaked past Endicott's guard, and clamped its teeth around his left vambrace. He struggled to gain enough leverage to swing his sword with his other hand.

Can't let it pull me out.

Endicott resorted to a memorized calculation. He innovated a cup-sized portion of the skolve in the middle of its chest, borrowing energy from another portion of the creature's abdomen. It was a fast, desperate move. As its chest heated, the skolve spasmed, released Endicott's vambrace, and vomited a slushy, pink, foul-smelling fluid all over the young man's face. At the same time the error waves rolled over him: waves of intense cold and heat, one after the other. The skolve continued to shake, and Endicott stabbed it in the left shoulder with his sword, which pushed it back into the chaos of its peers.

The second attack ended as quickly and with as little warning as the one before. One second Endicott was thrusting the dying animal away, the next all the skolves were gone. The other half of the gate was also missing, having been ripped out at some point in the poorly illuminated scrum. No one moved for a moment, unsure if another attack was coming, praying it was not.

Endicott set his bloody sword down and with shaking hands tried to wipe the pink slush out of his eyes, nose, and mouth.

"Take a drink of water, Robert." It was Gregory. He had handed his shield over to someone else for a moment, who had accepted it like a gift from the angels. Gregory's face was drenched in sweat and a trickle of blood dripped slowly out of his hairline. Otherwise he looked well enough. Someone slapped an apple into Endicott's hand, and he took a crunching bite out of it. He was so hungry the little apple only made him hungrier.

"Thank y-you," he said to his unknown benefactor. Long arms wrapped around him. Not Elyze's.

"Come to Uncle Eoyan, Robert. Fuck, you're cold! Go away!" Eoyan pushed Endicott away, then hugged him again. "Uncle Eoyan didn't mean it." He squeezed him one more time and finally let him go. "Let's have someone go on up the hole and find us some wood. Robert here needs a fire, or he won't be able to fry us any more skolves next time they come."

"It would help us see too," said Eirnyn. "The tree is almost burned out."

Ida Yseult's hand had been mangled somehow, but that did not stop her and another soldier from scrambling up through the hole and tossing down whatever bits of wood they could find, mostly rotted planks and parts of old beams. The pile grew to an impressive size fairly quickly despite the fact that by now it was almost pitch black on the upper floors. They arranged the wood in the depression under the hole so the draft would take the smoke up and away instead of into their faces. There was no going up there again anyway. With no other way out it was a trap. When the wood was piled high enough, Gregory rubbed his hands together and started the fire with a slightly nervous innovation. "Good thing we practiced," he muttered, shaking slightly.

"Good thing you brought that shiny new shield," said Ildrys.

Gregory gestured at the wound on Ildrys's scalp, now being hastily sewn shut by another soldier. "You still got hit."

"Ha!" he said, clapping Gregory hard on the shoulder. "Better a flesh wound than a spear through the gizzard." No one mentioned the dead soldier who had been stowed out of sight under some debris at the back of the circular room.

"Sir Robert made that shield," gushed Rhysheart, stretching his legs by the fire. Elyze had volunteered to watch the front gate with the new group of soldiers. Thunder rumbled faintly, heavily attenuated by distance.

Endicott smiled, still shaking. "G-Gregory and I-I both made it. F-for l-love."

"Hey," said Ildrys, hands raised and scowling. "I wasn't asking, so you don't got to say nothing."

Elyze burst out laughing from her post all of ten feet away. "For Sir Gregory's fiancé, corporal."

Endicott couldn't help smiling too. "Thanks for heralding, Elyze." He did not know when or why Elyze had decided to get directly involved, but he was relieved that she had. Her heraldry of the skolves' rushes had made an enormous difference to the outcome.

"Make me one of those and I might marry you myself," yelled Ildrys, guffawing. It was strange how either blood or the threat of imminent death made such a positive change in his taciturn disposition.

"Me too," added Eoyan, "But let's get serious now and talk about what's going to happen later tonight. And don't get excited, I don't mean sexually. If we get out of this alive, though, all the grain is in the bin, so to speak, but let's not get all distracted or hopeful over any orgiastic celebration just yet."

"I've been thinking about that," said Eirnyn. "I have to now." She paused just for a moment, not mentioning Vaugn Somne but obviously thinking about him, dead and torn to pieces in the field beyond the tower. "There aren't many options. We only have water and food for tonight and maybe the morning, so we can't hold out here very long. The Line is over three miles away, but the route is dead flat. They've probably seen Sir Robert's fires from the tower, but they can't get to us tonight. Too risky in the dark. They'll probably also need reinforcements from down the Line. That will already be in process. But I can't see them being ready to come to the rescue before noon tomorrow at the earliest, if they're being careful. Which they will be."

"Hemdale might come sooner," interjected Eoyan, "but alone, not even he could get us out by himself."

Ildrys shifted. "Knights know there ain't nothing no one could tell him one way or the other."

"That's what he keeps saying," agreed Eirnyn. "So if Sir Hemdale comes earlier, great, but we are still stuck here until maybe late in the afternoon. Or later. The question is, can we last that long? Maybe. The gates are gone now. That's against us. But we have Sir Gregory's magic sword and shield and ten of the best soldiers in the duchy. That's pretty good, don't you say?"

The soldiers cheered. A few called out, "Redoubt Empyrean!"

"Damn right," replied Eirnyn, nodding energetically. "Now let's pile those rocks a little higher. Let's make it as hard as possible for them to beat us just through superior numbers. Keep one side open, though, in case help doesn't come and we have to make a break for it." She turned to Endicott. "You got eleven skolves that I counted, Sir Robert."

"He's the Lonely Wizard hisself!" exclaimed Ida Yseult to some chuckling and a few more cheers. Her hand was wrapped up in a thick strip from someone's shirt, but blood had soaked completely through the makeshift bandage.

Eirnyn waited until the laughter died down. "Can you do more?"

Endicott was still shaking despite the fire. "Y-yes, if I can get w-warmed up. But I h-have to hit them away from our p-position or some of us c-could be hurt or killed."

Ildrys pressed another apple into his hand. "Have a rest."

"We should expect the skolves to probe us again," Eoyan suggested.

"Agreed," said Eirnyn. "If we can get warning of it, Elyze, that could make the difference."

Endicott ate his apple and, still shivering, hunched closer to the fire with his back resting against one of the larger rocks. He closed his eyes. Lightning flashed, close by now, bright against his eyelids, but he did not hear the thunder...

It is dark except for the little pools of light from the streetlamps. Koria, Eloise, Heylor, Merrett, and Lindseth manifest out of the darkness, marching purposefully down the cobblestone street towards a set of gates: the arched gates of the Bifrost. Eloise, chest thrust proudly forward, presents her medallion, and the gate guards flit about, poorly lit shadows. The gate opens, and the entourage flows past.

They pass through the locked door and work their way through the vast building to a room with a long table. Koria is looking at something. She points at it, and Eloise walks to the wall and unhesitatingly pulls down a painting. Heylor punches the air in some silent victory. Koria talks excitedly, and they turn to leave with the painting tucked under Eloise's arm.

Two men approach the gate. One of them casually displays a medallion, and the shadowy guard signals for the gate to be opened. The man with the medallion pulls out a concealed dagger and stabs the guard. Dark streaks dart across the night, felling two other guards. A double line of men flows out across the street towards the gate. Most of them are armored in heavy plate. A few others wear dark civilian clothes. They join the first two men. At the end of the column walks a huge, cloaked figure with a spear in one hand.

No.

Koria, Eloise, and the others emerge from the Bifrost. Jeyn Lindseth points at the double column of men approaching them at a trot. The cloaked figure raises its spear. There is a flash, and an incandescent halo forms around Koria, Eloise, and their friends. But they do not burn. A ring of fire forms around them, engulfing one of the approaching men and immolating him, but Koria's group is unharmed. Koria has her hand raised. Her hair moves as if a wind has blown across it. Jeyn Lindseth draws both his longswords and launches himself past the burning man towards the others.

Merrett springs for the closing door to the Bifrost and catches it. He pulls it wide open, shouting. Koria and Eloise make it through, but Heylor trips. Merrett slams the door shut and draws his sword. With his other hand he pulls Heylor to his feet and shouts something at him, then pushes him away. Heylor stumbles off, looking over his shoulder and moving along the building past the loading docks towards the river. Merrett leaps into the fight, breaking into the circle of men surrounding his friend. He hacks down a man aiming a loaded crossbow at Lindseth. Another soldier swings his sword viciously at Merrett.

No.

The cloaked figure walks around the perimeter of the sword fight, leading half the remaining men towards the door of the Bifrost. He produces a key and they enter the building.

No.

One of the armored men does not enter. He follows Heylor.

No.

Soldiers stream through the Bifrost. Some go with the cloaked figure, trailing after Koria and Eloise.

No.

Heylor stands with his back to the river. A soldier approaches him slowly, sword drawn, shouting something. Heylor closes his eyes and moves his lips soundlessly. Nothing happens. Heylor's eyes open and he turns, takes three steps, and leaps off a boulder into the river. He is swept downstream, thrashing, panicked, and his hand catches on a bent piece of metal from a sewer culvert. He clutches it, head half under the water.

No.

A bloody hand lies, absent its arm, on the dark cement of the forge room. A ringing sound reverberates in Endicott's ear, the first sound he has heard. Someone breathes loudly. It is almost a honking sound, and it seems strangely familiar to Endicott. Koria backs into view, one of her shoes broken and half hanging off her foot. The enormous cloaked figure steps forward, and Eloise raises her shining sword with one hand. Her other arm hangs limp as blood runs down it and trickles from the end of her index finger.

No! Koria! Eloise! NO!

Chapter Twenty-Five.
Be Slow, Be Fast, Be.

"Robert?" It was Gregory's voice, but faint and far away. Endicott could barely hear it.

"Robert!" Gregory's muffled voice again. A great weight seemed to press Endicott down. He could barely breath against the pressure of it.

"Robert? Are you okay? Are you yourself?"

Endicott remembered the dream in a flash, the memory like a hot knife into his soul.

Koria! Eloise! NO!

No! No! No!

"Robert. You have to calm down."

It was his friend. It was Gregory. But not just Gregory. A mass of other people was holding him down.

"I can hear you, Gregory. I'm okay. Please get off me."

Koria! Be safe, be safe, be safe.

Slowly the weight lifted. Men and women unpiled from on top of him, but they kept watching him. They looked terrified, and he realized they were soldiers, the soldiers he was trapped with. In the tower. He was shaking uncontrollably, though not from cold. From adrenaline. The memory seared him, but he struggled for control. "What happened?"

Endicott could see that some time had passed. The lightning flashes were very close now and the wind was gusting. The tree he lit on fire was guttering in a wild rain that had started at some point during the lost time.

"You had another heraldic dream, Robert." Gregory crouched in front of him, brows deeply furrowed. "You screamed and tried to run out of the tower. We had to hold you down."

Elyze crouched by Eirnyn behind Gregory's shield, but she looked over at him with wide eyes. "It was harrowing. I thought someone had died."

"People have died. They are dying. They *will* die!" Endicott yelled the last part. Eoyan, squatting beside Gregory, put a hand on his shoulder.

"You're scaring everyone, Robert," Eoyan said, voice low. "You could have hurt someone." He shook his head ruefully. "Believe me—it's a miracle you didn't. Six of us had to pile on top of you."

"For the love of Leyla, go easy, schoolboy," Ildrys grunted from not far away. "We have to save our energy for the skolves now."

Endicott held his hands up, palms out.

I understand.

His heart still pounded, his body still overflowed with energy, and the dream continued to play out over and over again in his mind, but he held himself in a fragile equilibrium. "Let me tell you what I dreamed." As simply and unemotionally as he could, Endicott related his heraldic dream. He watched his comrades as he spoke. Gregory and Eoyan listened silently, breathing rapidly. The dream was as much about their friends and loves as his. The soldiers were also clearly fascinated. It was unlikely any of them had ever heard a direct account of a heraldic dream or seen what it did to the dreamer.

"I can guess what you want to ask." Endicott gazed at the perplexed faces that surrounded him, seeing the questions there.

"Do I know when it is going to happen? Am I sure that what I saw *will* happen?" Endicott looked out into the night. His face was suddenly lit up by a flash of lightning, and he waited for the thunder to pass before continuing. "The answers are: I don't know, and I don't know, but my instinct is that this dream has come because of its imminence. I must leave tonight. Immediately."

"Damn it, Robert, you'll die if you go out there!" Elyze shouted. "Then where will we be? You can't be replaced!"

Eoyan scowled "Just ignore her, Robert." He scratched his head and added almost in a whisper. "But she has a point."

Endicott stood up. Eoyan and Gregory followed suit. "I'm going. Now."

Gregory squinted at him, and his lips were drawn partly over his teeth. "Let's not rush, Robert."

"I don't have a choice."

"Wait!" Gregory reached out his hands and spread them against Endicott's chest. "How many times has it proven better to take a minute and think?"

"Almost every time," Endicott smiled as he replied. "But we have run out of time. We have used what time we had to prepare, to study, to practice, to build tools. I am going with the theory that I have to act now."

"And repeat your previous mistakes?" Gregory shot back, trying to smile too, but the attempt collapsed like a house of cards. "Do we have to endure forever your habit of rushing in again and again until you learn something?"

"Or more accurately, again and again without learning until it kills us," interjected Eoyan wryly.

"I understand, gentlemen," Endicott said, trying to stay calm, though his voice grew louder with each word. "But how can we delay responding to such a dream? What new information or insights are we going to miraculously receive by waiting?"

"Well … actually that reminds me of something." Gregory reached into his shirt and pulled out the now sweat-stained envelope. "Your grandpa wanted you to read this. I think we just passed midnight. Happy birthday."

Grandpa.

This stopped him. He took the envelope in fingers that shook from excess energy, opened it, and pulled out a paper covered in his grandpa's familiar, jagged script. It said,

"Robert:

I've fixed plenty a horseshoes, harrows, axles, and such. I could always reach into the sky and find the perfect shape and authentic form for them things. The forms could be wrenched out of even the most unlikely probability if done in the right mind and with the right preparation.

People aren't the same. They choose their own form. No one can choose for them. Maybe no one should.

I've seen you fight yerself. Are you too fast? Too slow? Too optimistic? Too green? It don't help when others say it either. Some of them there at your New School might be able to look into the smallest spaces, the very atoms of a hoe, but they can't see inside a person's mind or feel a thought or hear a feeling. They can't look upon you and know who you are. There's no mathematics for the mind or calculus for the soul. The worst of them know this all too well, while the best of them—misguided but well meaning—have no idea what they can't know. But all of them will try to change you.

Who are you? Are you perfect? I can't make you perfect, Robert. The closest to perfect there is comes from being the real you. Maybe the real you is imperfect. That don't matter much if you can find a harness for it and bring it into equilibrium. Not speed, not inspiration, not romantic idealism are wrong if that is who you are.

We didn't build the elevator in a day or grow the grain in a week. Everything has its time and season. Out there in the night of Ardgour's mistake, you don't have time to grow a lifetime's crop of wisdom or realize every expectation. You do need to survive, and you can by taking up just one right idea and holding onto it. That right idea is your harness. The right idea leads to the authentic you, the singular you. That you is simple, has beautiful, matchless affinity. Find that right mind and allow it all to be.

What are you, boy? One answer. Whatever of the infinite it is, don't question it. Be as much yourself as you can, and you will make it back across the Line.

On yer birthday be yourself, Robert.

Pa"

Skolving be myself? My authentic self? I might as well take advice from the Lonely Wizard.

Endicott's roiling mindset did not allow him to appreciate the letter the first time he read it. It was noise, the poorly written meanderings of someone who probably used to write in their youth but hadn't written—or spoken—much since then and had lost the knack for making sense. It was an incoherent mix of eloquence and euphemism. The first reading only made the already angry young man angrier. But it was a letter from Grandpa. Its provenance made him pause and think again.

That's about a month's worth of conversation from him. And an eternity of patience for the listener waiting for it to come at its own pace from out of his mouth.

Endicott chuckled inwardly.

I can't believe he wrote that. It would have taken more effort from Grandpa to write that letter than to make Gregory's unmatchable sword.

Then he read the letter again. It was no longer noise. And he was no longer angry reading it.

Who am I?

He passed the letter to Gregory, still pondering the question.

"That's quite a letter from someone you told me is a man of few words, Robert." Gregory handed the letter back to Endicott, but Eoyan reached out for it, a question in his eyes. Endicott nodded and Gregory handed it to Eoyan. Thunder rumbled in the near distance.

Be as much myself as I can be.

Endicott thought about that. He recognized many things in himself. Anger, fear, anxiety, frustration. His heart pounded with his fear for Koria.

Koria! I always feel so much for you. But why?

Endicott knew he was a mess, that he had been on the brink of madness since the first heraldic dream. He had fought the mania with thinking and analyzing, with calculating and planning, and with actions that had sometimes been as reckless as they had been well meaning. He had fought it with friendship and love too. He had tried to outsmart the future, but it had remained always there, menacing and unavoidable in its infinite, threatening variations.

"Who am I?" Endicott said. "Who am I more than anything else?"

"You're a hero, Robert," said Eoyan, not smiling now. "I told you before."

"Of course he's a hero," said Gregory, "but that's about actions and consequences. It's not who he *is*." Gregory laughed gently and turned back to his best friend. "You are so full of it." Endicott stared at him. "Don't you know, Robert? It flows over and out of you all the time. You are *love*, brother. That's who you are more than you are anything else."

"Well," said Eoyan March. "Under most circumstances I would have barfed a little in my mouth by now."

"Glad you didn't," murmured Ildrys from some shadowy spot not far away. "It smells a little ripe in here as it is."

The skolves had brought their abominable rotted meat smell with them, and it had not dissipated. It had only mixed with the odor of burned, moldy wood, pungent fear, sweat, blood, dirt, and too many people in one small space and created a truly repulsive stew that could almost be tasted.

Eoyan wrinkled his nose. "Yes, indeed. Not quite sure why no one is laughing. Not even you, Ildrys." But no one was, not even Ildrys. No one was saying much of anything. "Maybe *I'm* the hero here." He held up one hand. "No, hear me out. I *was* the right choice to come with you gentlemen on this little expedition. Jeyn would never have stopped talking philosophy once you started, and Merrett, oh yeah, he would call you both prissy little idiots and tell you to shut the hell up. But I have heard a lot of weird declarations from men and women going into combat. It isn't all stoicism all the time, and that's an understatement. So I'll call you whatever you want if it makes you feel better and gets you in the right mind to deal with our situation." Eoyan grimaced as if in pain. "You're always declaring your love for everyone you meet anyway, so sure, love it is."

As Gregory looked askance at Eoyan, perhaps not sure whether to clap him on the back or slap his face, Endicott went deep inside himself. Fear, anxiety, and hate still raged within him, held in abeyance by the letter, by thoughts of his grandpa, by his friends beside him, and by the ideas they were discussing, but still very much there. The turmoil remained. How could love be any kind of answer? He was viscerally horrified by the dream, by the thought of harm to Koria and Eloise. His mind still worked, churned, and spun.

Koria!

The idea of future trauma brought back a memory. "Do you remember that conversation we were having on the road? We were talking about how it is that I have never really spoken about my mother."

Gregory nodded, unfazed by the non sequitur. "You said you didn't remember what she looked like."

"That's right. Sir Hemdale said I needed to face that gap if I was ever going to change. He said I was lucky I couldn't remember my mother's face because that way all women could be her. Later Koria and I spoke about it and she felt the same." Endicott smiled. "She thinks that because I don't remember what my mother looked like, I mix things up when women are in trouble. I saw my father's face in one person, but I see my mother everywhere. *All* women are my mother, and when *any* woman is threatened, I react like it's *my* mother that's threatened."

"O-kay," Gregory's voice was patient. "That's ... interesting, but what does it mean?"

"Maybe it means I'm insane," Endicott whispered.

"Probably," stage whispered Eoyan.

"Maybe it doesn't matter. Or maybe this time we should embrace it. I know what Koria and Eloise look like. I would say *that* is what matters now."

"*I* would say we have firmly crossed the Line into skolve scat," declared Eoyan. "However I did see the door of the Orchid after you lost your shit that time, Robert."

"Yes," said Endicott with a tight smile. "And I do love Koria."

"I love Eloise," Gregory added.

Yes. Love. Endicott nodded. "I have to go. For love," he whispered.

"*We* have to go," declared Gregory, drawing Justice. It rang sweet and long.

Yes.

Endicott embraced the feeling, accepted it. It filled him. He did not care if it was skolve scat. He was not going to go out in fear or anger. *It must be love.* The other feelings, the feelings of fear and anger, indistinguishable and jumbled, felt wrong. They had always felt wrong, like a sickness. Love felt right. It felt pure. Endicott smiled. He was full of love.

Eoyan's brows went up. "Yah! Let's kill these fuckers for love!"

Gregory looked sharply at Eoyan, then laughed and agreed. "For love."

Endicott took the letter back and folded it up. He turned to Elyze and the others, who had been watching and listening closely but in total silence. "In a few moments I am leaving. I am walking out that gate, and I am not stopping until I reach Vercors. If you want to come with me, you may do so. You'll have to stay a little behind me. It is going to be ugly."

Elyze crossed her arms. "When I first saw you and Gregory, do you know what I thought?"

Endicott had little patience for rhetorical questions. He checked his scabbard, his boots, and his armor, saying nothing until Elyze continued.

"I thought you were rushing around for no reason. You ended up finding a reason for being out that night, but that entire debacle was just dumb luck." Elyze smiled her superior smile. "I knew you had talent. Anyone who knows dynamics knows the name Endicott. But I saw someone who was both the most intelligent person I had ever met and the most idiotic. That's you, Sir Robert Endicott. Think for a moment. We are surrounded. If you go out there, you'll be ground up like dog meat by those skolves." She turned to Eirnyn. "Help me out here, Sergeant."

Eirnyn smiled wryly. "For my own sake I would rather he stayed here. I would rather everyone stayed here. We are mounting an effective defense. This is a strong position."

"Well, that was a little less than I hoped for," Elyze said crisply. "But you're right about one thing, Sergeant, we must stay together. Here. And this is where I'm staying, so you and your men *have* to stay here."

"That's correct," Eirnyn said flatly. "But I cannot tell Sir Robert what to do."

"Independent command," muttered Ildrys just loud enough to be heard.

"This sword was made before I was even born," declared Gregory loudly. He held his probability sword high. "Justice was fated for this moment. *I* am going with him."

Eoyan laughed and hefted his heavy spear. "I don't have any magical weapons or old blood, but I trust Sir Robert. A little." Eoyan seemed to remember something else. "And I've been ordered to stand by him no matter what."

"So it's the three of you. I don't want to keep acting the cynic here," Elyze said with an undeniably cynical expression, "but you three are going to die." She said "die" like most people would say "shit," and she let it lie there and stink for a moment before she continued.

"It's great, Eoyan, that you are willing to follow the heroic Sir Robert and his squire to save their ladies, but is that what you *should* be doing?"

Elyze turned and took in Eirnyn, Ildrys, and the other soldiers before returning her gaze to Eoyan. "And for love?" she snorted. "Love isn't going to save anyone. You're going to *die*. Probably first. You shouldn't even *let* him go out there. You can be replaced, but Lighthouse needs him. You can't let Robert go. It's your duty to stop this."

Eoyan was unfazed. "Nice to meet you again, Elyze Astarte. You almost fooled me earlier when you were helpful. The fact is I've been instructed to do what Robert says no matter what." He looked off into the shadows. "And by people I respect," he added, glaring at Elyze. "Gerveault, Lord Kennyth Brice, the duchess." He smiled. "My duty is clear."

Endicott was equally unfazed. "I don't feel embarrassed about risking my life for love. What better reason could there be? You aren't coming, Elyze. That's fine. I never expected you to. The rest of you shouldn't feel embarrassed about staying either. You never had my dream or saw what I saw. There's no exigency in this for you, and staying here makes sense. Hopefully we'll clear out enough of the skolves as we go to make things easier for you until Sir Hemdale comes." He paused and took a breath. "Just tell me one thing, Elyze. Did you ever actually have a heraldic dream about me being here?"

Elyze bit her lip. Her face betrayed the merest hint of shame. "No."

It was the answer he expected. "Why did you want me to come, then?"

"I've told you why." Endicott thought about that, trying to understand. Into his silence she added, "I'm sorry about your heraldic dream. I'd heard about Keith Euyn's dreams, that they twist him sometimes, but what happened to you was much worse than I expected." She looked down. "It looks like a curse."

"It's a gift," Endicott said, meaning it this time. He looked at the soldiers. They were tired, dirty, hungry, and starting to get thirsty. A few were injured, two were dead out in the wheat field, and another body lay just a few feet away. Rhysheart looked down when Endicott met his eyes.

He's embarrassed. I can't leave it like this.

His time with Somne, Eirnyn, Rhysheart, Ildrys, and the others had seemed in some ways only a moment and in other ways as if it had lasted for ever. All the soldiers had some small injury, some mark of their time together. Endicott felt a moment of love for them too. He raised his voice so that it echoed off the stone walls. "By now you know that we are going, soldiers. We talked a lot of skolve shit about why we are going. Love, fear, anger, dreams."

He smiled at their dirty, dark, shadowed faces. "The words don't matter. We have to go. It's as simple as that. *You* have to stay."

"It has been an honor fighting here with you," he shouted, looking around at everyone, smiling again and catching each of their eyes in turn, ending with Ildrys. "And it's been a pleasure learning about the real world with you."

Ildrys laughed, his face orange from a mix of blood and sweat.

Endicott shifted his focus to Eirnyn and shouted once more. "So are you going to hold out here without us schoolboys?"

"You're damned right we are!" Eirnyn roared back. "Redoubt Empyrean, Robert! Redoubt Empyrean, Gregory! Redoubt Empyrean, Eoyan!"

"Shout, shout!" Ildrys shouted.

"Redoubt, redoubt!" Rhysheart and Ida shouted back.

"Redoubt Empyrean, it's echoed, echoed, in the halls of Elysium!" The other soldiers sang, their voices ringing in the small stone room of the tower.

"I guess that's where we will see you then," said Eoyan. "In Elysium."

Rhysheart held the shield out to Gregory. It reflected the firelight, gleaming red and orange.

Gregory shook his head. "Give it back to me when next we meet. Wherever that is." Rhysheart nodded, speechless and practically hugging the shield, scarcely daring to believe Gregory would leave such a precious weapon behind. Endicott guessed that Gregory had decided to both help the soldiers and reserve two hands for his sword.

It's time.

"Wait a moment," Endicott said as he passed the ruined hinges of the gates and stepped a few feet outside the tower. It was starting to rain. Lightning flashed, lighting up the surrounding fields for an instant. No skolve pounced while he opened himself to the empyreal sky, assessing the storm. Though caught up in his work, he could still just barely hear Gregory and Eoyan whispering behind him.

"That was surprising." Gregory's voice.

"What was?" Eoyan now.

"The way everyone saluted us like that."

"That's because they think we're about to die."

Endicott knew this too but put it out of his mind. He only needed to know what the storm might provide, what he was going to do, who he was.

Be myself. Love.

Another moment passed. Still no skolves. Gregory and Eoyan stood just behind Endicott, swords out, tense, no longer whispering. Behind the gate Elyze, Eirnyn, and the other soldiers breathed fast, eyes big, excited, scared.

Endicott was a young man of complex, sometimes contradictory, thoughts and feelings. He was generally cheerful but sometimes melancholy, often at the same time. Occasionally he was filled with a mix of rage and terror that was sometimes blinding, sometimes illuminating. Whatever the situation, even when he was almost overwhelmed with anxiety or impatience, he almost always had to think, analyze, calculate. The only times he ever acted with such complete internal uniformity, with so little thought that he could barely remember acting at all, were in those very rare moments of absolute purpose when he saw a woman being abused. He had no way of evaluating Koria and Hemdale's theory about his mother, of knowing if her absence had created such a trigger, but there was no doubting the phenomenon, no doubting that only under those circumstances had Endicott ever truly been able to act without thought, debate, or self-censure.

When Endicott stepped out of the tower into the rain, he once again entered that rare state of being. He reached it through the trigger of the chaotic heraldic dream but held it in equilibrium through love. While in this state of harmony he did not consciously feel anything else.

"Okay," Endicott whispered. "Let's go."

It could all have been so much trash. It could have been a joke that only someone with the credulity of an idiot would take seriously. If Endicott had led them charging out like a trio of fools to be overwhelmed at once by the skolves, it would have been these things. The difference between cliché and eloquence lies at the intersection of subjectivity and objective truth. Endicott was now in a state of absolute emotional harmony, but it *physically* mattered, enabling him to reach effortlessly into the empyreal sky, into the storm, and find power there. Power that was smoothly redirectable, probabilities willing to be flipped, potential energy waiting on the precipice of the future, ready to be nudged over the edge and manifested into action. The cost could not be calculated, but Endicott sensed it intuitively; it was low and there was energy to spare.

"Sheathe your sword." As Endicott said this to Gregory, he made the signal for calculating, though in this case there was no calculation at all but only an intuitive grasp of the location of the skolves. They were not as clustered as they had been in the fields earlier. He imagined a slowly undulating curtain connecting them, and he saw how the potentials and pathways of these connections could be reorganized along the curtain between the ground and the thunderclouds above. He made the raised fist sign for innovating and executed his instinctive manipulation.

A sheet of electrons staggered downwards in the tiniest sliver of a second along the imagined curtain. Plasma and positive charge were instantly blasted back along the same path from the ground to the sky.

CRRRACKKKKKKKKKKKKKK

The flash was blinding, the sound deafening. The earth shook and kept shaking. Gregory clutched at his head. Eoyan dropped his spear. Burning skolves smoked along a roughly arcuate line, half circling the three young men.

Gregory's lips were moving, but Endicott could not hear him. He was still deep in the empyreal sky. He held his hand up in the innovating signal again.

CRRRACKKKKKKKKKKKKKK

He saw five skolves charging them from the left, closing fast.

CRRRACKKKKKKKKKKKKKK

The last detonation was so close that Endicott felt the charge pass through him, nearly knocking him off his feet. He staggered and saw Gregory and Eoyan crouching in a deep squat, low over their boots, almost sitting, hands over their heads. They may have been screaming. Endicott stood tall again and surveyed the carnage. The other half circle had now been described in plasma, broken only by the tower, which he had spared. Small fires burned here and there along the arcs, signs of the bushes that had lived there one moment before.

"Let's go!" Endicott roared, pulling Gregory up. Eoyan found his spear. They set off at a quick jog towards the Line. As they emerged from the boulder field, Endicott looked back on the tower. Four skolves were rushing towards the entrance, two on each side. He looked up into the empyreal sky and made the signal for innovating.

CRRRACKKKKKKKKKKKKKK

CRRRACKKKKKKKKKKKKKK

Skolves burned for a fleeting period of time if made hot enough. As those four exploded into flame, they illuminated the faces of the soldiers huddled within the tower for a moment. Feeling nothing, Endicott pivoted and ran, leading Gregory and Eoyan into the darkness.

THE STORM WAS PASSING NOW, ITS NOISE AND POWER FADING. LIGHTNING FLASHED FURTHER and further away. They were halfway back to the Line before Endicott saw another group of skolves, seven this time, charging through the fields just ahead and to his left. He made the innovating sign without hesitating.

CRRRACKKKKKKKKKKKKKK

The flash was enormous. Again the ground shook and heaved. Endicott also shook but from cold this time. The weight of probability had moved beyond him.

"Two alive!" Eoyan roared, stepping forward to meet one of the skolves with his spear. It surprised him by swinging its heavy hammer sideways instead of overhead. The hammer nearly took off Eoyan's head. He ducked just in time and only grazed the skolve with his spear, then parried the ferocious overhead swing of an axe, slicing through the haft. Endicott drew his sword but nearly lost it when the hammer came around again, knocking his blade to the side. The blow was hard, and the sword's hilt was wet from rain, but Endicott managed to regrip and cut the skolve's snout in two as it was brought up short by a recovered Eoyan. It screamed, clutching at its face. Eoyan stabbed it repeatedly as it thrashed and rolled. Endicott whirled to help Gregory, but his Skolve was already down, one hip cut clean through. They ran on through the rain, unable to see the Line through the storm's black, filmy cloak.

Chapter Twenty-Six
Battle of the Bifrost

"Open the gates!" Eoyan's hoarse shout brought Endicott's mind back to earth. He had lost time somewhere in the fight, perhaps halfway back. Now he saw the Line only about three hundred feet away, the tower looming behind it, both glimmering in torch and lantern light.

"Open the gates!" Eoyan roared desperately.

Endicott was breathing heavily, but his sword, he noticed now, felt light. He looked down at it. The blade was broken. The last foot and a half was gone. Then he saw he was also missing the greave from his right leg.

When did I break my sword? How?

Endicott was not the only one showing signs of wear and tear. Eoyan was limping badly, and his spear was gone. He was cradling his right arm too, hunching tightly over it whenever he was not yelling for the gate to be opened. Gregory, also limping, his face streaked with blood, stumbled backwards behind his two comrades, amorphous blade out and fanning from side to side.

A tall armored figure charged out of the gate straight towards them. No signs of age, infirmity, or second thoughts were visible on the enormous knight. His eyes were bulging and ferocious. He came on so fast Endicott thought he might run them down, but the exhausted young man was too worn out to flinch.

The big man shocked them by suddenly flinging himself on both knees and crying out, "I'm sorry, boys! I should have come. I should have come!" He was weeping and his face was blackened and filthy from who knows what, his big, crazy eyes red as fire, hands clenched and trembling, hair wild and torn. Endicott gaped at the spectacle, unable to speak. Hemdale's grief and desperation were even more surprising and disturbing than Eloise's had been.

Guilt? Even in him?

It was a revelation, though not a welcome one. For all his high talk and imperious manners even Sir Hemdale could not always embody his ideal of knightly self-control. Was he punishing himself retroactively now that he realized they had been on their way alone all this time?

"How could you have known?" asked Gregory wearily.

"I saw the lightning. I … thought it might be you."

Time was passing and Endicott's sense of mission could not allow him to dwell for long on Hemdale's shocking transformation. "Let's talk about it on the way in," he said, grasping the big knight's pauldron to steady himself. Hemdale nodded, a long string of snot dangling, unnoticed or disregarded, from the end of his otherwise autocratic nose, and stood up.

The big man put his arm around Gregory's shoulders for a moment. "Well done, nephew."

"What?" Gregory's face betrayed his exhaustion and confusion. They passed under the first gate, where a troop of soldiers waited. Endicott saw Emyr Wynn's honest face at the head of them, looking honestly concerned and relieved. Hemdale disregarded the soldiers, his dark eyes fixed on Gregory at his side. "Ha! You crossed the great no-man's-land in the dead of night despite storm and skolves. You are a man now!"

"Fuck that," muttered Eoyan, limping and grimacing in pain. He did not elaborate.

We don't have time for this.

"I normally like to hear all about your culturally backward traditions, Sir Hemdale, but action needs to be taken right now." The words came out without thought or editing, but rude or not, Endicott regretted none of them. "We must push through to Vercors tonight, and you, Sir Hemdale, must relieve the soldiers we had to leave behind."

To his credit Hemdale did not squash Endicott where he stood. He turned and looked back through the gates. "They are still alive? Where?"

Endicott understood the big man better now.

He thinks we all came together and only the three of us survived. He was proud we survived but grieving the loss of the others … and trying to console us in his awkward, old-fashioned way.

Eoyan chose that moment to collapse. One moment he was muttering incoherently under his breath, and the next his eyes rolled up into his head and his legs gave out. His mail kept the fall from being completely silent, but his consciousness had clearly departed before he hit the ground. Endicott opened himself to the empyreal sky and looked closely at Eoyan's prostrate form, seeing past the huddle of soldiers crowding in to tend to him. "His leg is broken. And his right arm," he said.

Gregory was aghast. Hemdale only nodded approvingly at the young soldier where he lay.

"Get a stretcher!" shouted Emyr. She put a hand on Endicott's shoulder. "What is the situation out there?"

"We had to hole up in the tower." Endicott said it flatly, looking back. "Three dead, the rest still holding out. At least when we left."

"I *told* you it was the tower," exclaimed Gail Guise, a soldier Endicott barely knew apart from her name. "We saw the fire and then the lightning." She made two fingers and darted them down sharply. "It came again," she gestured sharply with her fingers several more times, "and again and again. It was like Elysium itself had come to battle. We all argued about what on the Knights' earth was going on out there. Then Sir Hemdale put his armor back on in a frenzy and told us to open the gates. But it all happened so fast! We didn't thi—"

"Thank you, Corporal." Emyr's voice was precise and sure. "Who is in charge there?"

"Eirnyn," Endicott said.

The only sign that the lieutenant understood what that meant was the blink-length pause before she spoke again. "How many skolves?"

Endicott looked at Gregory, nodding to him, not trusting to the gap in his memory.

"We don't know exactly," Gregory said thoughtfully. "Enough to surround the tower. We might have killed eighteen or twenty before we broke out. On our way out we thinned what was left pretty heavily. Probably another forty of them perhaps, mostly with ... Elysium, injured a sizable number more certainly." Gregory thought for a moment. "I doubt there's many of them left. If they are still there at all."

There was a lot of muttering and cursing from the soldiers, some disbelieving, others clearly excited. Emyr's face, all business, betrayed neither of these reactions or any other. "But why did you three leave? Why take that risk? And why tonight?"

"I heralded an attack on the New School. It's imminent." Endicott allowed for no uncertainty about the attack's timing. He had already made his decision. He saw Sir Hemdale nodding at him as if he understood.

All women can be your mother.

The young man turned back to Emyr. "We are riding out immediately to deal with it."

The lieutenant looked at him for all of a second before turning to a group of her soldiers. "Go saddle their horses. Load their saddle bags with food and water." She turned to Gael Guise. "Corporal, you're going with them. Get your gear ready."

"Good luck, nephews," said Sir Hemdale, starting to walk back out under the gates. "We will resume our *backward* cultural celebration when everyone has returned safely."

"Wait!" shouted Emyr Wynn.

"See you in the morning," the big knight shouted back as he broke into a run. In moments he disappeared into the darkness.

"Damn it," breathed Emyr Wynn.

"I think he means to help them until you get there tomorrow," said Gregory wearily.

"Yeah, I harvested that."

"What's the Bifrost?" asked Gael Guise. "I know you can't mean the old Metheuyn Bridge."

Endicott did not reply, his eyes on the road ahead, but Gregory answered. "It's a part of the New School but off campus. You might know it as the Vercors Ice Company warehouse."

"Oh, I've heard of that." Gael frowned ever so slightly. "Do you know why the lieutenant sent me with you?"

For your open-eyed enthusiasm?

As focused as he was, Endicott could not help but enjoy Gael's ebullience. She had fired off an unending series of questions and observations ever since they set out. This time she answered her own question. "Because I am the fastest rider she has. The most experienced too." Her nose scrunched up. "But we should slow it down a little, gentlemen. At the start of a journey everyone goes too fast. All full of energy. Feeling strong." She curled her left arm in a biceps pose that reminded Endicott of the time he had first met Koria and Eloise. "But if we don't take it just a bit easier, we're going to blow our horses."

"It doesn't feel much like the start by now," muttered Gregory, flagging. It was late morning. They had been riding hard for five hours or more, which in most circumstances would be considered a fairly long time in the saddle, but they were still only a fifth of the way to Vercors at best.

We must pick up the pace, not slow down. There is no time for pacing ourselves.
But we can't risk losing the horses.

"Let's dismount and run," Endicott said. Emyr Wynn had given him a new sword, and he left it strapped to his horse as he sprang to the ground. Gael dismounted with expert gracefulness, patted her horse, and followed Endicott. Gregory's dismount was not nearly as graceful, and he had much less spring in his step as he struggled to keep up with the others. He had already been exhausted before they departed from the Line. Neither he nor Endicott had enjoyed any real sleep or even rest for two days. The few winks they had caught between skolve attacks and heraldic dreams did not amount to much. Endicott did not feel it yet, but he knew he would pay at some point.

Running or not Gael did not seem tired, and she still had more questions. She wondered how they had known the skolves were coming, how they knew to shelter in the tower, what a heraldic dream was, why they had not helped Eoyan after his leg was broken. Finally she asked, "How did you break your sword, Sir Robert? I thought your sword was magical."

Endicott looked helplessly at Gregory, who may or may not have realized his friend could not remember how he had broken the sword. Gregory did not pick up on the wordless plea for a moment. He was in his own misery, huffing and puffing as he ran. "What? Oh. It all happened pretty fast." He took in a few big breaths. "Though some of it seemed slower than grain grows. After the storm moved on and we lost the lightning, we sustained several more skolve rushes.

Robert immolated the first of them right to ashes, but two rushes got right through and we had to fight." Gregory ran on a few more steps, Gael's head switching like an owl's between him and Endicott. "Robert here fought like a maniac and broke his sword right off on one of their thick skulls."

"But I thought it was a *magic* sword," Gael complained. Endicott gathered she must have noticed its glassy appearance and equated it with Gregory's superior blade. It took some time to explain the key points of metallurgy and dynamic manipulation to her and she eventually tired of the subject and changed tack.

"Do you think Sir Hemdale has found them yet?"

Endicott looked at her. "I'm sure he has. Probably before we even left. He had a pretty good line and some of the bush fires were still smoldering."

"He can run pretty fast for an old man," added Gael, smiling. "I don't suppose the skolves could have gotten him."

"I don't suppose so either," said Gregory huffing raggedly. "There weren't that many left."

"Hmmf. Well, gentlemen, I guard the Line every day and I can tell you skolves are just like angry people. There are always more of them." Gael was not even breathing hard.

Not for long if the grain works and we starve them out.

"I think I should come with you to the Bifrost when we get to Vercors."

Gael had already proposed this several times without getting an answer. Now Endicott took a big deep breath and responded. "It will be better if you go to the constabulary and rouse them. I saw a lot of soldiers in the heraldic dream. We'll need help."

"Knights of Armadale?" she asked.

"That's what most of them looked like."

"How sure are you about the timing?"

Sure enough to die trying to get there. Or not sure at all.

"It'll be strange," puffed Gregory a little later. "Strange if we save Eloise." He coughed several times. "She'll be sooo pissed off."

"It'll be a change," agreed Endicott. So far it had always seemed to be the girls doing the saving. He clung to the hope that Eloise and Koria would end up not even needing their help, though scarcely believing it possible. He looked over at Gregory, who was drooping seriously now. "Let's mount up again."

They rode on, Gael quiet for a change and the two men too tired to talk. Then Endicott noticed Gael staring at him and Gregory. Her face had a sharp, evaluative expression that contrasted markedly with the open-eyed, incessant stream of questions she had asked earlier.

She is not just a naïf.

This crystallized an idea he had been ruminating on half consciously for the past week.

A person can be simultaneously mature and immature, wise and foolish, good and evil, strong and weak, all in different ways. Like my broken sword, unlike Gregory's. Few indeed are strong in every way, all one thing or the other.

"You two should be eating and drinking more." Gael frowned as she admonished them. "Every hour. Better yet every forty-five minutes."

"I don't have a pocket watch on me," muttered Gregory.

"You've got me," she said pertly. "Eat something, schoolboys!"

They changed horses at the tiny constabulary in Byrste, which cleaned the local garrison right out and then, with a little more food and water packed in great haste, were off again. Even Gael fell silent after a few more hours, time and distance finally eroding her verve.

Exhaustion makes dullards of us all. When it doesn't make us sentimental.

Clop-clop-clop-clop.

They passed a farmer harvesting his crop. The dark, yellow wheat had survived last night's storm, and the farmer might have been waiting for it to dry properly. Endicott watched the man work as he trotted by, wondering if it was the new wheat, the poison wheat. Later, on foot again, pulling the reins of his horse, he thought about their own tests of the new grain back at home. It had seemed fine. Better than fine. The cattle had fattened up unusually quickly on it. The yield was higher too, the protein content as well. And it was easier to thresh, easier to winnow. And now he knew that skolves could not digest it. Everything about the wheat was better.

As far as they could tell.

Do we know everything?

Clop-clop-clop-clop.

Somewhere after the second town and second change of horses, somewhere before Kuiyp, Endicott fell asleep in the saddle.

Koria was pointing at the painting on the wall. She was excited. Eloise pulled the picture off the wall and carried it out of the Bifrost towards the cloaked man who was coming for them or for it. Koria looked up and recognized the colossal figure.

Koria!

He woke with a start, the fragment of a dream momentarily fragmenting his senses. Then he came to himself.

"We have to pick up the pace," he said in as even a tone as he could manage.

"We can't," replied Gael.

Endicott shook his head vehemently. "We need to try harder!"

"Gregory's horse is lame."

"*I'm* skolving lame," Gregory said under his breath.

Endicott leapt off his horse. Gregory could not move as quickly, but he managed to climb off awkwardly, looking like an old man. Gael crouched down and applied her expert eye to the beast. It *was* laming. Anyone could see it.

"I can't wait," Endicott exclaimed, still in the grip of the dream. "Time is almost up."

"You don't know that," Gregory whispered, hands on the horse's leg. Gael slapped his hands away from the sore limb and began her own tactile examination, touching and kneading it.

"I do," declared Endicott. "I just dreamed again. Just now."

Gregory's face scrunched. "You can't go there without me. I have to be there!"

"Take my horse," said Gael Guise.

"Really?" asked Gregory hoarsely, perhaps wondering how they could leave a woman behind.

"Really," she said flatly.

Gael was a soldier.

"Thank you!" Gregory practically shouted, though his voice cracked. He unstrapped his sword and moved it to Gael's animal, while the talkative soldier moved her head from side to side in unsubtle mockery. "Well, I don't want you two boys crying. Or fighting. Besides I bet I can still catch up with you before Vercors."

They left her, and she disappeared from view behind them as quickly as a rock dropped from a great height. The brief dream had sharpened Endicott's mind. He was focused and singular again. Only the goal mattered, only Koria and Eloise.

Gregory loved the girls as much as Endicott, but he lacked his friend's compounded mental trauma, his dream-induced mania. The tall young man who had fought so bravely against the skolves, who had felt such pride wielding the sword made solely to help his friend, the young man who had come to believe *he* had been made solely to help that same friend, was utterly exhausted. And because Gregory felt all those things, his exhaustion made him ashamed, and he fought it bitterly, especially as it became apparent that Endicott was, on this mission at least, indefatigable.

"Drink."

"Dismount."

"Run."

"Mount."

"Eat."

Endicott's continually cycling instructions seemed vaguely familiar to both young men, though they missed the connection for vastly different reasons, single-minded task orientation for one of them, numbing exhaustion for the other. Not far from Kuiyp, Gregory simply face-planted onto the road. Luckily he was running at the time instead of up on his horse.

Endicott heard the impact and whirled. He observed the collapse of his best friend dispassionately, saying nothing. The mission had priority now. He tied Gregory's horse to his own and calmly—though not easily given his own exhausted condition—heaved his comrade across the saddle of his horse and resumed running, leading both horses now.

When they arrived at Kuiyp, Endicott made Gregory first eat and get an hour's sleep at the Inn on the Rill. Meanwhile he got fresh horses and provisions from the constabulary. He barely remembered speaking with Daeg, with the innkeeper, with the local constable. He could not remember asking them to prepare a horse and supplies for Gael Guise when she arrived. His heraldic dream and the urgency of countering its foretold horrors engaged his conscious mind to the exclusion of everything else. As soon as the new horses were ready, Endicott shook Gregory roughly awake. His comrade lurched laterally and collided painfully with the wall, blinking his owlishly wide eyes as he tried to wrench himself awake and mumbling, "Where are we?"

They were back on their horses and galloping down the road in moments. As they left the inn behind Endicott thought he saw Gael Guise trudging towards them in the distance but said nothing. It was already past noon, and time was short.

"Eight Knights, I am sore all over." Gregory clutched at his abdomen, then his back, and squirmed in the saddle trying to find the least uncomfortable position for his aching bottom. He did not remember being flung over his saddle and carried into Kuiyp like a sack of wheat, and hearing about it from Endicott made him laugh. "If that peasant Eoyan March had been there, I would fear the worst," he quipped.

Gregory has recovered a little.

They rode on quickly, pushing the new horses to their limit, energized by knowing this last leg of the trip was the shortest.

"What do you think Eloise would have said if she had been with us in that tower?" Gregory's smile looked incongruent on his gaunt features. An hour's sleep had not erased the stresses of the tower siege, their embattled retreat in the night, and this long ride. Still, Endicott could see that the smile was genuine.

"She'd have said you were Heydron herself, holding your shield against anything and everything."

Gregory sighed. "I had a moment, didn't I?"

"Quite a few of them." *Strung out over quite a few hours.* Endicott knew they would all be dead were it not for Gregory and his superlative sword and shield.

"We're really going to rescue them, aren't we?"

Please be safe, be safe, be safe. We must *arrive in time.*

Endicott pushed down on his rising anxiety. It had started creeping up as the ride grew longer and longer, fighting his will like rubbish spilling out from underneath a tarp. His sense of unity, of harmony, of love was fraying bit by bit. Despite all his efforts it was being slowly eroded by relentless exhaustion.

Asserting his self-control again, Endicott replied. "It'll be the role reversal of all role reversals."

"Do you remember what that old lady said?"

"What old lady?"

Gregory cleared his throat. "When we found Konrad and Rendell. She said I would see Nimrheal several times, and the last time I did, he would mount me on my own sword."

Endicott barked a laugh. "She was crazy, Gregory."

Gregory said nothing. Endicott amplified his position. "*I* will make sure Nimrheal does no such thing."

"Oh well, if *you* say so …"

On the final leg of the journey their old companionship revived and helped both of them stay alert. They talked about the constabulary and how they never seemed to get anything done and about why soldiers from Armadale were still in Vercors when it was obvious they were the villains. But it was the smaller things that really helped. Talking about the girls, the sharpness of Gregory's sword, the resilience of his shield even though it was only a prototype, and their hopes for the day *after* the long ride, what they would eat first and what they would drink afterwards, whether there would be ice … It all made the journey pass quickly. Before they knew it, they had skirted the hills near Aignen and could make out Vercors shimmering in the far distance. It was a heartening sight, even if the sun was setting on it.

As they gazed at their adopted hometown on the horizon, they heard a horse galloping up from behind. "I told you I'd catch you before town," Gael shouted as she approached, still riding easily, though even in the failing light Endicott could see that her eyes were bloodshot and her features drawn and stressed. "You don't look so good, Sir Gregory," she ventured with a cheerfulness that on anyone else would have sounded forced.

Gregory straightened. "I'm as good as your favorite saddle. I can ride all day."

Gael produced an exaggerated frown. "Not sure what that means exactly, but you *have* ridden all day. That's obvious."

Endicott's sense of humor had evaporated again with the immediacy of the mission. They were achingly close to their goal now. "We're only a couple of hours out. Let's eat something now so we can get straight to work when we reach there." He twisted in the saddle and unbuckled a saddlebag as he spoke. "When we make Vercors, Gael, ride to the constabulary headquarters and ask to see either Erika

Lyon or Edwyn Perry. Tell them to bring everyone they can to the Bifrost as fast as they can. Everyone."

It was fully dark when they reached the edge of town. It was strange seeing people on the streets walking by lantern light after having been across the Castlereagh Line, where there were no lanterns or people, and then on the road back, which had been dead quiet except for a few farmers they had ignored in their single-minded focus on getting back. Except for the time it had taken to change horses and the one short rest period for Gregory, they had been travelling non-stop for thirty-nine hours, Endicott reckoned, turning four normal days of travel into less than two. And before that they had been fighting to survive in the tower and on the road back to the Line for the best part of another day and night.

They rode down a familiar street. A group of revelers lounged outside a tavern, dressed casually, laughing. Unafraid. It was almost time to part company with Gael.

"Does it feel to you like we just lived a lifetime in that tower across the Line?" Gregory mused.

Yes.

He had echoed Endicott's thoughts precisely.

But we don't have another lifetime in front of us. We're here.

He pulled his horse up, stopping both Gael and Gregory. "Thanks for riding with us, Gael. We are close enough to run for it now."

"Thanks for not waiting for me," she replied. Her face was dusty and rimed with the white salt of long sweat.

Endicott thought he understood. "Count on us to abandon you any time."

"Because I can take care of my business," she said with the first real edge they had seen from her. "I'll catch you up again soon. At the Bifrost."

Endicott wheeled his horse. "Don't come unless it's with the constabulary, and don't charge on ahead of them."

She winked at them both and put her heels to her horse. They watched her post away for a few seconds.

"I guess we don't need to worry about blowing the horses now," said Gregory. They were only about two or three miles from the Bifrost now. The thought triggered a surge of both rage and love in Endicott. Anxiety rose again too, and kept rising, threatening to unhinge him.

Just a few more minutes. A few more. Be safe, be safe, be safe.

They were so close, and the ride had been so long, too long for him to hold onto his self-control after the threat of the heraldic dream. Now the last of it slipped away like the blocks of ice the Vercors Ice Company transported. His equanimity fractured, and he scrambled desperately to hold the pieces of his composure together.

Love.

Endicott remembered love. He reached for it like a drowning man would reach for a tree in a raging river.

I will not arrive as a slave to fear. It will do no good.

Endicott took a breath, accepting the situation. They had done all they could. He *did* love Koria and Eloise. He loved impulsive, out-of-place Heylor. He even loved tall, philosophical Lindseth and grumpy, broad-backed Merrett. He would see the both of them wear his aunt's shirts again.

He smiled. "You're right. Give them everything we've got, brother. Hah!"

Endicott kicked, his heart pounding as they picked up the pace for one last charge. The streets were quiet except for their horses' rattling hooves and snorting breaths, and their own ragged breathing. They passed the fountain where Endicott had first met Koria and Eloise, raced across the square and down cobblestone roads towards the river. The Academic Plateau loomed on one side as they entered the warehouse district, horses' chuffing as they galloped.

The arch of the Bifrost was just ahead.

A flash of light.

Whump.

Some sort of detonation. Endicott smelled burning and glimpsed small, isolated fires in the near distance. Then he heard the urgent clanging of swords. The two comrades charged towards the wide-arched double gates and saw a knot of soldiers fighting a little further on. The gates were wide open, and as they swept through, they rode past the bodies of the Bifrost's guards.

Lindseth stood surrounded by four or five dead or incapacitated soldiers and perhaps seven more standing ones. He had a long sword in each hand. A second later a broad man slowly rose up beside him. It was Merrett, regaining his feet. Their plate-armored opponents allowed this for reasons Endicott had no time to wonder about as he galloped headlong towards them.

He did not think to show quarter to the heavily armored soldiers. He did not think at all. He did not hesitate or consider but charged close in on one side of the rough circle, his horse's shoulder roughly colliding with one of the metal-encased men, flinging him violently aside. Endicott brought his sword whistling around and into the gorget of another knight, collapsing it, and cutting deep into the knight's neck. The man's head flapped forward, possibly only held in place by the posterior side of the metal gorget, and his body flew back, listing laterally and falling. Charging out the other side of the tangle of men, Endicott wheeled his horse around to attack again. He absently noted a heat-scored, plate-armored knight lying right where his horse's feet had danced.

Gregory had stopped among the armored knights and was slashing down with his probability blade. The sword rang as it cut straight through the middle of one knight's helm. The man's nervous system was instantly snuffed out and only his armor controlled his fall, which proceeded in fits and starts as the metal sections collapsed according to their joints and degrees of freedom. Gregory pulled his sword out of the mess just in time to intercept a heavy two-handed blow from an enormous sword. The massive weapon parted cleanly in half, one piece flying off to bounce and skip across the cobble. Gregory swung laterally and took off the attacking knight's arm at the elbow. Blood sprayed black in the dim light.

The armless knight's helm-muffled scream stopped abruptly when a stumbling Merrett forced a dagger up at an angle under the back of his helm. Merrett at first looked like he was wearing a shoulder-length wig until Endicott realized that what he was seeing in the poor light were actually long, twisting streams of blood flowing from a head wound the heavyset man had suffered.

Lindseth moved smoothly, both of his swords beautifully compatible, working together to block and strike again and again until he had found a weakness in one knight's armor and struck there under the armpit, all while using graceful and easy footwork to avoid a second knight until he had a chance to deal with him alone. Endicott knew Lindseth would have no trouble with his second opponent, so he leapt off his horse and jumped further into the fray. Seeing him approach, a knight fell on one knee in front of him. Without hesitating Endicott lunged and slipped his sword through a gap in the man's armor into his eye and brain.

"I think he was surrendering, Robert," Gregory gasped from nearby. He too was on foot now, standing over the last surviving knight, who was also kneeling in submission. Endicott turned on his heels. He strode without thought towards the survivor and brought his whining sword down ferociously on the man's armored head. The helm caved in with an awful clang and the knight shuddered and fell sideways, jerking spasmodically.

Endicott ignored Gregory's shocked, open-mouthed expression and examined his sword blade, which now had a thumb-sized notch in it. Endicott tossed it aside and picked up the still spasming knight's weapon.

Off to his right Merrett gave in to his injury and collapsed on one knee, gasping in pain and barely holding himself up with one arm. Blood from his head wound coursed down that arm and dripped onto the cobbles beside him. Lindseth rushed to tend to him, but Endicott called out and pointed the appropriated sword towards the river, past a Vercors Ice Company wagon that was backed up to one of the loading docks. He had not seen the rig in his heraldic dream. "Heylor is drowning there. Help him instead, Jeyn. Merrett will make it." Lindseth nodded and jogged towards the river, still holding his two swords.

Endicott turned to the Bifrost, forgetting Lindseth and Heylor, forgetting Merrett, who still struggled to rise off his knee. He feared the door would be locked, but it was jammed open by the severed arm of one of the knights. The cut through armor, skin, muscle, and bone had been clean and instantaneous, Endicott noted as he stepped over it and grasped the half-open door.

Only one of Grandpa's blades could have done that. Eloise's.

"Blouse! Where is Eoyan?"

Endicott wrenched open the door and entered the building. He did not acknowledge Merrett or pause to answer his question. It was not germane to his purpose. The remainder of the armless knight's body lay just inside the door. Endicott heard Gregory, a few steps behind him, tell Merrett that Eoyan had been injured and left behind at the Line.

"Slow down, Robert!" Gregory slipped on the knight's blood as he tried to catch up, but

Endicott only looked over his shoulder and shouted fiercely, "Twelve against two, Gregory, and those two still alive. Don't you know what that means? This fight started only moments before we got here! Probably only seconds! The detonation we heard must have been the innovation I saw in my dream. There's still time!"

"Those knights surrendered, Robert!"

Endicott did not care. His eyes had adjusted to the interior darkness now and he was already moving forward. "I don't give the gift of honor to those that act without any."

By guile and treachery they came to murder those we love.

He was unaware of his own self-righteousness. The young man barely thought at all. Weariness had eroded everything but his goal. Even if he had been capable of objective self-reflection, events were moving too quickly and too exigently for it.

Desperate shouts, clashing swords, and smashing objects filled the Bifrost with an auditory chaos that assaulted and disoriented the two young men as they made their way further into the complex. Acrid smoke pervaded the air and attacked their throats and lungs. The floor was slippery with blood and littered with the wreckage of battle. The Bifrost had been transformed into a replica of hell. Endicott and Gregory jogged through the building, trying not to slip on the bloody floor or trip on the broken pieces of furniture and apparatus that had been flung about. They passed through the ruins of the classrooms in which they had practiced heraldry and probability manipulation. Chairs and tables had been knocked over or hacked in pieces everywhere. As Endicott brushed by one of the few tables that remained upright, he noted a small pile of dice sitting there undisturbed. He absently grabbed a handful and put them in his pocket.

They turned left at the sounds of a nearby struggle. "That's Jeyk Johns!" Gregory exclaimed as they came upon the prone form of one of the Bifrost's mail-armored guards. He was still moving, instinctively crawling towards them, face grimacing in pain. "Hang on, Jeyk!" Gregory whispered, kneeling beside him. "Help is on the way."

Endicott did not stop to aid or comfort the injured man. He turned a corner into the corridor leading to the greenhouses. Five armored men were leading a woman, crudely bound with ropes and wires, along the corridor towards them. A burlap sack was tied over her head.

Koria!

The corridor was wide. It had been built to transport soil, ice, and grain to the loading docks on the other side of the building, and it had a stone water channel running down the middle to ensure the dynamicists would have water on hand wherever they worked. Endicott had walked along this corridor many times. He had been everywhere in the Bifrost and had memorized the calculations necessary for the manipulation of every standard volume of water within the various containers, troughs, and channels in the sprawling complex. He had heated and cooled water exhaustively, far past the point of boredom, and manipulated it at every temperature, safe and unsafe. His knowledge of the place was so complete that he could instantly apply the cool and detailed calculations of dynamics with the instinctive speed of wizardry. Here calculation and wizardry were the same for him. And at this moment Endicott lacked all restraint.

There was no question of how or why. He knew exactly what was required and how to do it. He made the agreed signal for calculating but calculated nothing. He did not need to. Before the soldiers could cross the remaining distance between them, before Endicott could even get a proper look at their prisoner, he made the clenched fist signal for innovating.

Five soldiers ignited instantaneously inside their armor. In the first half second thin, dazzling spurts of flame shot out from their visors and some of the armor joints, but after that they emitted only strange, raw screams, shook, stumbled, tried to run, and fell. The water channel cracked, and a massive error wave of heat and cold lashed the corridor in both directions.

"Eight Knights!" Gregory exclaimed behind him. Endicott smiled. He had not been sure if his tall friend was still with him or if he had stayed behind to help the injured guard. They rushed to the bound woman, who had slipped on a line of frost and now lay on her side, feet scrambling. Endicott put his sword down and cradled her head while Gregory pulled the sack off.

It was Lil Hilliard! She blinked sticky, frosty tears at them, obviously struggling to comprehend what had just happened. Her hard, spare, muscular body was shaking uncontrollably.

Koria!

Gregory stooped to examine one of the knights while Endicott helped Lil to her feet.

"Black longship sigil on his armor." Gregory rolled the motionless body over and tried to remove the helmet. Suddenly he jumped back. "His skin has melted. It's all stuck to the visor. It's stuck to his gauntlets. Eight Knights!" Gregory sat back, his face ashen, breathing shallowly and making fish shapes with his lips. Then he vomited.

"Bwooh. Bwooh. Alllach Bllaahh!"

Endicott ignored him, desperate to get some information from Lil.

"Where is Koria?"

Lil blinked again and in uncharacteristically weak tones, said, "Is s-she here?"

Heydron! Endicott could hear other sounds of nearby fighting now. From the other direction.

"Help is coming. Stay here," he said, picking up his sword and turning back in the direction of the forges and loading docks. There was no time to look after Lil. He started running again. He heard Gregory following a few steps behind him, breath labored and loud, apparently done vomiting.

Whump.

A bright yellow light flashed not far away, followed by rolling black smoke and the sounds and smells of burning. Metal clashed on metal from the same direction. Endicott sprinted through a broken door, across a wrecked conference room, over the detached head of a man he did not recognize, and out another broken door. The head was helmless. The man had not been a guard. Endicott remembered that in his heraldic dream the cloaked figure had been accompanied by another group of men. They had not been dressed in the plate armor of Armadale.

Who are they?

He nearly tripped on another man whose left leg had been sheared cleanly from his hip. He was also unarmored. An unloaded crossbow was illuminated by the light from Eloise's shield, which lay nearby. Spatters of blood marred that perfect reflective surface and puddled heavily on the floor.

Eloise's shield!

Endicott thought about picking up the shield, but in his haste kept going. Skidding in the blood, he ran on.

"Heydron herself!" Gregory's voice. Had he also seen his love's abandoned shield?

Shouts and screams. More clashing of metal. Much closer now. Endicott leapt over the still body of a woman. It was Myfan, one of the Vercors Ice Company workers. She had been struck over the head with something sharp, a flap of skin above her temple hanging, blood flowing out from it. Still alive.

"You killed my brothers! Haaggh." The voice was male, shrill, and loud enough to rise above the clamor, but the words were poorly pronounced, with a weird honking tone that was strangely familiar. Endicott sprinted around a corner to find a knot of armed men in civilian clothes crowding around the wide stone door of one of the forges. Smoke billowed from the doorway, and as one of the men turned away, coughing, he saw Endicott and yelled something to his companions. Four of them charged towards the young dynamicist.

"Take my sword."

It was Gregory. He was leaning against a stone water basin.

What happened?

Blood had soaked the front of Gregory's jacket. He had been cut somewhere on his left side. Endicott looked down at the still form of one of the men who had charged him. He was crouching over the man's corpse, and his right hand was covered in blood. A single tooth sat improbably on the stretched skin between his thumb and index finger. His entropic dagger was clutched in his left hand, bloodied up to the hilt. He had lost his sword somewhere. He had lost a piece of time too. What had happened here in that interval?

He struggled to his feet, wobbly at first, and shook his right hand impulsively, flinging the tooth somewhere out of sight. Then he changed hands with the dagger and wiped its dripping blood on his pant leg.

"I should have had it, Robert, but I was too tired. I didn't see. It was easier fighting the ones in armor. They were slower." He struggled to pass his sword to Endicott. He looked exhausted. And deathly pale. "Save them."

"You keep it," Endicott whispered, knowing he could never take Gregory's sword. There was no time to explain the instinct that drove this feeling. "Watch my back."

Stay alive.

Endicott turned away from his friend and stepped through the door into the forge room. Koria was crouched near the forge itself. In front of her stood Eloise, holding her entropic sword in her left hand. Her right arm dangled, blood trailing down it, down her hand, down her fingers, and onto the stone floor. A crossbow bolt was lodged in her shoulder.

The room had clearly been heat-blasted. Every surface, except for a tight circle around the two women, was blackened and smoking. A charred corpse, barely recognizable as human, lay a few paces from the women. A towering, cloaked figure stood by the water reservoir, facing the girls, side on to Endicott. His cowl was down. Endicott knew him. In a flash, the memory that had been buried by that blow to the head at the Black Spear resurfaced.

He was the man from the Nimrheal cult meeting, the man who had struck Endicott from behind, the man who had breathed, and breathed now, in great honking gasps. He was the man who had taken Endicott's medallion. Endicott knew who he was. This huge man who stood gasping and honking with a great spear in his hand and tears running down his face was the third brother of the two students who had died. The slow brother. The one who despite his soft head was unaccountably gifted at heat manipulation. He was the affinity anomaly Gerveault and Koria had spoken of.

Endicott remembered the power of the spear throw he had caught with Kennyth Brice's shield, the strength of blow he had taken to the head, the incredible, improbable heat that had been brought into being in the first murder.

I must not give him a chance to innovate.

With his left hand Endicott pulled out the dice that had been in his pocket and threw them at the giant's feet, innovating a familiar kind of probability, a cheap trick in any other context. The dice danced and spun on end under the third brother's feet. He looked at them for a moment as if fascinated, then scrambled and stumbled backwards. Eloise seized her chance. Ignoring the arrow in her shoulder, she leapt forward and drop-kicked him hard in the chest. He fell awkwardly into the trough, and before Endicott could blink, the water flash-froze with the big man still sprawled in it. Simultaneously the forge roared to momentary life, its coal igniting with a thunderclap. A sheen of ice covered the body of cloaked giant, but his head was just out of the water, eyes frozen and cracked. The saliva in his gaping mouth looked like clear glass with several foamy bubbles preserved in it like flaws in crystal. The error wave that blew over Endicott was tiny, as Koria's error waves always were.

Endicott saw nothing more for a moment. It was as if a light went out in his head. Then he found himself being pressed into a fierce hug by the two women. "Gregory is just out the door," he gasped, feeling the weight of exhaustion pushing him down. He sensed rather than saw that Eloise had left the hug, but he hung on to Koria, struggling to stay on his feet, pulling her into himself.

The heavy feet of the constabulary sounded down the hallway. A moment later Edwyn Perry strode into the room, a frowning, confused-looking Sir Christensen in his bright, polished armor flanking him on the right and Gael Guise behind them with an expression jumping between horror and triumph. Only Perry seemed to take the widespread death and destruction in stride. "There are bodies everywhere," he said casually, shaking his weirdly long neck. "I said to myself, Robert Endicott has got to be back in town."

Endicott looked up from hugging Koria to smile as best he could at the vice constable's lame joke. Then he clutched her even tighter and held on for a few more seconds before passing out.

She is safe, she is safe, she is safe.
Safe.

Chapter Twenty-Seven
The Lonely Wizard

When most people are surrounded by their family, they feel loved. I do not.

It is my belief that love is only a romanticized projection, the romanticization itself being a hypocritical denial of underlying needs. *Romantic* love? A deliberate or unconscious sop for the need for sexual fulfillment. The instinct to propagate the species translated into a glorious hallucinogen. For some a proxy for validation or power. For a few the pathetic proof they are needed for something.

Platonic love? Validation from a friend for some, an extra chance at survival for others. It is the emotional payout for the competitive advantage of having a team of peers.

Familial love? The instinctive need to survive as a species projected as a subjective feeling of belonging.

Why can we all not simply admit that every kind of love is a delusion lacking any real or objective value? Why did I not simply walk away from my father's cold, cold gaze?

But I did not. I walked around the balcony towards the stairs. All their eyes were upon me. My sisters' tearful, my father's angry. The other townsfolk were harder to read, closed off in the typical small-town reception of the outsider. I had *become* an outsider.

Becoming an outsider to insular, ignorant groups is a straightforward matter. Simply hold a different opinion than they do. It does not matter if the opinion is old or new, conservative or progressive. If it is out of step with that of the group, you will be an outsider. Know something they do not and let them suspect this? Outsider. Seen something they have not seen? Outsider. If there is anything different about you, and the collective holds any hate or frustration in their hearts, you will be treated as an outsider. Like the delusion of love the emotions provoked by an outsider are also a projection of something primal. Just not so positive. Perhaps the difference has to do with the primal needs being addressed: the former being about successful propagation, safety, and security, the latter about fear and a threat to survival.

I descended the stairs under their unfriendly gaze and approached the table on which they had laid my mother's body. Even under the blanket they had covered her with, it was clear what a tall woman she had been. She had been almost as tall as me. She had towered over everyone else, including my father. I remembered her long dark hair and her smooth, perfect skin. I gently folded the blanket down to her neck so I could look on her one last time.

She breathed still! Her face was red with heat, her breaths shallow and quick, slightly hoarse. How had I missed that sound, that movement until now?

"She still lives!" I exclaimed. It was an objective fact, obvious to even the most cursory inspection. Why had they covered her?

"Leave it be, wizard!" my father said roughly, throwing the blanket with imperfect gentleness back over her face. I have a name, but he would never say it. Not when he could insult me.

I turned and looked closely at him. His face was ruddy and angry. Liver spots darkened both cheeks in scattered, elliptical patches. His temples and forehead also showed the damage of sun and time, but his emotional state was the most damaged of all. He looked brittle. I moved my hand toward the blanket once more.

He reached out and grabbed me, trembling with the force of the effort to restrain me. To me it was nothing. I turned my head slowly towards him again, considering removing *him* from the building.

"Please!" It was my sister, teary and pleading. "She's had the fever for a week. The goose fever. Everyone knows she's on her last few hours."

Goose fever is a virulent infection, generally fatal, that presents as a wasting fever, often making its victims breathe hoarsely and honk like geese. It kills by dehydration. The few who survive are left devastated, usually reduced to a state of idiocy.

"She is still alive," I replied.

"There's nothing left inside!" My father let go of my hand.

I opened myself to the empyreal sky, looking past the blanket into my mother's ravaged body. It was not the kind of examination I normally engaged in, but I could see the disease clearly. It was in her brain, in her lungs, it was everywhere. She was dehydrated, burned up inside, but all that heat had not managed to kill the infection.

If I burn it out, will she die from the heat?

"She can be saved." No one said anything to this. "Get me a tub of water," I said. "Bring it here. Quickly!" I turned my cold gaze on the gathered townsfolk and they scrambled to obey. My father and my sisters stayed close.

"Can you really do it?" My younger sister's arms were wrapped around herself. My older sister clutched at her shoulders.

"Yes." It would be objectively simple, merely physical. I could do it.

There were several large tubs in the tavern, and one was quickly brought and filled up in moments by a bucket brigade. I ordered a final set of buckets to be arrayed around the tub and also filled with water.

"Stand well back," I instructed. Only my sisters and my father remained near. I did not know what my father's closed-off expression portended, but he did not interfere. I removed the blanket entirely and set it aside. My mother was dressed in a thick, white gown. I easily pierced the first veil and entered the empyreal sky, observing her temperature and calculating the energy I would need to raise it seven more degrees. I executed.

The water in one of the buckets froze instantly. A wind blew over the room, cold, then hot, then cold again. I hesitated for two long seconds as frost crystallized out of the air and drifted down. My mother steamed as the flakes landed softly upon her.

"Into the tub," I said, picking my mother up. Her skin was extremely hot. She was much longer than the vessel, and my sisters each hesitated over what to do but finally held her arms up as I lowered her upper body into the water first. My father lowered her legs in last, gently and carefully.

I executed a second innovation, cooling the water rapidly. Not even I dared manipulate her core temperature a second time. The array of buckets steamed, but the tub remained cold, almost painfully so.

We watched my mother as she lay, still and peaceful in the cold water of the tub. Her red face gradually turned a healthier shade. Her breathing slowed. She looked like an angel. With great care for her dignity, we raised her out of the tub, and my sisters and some of the other women removed her gown behind a blanket and dried her. They wrapped her in the old mourning blanket and set her on the softest and most comfortable chair in the tavern, brought out specially from the best guest room.

Later, much later, my mother's eyes opened, fluttering gently. We leaned forward to hear her speak.

"Blehh glsddhgsj bwhygdu wqdr."

☾

I had been arrogant. I thought I could achieve anything I set my hand to, that I could write a new chapter in the Book of Nature. I had tried to change what I failed to understand and thus I failed to control the change. I should never have come home. I should have stayed away and allowed nature to follow its course.

I wish I had never seen my mother's face as she lay dying.

There is no love for me anywhere. I know it for the delusion it is, and I do not deserve even that.

It would be better if I was forever alone.

Chapter Twenty-Eight

I Am the Lonely Wizard

"What have I learned?" Endicott opened his eyes, one arm under and around Koria's back as they lay in bed together, the slight weight of her not yet able to put the limb to sleep. "I've thought about that a little." He had thought a lot. And slept a little, some of it voluntarily. There had been questions and chaos at the Bifrost for quite some time. Most urgently there were the injuries to Eloise, Gregory, and a great many others who were eventually carted off by hand stretchers. As he had watched his friends carried away, he had wondered less what he had learned than what it had all meant. But he realized these questions were related.

"It isn't to be slower, is it?" she said softly.

"I don't think so." A strange numbness settled over him. It was as much emotional as physical. He blinked, trying to clear the unwelcome feeling away so he could consider Koria's question more clearly.

What was it I learned from Grandpa's letter? It came back to him, though not as clearly as it had been that night across the Line.

"No. Not slow. But not fast either." He almost laughed.

What if there is no lesson?

Endicott could not accept that. He reached through his deadened feelings for something better.

Love?

Embracing the feeling of love had helped him maintain something like an equilibrium on that awful night across the Line, but he was not sure it qualified as a lesson. He did not know the answer, so he spoke, hoping that in speaking he would unconsciously give voice to the answer.

"It isn't about somehow being in a state of graceful unity, as if that was realistic in the long term. It isn't even about fears or misplaced instincts or emotional trauma. Sometimes we do need to charge in, and we are never fully free of old pain or lessons. That is okay if kept in perspective."

"And what perspective is that?"

"I'm not sure. Maybe it is … humility. Maybe it's that we need to remember that not only do we not know everything, but we can't control everything."

Or anything?

"Perhaps." Koria rolled over and kissed him. "Though it's not really more of a lesson for you than it is for the rest of us too."

"I feel it, though. Even when I think I know what is going to happen, I end up reacting. I end up desperate. I know I shouldn't take such reckless chances, but I keep finding myself on the wrong side of events."

"I know what you mean," Koria said with a rich, knowing timbre.

"You?" Endicott sputtered. "You're always ahead of everything. You figured out that the cloaked figure was Eldred before I did."

Koria laughed. "Just in time to get trapped by him and thirty of his friends?"

"Hmm."

"It happens to everyone, Robert. If we are not humble, we will *be* humbled."

"I suppose so. Remember what I told you about Elyze Astarte and her plans for world domination?" Endicott asked with a snort. "She sure wasn't so confident trapped in the tower."

"How about Gerveault ever allowing Eldred into the New School? Or even his two brothers." Koria rolled away. She climbed out of bed, threw on a robe, and walked across the room, heading towards the baths. She was due in the Citadel. Endicott watched her go, not ready to stand up yet. She looked back at him, smiling wryly. "A lot of mistakes were made in the dynamics program early on."

And are still being made. Endicott remembered the trip to Aignen and how Heylor had almost flooded the town. He remembered his own far more numerous mistakes, errors arising from arrogance, fear, and impatience.

How many times do I need to learn the same lesson? What place in the Hall of Incompetence will I be awarded for my failure to remember what I thought I had already learned? Learning that in all our difficulties we don't know everything.

Endicott thought about it as he lay there on the edge of sleep. Koria had learned the lesson, though it had cost her the precious gift of childlike enthusiasm and joy. It had cost her that thoughtless leaping in the air.

He realized that people who claimed they had learned their lesson after one mistake were probably liars. No one learns the first time, unless that first time is unalterably damaging, unless the lesson is perfectly congruent with their personality, which would mean they did not really need it in the first place. Unless the lesson required only a thin and immaterial change.

The important lessons are so orthogonal to our nature and instincts that they are almost impossible to learn. It is as if they are invisible, inscrutable. We don't perceive them, and even if we do, we do not retain the memories. They slip away. What was it Eoyan said? "Repeated until it kills you." And what was that other saying? "What doesn't kill you makes you stronger." Maybe what doesn't kill you doesn't kill you until, well, it kills you. Or it doesn't kill you at all; it just alters you beyond yourself and, only by destroying the inner you, finally teaches the lesson.

I need to cheer up. We got him after all.

⦾ ▽

WHEN ENDICOTT FINALLY RETURNED TO THE BOYS' FLOOR, HE FOUND IT GUARDED BY two military school students he did not recognize. The tall, chain-mail-armored woman smiled at him as he moved slowly down the stairs towards her. Every single one of Endicott's muscles were debilitatingly sore. His hips were so stiff he could barely move his legs far enough to reach each step. "Tough day yesterday, Sir Robert?" she said.

Endicott noticed a small mole on her lip. "Tough three days." He limped past under her gaze and that of her silent male companion. As he shuffled ever so slowly into the common room, Heylor sprang up from the couch. Sitting in chairs opposite to him were Lord Jon Indulf and Jennyfer Gray. They were startled by Heylor's energetic and unexpected leap, but when they saw Endicott, they also stood up. Endicott was nearly knocked off his feet when Heylor collided with him. The skinny young man wrapped him in a tight hug.

"Robert, you're back!" he exclaimed unnecessarily. Endicott noticed that he had grown taller and was a little heavier than he had been. There was even a sparse tuft of brownish hair on his chin.

When did this happen?

Heylor was still short and lean but a little less so now. Unaffected by the sneaky passage of time was his essential nature. He stood just a step back from Endicott, still jittery, face transparently shifting between delight and chagrin. "Jeyn told me you sent him to help me. I almost drowned!" His expression shifted. "How did you know? Did you dream it? Was it as bad as last time?"

Endicott exchanged a look with Jon Indulf. The tall lord's demeanor was very different than it had been when they had first met in the late spring. He exuded a kind of tolerant exasperation towards Heylor. Jennyfer's smile was pure indulgence towards the edgy young man. The only things that had changed about Jennyfer Gray were her dimples, which seemed a little more noticeable.

"I'll tell you all about it, Heylor, but first I should perhaps say hello to our guests." He extended a hand to Indulf, who slowly and carefully shook it. Jennyfer gave him a hug, which was also on the careful side.

I look that bad, do I?

"We just came by to tell you that we will finish carving the Lonely Wizard poem this morning," Jennyfer said brightly. She reached for her notebook, which had been set aside in favor of hugging.

"You're carving it somewhere?" Endicott had known nothing about this.

Lord Jon Indulf winced marginally. "My family. I … requested permission for it to be inscribed in Mathematics Square."

Endicott pursed his lips. "O-kay. That sounds lovely." He evaluated Jennyfer. "I take it you came to some decision on the rhyme and meter?"

"You remembered even after all this happened." Jennyfer smiled broadly now. "I changed it again. The second iteration had more the form of an essay. It represented what I thought *The Lonely Wizard* was really trying to say. Between the lines. But that ended up feeling too pedantic, just as the classic form felt too artificial. So I went with this." She opened her notebook and removed a folded piece of paper, which she handed to Endicott.

Endicott took the paper with a feeling of trepidation. It reminded him of that moment back in the tower when he had read his grandpa's letter, of the state he had been in then, of the weight of fear he had labored under.

He's dead. Eldred is dead now.

The thick paper unfolded crisply. Endicott read the poem under the watchful gaze of its author and thought about it for a moment. He could feel the intensity of its theme even through the heavy numbness.

What will Gerveault think of this?

Endicott refolded the paper. "I can see your point, Jennyfer. I am glad you did not make it too opaque."

"Is it too obvious?"

Endicott slowly shook his head. "No … not too obvious. But I have read the original edition. Not many others have."

"Thanks." Jennyfer deftly retrieved the page from Endicott's hand. "Maybe it'll encourage Gerveault to try publishing the real story again. It's wrong to leave us with only the watered-down version."

Or the children's version.

Jennyfer and Jon Indulf left shortly after that, giving Endicott a chance to clean up and find some fresh clothes.

Someone had been in his room. A dark set of plate armor stood in the center of the small chamber, missing only its helm.

No. Not just the helm.

Four fingers were still missing from the left gauntlet. They had been sheared cleanly off. Endicott knew who had done the shearing, but he did not know who had cleaned, oiled, and assembled the entire kit and placed it on an armor stand in his room.

Sir Colborn Vig's armor. Who put it here and why?

He shrugged. There was a lot to catch up on, and no one seemed to be in a hurry to have him do anything, so Endicott took his time reorganizing himself. He even managed to oil his heavy riding boots before Heylor's eager dancing around made him realize it was time for lunch. He thought eating would be a good idea before he tried to make the walk over to the military school where Gregory and Eloise had been taken for medical treatment.

Heylor kept getting ahead of Endicott on the walk to the Lord's Commons. The energetic young man just could not seem to limit himself to Endicott's slow, stiff, short strides.

"You don't need to wear that anymore," Endicott said, pointing at the light, narrow sword Heylor wore on his right hip. Endicott had belted on Sir Colborn Vig's sword but only because wearing a sword was expected of him as a Knight of Vercors. He could not imagine he would have any need or use for it. If he did, he was unsure he would have the energy to draw it, let alone swing it in battle. Today the sword was merely ornament. Their soldierly escorts stayed a few paces behind them and did not join in the conversation. It seemed strange to have such silence from the military school after spending a week with Eoyan March.

Heylor ducked his head. "Koria said I should wear one."

"Koria said so? Okay."

"I ran away last night, Robert. Did you know that?" Heylor seemed to be trying to look at Endicott but could not quite meet his eyes. "The fighting started, and I just ran away. I'm a skolving coward."

"I did see it, Heylor. Look at me." Endicott waited until Heylor met his gaze. "I saw it in my heraldic dream, and I was *relieved*. I was glad you weren't killed outright, because that's what would have happened if you had stood your ground."

"But I left the girls!" he sputtered, tears flowing now.

A few other students, probably returning early from the break, turned to stare. "Heylor. You can only do what you can do. Besides, do you really think Eloise and Koria needed help?"

That proved to be an unwise question, for Heylor lunged forward and grasped Endicott's last clean shirt with both hands. "You thought so! You nearly killed Gregory and Eoyan to get back here as fast as you did. You accepted no surrender you were so sure. Stop lying to me, Robert! I *am* a coward!"

Endicott wrapped the struggling young man up in a tight embrace. "It's okay, Heylor. I didn't have any choice in the matter. I hardly even remember my part in what happened. It was like a dream." Heylor's struggles slowed. "In all our lives we will probably never be in a worse position than the one you and the girls were in last night. Give yourself some credit."

"For what?" Heylor whined into Endicott's now slightly soggy shirt.

"For not dying. Now straighten up." Endicott let him go, brushing off the wrinkles around the smaller man's shoulders. "Your time is yet to come, little brother."

They resumed the slow shuffle towards the Lord's Commons. Wiping his eyes with the back of his hand, Heylor spoke up again. "Are you still going to make me a sword?"

"Sure," Endicott affirmed. "I'll even emboss "Style" onto the blade just like you asked."

Constable Lynwen held the door to the Lord's Commons when they eventually arrived there. "Sir Robert," she said. Her gray eyes were very large and round. "You are expected in the Duke and Duchess's Lounge."

I am? Endicott turned around and saw that his two escorts had become one. Only the tall woman remained. *Oh.* One of them had run ahead.

Lynwen looked just as tall and young as she had the last time he had seen her, which was at the scene of the first murder. Those killings had been the worst ones, and under orders she had tampered with evidence to preserve the dignity of one of the victims. She had hidden the spear that had been shoved up Konrad Folke's bowels. At the time it had seemed important, but with the cloaked man gone, Endicott found it mattered much less to him.

I wonder if she felt just as over her head as I did at the time. He doubted she would appreciate being asked. "Lead on, constable."

With a flash of a smile and a brisk walk, she did just that. Lynwen quickly brought Endicott, Heylor, and their single military school escort to the private lounge in the Lord's Commons, where Endicott was surprised to see a reclining Lord Kennyth Brice and Vice Constable Edwyn Perry. Brice smoothly came to his feet and shook both Endicott and Heylor's hands. "Sir Robert. Heylor Style. Welcome."

Edwyn Perry pushed a high-backed, heavily padded chair over for Endicott to sit on and whispered, "Good to see you vertical, kid. Again," and patted him on the shoulder. Endicott looked over at Heylor, who was being helped to an identical chair by Constable Lynwen. Endicott observed Perry motion Lynwen towards the entrance once Heylor was seated. Her eyes seemed to linger for a moment on the skinny young man before she turned to go and stand beside the military school escort, which had reverted to two again.

Hmm.

It was always a pleasure listening to Kennyth Brice with his beautiful manners and mellifluous voice. He always gave his complete attention to whoever he was speaking with, and it was impossible to feel uncomfortable with him. He opened the conversation with pleasantries about Endicott's health and regrets that Armadale had once again troubled his citizens. Apparently it took time to expel the embassy of a country without hard evidence. They had found Terwynn dead in a warehouse near the Hanging Man, just as Conor had said, but they had not captured the two Knights of Armadale who had fled the alley when Endicott had fought and killed Sir Colborn Vig. Lord Quincy Leighton and Steyphan Kenelm had not seen the actual murder of Conor, and there were no surviving witnesses that could testify against Armadale except for Endicott. All this meant that the embassy still operated in Vercors.

Heylor, never one for sitting, could not contain himself. "But how? You had the body of that knight, Sir Colborn, that Robert fought. He is known as a Knight of Armadale, some kind of royal knight, whatever that means. Isn't that enough, along with Robert's say-so, to kick Armadale out?"

"Not immediately, Heylor." Kennyth directed a warm, sympathetic smile at the nervous young man. "Not without a trial. And a trial will not succeed without more evidence. You see, the ambassador claimed that Colborn Vig had broken with his government and acted alone. He was disavowed, and that is why we kept his body and his armor," he added, glancing at Endicott, "which would normally have gone back to the embassy."

So I was given his armor?

Heylor kicked his left foot out from under his chair. "What about the two protestors Robert fought at the Black Spear? The ones that lived at the Armadale embassy."

Those two. Endicott had almost forgotten the two bald ignoramuses. They had been the original protestors in Vercors with their misspelled signs and bizarre claims. It was amazing that events could become so bad that those two men could be forgotten.

"Halvor Vande and Iver Ottaker," said Edwyn Perry with a shake of his head, "did not live at the embassy. They are not even brothers, though they looked and acted as such. We investigated them. They immigrated from Armadale over twelve years ago and have lived uneasy lives here in Vercors. They have a long history of minor disturbances but nothing that resulted in imprisonment. They did visit the embassy on several occasions, one of which Sir Robert and Sir Gregory observed. The Armadale ambassador claimed they were merely expatriates visiting for legitimate purposes and that his officers distanced themselves from them after their radical attitudes became known."

"That almost sounds like it could be true," mused Endicott tiredly.

"Perhaps it is true," Edwyn Perry interjected with a sad smile. "Perhaps several things are true, as Lady Koria implied. Perhaps they really are just maladjusted, angry men unhappy with the new ways of the world. Perhaps at the same time they were also nudged by Armadale. Nudged and then set loose."

"The time for nudging has passed," Kennyth Brice continued in his carefully modulated tones. "All that happened before last night was in the nature of a covert war, gentlemen. But last night ended up being quite a bit more overt. From an evidentiary perspective you can imagine how last night's events change things, Sir Robert. We have most of the picture of what happened now, but we would like you to help us by testifying yourself."

"Of course," Endicott said. "But can you tell me if any couriers made it in from the Castlereagh Line yet? What happened to the soldiers in the tower? Is Eoyan March okay?"

Kennyth Brice laughed and turned to Edwyn Perry. "I told you that would be his first question, Ed." Turning back to Endicott, he adopted a more serious expression. "Yes, Sir Robert. A courier made it through a few hours after dawn. Apparently Sir Hemdale found the soldiers, as well as Elyze Astarte, safe in the tower where you left them. They reported very little pressure from the skolves after you departed. They asked that you, Sir Gregory, and Eoyan March be thanked for breaking the back of the skolves. Quite spectacularly, they emphasized."

"And Eoyan?"

"Eoyan March is stable."

Endicott closed his eyes. *Thank you.* He had other questions about the soldiers and friends he had left back at the Castlereagh Line but decided they could wait.

"He will not be travelling for some time, though." Brice gave Endicott a very direct look. "Leaving the tower like you did was very brave, very committed."

Very desperate. Thank the Knights I am not likely to be so desperate again.

"You did it because you had another one of those heraldic dreams. Was that it?" Edwyn Perry had produced a small hardback notebook from somewhere. He rested it on a small drinking caddy and began writing notes in it.

Endicott remembered the trial and Keith Euyn's lecture on heraldry there, of the more recent ducal announcement at court about public works. *Heraldic dreams and the duchess's program are transforming from a poorly kept secret to public knowledge.*

"Yes. It was a continuation of the one I had shortly before leaving on the agricultural mission."

"And it showed Knights of Armadale attacking citizens and soldiers of the duchy?"

"Yes."

"Did it show them invading the Vercors Ice Company building?"

"Yes."

Edwyn Perry scribbled furiously, his head askew on his long neck. "Sir Gregory Justice reports that you came across the Castlereagh Line and rode in one continuous journey straight to the Vercors Ice Company in under forty hours?"

"Yes. We stopped three times very briefly to change horses and resupply."

"That's normally at least a four-day journey, Sir Robert. Why were you so rushed?"

Endicott considered that he was speaking more to some form of legal entity than to Edwyn Perry, that Edwyn Perry could not possibly be so obtuse, so he kept his patience. "The heraldic dream was quite explicit. I believed that Koria, Eloise, Heylor, Merrett, Lindseth, the guards at the Bifrost, as well as anyone else who might be there, was in grave and immediate danger. As indeed turned out to be the case," he added pointedly.

Edwyn bounced the feather against his lip, leaving a blue stain there. "How could you be so sure?"

"It was the second time I'd had the dream. That made me pretty sure of the imminence of the danger. I dreamed it a third time on the way, which made me absolutely certain. And when we arrived, the situation was largely as the dream had indicated."

"I see. Fortunately we have direct testimony from survivors of the ... Battle of the Ice Company, if I may call it that. Everyone that you or Sir Gregory personally fought is now dead, you know. But some of the other soldiers from Armadale, as well as Lil Hilliard, Bat Merrett, and Jeyn Lindseth, have spoken at length about what happened. Jeyn Lindseth says you killed two Knights of Armadale who may have been trying to surrender. Is that true?" Edwyn's face was leaning forward, both his eyes comically wide open as he stared directly into Endicott's.

"Two Knights of Armadale outside the building may indeed have been attempting to surrender. I *think* they were trying to."

"So," Edwyn said, still staring weirdly, "why did you kill them?"

Endicott shrugged dully. "I could not accept their surrender. They had already murdered the gate guards. I knew that a significant number of their ... associates were inside the Bifrost, still working to kill or, as I now know, to kidnap people I cared about. There was no time to take their surrender, and I could not leave them with Bat Merrett, as he was seriously injured."

"What about Jeyn Lindseth? Could he have not taken their surrender?"

"No," Endicott sighed. "He was needed to rescue Heylor Style who, as a result, is now sitting beside me."

"And you also knew that from the heraldic dream?"

"Yes."

"I was in the river!" Heylor blurted. "Chased there by one of those Knights of Armadale." He jumped to his feet. "What is this, anyway? Why are you asking Robert all these questions? We'd all be dead if he hadn't rushed there and did what he did."

Kennyth Brice stood up and put his hands on Heylor's shoulders. "Be at ease, Heylor. We just don't want someone later accusing Sir Robert of being a murderer or a war criminal. This is the best alternative to a tribunal we could come up with."

"Or a day in open court," Perry added.

"*That* my mother would never allow." Brice nodded to Heylor. "And neither would I." he released the young man and gracefully sat down.

Edwyn put both hands up placatingly, one still holding his feather pen. "Just one more question. How much of the journey back do you remember?"

Endicott had to think about that for some time. He could only recall isolated moments of the journey, perhaps about half of it in all. When he reported this, Edwyn Perry exchanged a look with Kennyth Brice. "What do you think? Automatism?"

Kennyth Brice pursed his lips. "I would rather not have people focusing too much on that aspect of heraldic dreaming. We could simply go with a ... broad interpretation of the right of martial defense. Even absent the heraldic dream one of the knights was lodged in the doorway, indicating that the fight went into the building and might still have been going on."

"We might argue that he could hear the fighting within too." Edwyn squinted at Endicott. "Yes, that should work, legally speaking. But we could just as easily argue for summary execution, don't you think?"

"Both, I think." Kennyth nodded ever so slightly. "And both legal under the First Precept, since he is a knight." He turned back to Endicott and Heylor. "We are likely going to war, gentlemen. Our soldiers have been mustering since you left. The Armadale embassy is under siege right now."

Under siege?

"We need to make sure our records are complete. Even my father answers to someone." He stood up, smiling at Endicott. "You have done far more for us than we can repay, Sir Robert, and we will talk about that in due course, but right now I have to visit the Bifrost one more time and then observe the siege."

"Don't forget your magic shield," said Heylor, uncharacteristically making a deeper point.

Kennyth Brice smiled again at the young man and then was out the door without another word.

"I should be off as well," said Edwyn Perry, standing up. "Eryka will be expecting me at the Vercors Ice Company."

Endicott raised his eyebrows. "Not yet."

"No?" asked the vice constable.

"No."

"Not so fast," added Heylor.

Edwyn Perry grimaced and sat down. "You answered my questions, now I answer yours?"

"Right."

"Damn right," echoed Heylor.

Edwyn raised both his palms facing up. Endicott smiled and spoke. "What is your prevailing theory? Why was Eldred Derryg working with Knights of Armadale?"

"Simple enough once you know the back story," said Edwyn. "Eldred's two brothers die while in training at the Bifrost a year ago. Eldred is either not intelligent enough to understand, or doesn't want to understand, that their deaths are an accident. They died because they were careless. And because dynamics is inherently dangerous. Eldred leaves the New School when his class is suspended. He never should have been a part of it, but he had two brothers with talent, and I am told he had an unusual gift as well. He bounces around like a little seed in a big wheelbarrow until he finds a place in the Cult of Nimrheal, which is being funded by certain local business interests who have benefited from, shall we say, the older economy. They would like to see things slow down or even stop changing. Okay, some of that is unproven due to certain deaths, but we are still investigating. You'll be happy to hear, by the way, that we agree that Cyara Daere was not part of the conspiracy, and we have released her. We are just as sure that Eldred's hatred was encouraged by some of the other members of the cult and that as a result he began stalking students and faculty on campus. We think he had been at it for months but only recently escalated to murder for reasons unknown."

"Koria told you all that!" interrupted Heylor.

Edwyn Perry laughed. "Yes, she did, though as of last night we also had heaps of incontrovertible physical evidence to back it up such as Eldred's frozen body in the Vercors Ice Company warehouse. Some of the men who were with Eldred also appear to be members of the Cult of Nimrheal. Eryka Lyons is working to confirm their identities and affiliations even now. But that is less than half the story. There is another important player: Armadale. They have also been funding the Cult of Nimrheal."

Heylor whistled. "Was anybody *not* supporting the cult?"

Edwyn raised an eyebrow. "It was an easy group to suborn. The group, as its name implies, already attracts people who are resentful of development and in some cases of unsound mind. Since the cult has no formal organization, it was relatively easy to insert agents to help foment members' resentment into protest and eventually recruit a few of the more desperate or mentally disturbed into actions of a... more escalated nature. Armadale participated because they fear the commercial power of the new strain of grain and the future power of the New School as a driver of other innovations. Perhaps they also have some idea of how the new grain fits into the plans to annex the Ardgour Wilderness. With me so far?"

So far that was exactly what Koria and Endicott had discussed. Heylor was shaking his head and fidgeting from an unstable mix of anger and fascination.

"During the fight at the Black Spear," Edwyn continued, "Eldred steals your medallion because it reminds him of something he has forgotten about—the New School's facility at the Vercors Ice Company warehouse. He is injured in that fight, but by the time he has recovered, a certain agent of the Armadale ambassador, one Alfrothul Gudmund, has found out who Eldred is and approaches him with the idea of exploiting the boy's desire to avenge his brothers. In the course of their discussions Eldred reveals what he has remembered about the nature and location of the secret school, the Bifrost. He also tells Gudmund he has a medallion that can get the gates opened. Armadale wants to kidnap at least one of the dynamicists at the Vercors Ice Company warehouse and kill as many others as possible. We think Gudmund plans to burn down the facility on his way out. Eldred cooperates in the hope of some blood revenge of his own. When he sees Koria there, a girl from his own class, someone his addled brain can blame for his brothers' deaths, he is delighted to have a chance to kill her."

"So it's not all about the grain?" Heylor asks incredulously, face red.

Edwyn smiled thinly. "It's about money for some. Grief and frustration for others."

And Koria went there that night because she made an intuitive leap. She pieced together my descriptions of the giant and came up with Eldred. Then she came back to town early to pick up the painting to show me when I returned.

Endicott cursed himself for forgetting his own recognition of Eldred, lost when he was hit on the head that night at the Black Spear. "What happened to this Alfrothul Gudmund?"

"Well..." hedged Edwyn Perry, "uncertainty due to melted skin aside, we believe he was one of the men you roasted in their own armor last night."

Herald

ⓒ ▽

"I find all this interest in legality a little strange when so many people have died." Heylor was playing with a potato on his plate. He balanced the fork across the back of his hand while flicking at the end of the handle with his thumb. The fork flipped, shooting a fragment of the root vegetable high up into the air and then onto the floor with a squishy plop.

Endicott held out his hand palm up. "How many times do I have to ask, Heylor? You must stop doing this. Give me my knife back." He had only noticed its absence when he had turned to track Heylor's latest ballistic vegetable.

"Sorry." Heylor produced Endicott's glass-like dagger. "I mean I almost drowned. *You* could have died. If that was possible. Gregory was badly hurt, Eloise was hurt. Even Bat was hurt. Jeyk's dead. There must be thirty dead in all. And they want to do some legal tiptoeing around your killing a couple of the murderers."

Endicott was tempted to join in lamenting the absurdity of it all, but he knew very well that some would call what he had done murder too. The continuing anesthetic haze that clouded his mind and body made it difficult for him to decide how he really felt about what had happened. Perhaps it was just too soon.

There just was no time. Endicott had hardly thought at all during the battle. He had only acted.

"Well *I'm* glad you killed them!" Heylor said with some heat, his left hand trembling.

Even in his present fog, Endicott worried about Heylor's agitation. "It's over now, Heylor."

"Yes," Heylor said, taking an even bigger forkful of food than usual as his demeanor rapidly changed again. "I guess we now know everything. It'll all be fine from here on."

You mean besides probably going to war? Endicott left the thought unsaid. They had solved their immediate problems. The bigger one could wait.

As they entered the grounds of the military school a short time later, their two escorts still trailing at a short distance, Endicott felt almost strange to be there again after everything that had happened. They passed the training hall where he had spent so much time with Merrett, Lindseth, and Eoyan, and he remembered

Eloise sparring with him, and usually beating him, once with a very uncompromising message about Koria. He hoped to see the tall girl back to her fierce self again soon. As they turned left towards the barracks and infirmary, Endicott gazed up at the great shield-bearing statue of Heydron. This was where he had walked with Koria the first time they held hands. Now that seemed an age ago. He felt an enormous urge to touch her once more, but she was at the Citadel for the day, working on Lighthouse, out of the reach of whim or sentiment.

The urge to rush to Koria, to feel her soft, smooth hand once again, was strong but gentle. They passed across a green, fresh cut lawn and through the infirmary doors with Endicott still feeling that inexorable, if soft, pull. The shock of seeing Eloise, Gregory, and Bat in the infirmary was more like a sharp, visceral stab, like being knifed in the stomach. He had held Heylor back from rushing into the clean, white room, but craning his head around the open door, he experienced the apparition of them like a blow. Eloise's head was tilted to the right, bringing her large, aquiline nose into profile. Her eyes were closed. Endicott stifled the contradictory urge to burst into tears or give a wild shout at the sight. She lay peacefully, breathing gently, mouth relaxed in what looked like a faint smile. It just seemed all wrong.

Taking a tentative, silent step into the room, Endicott got a better view of Gregory in the bed next to Eloise and realized that her head was turned towards him. Gregory's face seemed contorted. Though also asleep, he was propped in a sitting position, presumably because of the wound to his ribs. Endicott imagined the bandaged chest under the sheets. It was easier to see Eloise's bandaged shoulder because it was above the white sheet someone had tucked her in with. A patch of blood had soaked through the bandage. The site of Eloise's blood shook the young man. It was only about an inch across, but from it there emanated a great wave of rage which rose and washed over Endicott, submerging his numb mind. He started to turn, ready to march on the Armadalian Embassy and do battle there. The simplicity of violence seemed preferable to the horror of seeing what he loved hurt. As he struggled to calm himself and breathe evenly, Eloise's eyes opened.

"You finally made it, stupe!" Her voice was no infirmary whisper. It was not the sound of someone facing impending morbidity, or how someone sick would speak at all. Endicott's knees buckled but he caught himself on the way to the ground.

A new tide of feelings swelled, thanks to her voice. Both Gregory and Merrett, who had also been sleeping, started awake, also affected by Eloise's exclamation. Heylor nearly jumped all the way to the high white ceiling.

"We rode as fast as we could, Eloise," Endicott replied ruefully. Despite his joy at her animated face and confident voice, he approached her bed cautiously.

Eloise made a dismissive gesture with her left hand. "Oh, I know that. Gregory has been going on and on about it, as if either of you were the heroes of the story. I mean, you should have gotten *here* sooner. It is stultifyingly boring, and I need some entertainment. I just have these two idiots for company. Bat hardly says a word, and my fiancé here keeps trying to hog all the glory."

"That's not true," Gregory protested in a whispery, barely audible voice.

"He's trying not to breathe too deeply," explained Eloise, "because his ribs were cut and a couple of them cracked. Apparently that hurts."

I wonder what you are going to be like in childbirth, Eloise.

"Look, look down there," whispered Gregory.

Eloise laughed at Endicott's evident confusion. "He means beside the bed. The courier finally got here a few hours back. She brought Gregory's shield."

The shield was there, leaning almost vertically on the far side of Gregory's bed next to Justice in its sheath. Someone had even polished it. Endicott opened himself to the empyreal sky and examined the shield more closely. It taken some microscopic damage in the fight with the skolves, and Endicott could see where the metal would fail at some point in the future.

"Take it," Gregory whispered. "Just until we're better."

"Sure." Endicott picked up the shield a little reluctantly and placed it at the foot of Gregory's bed. *At least I can repair it while he recuperates.*

"Take Justice too."

The suggestion felt deeply wrong. "No, Gregory. I don't think I can do that."

Get better.

Gregory tried to sit up but winced and lay back down. His eyes were watery. "You were like a god out there, Robert. Like an angel from Elysium."

"I don't feel like one today, Gregory."

"He can hardly walk!" blurted Heylor, his voice warbling between a whisper and a shout. "I think *I* could beat him in a fight!"

Gregory kept his eyes locked on Endicott. "You have to think carefully about how powerful you have become."

"No. It was more like an accident, Gregory." Endicott sighed, forcing himself to stand straight. "I was not in my right mind. It was the storm. And I knew the Bifrost inside out. I doubt I could reproduce what happened at any other time or place."

Gregory's head moved with painful slowness from side to side. "I don't believe you, Robert. You have been changed by all that's happened, and it worries me. There has been a cost." Gregory tried to reach out to grasp Endicott's arm, but his reach was short. "You killed those knights. You mustn't become like *him*."

Actually, the Lonely Wizard protected his *prisoners.*

It did not make for a comfortable comparison.

"Leave off, Gregory." Eloise's strident voice cut across Endicott's thoughts. "He did it for Koria and me."

Gregory shook his head at her, but Eloise continued. "It was for love."

At that moment a short, slight doctor in her middle years entered the room carrying a tray of medicines and bandages. She had dark, curly, shoulder-length hair, an olive complexion, and startlingly thick eyebrows. "Are these two gentlemen bothering you?" she asked in a firm, almost sharp voice.

Gregory and Eloise laughed and assured her there was no problem, but Merrett seemed to consider the question for a moment and then growled, "Yes. They bother *me*." He glared at Endicott and Heylor, and for once it was difficult to tell if he was just being sardonic. "But they can stay for now," he added grudgingly.

"Well," the doctor said briskly, "you all need to sleep anyway so they had better be on their way soon." She worked on Gregory first, changing the dressing on his left side. Endicott winced when he saw the wound. Heylor stepped back and sat on an empty bed, covering his mouth and breathing oddly.

The doctor made Gregory drink from a small bottle she produced from her pocket and then came to the foot of the bed to enter something on his chart. "Will he ... be all right?" Endicott whispered to her. After seeing the condition of the wound, he was worried about infection.

"We shall see," was all she said.

I'm so sorry, Gregory.

The doctor attended to Merrett next. The broad man had stitches in his head that needed checking as well as a lateral cut across his right ear that had nearly detached the whole organ. It was also heavily stitched. Despite the pain he must have been in, Merrett seemed proud of the wounds, and even called Heylor over to touch the coarse black threads in his ear. The sensation made Heylor's knees buckle.

"Blouse, I forgot to tell you you're supposed to go get Jeyn from the barracks when you're done here. He'll be sad if you don't go see him."

Sad? What an odd thing for Merrett to say.

Endicott looked past the man's grossly stitched ear and saw that his eyes were blinking sleepily. Gregory was already asleep.

The drink the doctor gave him.

"I'll go," volunteered Heylor with a sheepish look on his face. One of their escorts, who had lounged just outside the door, left with him.

"Are you sure you want this gentleman here while I treat you, Mrs. Kyre?" The doctor had made Eloise drink from several small bottles instead of just one and was about to pull the blanket aside to work on Eloise's shoulder.

Eloise smiled with her old predatory look. "He's seen it all before. We bathe together all the time, you know."

The doctor made a tutting sound, and Endicott's face turned instantly red. "That's the medicine talking," he said quickly. "We don't *bathe* together. Well, not often. I mean, not regularly."

"I see," the doctor said, though Endicott was unsure who she was addressing. "That's nice." She peeled the bandages away and nodded approvingly. "You're a fast healer, Mrs. Kyre."

"That's *Sir* Kyre, to you, doctor." Eloise's voice slurred a little.

"Not here you're not," the doctor said, finishing with the new bandages. "Don't keep her awake," she ordered Endicott as she left with her tray.

Endicott found a chair and sat down beside Eloise. Her long blond hair fell partly over her face, softening her customarily ferocious expression into something more ambiguous, something Endicott did not quite recognize.

"Take my sword. It's with my stuff," she glanced down over the side of the bed, "down there."

Everyone wants to give me their sword.

"Just until you are better," Endicott replied. There was no question of refusing this time. And he was sure that in Eloise's case he would not be accepting a deathbed gift.

"That'll be tomorrow or the next day. I won't be held back, Robert."

Endicott smiled.

"Thanks for helping Gregory," she said.

"How did I help?"

"By making him feel the hero. For helping him make it back to me."

The last of Endicott's emotional numbness evaporated. He felt ashamed. "I nearly got him killed."

"You respected his choice." Eloise's left hand reached out to touch his hair, his jaw, dropped down his shoulder and ran along his arm, and then finally found his hand. "You can't save everyone, Robert, not your enemies, not even everyone you love."

Endicott felt hot tears roll down his face. "But I was obsessed. I wouldn't stop. I did things. Gregory is right about me." He had told himself he was not sure how he felt about executing the two knights who had surrendered. He had felt numb, without shame. When speaking with Kennyth Brice and Edwyn Perry, he had not felt much at all, but he did now.

Eloise blinked slowly, but her grip was still there on his hand. "Would you do it again?"

Endicott could not answer her for a few moments. He tried to remember exactly how he had felt at the time. Righteous? No, self-righteousness was after the fact. At the precise instant of action, he had felt... Nothing? *Could I really have felt nothing, thought nothing beyond the doing of it?* His emerging shame urged him to say no, but as he thought more about it, he could not do so. After some thought he said "Yes," finally. *I would do it again. But please, I should feel something.*

"Ah."

"But when it happens, when I am absent of thought, when I... lose time like that, I think I might be mad."

"You just think that because you're a man and haven't grown up."

Endicott did not know what to say to that.

"Listen," Eloise whispered, fading now. "I owe you something."

"Owe me? I doubt that." He knew it was *he* that owed *her*.

"Yes …" Her eyes closed, then slowly, very slowly, opened again. "W-what?" she said, confused.

Endicott was unsure he should answer her, that he was keeping her awake when she should be asleep, recovering, but then he remembered that she was Eloise and would want to make her own choice. "You were about to tell me something, I think."

"That's right." Her words were thick. "I will tell you something only women know, Robert. Life's hard. It gives us hard choices. What have I been telling you since we met, stupe? Women learn this every month during their time."

That's the elixir talking for sure. Eloise never spoke of such things with him.

She continued her lecture with no trace of self-consciousness. "The smart ones anyway. What does blood teach us? You must accept the realities of the world. The blood doesn't stop just because you don't like it. Ask any woman. You think everything to death. You think, debate, feel guilty. Think some more. You stand in your own way most all the time. Only when you're mad with grief do you stop thinking and do what you know must be done. You aren't crazy then, Robert. You're meeting the real you."

Her hand went limp, leaving Endicott aghast.

The real me? A merciless executioner? A powerful, reckless wizard?

I thought I was love.

Endicott considered the question some more, not sure he accepted her theory, quite sure that Koria would not like it. That it was meant sincerely he had no doubt. It reminded him of something Sir Hemdale had said the first time they had crossed the Castlereagh Line.

This is where you find out who you really are. Out here, beyond civilization and rules. When no one is looking.

Endicott thought they were both wrong. He hoped they were. Eloise probably did not really mean he was a heartless murderer. She probably only meant that he had acted without deliberation and found strength because of that. At least Endicott hoped that is what she meant.

Violence is the last refuge of the incompetent.

Standing on the other side of the old proverb, Endicott could not help but feel it was just a little uncharitable. Perhaps even a little smug. He had *tried* talking with the protestors, but there had been no time to speak with the surrendering knights. Even with his heraldry, events seemed to outpace him. Even with his attempts to plan against the threat of the cloaked figure, he could not seem to consistently hold the initiative.

Because I have been ignorant.

It came back to the conversation with Koria that morning when they had agreed that no one could know everything. He certainly did not know enough. He knew so little that every event was a crisis and all choices were mortal ones. He had never known who his real enemies were or what they were trying to achieve. Endicott desperately hoped that was in the past now. He released a long sigh and looked at his three convalescing friends.

I am not love, but I do love.

Still holding Eloise's hand, Endicott stood, brushed her long hair out of her eyes, and gently kissed her forehead. "I love you, Eloise Kyre, Knight of Vercors." He looked over at Gregory, who was asleep with his mouth open. "I love you too, Gregory Justice."

Please, please get well.

"For the love of Knights, don't say that to me," whispered Merrett, not asleep after all.

Heylor returned a moment later accompanied by Lindseth now, and the two military school escorts were dismissed. Endicott strapped on Eloise's cold-forged sword, leaving her Colborn Vig's weapon in exchange.

For a day or two.

As they walked slowly out of the infirmary, Endicott related the salient points of his conversation with the two men.

Lindseth listened, expressionless. "Love. Some would say talking about it is indulgent, Robert. I would not agree. I think it is unfortunate that we cannot speak so honestly all the time, that our friends need to be injured before such truth is spoken."

"Really?" Heylor shot back, grinning. "Did you tell Merrett you loved him, Jeyn?"

That made the three young men laugh. Endicott was starting to feel a little better; a little more hopeful.

All will be well. Please. All will be well.

As they passed the great statue of Heydron again, it seemed to Endicott that all would indeed be well.

SSHHRRACK!

An instantaneous shockwave paralyzed Endicott. The jolt was not dissimilar to what he had felt when he had called down the lightning strike on the skolves. His entire body had spasmed sharply, right down to his toes, and only slowly released.

Heylor spasmed too. "What the Hati was that?" he exclaimed.

Lindseth had drawn both his swords but was clearly confused. Evidently he had felt nothing.

"It was a huge shock wave," Endicott explained. "A massive breakdown in the empyreal sky." He thought quickly. "I bet it was from the siege of the embassy. Gerveault must have gone down there and given them a taste of his mathematical precision." As if in reply a thin wisp of black smoke began to rise in front of them, but it was much closer than the embassy. Whatever had caused the shock wave was somewhere on the Academic Plateau.

Ignoring the protests from his still sore legs and the systemic weight of physical and mental lethargy that had plagued him all morning, Endicott began jogging in the direction of the smoke, struggling to avoid tripping on Eloise's sword which hung from his hip or bashing himself with Gregory's even more ponderous shield. The sounds of screaming pierced the air. Two students raced by from the direction of the smoke but refused to say what they had seen. Heylor and Lindseth, fresher and less encumbered, passed Endicott and sprinted ahead towards the column of smoke.

"Help!" a female voice screamed from Endicott's left. It was Annabelle Currik. Endicott stopped but quickly saw she was uninjured. She clutched his arm, weeping uncontrollably, and pointed towards Mathematics Square. Endicott squeezed her hand and continued into the square. At first nothing seemed amiss. A group of people were milling about randomly, looking almost casual until Endicott realized they were in shock and did not know what to do, who to help, where to go, or perhaps even where they were.

Then he spotted Heylor on his knees, shaking beside a smoking heap of … something. Lindseth stood nearby, head turning from side to side, face rigid. The smell was overwhelming, like spit-roasted pig but different, more burned than any pig had ever been. Endicott staggered painfully over to Heylor and Lindseth, avoiding collisions in the milling crowd with difficulty. The heap was a person, had been a person. But whoever it had been was unrecognizable now. The corpse was charred all over, melted in places and in others burned almost to ashes. Only a step or so away from the ashy ruin lay a blackened notebook.

It was Jennyfer Gray's book of poetry.

Endicott realized that his vision had narrowed. By force of will he opened his eyes wider and took in the rest of the scene. Tools for carving stone lay scattered all about. A bucket lay in a twisted pile. The mathematics monument had also been seared. A tremendous thermal event had taken place. Still standing not far from the monument was the corpse of Lord Jon Indulf, a dark spear rammed up through his body, its butt somehow jammed into the stones of the square to hold him upright like some hellish scarecrow. For the second time in a matter of days Endicott remembered the image in the original edition of *The Lonely Wizard* of the Methueyn Knight left murdered by Nimrheal in the wilderness.

Carved on the stone at the base of the monument, now stained by the bubbling grease of a horribly immolated human being, was the last poem of Jennyfer Gray. It read:

> "Fear me!
> I have an eye
> As keen as
> Expectation,
> Sharpened by evidence
> Undulled by narrative,
> Bereft of
> Feeling.
>
> See Me!
> I have fled
> Across the Line,
> Alone with skolves
> And bones of angels.

Looking for facts,
Blind to wisdom.

~~H~~elp me!
I am Alone
Even here,
~~H~~ome,
Back across
The Line,
With you.

Save me!
I have denied
Love,
Friends,
Family.

I have made myself
Alone."

                    .Adapted from *The Lonely Wizard*

                               by Jennyfer Gray

Roughly slashed in a diagonal through the middle stanza of the poem was a newer message:

"The price is paid."

Gregory's shield slipped from Endicott's hand and fell on the cobbles.

BRAAHHHH.

Chapter Twenty-Nine.
I Am the Furthest Herald

"It *is* Nimrheal!" Heylor cried, still shaking beside the smoking pile that had once been Jennyfer Gray. Lindseth had decided there was no one to fight and sheathed his swords. He crouched over Heylor now, speaking in a low voice as if comforting the stricken young man. Endicott thought about Heylor's outburst even as people continued milling about, crying, screaming, and arguing, saying strange, unaccountable things as they emerged from shock. He tried to ignore what they said as he considered the problem, but this proved difficult. He had heard words like these before but had never expected to hear them from students or faculty of the New School.

"That's what we get! That's what you get! The price. This is the price. The demon comes for a reason!"

There was a scuffling sound, a slap, and hysterical yelling.

"Who's he coming for next? Who?"

Endicott thought about Armadale. This horrible new event would undoubtedly further the dissent and unrest that Armadale craved. It would affect many people, but after Jennyfer Gray and Lord Jon Indulf, none would suffer greater injury than the community of the New School. Did Armadale have their own wizard? Was he or she *this* powerful? It made no sense. If they had such a resource, why not use this wizard in the raid on the Bifrost? Endicott doubted he could have prevailed over whoever had done this. Of course he had been a fool to believe that Eldred could have been responsible for all the murders. The first murder especially. The second had involved much less energy and might have been perpetrated by Eldred. There had been no ritualistic element to it, no spear. He understood at last that there had been two murderers, not a single killer merely refining the method.

So obvious now.

And also obvious was that this wizard had to be an independent party. This wizard was a Nimrheal player unaffiliated with Armadale. Otherwise he or she would have broken the embassy siege by now rather than waste energy on a sideshow. He or she would have burned the entire Bifrost complex to the ground.

"Did we do this Robert? Did we bring this on?" Annabelle Currik was back, clutching at him, shaking him out of his thoughts. She looked years older. Her long blond hair was limp and looked suddenly gray.

Ash?

"You would know better than me, Professor." The words were out his mouth before he could stop them. They came instinctively, from a place below thought, and the question that followed surprised him even more. "Is the grain truly safe?"

She let go of him and stumbled back a few steps. "What? The grain? Safe from whom?"

"Yes, the grain" Endicott repeated, calmer now, rational thought processes catching up with instinctive impulse. He still thought that Conor, despite his obvious sincerity, must have been wrong. But now he had to ask. "I mean safe for consumption. How well was it tested? Do you know?"

She composed herself. "It was very well tested, Robert. Very carefully." Perhaps the question had helped compose her. "In any case how could the invention of a new strain of grain ever justify *this*?" She waved at the burned and melted corpse of Jennyfer and the horribly mutilated scarecrow that was Jon Indulf.

"It couldn't," Endicott said, not sure if he felt better or worse for answering. In some ways, despite his association with the New School, it would be so much easier if there were something simple he could blame for what was happening. "Even if there is something wrong with the grain, it could not justify this. This is madness." He looked at the carved poem.

An awful price for an act of poetry. An awful asymmetry of violence.

It made no sense.

Why kill these two? They were never involved in the agricultural project. They were just writing a poem about the Lonely Wizard.

"The Lonely Wizard," Endicott whispered, struck by a new idea.

"What?"

Endicott grabbed Annabelle's shoulders. "You have ash in your hair! You were standing close by! What did you see? Was Gerveault here?"

The professor screwed her eyes up tight. "I don't know what I saw. It happened too quickly."

Endicott kept his hands on her shoulders and his eyes on her face, but said nothing more. He desperately needed to know what she had witnessed but recognized she was still in shock. She needed time to compose herself. There was movement around him, some of it the disjointed actions of the crowd, but a new order in the background movements suggested that order was being imposed.

Endicott continued to hold Currik and watch her face. Finally she started speaking again. "I saw an ... incandescence. No, I saw two. Two flashes of light, one immediately after the other. Then I felt two waves of heat." She opened her eyes and locked her gaze on Endicott. "One was the monument, the other was ... Jennyfer." She screwed her eyes up again and started sobbing.

"You are doing wonderfully, professor," Endicott said in as soothing a voice as he could with his nostrils full of the overpowering smell of his friend's charred flesh. "I know it's hard, but it will help enormously if you can tell me absolutely anything you remember."

Her jade eyes had regained some of their fire, but her forehead was creased with parallel wrinkles that looked to Endicott like a set of standing waves as she struggled to remember. "I heard someone scream. I think ... yes, it was Jon. It was Jon screaming. He was running. At a tall man, very tall, in a cloak and a hood."

Too tall for Gerveault? Perhaps, perhaps not. Gerveault was by no means short.

"The tall man killed him and—" She burst into tears again. Endicott waited patiently for more details, but Annabelle had not seen the cloaked figure's face, and she couldn't say for sure how tall he had been. She thought she had seen a sword belted to his hip and a spear, perhaps two spears, in his hands. Endicott looked up from comforting her and saw that the constabulary had finally arrived at the center of the square after dispersing the crowd. He made a gesture to one of them and gently handed Annabelle Currik to her, explaining that she had seen the perpetrator and needed to be protected at all costs. Then he reached down and picked up Gregory's shield again.

Sir Christensen had also arrived. He was speaking quietly with Jeyn Lindseth and a drooping Heylor Style. As usual Sir Christensen wore shining plate armor and his face was impassive and, unlike Sir Hemdale, unreadable. He was a perfect blank slate, his suave demeanor giving no sign of any urgent or troubling agenda. There had only been that one moment at the Bifrost when Sir Christensen had frowned as if confused.

About what? About everything maybe.

There were no senior members of the constabulary at the scene yet. With the embassy siege and the ongoing investigation of the Battle of the Bifrost, internal resources were stretched thin. Endicott approached Christensen, Jeyn, and Heylor. "I have a thought about who might have done this and why."

Heylor whirled to face him, face ugly with tears. "Skolving Nimrheal did it!"

Jeyn Lindseth said nothing, just stared at Heylor sadly. Sir Christensen's face was harder to read. He was calm. "Who would that be, Sir Robert?"

Endicott's right index finger went up, though he did not realize this. "It's only an idea. I am not certain, so let me walk you through it. I'm thinking aloud. Okay, who has the power to do such a thing? Who has a history of doing what they think is right, regardless of the consequences? Who is so utterly confident of their own abilities and assessment of what is needed that they could do this?"

"You," whispered Heylor.

Endicott flinched, almost as if he had been hit by that jolt of power again.

Touché, Heylor.

"Really?"

"Robert helps people," Jeyn said in his soft voice.

"Sorry," Heylor muttered, looking down. "I know you wouldn't hurt innocent people. I don't know why I—"

"Thanks for that, Heylor," Endicott interjected before his nervous friend could dig himself into a deeper hole. "I was with you when this happened, remember?" He shook his head, smiling despite his irritation. "Shall we continue? Who is connected to the New School? Who understands what we have done here and the long-term implications of our innovations?" He raised his index finger again. "And who is also deeply connected to the Lonely Wizard story? Who is so connected to that story that seeing this poem could have enraged him to madness? Nimrheal didn't commit this atrocity. The Lonely Wizard did."

Sir Christensen frowned. "There is no Lonely Wizard. It is only a story, Sir Robert."

"Aha! No, it is not." Endicott set his jaw. "The Lonely Wizard was based on events that actually happened. It was written by Gerveault. About himself."

"Let's get him!" exclaimed Heylor, vibrating in place.

"That makes no sense," said Sir Christensen incredulously.

Heylor bounced on his feet, irrepressible again. "I bet you haven't read the original edition. It is much darker. He kills his own mother. After scrambling her brain."

Jeyn's face also proclaimed skepticism. "Gerveault is the brains behind the development of the grain. And I cannot believe he could be capable of this. I've watched him train you, Robert, and you, Heylor. He is a deeply humane and caring man."

That stopped Endicott like a punch in the stomach. He *so* wanted an answer. "Yes, you're right. Gerveault wouldn't do this. Something is wrong here. But what?"

"Let us go speak with Gerveault anyway." Christensen's smooth voice was as calm and unreadable as ever. "Perhaps he can at least help us understand what is going on."

It turned out that Sir Christensen had recently escorted Gerveault back to his offices from the embassy siege, which meant they did not have far to go to find the professor. They had only to walk to the entrance of the building that currently cast its shadow on them. It was literally within a spear's throw of the murders.

Why didn't Gerveault come out and investigate? He was right here.

"We should take him by surprise," suggested Heylor as they started ascending the stairwell of the mathematics building.

"What?" all three of his companions exclaimed together.

"Were you not just at the square!" Heylor shouted. "He is too powerful. If we give him a chance, we're all going to die."

Heylor had a point, but Endicott could not imagine simply clubbing Gerveault over the head with Gregory's shield or the butt of his sword when the old man answered the door. That was not how students treated their professors. And after what Jeyn had said, he could no longer imagine Gerveault as the murderer. *But still.* His hand went to the hilt of the entropic sword at his hip. It felt slippery.

My palms are wet.

Christensen put his foot down. "We are going to talk to him," he said firmly. "That is all."

"Fine," muttered Heylor. "I'll just stand behind him you while we talk."

The door to Gerveault's office was closed. Endicott knocked on it. There was no answer.

"Let me try," Heylor said and squirmed in front of Endicott to knock more sharply. Endicott scowled down at him. They waited. Finally Endicott put his lips next to the door and shouted, "Professor, we need to speak with you."

There was no answer. Heylor tried to open the door. It was locked.

"Stand aside, gentlemen."

Endicott pulled Heylor away from the door and led him a few steps down the hall and out of the way. He held Gregory's shining shield in front of them both. Jeyn stood in the hallway on the other side of the door. Sir Christensen charged forward, back foot making the stone floor ring as he launched himself at Gerveault's heavy, hardwood door. With a loud crack the door fell straight back—*it must have been laterally barred*—and fell with a tremendous crash onto the floor of the old man's office. The bar flew across the room and landed sideways on Gerveault's desk, where it knocked a book and some papers to the floor.

Gerveault sat in his large padded chair, a look of pure surprise on his face. He blinked at them three times and then declared, "I have to go to the Citadel."

What?

Heylor stepped past Christensen, and standing just beyond the doorway, proclaimed, "You're not going anywhere, Lonely Wizard, until you answer some questions."

"What?" Gerveault looked genuinely surprised. Endicott and Lindseth shuffled through the wreckage of the door. As they got closer it became apparent that Gerveault had simply been sleeping. The older man's hair was disheveled, and a small patch of drool glistened high on the leather chair back.

This does not seem right.

"Something terrible is going to happen if I don't get to the Citadel immediately," Gerveault said. He began to stand up, but Heylor rushed forward to block his path. "Move out of the way, Mr. Style," the exasperated professor barked, half out of his chair.

Endicott foresaw a rapid descent into farce. "Something terrible has already happened, professor."

Sir Christensen raised his right hand towards Gerveault. "He's right. We need a moment with you."

Gerveault looked at the four of them, taking in their distress, and looked down at his broken door and the bar lying sideways across his desk. "Very well." He settled back in his seat, motioning Heylor to step back and watching the rest of them through thick gray eyebrows.

Sir Christensen glanced at Endicott. "It is your theory."

Endicott squared his shoulders. "Jennyfer Gray and Jon Indulf were killed just minutes ago in the square outside this building. Their killer, a tall, cloaked, hooded figure who unfortunately escaped, used two nearly simultaneous acts of thermal manipulation of such magnitude that one of them may have involved an extradimensional breakdown. Jennyfer Gray was immolated. Jon Indulf was impaled on a spear. The scene was a replay of the first Nimrhealesque murder. They were killed while carving a poem on the Heydron monument with the Lonely Wizard as its subject."

"Knights," the old man muttered, swallowing hard.

"Where were you during all this, Gerveault, I mean professor?" Heylor snapped, passing an acorn-shaped paperweight from hand to hand. It was heavy enough to be used as a blackjack. Endicott had not noticed Heylor pick it up. He could only hope his light-fingered friend would not leave with it. Or hit the old professor. "You had to feel it. The breakdown was incredible."

Gerveault frowned at the golden metal acorn and the menacing way in which Heylor was handling it. "For your information, Mr. Style, I was deep in a heraldic trance. I did feel a ... jolt from within the trance, but I must now assume it was folded into the events I was attempting to interpret." He looked from Heylor to Sir Christensen, then to Jeyn Lindseth, and finally to Endicott. "You think *I* perpetrated these murders? Is that your brilliant theory?"

Endicott did not believe the theory at all any longer, but Heylor's eyes were red and building. He was clearly desperate to cling to the theory. "You *hated* them writing a poem about the Lonely Wizard, didn't you?"

"Well, it *was* annoying."

"You—" Heylor began again, but Endicott grabbed him roughly by the shoulders. "He didn't kill anyone, Heylor. Look at him. We knew he didn't do it before we even got here."

"Thank you kindly, Mr. Endicott. Now I should tell you what I herald—"

"But there *does* seem to be some connection to *The Lonely Wizard* story, professor," Endicott said, interrupting the professor himself.

"And you're the Lonely Wizard!" shouted Heylor.

Gerveault glanced contemptuously at his accuser, almost cracking a smile, then blew out a huge breath and turned back to Endicott. "Yes, you are quite right, but not in the way you think. I really must get to the Citadel right now. *Right. Now.* I am *not* the murderer, as you have just acknowledged. Now will you trust me, please? I will explain on the way."

"Yes." Endicott did not have to think about it. He did trust Gerveault. He was his grandpa's friend. Gerveault was *his* friend, or as much a friend as a professor can be. Sir Christensen nodded his agreement, as did Lindseth. With some reluctance Heylor put the golden acorn paperweight down and stepped out of Gerveault's way.

They could not help but pass through the square on their way to the Citadel. Gerveault's face paled at what he saw there. "So it's true," he whispered. Looking up with haunted eyes, the old man spoke louder, "We have to hurry now. I need all of you." He looked at Sir Christensen. "See if you can persuade the constabulary to send as many constables as they can spare to the Citadel as fast as they can."

Endicott caught a glimpse of Edwyn Perry and Eryka Lyon conferring amidst a growing crowd of constables. Perry cast a quick questioning look at Endicott, but the young man had no opportunity to reply. He tried to ignore his stiff muscles and the weight of Gregory's shield. He was barely managing to keep up with a sixty-year-old man on a slow run. Sir Christensen broke off and stopped to speak with Eryka and Edwyn. Heylor watched Gerveault out of the corner of his eye, which the old man soon noticed. "Yes, yes, I know what I promised, but wait for Sir Christensen to rejoin us. I only want to explain this once."

A short while later the tall knight caught up with them. He seemed to be barely winded.

"Fine," Gerveault said, puffing almost as hard as Endicott. "I will tell you everything now. Be calm and listen. Promise me that." After a chorus of assent he continued. "I am *not* the Lonely Wizard. The story is not about me. It is about Keith Euyn. After his mother died, Keith went off into the Ardgour Wilderness for several months. When he came back, he ended the war with Armadale and founded the dynamics school that predated this one. He allowed me to write the book for many reasons, one of which was to help the next person like him avoid his mistakes."

"But Keith is *old*! He's got to be ninety!" exclaimed Heylor.

"Eighty-two," Gerveault corrected.

Heylor's face scrunched up. "That's really old. And he's been sick most of the time we've been here." Unsaid was the obvious question of how such an old, sick man could wreak such destruction.

Gerveault laughed mirthlessly. "You have no idea what you are talking about. None. Keith Euyn was both wizard and Deladieyr Knight, perhaps the greatest of both. If even a fraction of his old strength remains, he will be more powerful than any of us."

"There are other people like Keith?" Lindseth's slow, soft voice barely carried over the sound of Endicott's labored heart pounding in his own ears. "Both Deladieyr Knight and wizard?"

"Knight and wizard both, yes. Very, very rarely. Powerful, arrogant, and rigidly literal far too often. The book is for them. Or rather the original edition was meant to be. But let me get to our current predicament. Keith is ill, but not physically. He is suffering from … a mental disease of the elderly. It has made him not himself, or rather, which may be worse, it has at times made him who he once was in his youth, but now mad with pain."

"It's all pretty Knights-damned obvious, though, isn't it?" declared Heylor stridently, apparently forgetting the skepticism he had heaped in Gerveault's direction moments earlier. "Keith is the Lonely Wizard. Keith is the murderer. How come you didn't tell us?"

Endicott could not help but scowl. The idea that Keith Euyn was the Lonely Wizard he could easily accept. After Gerveault, Keith was the likeliest candidate. But Keith as a murderer still did not seem right. Keith Euyn, founder of dynamics, acting in the role of Nimrheal was preposterous. It was against everything the man stood for.

Can dementia change a man so?

"Well, Gerveault?" Heylor persisted bitterly.

"Heylor." Lindseth said in a low, admonishing voice.

"Heylor what?" asked Heylor. "We've been running around looking for a cloaked man practically since the terrible night, and Gerveault here has known the entire time."

Gerveault's brows furrowed and his eyes hardened. "Oh, I see, it was obvious the whole time, was it? Because every woman or man who gets old, who suffers from dementia, is a potential murderer! Yes, that is what always happens. That is why we have so few old folks' homes: it is not because people die young, it is because *old* people all end up murdering each other. Think again, Mr. Style. This was not at all an obvious or easy conclusion to come to. There were many variables that confused matters until now."

"Hmmm," Heylor said grudgingly. Not much time passed in silence before he asked, "Such as?"

Gerveault's disgust was palpable, but he *did* like explaining things. "It did not help that there seemed to be a swelling of protest against progress, against the new grain, and against our New School altogether. It did not help that so many people have been acting as if they really wanted Nimrheal to come back. It did not help that it was Keith who was asked to herald the first murder. It did not help that Armadale has been operating in the city, and we suspected a wizard from that country. It did not help that I even considered the possibility of a wizard from Novgoreyl playing some long game associated with the treaty. It did not help that there was a second cloaked figure, Eldred, who I now think acted as mimic to Keith. It did not help that Keith was with me when the second murder happened. Even if I had suspected Keith, which I did not, the murder of Lady Gwenyfer would have eliminated him as a suspect. The whole business reminds me that I. Much. Prefer. Mathematics." The old man shook his head. "I have been wrong again and again about this."

I know the feeling.

"So why are you so sure you're right this time?" Endicott asked. Gerveault had seemed to know as soon as he woke from his dream, before he had seen what happened in the square.

"I will tell you. Returning from the siege of the embassy of Armadale, I decided to try a specialized form of heraldry. I visited the Bifrost last night and was surprised to see the level of carnage there. Armadale has been engaging us in a covert war for some time. I did not like this sudden change in tactics. Real war seemed to be coming. I have seen war, and I know it to be the refuge of the ignorant. I thought perhaps I should try once more to see a way through that did not involve storming the embassy and igniting a fire we might not be able to put out. So I attempted a heraldic trance. That is a technique of the far heralds which you have yet to learn, gentlemen. It is a state halfway between heraldry as you know it and a heraldic dream. But I was very surprised when the locus of events took me not to the embassy but to Keith Euyn's estate. A folded paper sat on Keith's desk, though the man himself slept. Then I saw him thrash awake from some nightmare, screaming, and run madly around his house rather like young Robert here when he had his first heraldic dream. In the midst of this Keith suddenly went deathly still. After a time he moved again, but now with a stately calmness, tall, and easy. He dressed and walked to the Mathematics Building, to the floor above me, belted on his entropic sword, Likelihood, and donned a dark cloak. He pulled up the hood and collected two dark spears from the corner. He descended the stairwell only moments after I barred the door to my office. Keith walked to the square where he saw Jennyfer Gray, Lord Jon Indulf, and the poem they had etched in the stone."

"So you saw what happened in the square," said Christensen. The statement seemed unnecessary until he continued. "We must stop Keith Euyn."

"If we can," replied Gerveault, huffing.

If.

The story of Keith Euyn's heraldic dream chilled and horrified Endicott. He imagined himself having another heraldic dream and becoming yet another crazed murderer, a third cloaked figure. The idea seemed alarmingly plausible. Then he shook himself out of this reverie. There were far more urgent matters to consider. "Tell us what you saw at the Citadel before we get there."

"I saw Keith going to the Citadel and murdering the duke, duchess, and the entire Lighthouse planning committee."

Koria is at the Citadel. And Bethyn, Deleske, Davyn, and Syriol. This is a nightmare.

Fear and anger, sick and painful, shot through Endicott. He felt the wrongness, the slightly off-center flow of adrenaline, the narrowing of vision that he had felt too often since coming to the New School. It made him forget his exhaustion, but it also threatened his reason.

Again.

That Endicott had been through similar trauma in the recent past did not make this new problem easier emotionally. Saying that he felt extremely stressed and concerned over the possible murder of the friends he loved and the woman he loved even more would scarcely do justice to the deep, searing feelings that coursed through him. No one else could truly understand how Endicott felt. It could not be measured or explained, imagined or described. Endicott himself did not understand it despite all the thinking he had done about it. What was happening to him was as indescribable as it was authentic. Nevertheless Endicott had learned to manage his response to a certain degree, to take the indescribable and angle it towards something quantitative, something measurable. Towards an action.

How do we kill the great man?

∞ ▽

The grand entrance to the Citadel was unchanged. The guards were still on duty just as Gerveault had said they would be. Nothing had happened yet. A visiting Keith Euyn would have been considered unremarkable. The great man would have passed through the Fool's Way unhindered, even fully armed. And he had, only moments before.

Christensen spoke softly to the guards as Gerveault, Endicott, Lindseth, and Heylor pressed on. Christensen would race ahead with the guards through little-used, little-known posterns and back routes while Gerveault's party took the steps of the Fool's Way past the eight wide-open gates and their snippets of advice carved so beautifully into the polished stone floor. As he passed the etchings once again, Endicott felt anger and frustration.

"Know the cost"

Who would want to know this *cost?*

Endicott remembered the square and the burned ruin of a brilliant and beautiful woman, the horrific and humiliating murder of her companion.

What did we do to pay for this nightmare?

It was worse than a nightmare. Their enemy was not some foreign agent or local malcontent seeking fictitious justice. It was not even about the grain's economic effects on the world or the dark possibility that it was poisonous to more than just skolves. Their enemy was an old friend, a person who had helped found institutes of learning. Their enemy was apparently a man who had simply grown old and sick and could no longer withstand the trauma of glimpsing the future. Their enemy was both their friend and a victim.

But what had Keith Euyn seen?

Endicott remembered the panic, the mania, of his own heraldic dreams. He remembered the pain of foreseeing something terrible that had not yet happened, the simultaneous, soul-crushing feeling that it had already happened, and the exigent, unstoppable, hysterical need to keep it from happening. It was a destructive and self-perpetuating cognitive loop.

What had Keith Euyn dreamed? What had triggered it?

He hoped the old man could be pulled out of his hysteria, that further violence could be avoided. He remembered the square and the smoking puddle that was Jennyfer Gray, the scarecrow that was Lord Jon Indulf, and shuddered. He wondered if reason was possible after such violence. He also wondered if his own actions the night before against the surrendering knights had been a small step in the same terrible direction.

It must not be so. This must not be who I become.

He let that vow settle over him. It calmed him just a little.

Suddenly they caught a glimpse of the cloaked man ahead, then lost him around a corner, the first turn in the predominantly straight Fool's Way, the turn that marked the end.

"We should just attack!" hissed Heylor.

Endicott glanced sideways at the skinny young man. Heylor was shaking, but a pregnant bead of sweat gathered on the end of his narrow nose. *He shakes from his own fear and anger.*

"I agree," said Endicott softly, his perception narrowing again and only tenuously within his control. He was ready to set aside thought and conscience, dulled already from exhaustion. He was impatient to act, but he remembered the conversation with Koria this morning. He remembered the vow he had just made. Those thoughts gave him pause.

I've been wrong so many times. What if by talking we can break Keith out of this episode of madness?

What if by talking we save everyone, including him? We must try.

They rounded the corner and saw a tall, hooded, cloaked man striding through a doorway ahead. He held a dark spear in his right hand. The cloaked figure passed into the throne room and marched towards Sir Christensen and a column of guards. Another group of guards were still racing in from a side door, making a great, jangling noise. They had outraced the confrontation.

Just.

Not far away, elevated by a few steps, sat the duke and duchess on their thrones. A small group of lords and citizens clustered just below the steps. The cry of a baby reverberated off the high stone ceiling of the throne room. The sound felt like a knife in the soul, sharp, unwelcome, horrific.

What intimate meeting are we interrupting? Parents presenting their new baby to the duke and duchess?

With a frustrated growl and a surprising burst of speed, Gerveault raced ahead into the throne room.

"Keith, stop!" Gerveault roared as Sir Christensen drew his sword and the duke and duchess both rose from their great chairs.

The cloaked figure did stop. A moment passed in frozen silence, and then he lowered his hood with his left hand. It *was* Keith Euyn. The great man, his thinning hair wildly askew, turned and looked back at Gerveault with blazing eyes. Endicott could not decide if the eyes were wilder than normal, but they were certainly wide. Professor Euyn had always been intense.

As he raced forward, Endicott saw motion in the far distance, behind and to the side of the duke and duchess. It was Koria! She had entered the formal throne room from the smaller, informal meeting room at the back. Davyn was behind her. Even from the far side of the vast room Endicott could see the big man's eyes, large as teacups. Endicott stopped next to Gerveault and motioned violently to Koria.

Go back and bar the door!

But he knew she would not obey. Her quick mind would rapidly process the unfolding confrontation. She would try to help. But in this battle, she would be missing her best knight, Eloise. Endicott also missed the tall, fierce woman. But she and Gregory had been spent at the Bifrost in what they had thought would be their last battle. Thinking about them back in the infirmary was like another knife in Endicott's soul.

Perhaps it is better they are not here.

He wondered what Davyn would do when he fully grasped the situation. The fat boy would not fight. He hated fighting, felt it solved nothing, had no intrinsic honor. In his visits to the military school he had participated in physical training but refused even to pick up a weapon.

He won't fight, but he won't run either. He will try to help without fighting.

"You think I will be talked out of this, Gerveault?" Keith Euyn's voice echoed, reverberating from the high ceiling of the vast chamber.

Gerveault spread his hands out. "These are your friends, Keith! If you would just recognize them, you would see that. Open your eyes!"

Gerveault's plan had been three-fold. First to get Sir Christensen and as many soldiers as possible into the room ahead of Keith Euyn. If necessary, they could slow down or even stop the old man and their presence would at least warn the duke and duchess and Lighthouse team. The second part of the plan was to try to make Keith Euyn recognize what he was doing and end the episode without violence. The more time that passed the better the chances of this. The constabulary would trickle in eventually, and the Lighthouse team might use the time to escape. The third part of the plan, the part they hoped to avoid, was for Gerveault to suppress the great man's dynamics so that he could be brought down by force of arms. Endicott did not know exactly how that suppression would happen, though he wondered if it could be brought about in something like the way Koria had resisted Eldred's thermal manipulation.

They had gotten the idea of how to suppress certain dynamic innovations from the dice experiments when they found out it was not only possible to interfere with someone's manipulation but that it was often less expensive in energy to do so. If Heylor was trying to manipulate a one-one-one roll, an effort of suppression was as inexpensive as Heylor's manipulation was improbable. The leverage of probability was usually with the suppressor. But to succeed, one would have to camp in the empyreal sky and have virtually perfect timing and concentration. Koria had practiced defending against Eldred's attack before ever facing it. She had used Endicott's temperature estimate data to do so. This was a very different matter. No one knew what Keith Euyn would do or could do, or what the cost would be. Was Gerveault up to the task?

Keith nodded slowly to Gerveault. The duke walked onto the stairs, the duchess only a step or two behind him.

Oh, thank the Knights. He recognizes his old student and friend.

Endicott's right hand was slick on the grip of Eloise's still-sheathed sword, and his left dripped as it held Gregory's amorphous shield. His heart pounded. He tried to see the whole room, to see Keith Euyn and Sir Christensen, to see the duchess, Koria, and Davyn off to the side, but his vision kept narrowing. Beside him Heylor's teeth chattered.

"I know who they are!" shouted the great man.

Thank them.

"But the furthest herald sees a different war!"

Furthest herald?

With astonishing speed Keith Euyn hefted and ferociously hurled his black spear. It passed a half foot over a guard's head on a dead flat trajectory into the duke's chest. The old man was flung backwards and nailed in a standing position to the back of his throne.

The duchess screamed. She had been knocked aside by the flying body of her husband, and was sprawled on the stairs, staring at his pinned corpse.

Eleanor!

Davyn covered his face with his meaty hands for a moment before setting his shoulders and charging towards the crowd of onlookers, who stood frozen in a state of shock. Koria rushed towards the duchess. A blinding incandescence flashed, and at almost the same time, an electric jolt struck Endicott. Two guards to the left of Sir Christensen and one guard on his right burst into brief flames.

They had no time to scream. Their companions did that instead. A wind raced through the throne room carrying alternating waves of hot and frigid air and the now sickly familiar porcine smell of roasted human flesh. The frost pattern on the floor was different than anything Endicott had seen before, a weird mix of angles and circles, repeating oddly and unpredictably.

He must be using different transforms than I know.

The baby cried again, somewhere in the crowd below the thrones.

"Hati damn it!" Gerveault hissed, face screwed up in concentration.

So much for suppression.

Endicott drew Eloise's sword. Then he became aware of his friend beside him. Heylor had not been himself since he had seen the remains of Jennyfer Gray and Jon Indulf in the square. At first he had been jittery and nervous, blaming himself for running away the night before, but after that he had become enraged. Heylor was angry enough to get himself killed.

How many of my friends will die today?

As Endicott leaped forward, he acted thoughtlessly. With all the strength he had, he pushed Heylor with the back of his sword hand, sending the shaking young man sliding backwards on his behind across the polished limestone floor.

Stay alive, Heylor Style.

CRACK!

The instinctive maneuver probably saved both his and Heylor's lives. With a sharp explosion of sound Keith Euyn abruptly materialized into the space Heylor had previously occupied, swinging his great sword, Likelihood, in a wide, whistling sweep, but missing both young men.

Probabilistic teleportation?

Endicott skidded to a stop, attempting to reverse his charge and engage the great man. Instead of doing that, he was blown off his feet by a massive detonation.

CRRRACKKKKKKKKKKKKKK!

Only the blue-white afterimage allowed him to piece together what must have happened. A sheet of lightning-like electricity shot like a jagged and angular curtain from Gerveault towards Keith Euyn, then abruptly changed directions before it could reach the cloaked figure, exploding into the limestone near Endicott's feet. Endicott tried to rise but found he could not uncurl or move. His muscles were locked in a powerful, painful spasm. But he could still see and hear. Gerveault tried reasoning again. "Keith! You can't keep this up! You'll kill yourself and the rest of us!"

This had no effect on the great man. Without a word he stepped forward to strike down Gerveault, but Jeyn Lindseth leapt smoothly into the fray, his two swords moving independently. Gerveault scrambled out of the way leaving Lindseth and Keith Euyn to duel at a nearly blinding pace. Endicott could barely follow the older man's moves, but he could hear Likelihood's high-pitched screaming and whining. Lindseth was not as impossibly quick, but he was fluid and poised and made excellent use of both his weapons.

Keith Euyn suddenly leapt forward, stepping hard on the mid-section of the still prone Heylor Style and somehow pinned both of Lindseth's swords against his body, then smashed his forehead down on the younger man's face.

"Keith, stop! You are *not* Nimrheal!" Gerveault bounded recklessly forward and grappled with his old friend before the deluded wizard could deliver the coup de grace to the half-stunned Lindseth. Keith Euyn proved faster, striking Gerveault in the jaw backhanded with the pommel of Likelihood. Both Gerveault and Lindseth collapsed to the ground. Keith Euyn paused, seeming to consider who to kill first. Endicott struggled desperately to rise, but his muscles were still locked in contraction.

Is he going to murder Gerveault while he's helpless?

The clatter of metal-clad feet rendered the question moot. Sir Christensen and a handful of the surviving guards charged towards Keith Euyn, and the old man turned from Lindseth and Gerveault to face the charging mass of armed men. A wall of blue fire shot out to meet them. It parted around the Sir Christensen but engulfed the guards. Gouts of fog and frost, waves of heat and prickles of electricity washed across the room. The error field from a rapid series of innovations was a hazard all in itself, even if it was nothing compared to the manipulations of the Lonely Wizard.

Endicott saw the great man's lightning in the empyreal sky. He felt the jolt as Keith Euyn broke through to Elysium, which was the only place he could summon the power to make lightning in an enclosed building on a sunny day. He did not understand the mathematics or precise techniques that were being used, but he saw how it might be possible to interfere with the great man's manipulation of even so vast a supply of energy. Disruption of such fine work could be done without complete understanding

Possible, but unspeakably dangerous. And not *possible without complete, perfect focus.*
This reinforced an aspect of the plan they had made.
We must keep him busy!

Struggling against his own overloaded nervous system, Endicott heaved himself off Gregory's shield and regained his feet. The guards had lost theirs and collapsed, smoking, to the floor, but Sir Christensen now traded heavy blows with Keith Euyn, their footwork carrying them back towards the thrones.

Endicott's body began to recover. He found Eloise's sword, picked it up, and took in the situation. Eight of the guards were dead, grossly burned in two heaps of smoldering bodies. The two survivors seemed frozen in shock. One of them turned towards the duke and duchess, gaping wordlessly, while the other stared at his sword where he had dropped it on the floor. Gerveault was rolling around on the floor, clutching at his mouth, Lindseth lay motionless where he had fallen, and Heylor was curled up around his own abdomen. Only a few moments had passed since the fight had started. Davyn cradled a baby in his arms and was pushing a woman towards the door. Koria was with the duchess, trying to help her off the stairs.

Endicott saw and felt the breakthrough into Elysium. It was fast, like a jab. On instinct he pushed on the improbability.

Lightning should not flash here!
CRRRACKKKKKKKKKKKKKK!

Lightning did strike. The binding blue flash manifested instantaneously near the door, bifurcating and shimmering, part of it exploding against Davyn's back and flinging him into the woman and through the doorway.

Did I help? Or did I just kill my friend?

Shivering, Endicott lost his grip on the empyreal sky and could only see with his eyes. Davyn was gone, thrown into the other room.

Did I do any good at all?

He could not tell.

The last refuge of the desperate is when you know better but have no choice except to do it anyway.

Endicott searched for Koria. In the smoke and after glare he could not make out what had happened to her.

Koria!

Endicott came fully back to himself and, gripping sword and shield, ran towards Keith Euyn and Sir Christensen. The exchange of blows between the two tall men was ferocious, but the older man was more powerful and at least as fast as his much younger opponent. He flowed from stance to stance, graceful and functional, always in a position to strike with maximum efficiency. And with each blow Sir Christensen's sword was further marred and notched. The tall Knight's left cuisse was dented, and he limped badly. Endicott raced to close the distance but could only watch as a wide lateral blow from the great man cut straight through Sir Christensen's sword and halfway through the younger man's left pauldron, hurling him from his feet with a crash.

Endicott raised his shield, deflecting the end of Sir Christensen's blade which had flown into the air, spinning wildly forward once parted from the rest of the sword.

BRAAAHHHH!

An instantaneous bite of cold came and went almost too fast to feel at all, its full force bypassing Endicott, who otherwise it would have frozen and killed.

Koria?

Endicott accelerated despite the thermal pinch and crossed the last few paces between him and Keith Euyn. As he bashed the great man with Gregory's shield, Endicott saw, for an instant, Koria's satisfied expression at the far end of the room, where she had paused in the act of pulling the duchess towards the small door there.

Thank you, love.

Endicott and Keith Euyn tumbled to the ground, sliding on the blood-slick flooring beside Sir Christensen. Keith Euyn was up first, springing to his feet with a sickening and unnatural speed. He brutally stamped down on Sir Christensen's injured leg.

Did I just hear it snap?

An image of Eoyan March flashed across Endicott's mind. Keith Euyn kicked Sir Christensen in the helm and tore the remains of the tall knight's sword from his hand, only to hurl the broken blade towards Koria and the duchess, who were not yet through the door.

No!

Endicott's vision narrowed instantly and locked on the spinning sword. He innovated instinctively, ignorant of the cost and uncaring. The sword spun to the left as if seized by an invisible hand and smashed into the wall beside the door, narrowly missing both women. He struggled to shrug off a wave of cold from the innovation and rose to face Keith Euyn, who had whirled back in his direction. The first blow from the old man was so fast and hard it nearly knocked Endicott's sword out of his blacksmith-strong hand. He stepped back, retreating from an octogenarian who appeared to be faster, stronger, and more powerful than everyone in the room, perhaps more powerful than all of them together. Endicott's exhaustion, his mental and physical fog, had been pushed aside by the exigency of events, but it still clung to him. He struggled against hypothermia and fatigue to find either the rage or the peace he needed to match the old man.

Eleanor.

Koria.

Love.

Only a quick sidestep and roll of his wrists kept his sword in his hands and his head on his shoulders as Keith Euyn advanced and swung his blade with lightning speed.

Eleanor.

Thinking of her made him think of his own, faceless, unremembered mother. Thinking of her made him remember the mother of the Lonely Wizard.

"Would your mom be proud, Keith?"

The old man stopped at once, sword held high, face tight, veins standing out. His lips moved soundlessly for a moment. Then he shook his head violently and grated, "If she knew the future, she would say it would have been better if we were never born!"

With an incoherent scream, Keith Euyn came on again, striking with a series of vicious overhand blows. Endicott caught them with his sword, more easily than before, more calmly now. He stopped struggling and gave himself to the fight, and this time did not lose time as he had at the Bifrost. Time simply became meaningless to him. What happened outside the fight did not register. A series of detonations around him were ignored, did not affect him. He saw the great man's movements milliseconds before they happened, and as he had done only briefly a few times before, he instinctively used this to his advantage, trading blows with the old Knight with lightning speed and precision. For Endicott at least, the fight had become effortless.

But in a strange way it also became meaningless. So little thought and so much instinct made all time irrelevant. There was no memory, only the moment and the few milliseconds before each move. Endicott was not perfectly made for a mental space like that. He could not maintain such a state indefinitely, and after some indeterminable period, he looked out. He had to know what had happened to the others. In that moment he saw himself and Keith Euyn standing, swords locked, within a circle of cracked and blackened rubble. Koria and most of the crowd were gone, and the door was closed behind them. Endicott smiled in relief. His love had escaped. The great man did not smile, felt no love.

It was almost a stalemate now. They were both fast, they both held entropic swords, and they both held nothing back. Endicott smiled again, satisfied with himself, with who he was and what his efforts had wrought. He knew time was his ally. He might die, would probably die, but more soldiers would come soon. The constabulary would arrive. The thoughts were heartening, but perhaps unwise, as they also gave Keith Euyn time to act. The great man's eyes narrowed, and he stepped back and gestured sharply with his left hand. A sheet of blue-white electricity flashed into being and just as quickly evaporated from perception, leaving another eerie afterimage in Endicott's eyes.

Gerveault?

The young man had no opportunity to find out who had helped him this time, for the great man blinked and raised his sword high above his head. With a high keening whine, Likelihood came crashing down. Endicott raised his shining shield, angling it just slightly off the norm.

BRAAAHHHH.

Likelihood bounced back from the shield and hit the great man in the face, cutting him vertically from his chin to his hairline. "Aaahgg!" Blood sprayed out in thick jets. As Keith Euyn staggered back, Endicott attacked, swinging laterally so fast the air shrieked. Somehow the taller man blocked most of the blow, taking only a partial cut on his hip. Endicott brought Eloise's sword around again and into a high guard.

I can end this now.

He thrust his sword at the great man's bloody face, but despite his terrible wounds, Keith Euyn flicked Endicott's thrust aside and turned his sword around the young man's twice, rapidly, in an almost feline motion controlled from his wrist. Endicott's blade was pushed roughly to the side and then viciously pounded right out of his grip on the great man's follow-up stroke. The young man raised his shield with both hands to block the blow he knew was coming.

BRAAAHHHH!

Endicott found himself on his back, alive. Keith Euyn was striding towards him, this time uninjured from his sword's deflection off the entropic shield.

"Keith, no!" Gerveault's roar was followed by an electrical discharge that flew faster than the eye could see from over Endicott's head towards the great man, but it missed him, jagging sideways into the two surviving guards, who still stood frozen in shock. They were blown off their feet and fell yards away, rigidly spasming.

Keith Euyn gestured, and Endicott heard an explosion behind him in the direction of Gerveault. The great man took his final steps towards Endicott and paused as he raised Likelihood over his younger adversary. Endicott did not flinch.

I won't close my eyes.

Likelihood vanished. Keith Euyn looked up through streams of blood at his hands, confused. Likelihood reappeared, thrusting towards the great man's chest and into it. The blow was too fast and too sudden to evade.

Endicott looked to his right towards the hilt of Keith Euyn's sword, towards Heylor who was holding it with both hands. The Lonely Wizard fell to his knees in front of Heylor and Endicott, blood spraying from his mouth as he tried to speak. "I saw. The furthest herald…"

Endicott did not wait to hear the dying words of the great man or the end of the prophecy, if that is what it was. He was already on his feet, running towards and through the back door, desperate to see Koria, Eleanor, and Davyn.

Koria and an attendant hovered over the duchess' prone form, which lay just within the room. Three armed guards stood beside the door, eyes wide, still not entirely certain the fight was over. Endicott skidded onto his knees next to Koria and looked down at the duchess. Her eyes were fluttering, and the skin of her face and hands had never looked so thin and transparent. Her veins and her lips were almost the same blue-purple color as the bruise spreading out from her right temple. She breathed in sharp, shallow gasps. Endicott felt he also could barely breathe.

If only I could help her!

She could have been his mother. That Eleanor was not his mother hardly mattered since he had never known his own. It hardly mattered. Eleanor had been supportive, helpful, and loving. It hardly mattered that she was not his mother since her face was the only one he knew when he thought the word. Endicott had little doubt that Eleanor had taken a risk, likely against advice, in her closeness to him and the other students. She had taken a chance for him. She had trusted him. And now she lay wheezing and blue. Dying.

I can save her.

But he could not. Koria saw his face and reached over the duchess to hug his stiff body. His arms stuck out to the side, his fists white from clenching. For all his intelligence and sharp instinct, for all his occasional flashes of power, Endicott's grasp of subtlety was weak. He could destroy quite easily but heal not at all. Sobbing with Koria over Eleanor's gasping form, he knew better than to try. He had just fought the man who, despite being far more talented and knowledgeable, had destroyed his own mother in such an attempt. Endicott could not have been more desperate or more in tune with his absolute powerlessness as he hovered over the Duchess.

On a few occasions she had called them her boys. His matching gasps for air, his visceral pain, his bottomless misery told him that he *was* her boy.

ⓐ ▽

How do you celebrate a victory in which so many others died? How do you celebrate when your adversary was once a mentor and a friend, and one of the greatest of men? What emotions do you feel when a celebration is also a mourning, when both are the same, when anger and fear cannot be distinguished from joy and thanksgiving?

The duke was dead. The duchess was gravely ill, probably dying. Most of the guards had died of immolation or electric shock. Lindseth was wounded, though he would survive. Propped in a chair, he winced as Bethyn administered crude first aid. Gerveault had also survived but had been rushed to the infirmary, his injuries serious, their full extent still unknown. Endicott had not seen what Keith Euyn had done to Gerveault or what had made the last explosion. He could only hope that Gerveault had been able to deflect the blow at least partially.

Sir Christensen still lay on the floor, but he was conscious now. The sound Endicott had heard was only his cuisse snapping, not his leg. The leg was bruised and swollen, but he would be able to walk. He would certainly need to. To begin with he insisted on briefing Kennyth Brice in person about what had happened, and he wanted Endicott to go with him. "Lord Kennyth always spoke about the feather pen you caught out of the air that would have hit his mother," he gasped as Endicott helped him to his feet. "Kenneth keeps it in his chambers and...looks at it from time to time. He...likes you, Sir Robert. It would be a comfort to him if you were with me."

He would go.

Davyn had not yet woken, might never wake. Endicott had found the big man on the floor, being comforted by Syriol, with blood leaking from his ears onto her lap. His shoes had been blown right off his feet. Endicott could hardly believe Davyn could even be hurt. He remembered when Davyn had been slapped and how the pacifist had simply accepted it. He hoped Davyn at least knew that the baby he sheltered had lived. Whatever his fate Davyn had done what he would always do.

Better than dying a monster. Better than going insane and betraying everything you had lived for.

He remembered Keith Euyn's cryptic prophecy, if that is what it had been. *The furthest herald?* He may as well have spoken gibberish. Traumatized, demented, and violent, there had been no point to the great man's final desperate acts, no meaning to them at all. Endicott had once thought the skolves were imaginary monsters, out there beyond human understanding across a near-mythical Castlereagh Line. The skolves were nothing compared to men.

No wonder Grandpa was happy to send me across the Line.

Men were the real monsters.

Nimrheal?

Conor had thought Nimrheal should come back. Some of the people protesting the grain thought so too.

Nimrheal.

Eldred thought he could revive the gospel of Nimrheal: punish progress and avenge mistakes. Keith Euyn wanted to do Nimrheal's work too. That seemed to have meant killing the duke and the person most responsible for the New School, the duchess.

Who needs demons when we have human beings?

"Still vertical, kid?"

"What?" Endicott found himself holding Koria now. The speaker, Edwyn Perry, had surprised him. His eyes had still been roaming the room, but he realized he had not really been seeing it anymore. *I am in shock.* It was obvious, even to him in that state, that he was not the only one. Constable Lynwen was standing nearby, staring at Heylor, a notebook upside down in her left hand and her mouth open. *The last time she saw us was at the interview with Kennyth Brice.* It seemed like that meeting had happened days ago, but it had only been hours. So many things had been better then. So many people had still been alive.

Almost alone, Edwyn Perry was unaffected. He smiled at Endicott. "You're still alive. Again." He started walking towards the body of the Duke. "I'm glad, kid."

Endicott tried to say something to the vice constable, but his immobile lips and tongue told him he was not ready to speak yet. He held more tightly to Koria, overwhelmed.

"I can't believe your little thieving trick saved the day." Deleske still had a dry edge to his voice, but it held a little wonder now as well. "You're finally a hero."

Heylor's head was bowed. It was his moment. He had saved everyone, but he did not look ready to celebrate. In fact he looked miserable. His face and chest were covered in droplets of dried blood, but they were not his own. They had come from Keith Euyn. Heylor alone had heard the old man's final words after Endicott had raced away to find Koria and the others.

"So what did the great man say?" Deleske asked, either not reading or not caring about Heylor's state of mind.

"I don't … it didn't make any sense." Heylor frowned and his mouth moved as if he was fighting to say or not say something.

"Why don't you leave him alone?" Endicott unwrapped himself from Koria and whispered in Heylor's ear, "Thank you."

It was all he could come up with, even if it was so much less than Heylor deserved. But big words and backslapping hardly seem right after what had happened. The throne room was a shamble. Bodies lay everywhere. Even the duke was still impaled on his throne like a ghastly centerpiece in a banquet from hell.

Endicott could not have been more eager to know what Keith Euyn had said. He needed to understand what the great man had dreamed, what he thought he had learned in that dream, and what had triggered it. He desperately wanted to know how the dream related to the Lighthouse project and the grain. More than anything else he wanted to know what Keith Euyn had *failed* to learn, the failure that had made him a monster. Or perhaps what he did learn, and in learning was changed, deformed.

But now was not the time. He thought of Eleanor lying on the floor before the attendants had torn her away from him and Koria. He thought of her blue lips and the sound of her gasps.

Deleske, who had missed all the fighting, who had disappeared at the first sounds of combat, followed Endicott's gaze. "What narrative are we going to put around this tragedy?"

Endicott looked at him sharply.

Who gives a skolve's turd?

Endicott did. But right now he was just exhausted, overwhelmed, and very, very angry.

Are we going to make up some moral about dementia and old age, about reckless youth, the dangers of madness and heraldic dreams, the arrogance of acting without restraint to change the world, or the many hangman's ropes of traumatic memory? What actually mattered here?

"Narrative? I wish I knew," Endicott managed to say.

But something more needed to be said, something better than denying that he cared. "I don't know how we can make up a narrative when we don't really understand what motivated Keith Euyn or if motivation even applies to the mad. And even if we knew why he tried to kill everyone here, I don't know if narrative would be important. What's more important? What happened or the story we make up about it? The duke is dead. Eleanor …"

He stopped, unable for a moment to continue. "She may soon follow. Davyn too, perhaps. Those facts at least are measurable. The dead can be counted, the damage can be categorized and logged." He choked. "I-I don't need to make up a narrative to know how bad all this is."

He stopped for good then, realizing that more talking was pointless for now and that he should stop moralizing, realizing that he could barely see through his own tears. He wanted to go home, he wanted to see his injured friends, and he wanted to go back to school, all at the same time.

Koria's hand slipped into his. "Everything matters, Robert. The facts matter. Yet acts of love and joy, Davyn's for instance, are not quantitative events. That is why we need narrative. It tells us what events mean. It tells us what value we should put on the facts. Our happiness—the happiness of everyone still alive—is part of a choice. Human beings have a gift we can give ourselves, a wonderful gift. We can find meaning in events. And through that, joy in our lives."

And love.

Koria smiled as she finished. It was a forced smile, but genuine, nevertheless. "Without some kind of positive narrative, some kind of charity in how we view the world, we are all in danger of becoming the Lonely Wizard."

Endicott's jaw involuntarily clenched.

What. Positive. Narrative.

He loved Koria. He knew why she had said what she did, but in the aftermath of so much death, he feared he might never recover the optimism he had brought with him to the New School. Or perhaps he was just not as clever as Koria and could not pretend…

The off-kilter sounds of heavy, armored boots interrupted Endicott's muddled thoughts. It was Sir Christensen limping towards them, the hitch in his step echoing loudly through the devastation of the room. It was time to go to the embassy siege and speak with Kennyth Brice.

It was time to tell the new duke his mother was dying.

"ANY FOOL CAN CHANGE THEIR MINDS. SAGES CANNOT CHANGE ANYTHING THAT CANNOT BE CHANGED, AND ONLY A FOOL WOULD TRY."

Selected people and places

⚭ WITHIN THE STORY OF THE LONELY WIZARD

The Lonely Wizard, a Deladieyr Knight and wizard of immense power

Sir Ameleyn Forteys, a Deladieyr Knight

Aungr, Marshall of the Army of Engevelen

Feydleyn, squire to the Lonely Wizard

⚭ BRON- A SMALL FARMING TOWN WITHIN THE DUCHY OF VERCORS

Lord Latimer, agent of the Duchess of Vercors

Meycal Endicott, Robert's dead father

Finlay Endicott, Robert's grandfather

Grandma, Robert's grandmother

Arrayn Endicott, one of Robert's many uncles

Deryn Endicott, one of Robert's many uncles

Aunt Ellys, one of Roberts many aunts.

Ernie, an old man who works at the Bron elevator

Paul, a young man who works at the Bron elevator

Mair, a young woman who works at the Bron elevator

Glynis, a young woman who works at the Bron elevator

- **N**YHMES- *A SMALL CITY WITHIN THE* D*UCHY OF* V*ERCORS*

    Laurent, a farmer

    Aeres Angelicus, owner of the Nyhmes Registered Seed Office.

    Terwynn, agent of Lord Glynnis

    Conor Karryk, an old bum

- **A**IGNEN- *A SATELLITE CITY TO THE CAPITAL OF* V*ERCORS*

    Adara Torrinton, Chief Engineer

- **V**ERCORS- *THE CAPITOL CITY OF THE* D*UCHY OF* V*ERCORS*

    The Duke of Vercors

    The Duchess of Vercors, Eleanor Brice

    Lord Kennyth Brice, the heir apparent to the Duchy of Vercors

    Eryka Lyon, chief constable

    Edwyn Perry, vice constable

    Cyara Daere, a woman, former student at the New School

    Myfan, a woman who works at the Vercors Ice Company

    Jeyk Johns, a guard at the Vercors Ice Company

    Vard, a young man

    Lynal, a young man

    Syriol Lindseth, a young woman, cousin to Jeyn Lindseth

    Lord Arthur Wolverton, commander of the military school

- **D**ELADIEYR K*NIGHTS*

    Sir Hemdale, formerly a citizen of Armadale

    Sir Christensen

At the New School

Eleanor, associate professor in the Duchess's Program

Lady Gwenyfer, administrator of the Duchess's Program

Gerveault Heys, senior professor of dynamics

Keith Euyn, professor emeritus

Meredeth Callum, senior professor of mathematics

Annabelle Currik, senior professor of physics

Robert Endicott, a student, Knight of Vercors

Koria Valcourt, a student, Lady of Engevelen

Eloise Kyre, a student, Knight of Vercors

Davyn Daly, a student

Heylor Style, a student

Lord Gregory Justice, a student, Knight of Vercors

Bethyn Trail, a student

Deleske Lachlan, a student

Freyla Loche, a student

Jeyn Lindseth, a senior student in the military school, cousin to Syriol Lindseth

Bat Merrett, a senior student in the military school

Eoyan March, a senior student in the military school

Lord Jon Indulf, a student

Lord Quincy Leighton, a student

Steyphan Kenelm, a student

Jennyfer Gray, an arts student

Elyze Astarte, a dynamics researcher

Vyrnus Hedt, a dynamics researcher

Lil Hilliard, a dynamics researcher

Konrad Folke, a dynamics researcher

Rendell, a dynamics researcher

⊗ At the Castlereagh Line

Vaugn Somne, a lieutenant on the agricultural mission

Eirnyn Quinn, a sergeant on the agricultural mission

Ildrys, a corporal on the agricultural mission

Rhysheart, a private on the agricultural mission

Ida Yseult, a private on the agricultural mission

Emyr Wynn, a lieutenant at the Castlereagh Line

Gael Guise, a corporal at the Castlereagh Line

⊗ Methueyn Knights

Urieyn, Angel of Music. Symbol, a blazing sun. First day of the week, Ursday.

Sendeyl, Angel of Endurance. Symbol, a broken sandal. Second day of the week, Senday.

Michael, Angel of War, usually male. Symbol, a great sword. Third day of the week, Michsday.

Heydron, Angel of Protection, usually female. Symbol, a shield. Fourth day of the week, Heyday.

Darday'l, Angel of Knowledge. Symbol, a scroll hung on a maul. Fifth day of the week, Darday.

Volsang, Angel of Righteous Vengeance. Symbol, an axe. Sixth day of the week, Volsday.

Hervor, Angel of Warning. Symbol, a bursting horn. Seventh day of the week, Hersday.

Leylah, Angel of Night, usually female. Symbol, a crescent moon. Eighth day of the week, Leyday.

Others

Sir Seygis, the heretical Ninth Knight. Symbol, a man in black plate armor or the number nine.

Secular orders of Knights

Knight of Vercors

Royal Knight of Armadale

Transcendental beings

Nimrheal, a demon who punishes creativity. Absent since the end of the Methueyn War

Skoll, a demon who appeared in the Methueyn War

Hati, a demon who appeared in the Methueyn War

Acknowledgements

Thank you to my test readers George Fairs, Dr. Greg Arkos, Serena Provincial, Cheryl Kendall, Graham Hack, Eric Street, Julie Rowe and Wendy Ross. My wife, Lori Hunt, was a test reader as well. You might think that being my wife she would automatically give my work a glowing review, but wives are not mothers, Lori calls it as she sees it, and she dislikes the fantasy genre. I will leave what Lori had to say as a mystery. No, actually, I won't. She liked it. Shawn Crawford, psychology professor at Mount Royal University was a very helpful resource; thankfully he never seemed to tire of my questions regarding trauma. John McAllister, my editor, also showed great patience and editorial acumen. He never tired of talking about commas, proper nouns and capitalization. Not many are willing to do that, especially for fantasy novels where the author can arbitrarily and perniciously decide what noun is proper and what is not. Jared Shapiro is the person responsible for the creative typesetting of the novel and Jeff Brown designed the equally interesting and unique cover. Nimrheal would surely slay both Jared and Jeff. The last person I must thank is Lyda Mclallen. She is my marketing advisor and, beyond being quite good at her job, was fun to work with.

And thank you, reader. I am selfishly glad you took the time to read my book. Having no one read your book is like having no one to tell a joke to. It is like talking to yourself. It's okay with me if some part of the book turned out to be upsetting for you to read because some parts were upsetting to me to write. If you want to argue about something in the book, so much the better. Reading, having some contrary thought, getting into a civilized argument, those are all good things. All those things get us out of the echo-chambers of our minds.

About The Author

After having the last rights read to him at the age of twenty-five, Lee Hunt came to appreciate the power of catharsis. He was born on a farm with only one working lung but has gone on to become an Ironman triathlete, sport rock climber, professional geophysicist, and writer.

As a Scientist, Lee has published close to fifty papers, articles, or expanded abstracts, has been awarded numerous technical awards, and was even sent on a national speaking tour. He enjoys discussing the amorality of science and is useful at parties in explaining the physics of whether fracture stimulation might be a risk to the fuzzy, cuddly things of nature. After 28 years trying to understand the earth as a geophysicist, Lee turned to writing fiction. He now spends time hiking, cycling, floundering in a lake, clinging desperately to a wall, or at his desk trying to write an entertaining story.

About The Author

AFTER HAVING THE LAST RIGHTS READ TO HIM AT THE AGE OF TWENTY-FIVE, LEE HUNT came to appreciate the power of catharsis. He was born on a farm with only one working lung but has gone on to become an Ironman triathlete, sport rock climber, professional geophysicist, and writer.

AS A SCIENTIST, LEE HAS PUBLISHED CLOSE TO FIFTY PAPERS, ARTICLES, OR EXPANDED abstracts, has been awarded numerous technical awards, and was even sent on a national speaking tour. He enjoys discussing the amorality of science and is useful at parties in explaining the physics of whether fracture stimulation might be a risk to the fuzzy, cuddly things of nature. After 28 years trying to understand the earth as a geophysicist, Lee turned to writing fiction. He now spends time hiking, cycling, floundering in a lake, clinging desperately to a wall, or at his desk trying to write an entertaining story.

CPSIA information can be obtained
at www.ICGtesting.com
Printed in the USA
BVHW030420060520
579146BV00001BA/9